MW00814995

ALSO FROM DIE MONSTER DIE! BOOKS

Mooncat Jack by James Chambers

The Dead Bear Witness by James Chambers

The Last Best Friend by C.J. Henderson

Pretty Female Assassin Pixie, vol. 1 and 2
by Vince Sneed and John Peters

The Dead Walk: Weird Tales of Zombies, Revenants, and the Living Dead
edited by Vincent Sneed

Dark Furies: Weird Tales of Beauties and Beasts
edited by Vincent Sneed

The Midnight Hour:Saint Lawn Hill and Other Tales
by James Chambers and Jason Whitley

Crazy Little Thing by Adam P. Knave

Sweat by Laszlo Q. V. St-J. Xalieri

Strange Angel 1: Genesis by Adam P. Knave

Strange Angel 2: Exodus by Adam P. Knave

Strange Angel 1: Revelations by Adam P. Knave

THE DEAD WALK AGAIN!

edited by Vincent Sneed

PADWOLF | NEW YORK

Cover art by Stephen Blickenstaff
Desktop composition by The Devil Genghis
(devilgenghis@yahoo.com)
Manufacturing by Lightning Source
(www.lightningsource.com)

Published by Padwolf Books

www.padwolf.com

Produced by Die Monster Die! Books
5082 E. Federal St.
Baltimore, MD 21205
www.diemonsterdie.com

ISBN: 1-890096-37-7

Printed in the United States of America

First Printing: August 2007
10 9 8 7 6 5 4 3 2 1

GUTS

Introduction: 2 Dead 2 Walk
Laszlo Xalieri 7
A Large and Rattling Stick
C.J. Henderson 12
Fast Eddie's Big Night Out
John L. French 35
Of Cabbages and Kings
Nate Southard 48
Laundry Day
Steven A. Roman 62
Married Alive
D.J. Kirkbride 80
High Noon of the Living Dead
Adam P. Knave 91
Ragged Bones
Bruce Gehweiler 116
The Spare
Laszlo Xalieri 142
Zombies on Broadway
Jack Dolphin 166
Zombie & Spice
Patrick Thomas 180
The Dead In Their Masses
James Chambers 190
Ode to Brains
Zombie Poetry by Adam P. Knave 257
Accomplices 258

Jack Dolphin

*For **TOM SAVINI**, the man who
makes the dead look so damn good*

Punchline number 3: "*GRAARARRGARRGHHH!!!*"

It's been a hellish couple of hours. Maybe quite a bit longer. I can feel the rigor mortis starting to wear off. The tingling-jangling is back, as bad as it ever was. The hunger is so bad that all I want to do is curl up into a little ball and rock and rock. But I'm too weak to move. I'm still just lying here in the position I was before. Oh, I wish I could move. Oh, I wish I could get up. The tingling. The burning.

Must move. Must move. Move something. Move *anything*. Must move.

Maybe it wasn't the blood I was given. Maybe this is nothing special at all. Maybe everyone who dies goes through this. *Everyone*.

That's a horrible thought. This is so goddamned awful! Maybe this is only for the people who die slowly…Maybe it's a hemophiliac thing. A blood lover thing.

Oh! Oh. Oh. Someone else just died. Oh. Oh, that's…*wonderful*. Wonderful. Not bliss, not ecstasy. Just…an abatement. A lessening. I'd be gasping with relief—if I could gasp.

"Uph."

Does everyone who dies go through this? Horrible for them, yes. But. But. But. For me? That'd mean I'm still...dying. That this will be over soon. Over soon. I hope. I hope.

Pain is coming back. Burning. Tingling. Oh, God. Oh, God. Ohgodohgodohgodohgod—

So hungry. Don't know what I'd do to put something in my stomach. Bucket of blood sounds great right now. Quick and easy. And warm. And, and, and...if I got it *fresh*, then...then there'd be the, the *lessening*. Ohgodohgodohgod.

Please, let me be dying. Please, God, let me be dying. Oh, God. Please.

"Uphphuph. Rrrrr."

It is now my honor to have coaxed not one, not two, but three *zombie tales from a terrific writer who professes to have no love (beyond the films of George Romero) for tales of reanimated, cannibalistic corpses.*

A LaRGE aND RattlinG STicK

by C.J. Henderson

"The incessant witless repetition of advertisers' moron-fodder has become so much a part of life that if we are not careful, we forget to be insulted by it."
–The Times, London, 1986

Now:

The large, bearded black man weighed the grenade in his hand, waiting for the sea of pursuers moving down the hallway toward him to draw closer. He did not, of course, really care for using shrapnel weapons within such a confined area—not when he, himself, was confined there as well. But, circumstances being what they were, he had to play for time as best he could.

"Have you not got dey combination yet, girl?"

"I need another minute."

The man groaned. Still, he knew his partner was doing the best she could. And, he had to admit, he could not have gotten nearly as far as he had without her—nor did he have the slightest talent toward the ends she was only moments away from accomplishing. So, choosing to be philosophical about their situation, he pulled the pin on his third to last grenade, counted off the correct amount of seconds, then let it fly. He skimmed the black steel sphere just over the heads of those approaching, letting it fall within their midst. The following explosion erupted nicely, flinging burst wire and burning metal in all directions. Those all around the disruption were shredded—limbs torn away, faces ruined, legs shattered. All but two in the front line were knocked over, and those the large man sent staggering backward headless with two careful bursts of his automatic weapon. Each burst released three rounds—more than enough to splatter a brain and drop a walker.

Behind those knocked down by the explosion, the following ranks continued on forward, of course. It was a wonderful mess. Those that had been broken still tried to rise, as always, even as those behind attempted to walk over top of them. The effect would have been more comical for the large man and his companion if those coming toward them were not doing so because of their ravenous desire to tear the two apart and devour their flesh.

Two grenades left, thought the man. Maybe twenty round. Not a big lot considerin' what be comin'.

Reaching into an inner pocket of the vest he wore, the man pulled forth a flask filled with a private stock, one made by friends on the island of his birth. It was a coconut rum, and it did indeed taste like coconuts—

Well, yes, the man thought cynically as he downed a hefty swig, flaming coconuts, maybe.

Sliding the flask back into his vest, he grimly assessed the situation at the other end of the hall. Those looking to murder himself and his companion were almost untangled one from another. It was obvious to him that it would only be seconds before those who could still walk would be lumbering forward once more. Hideously, those broken to where they could only crawl were already on their way. Unconsciously making the sign of the cross, the large man released a disheartened sigh. Then, his hands preparing another grenade, he said to himself;

"Blessed and sweet Mother of God, I have said it before, and I will say it again, oh, but...how I hate de zombies."

Only some twenty yards away, the screaming and growling dead began their slow but thorough march once more, all their glazed and vacant eyes fixed hungrily on the two living humans so tantalizingly close.

72 Hours Ago:

"Pa'sha Lowe," the woman's voice said the name with a mixture of surprise and delight in the lightest of French accents.

"Well now, why don't you bring your wonderful self into my home?"

Depressing the key on the control panel before her which unlocked the front door to her estate, Joan De Molina by-passed the usual security protocols she maintained when allowing anyone access to her private world. The large black man entering her front door was not an old friend, but he was well-trusted. Between them they shared a mutual acquaintance, a New York City-based private detective who was his best friend and her one-time heart throb. Though she had only known Pa'sha during a single encounter, the three of them had faced enough blood and death and terror together to make him an always welcome sight in her eyes. As he removed his drenched, oversized duster, she appeared from around a corner saying;

"It must be really coming down out there."

"Enough to make dis lad of de tropics glad he moved north a thousand miles."

"Don't worry about the dripping;" the woman said, indicating his duster, "just throw it over the railing there." Pa'sha did as directed, then accepted a hug from the much smaller redhead, giving her a squeeze tight enough to let her know he cared without crushing her.

"What strong arms you have, grandma..." she said, running a hand over the large man's biceps.

"Me Mama Joan, she feed all us boys well, don't you know."

"Perhaps I'd best just take your word on it. If I was to go home with you for a meal, maybe it would take a month in the gym to repair the damage."

"I would protest in my dear Mama's defense, but..." he made a gesture with his hands which indicated the swelling size of his own scale-tipping girth, then finished, adding, "well, such t'ings have been known to happen."

Joan laughed lightly, then began the usual ritual of hospitality, finding the correct beverage, the right snacks, and an appropriate corner of her home for the two of them to settle into so as to discuss what had brought them together that afternoon. The pair talked about simpler things at first, of course—generalities about the courses of their lives, mutual friends, the bizarre sudden change in the weather, that movie just everyone was talking about that week. Eventually, however, Pa'sha said;

"You are a lovely hostess, Joan my sweet, but as I am certain you must know, I did not come to sample from you wine rack—well, not exclusively."

"Oh," the woman said with a mock-startled surprise meant to be humorous, "are we getting to the point—already?"

"If you wouldn't mind; I think you might find dis t'ing I am going to propose at the very least...what is a truthful word...interesting? Yes?"

"Possible always," agreed the woman. Shifting her position on her couch, aiming her body at the large man, she added, "Let's see what kind of salesman you are."

Pa'sha nodded to his hostess. Of course, both of them knew he had not made the trip from lower Manhattan out to the southern end of Brooklyn merely to see Joan de Molina. He had come to visit with the woman's secondary persona, the one for which she was, at least in some circles, internationally famous.

"I know you will find this hard to believe, mon cheri, but dis t'ing I will be putting forth to you, it has to do with de supernatural."

Not that the large Jamaican himself did not have another face. For Pa'sha Lowe, that hidden face was the one of a seminary student who decades earlier turned his back on God and Heaven to sell weapons to the highest bidder. He learned far later in life that it was the lies of men and not the will of God which had disillusioned him with the church.

"The supernatural, you say?" The woman's voice was a delightful mix of teasing and giving in to the inevitable. "My word, what a surprise."

For her, for the girl christened Joan de Molina, the inner mask was that of the world's most successful thief—the Pirate Queen. She had never been mistaken over the source of her disillusionment. Stripped of her parents at far too early an age by cruel Fate, hers had been a long and vicious climb to the freedom adulthood offers so many others freely.

They were, the pair of them, terribly hardened people, both content to let the next guy over take the fall, shoulder the blame, carry the load, et cetera. Or at least, they had been, until each in their own time they had met the detective, Theodore London, whose very different outlook on things infected them both and changed their lives.

"A while back, not so long ago really," the large Jamaican started, "I found myself fightin' a bocor, a voodoo priest, but one who had put himself in league with terrible t'ings, elder t'ings—most hard to kill types of t'ings. I t'ink you have some small idea what it is I'm talkin' about."

"My memory is not that bad—no. I remember."

"I t'ought you might."

The weaponeer told his story quickly after that. The priest he had stopped had used fragments of an ancient gem, two halves of a crystal delivered to the Earth in the center of a meteorite long before man stood erect. The cursed thing throbbed with alien power, and the best the defenders of antiquity could do was split the vulgar thing in two and hurl the resulting pieces in different oceans. For a few thousand years, that had been enough.

When the halves were brought back to the same vicinity only a handful of weeks previous, Pa'sha and a few others had fought hard to keep the two segments from being rejoined. It had taken the deaths of more than a few of them, but in the end the immediate threat had been stopped and the large weaponeer had thought the crystal shards destroyed. He had been wrong. As he told Joan;

"It seems dese t'ings, maybe dey can not be destroyed; maybe you can only keep dem one from de other. Whatever—de t'ing is, I found out dat de pieces were recovered by some enterprising type after de battle. Dey at least were smart enough to sell de pieces to two separate museums, thousands o'miles apart. Dat keeps dem from startin' any trouble on their own."

"Let me see if I can't speed this up for us," interrupted Joan. "You want to break into the museums, steal the jewels, and make certain they don't fall into the wrong hands, so you've come to me to help you with the break-ins—*n'est pas*?"

"Well, dat was my idea a few days ago when I found out de damn t'ings hadn't been destroyed, don't cha know, girl. But, no offense, if my boys and I couldn't break into a simple museum and make off with one little piece of crystal, den for certain it would be time for me to hang up my hat, and just sit on de back porch and sip rum 'til I close my eyes for the final time, which I might still be tempted toward de way t'ings are goin' dese days."

"Then, Pa'sha," purred Joan, her interest climbing with every word, "tell me—just why are you here?"

"When we went after de stones, we hit both museums de same night, at the same time. Dey were textbook operations. Everything ran as smooth as possible. Except for one small possibility we had overlooked..."

Reaching for his glass, Pa'sha took a long sip of the not-too-tart afternoon wine Joan had served. Smacking his lips, he held the glass near his head as he added;

"De gems, we found we could not steal dem, but only because dey had already been stolen. The fragments on display in the museums...are copies."

---

48 Hour Ago:

Pa'sha watched the Pirate Queen as she stared at the single crystal shard on display in the Smithsonian. The museum had grabbed up the piece when it had been offered to them, knowing they would be hosting the German Manhoff Museum's traveling "Superstitions of the World" exhibit. Like all the other stops on the tour route, the curators there had pulled together everything from their basement storage vaults with which they could expand the experience of those visiting to see the tour.

Incredible workmanship—

Joan and Pa'sha had moved quickly through the rest of the exhibits, feigning interest here and there until finally reaching the voodoo section. Once they had located the crystal shard, the Pirate Queen set to examining it from all angles. After only a moment, she took Pa'sha's arm and the two walked on into the rest of the exhibit, Joan making comments about the beauty of precious stones and how few he had bought for her. Then, once away from any eyes that might have been made suspicious over the amount of time she spent studying the fragment, she whispered;

"I know who made this thing. We will need to head to the airport."

Once outside, the Pirate Queen explained that the duplicate shard on display had to have been sculpted by a woman named Ruth Bilfonte. Joan recognized a trademark insult the woman left in all her copies, a tiny set of scratches most would not notice, and only a handful would realize were actually a Chinese language character.

"She inscribes everything she does with it. It comes from one of the obscure Chinese mountain dialects."

"What does it say?"

"Fake."

"If it were not so annoyingly inconvenient," admitted Pa'sha, showing only the slightest trace of a grin, "I think I might find that amusing. But, c'est la vie, onward we must. Why do you mention a need for de airport?"

When the Pirate Queen explained that Bilfonte lived in Switzerland, Pa'sha corrected her, letting her know that what they needed to find was a restaurant, and that Switzerland could take care of itself. Getting a street designation from Joan which was the counterfeit jeweler's last-known-address, he dug out his phone, letting his partner know;

"There is no need for us to fly halfway around de world, not when with a call to one of my Murder Dogs, we can have our answer before dey bring to us de dessert cart."

The Murder Dogs was a mercenary band of the weaponeer's creation which remained in his employ. Although the force had been created mostly from the ranks of well-trusted fellow Jamaicans and Haitians, Pa'sha had seen to it that the assembly included men and women from around the world. As he had often explained it;

"There are times when only a blonde will do, don't you know?"

The Pirate Queen protested for a moment, explaining that Bilfonte was an artist and not a thug, but her companion assured her that his people did not always shoot first. His contact would simply track the counterfeiter down as soon as possible, and then get her on the phone with Joan.

"Whatever you could do in person, I trust you can do with a picture phone—yes? No?"

When the redhead assured Pa'sha such was the case, the large man nodded, then began the arduous task of dialing his cell phone. Large as he was, his hands were ill-formed for using one of the ever-shrinking devices. Taking pity on him, Joan took his large hand in hers and then finished pressing the buttons as he dictated. Pa'sha contacted his European Murder Dog cell, gave them everything they needed to know, then shut down his phone and returned it to his pocket, giving the thing an evil glare as he did so.

The Pirate Queen giggled. Ignoring her, the weaponeer slapped his hands together, completely dismissing the thought of doing anything else except tracking down dinner. Neither of them had any specific place in mind, but when both decided they would like seafood, Pa'sha snapped his fingers, saying warmly;

"Seafood in Washington, D.C.?" Snapping his fingers again, this time while waving his hand over his head, he called forth the car that had been waiting for them since they entered the museum. Rolling his eyes in an exaggerated fashion, then licking his large lips for comic effect, he announced in a voice that promised wonderment, "Den, true t'ings of true t'ings, der be only one place for us—Captain Vince's."

When the driver of the car demanded to be allowed to accompany them inside, and not have to wait in the car, Joan agreed there could be only one place for them, indeed.

Much to the Pirate Queen's surprise, getting to the establishment owned by Captain Vince was not something easily done. To begin, the restaurant was not even located within the borders of the American capitol. This was explained to Joan, but the eager anticipation of both their driver and her partner only made her more anxious herself. The trip was actually a thing less than forty miles, but escaping the dread, never-ending loops of Washington was always an adventure, even for the locals. After their break for the East was completed, however, the driver made a straight line for the Maryland coast, specifically, the town of Rose Haven in a tiny area known as Herring Bay.

"De Captain," explained the driver, "he want to be near de sea, take advantage o'de fishing boats. The fleets, they don't dock in Rose, but de Captain, he take his boat out every day in de late afternoon—den he anchor and wait. Dose what got de best, dey head his boat. Sell de best and de strange to Captain Vince."

Joan was willing to give Pa'sha and his driver the benefit of the doubt, even after seeing Captain Vince's from the outside which said much for her trust of the weaponeer. Even trying to be polite, there was nothing much good that could be said about the establishment itself. The wooden exterior had soaked up so much of the oceanfront's violence over the decades that the entire building seemed soft—spongy. Moss grew freely over much of it. On the other hand, she thought, the place had no sign, and yet the parking lot was nicely jammed at 6:30 in the evening.

The inside view did nothing much to sway her, either, however. The lighting was weak, the ceiling musty, the atmosphere filled with the stale aroma of many different types of smokers. As one who preferred a particularly harsh brand of Dutch cigarettes, that factor did not put her off much. Especially since the smell of smoke was not the overpowering one in the captain's establishment.

Despite the fact that their were people smoking at nearly every table, it was the fragrance of the kitchen which ruled over all. The warm, oily bouquet of the deep friers charged the room with the heavenly flavor of deep fried bread, while the skillets layered their wonder with the subtle scents of butter and wine, scallions and peppers and a score of wondrous other flavors, creating a perfume for the tongue which dispelled any further hesitation. Sitting back in her chair, tilting it on two legs, the Pirate Queen took a deep drag of a thin, long black cigarette, saying;

"If they serve wine older than our chauffeur, I might just consider moving to this Merry Land of yours."

One of the additional peculiarities of Captain Vince's—the one which discouraged the most walk-in traffic—was the fact there were no menus to be found. You did not order food; the Captain came to your table, spent as much time as he considered necessary with you, and then sent to you what he decided you would have for dinner that evening. One was allowed to refuse a dish, of course. But those would then be asked, politely, to leave. They would not be permitted to return.

When the Captain appeared at the trio's table, he turned out to be a man of medium height and years, a frosty fellow who shaved his bullet of a head but maintained a fierce moustache and pointed goatee. He chain smoked unfiltered Camels, even when he was cooking, and was immediately taken by Joan. Recognizing Pa'sha as well as his driver, he knew what he would serve them and thus concentrated his attentions and questions on the Pirate Queen. Once he had all he needed to know, he returned to the kitchen, having promised them a family-style dinner.

"You have made a favorable impression on de captain."

"How so," asked Joan, her mind suddenly roused to curiosity over Pa'sha's merry tone.

"Ohhhhhh, de daddy-man no lie," interrupted the chauffeur. "Cappy Vince, he no do de family treat, with de ten different dishes and de food 'til you drown for just anyone. He…" As the man trailed off, not finishing his comment, Joan smiled, adding quietly;

"Yes, I am quite used to men finding something they like when they see me. Don't worry, I am not the type to think of such as a curse." The two men remained silent for a moment. As the Pirate Queen stared, knowing something was wrong, Pa'sha finally said;

"It isn't quite that, mon cheri. When de captain serves family style, it means he feels he is serving a family…or those who should be a family."

"He be seein' fine banana sparks from dey two of you," interrupted the chauffeur, his face split by an enormous grin. "In de cappy's eyes, de love squid, he got all his big arms around de two of you…"

The man was about to say more, when his own eyes connected with Pa'sha's. The chauffeur's voice broke off at that point, the man waving his arms around, suddenly his attention taken with a dozen other points within the restaurant. His chatter only went on for a few moments as one of the waiters suddenly arrived with a large portion of cold seafood salad. Each of the three scooped bits of lettuce and celery, mussels, shrimp, scallops and crab onto their plates along with the olives, squid, peppers and everything else to be found on the heaping platter. Conversation dropped to the barest of comments as the trio feasted on the well chilled, wonderfully fresh opening course.

It was swiftly followed by others. Fresh fish sauteed in onions and butter served with pea pods came only minutes before a tureen of a wonderfully thick seafood gumbo. And, before those dishes could be consumed, their table was also graced with a large platter of steamed fillets and one of fried calamari, coated in a batter so delightfully thin, golden and crunchy it was as if the cephalopod had lived all its life with a potato chip skin, just waiting to be served up to someone that evening.

The trio sat after the feasting, cooling themselves with the wicker fans kept handy for just such occasions. Joan enjoyed one of her dark cigarettes while Pa'sha sipped at an after dinner concoction made from equal parts banana rum, dark rum, several fruit juices and a great deal of ice. Their driver had departed for the restroom some time earlier. When the Pirate Queen commented on how long he had been gone, Pa'sha a long pull on his drink, then told her;

"It was expected. De little one, he likes to dream he can eat with de big dogs. He has not de frame for it, though. He is most likely now still in de middle of tickling de back o'is throat, tryin' to relieve de pressure."

"He wishes very much to be like you," suggested Joan. "No?"

Pa'sha was about to answer when his cell phone went off, the ringtone he recognized as being from his main European contact. Not bothering to open it, he merely handed it to his companion instead. The Pirate Queen raised a single eyebrow as she took the phone. She was not surprised to find Bilfonte on the line. After a brief conversation, she handed the phone back to the weaponeer.

"This all seems to be going quite smoothly."

"We are rewarded with success—yes?"

"Apparently," Joan responded, taking another deep drag from her black cigarette. "Bilfonte did indeed make the replacements. It was a rush job she was delighted to undertake. Those involved paid top dollar because they needed the crystals as quickly as they could be acquired."

"She was delighted because de money was good?"

"Not entirely. Her greatest pleasure was being able to work without undue fear. Many times people in her line have to worry that those employing them will want to, as they say, clean up loose ends, when a job is over—considering those who have worked so hard for them as the loosest of ends..."

"Yes," interrupted Pa'sha, his voice a low growl. "I have known these types of employers."

"This time, however, her client was too clean, too mainstreamed to consider such tactics reliable."

"Oh, and so, who was dis client day make her so comfortable?"

"The Quench Corporation."

Joan said the three words with just the proper amount of innocence, lowering her voice to the perfect decibel to make her point. As the weaponeer's eyes went wide, then narrowed in dark suspicion, she asked;

"Quite the question, n'est pas? What could the world's largest corporate producers of soft drinks want with the secrets of reanimating the dead?"

"Yes," agreed Pa'sha. "Quite de question." Hefting his glass, he finished the last of his drink even as their driver appeared from around a corner, making his way slowly back to the table. "And, one we will have to answer I'm afraid—and soon."

24 Hours Ago:

Pa'sha handed the printout to Joan for which she had asked. The pair had taken rooms in Washington and immediately set to researching where the fragments might be at that moment. Since the Quench Corporation had factories in nearly every country in the world, and offices in all of them, the jeweled pieces could have been anywhere. Since time might be the most important factor in recovering the gemstones, they had decided even the few hours it took to return to New York City could not be spared.

"What truly bothers me," Pa'sha mused, rubbing his eyes, "is what they could even want with de power to raise de dead." Joan looked across the table at the weaponeer. Putting her hands to her glass of iced tea, she pressed her suddenly moist fingers against her eyes as she added;

"I understand. I have wondered about this myself. They control more money than most countries. Their executives wield more power than many of the most prominent world leaders. I admit this to you, in some ways the prospect of them having such power frightens me."

"Why so, *mon cheri*?"

"Because," she said in a low and angry voice, "I can not even begin to imagine what they would do with it. Fill their bottling plants with the walking dead to cut labor costs? Raise the dead and then put soda machines in every graveyard?" Staring at her large companion with a small, plaintive look, she said;

"Theft is my business—yes? I know how it works; why people do it. Robbing museums, stealing antiquities, for the rich and powerful it's a worse crime than murder. Very taboo. For them to risk the international censure, their need for these fragments must be overwhelming...but for all the devious and deceitful bends to which I can put my mind, I can not fathom their purpose."

Pa'sha was about to make a further comment of his own when one of his cell phones threw out the first few bars to the theme from *Jaws*. He grabbed it up quickly, knowing from the tune it meant the call was coming from his own home. After listening to the report being given for only a handful of seconds, he asked the speaker to hold for a moment. Turning to Joan, he thumbed the phone to its speaker setting as he told her;

"It appears my contacts have found our answer first. My boys back home, dey have stripped out several internal memos from Quench Corporate Headquarters back in New York. From der laughter, I have a feelin' we're not going to like what we hear." The Pirate Queen gave Pa'sha a look that said she expected laughter in their answer somewhere. Pursing his lips in frustration to frame his response, the weaponeer told his man to read them the pertinent memo. His voice leapt out of the cell on the table between them, reading;

"With dey death o' Donald Reynolds, it appears we have no choice but to go forth with Project Revive. His absence has crippled dey corporation to unacceptable limits. He must be returned to de living."

The Murder Dog in New York quickly read all the various pieces of memos their electronics expert had been able to hack away from the millions of corporate emails protected by the company's truly impressive firewall. Within a few minutes, he showed the pattern as discovered, and then where that pattern lead. Pa'sha gave detailed instructions while he began to pack. In less than ten minutes since the moment his phone had first rung, the weaponeer had taken in all the information his people had for him, had told them to await his arrival, and what to have ready for him when he returned. Looking across the table at Joan, he smiled a weary smile, telling the Pirate Queen;

"Well, mon cheri, it seems all is now clear. I told dem I will drive back simply because, you know, by the time a flight can be arranged...pufi...I will be home. May I ask your plans?"

"Yes, you may," she said, a dangerous edge suddenly making itself clear within her voice, "I shall accompany you in your vehicle, and then on into the bowels of Quench to put an end to their madness."

"Joan," answered Pa'sha, his manner stiff and somewhat bemused, "I came to you to help locate the missing jewels. We 'ave dem now. It was not my intent to endanger you with my concerns."

"Oh, how upright and so very decent of you," answered the Pirate Queen with a sneer. "Those in the cheap seats will applaud your nobility. I'm coming."

"But, it is too much for me to ask."

"No one heard you ask for anything. They heard me telling you what shall be—n'est pas?" Pa'sha eyed the redhead for a moment, not quite certain what to say. As he began to move his arms, looking for a way to explain himself, she held up a hand to stop him, saying;

"You listen to me; I was perfectly happy stealing from the rich and ignorant. It pleased me well to live like a queen by emptying the coffers of those who have everything and deserved none of it. Then I met you...you and your friend." Pa'sha's eyes went soft with sympathy at the mention of their previous meeting.

"Helping you stop the horrors that—aukh...you were there. You know what they were. But I doubt you know what it did to me. You and your save-the-world complex, the two of you, the white knights, his lousy, miserable sense of..."

Her face twisting, eyes blinking, upper lip starting to quiver, Joan de Molina, possibly the most feared woman in the world, suddenly found her steel resolve crumbling as she finally admitted to herself;

"It isn't fair—I was happy being me—goddamnit. It was comfortable, but he took it all away. He robbed me of everything, and then he, he...he went back to her!"

Pa'sha held open his arms as the dread Pirate Queen broke down into tears. He had indeed been there when his friend and adopted brother Teddy London had met the crying redhead he now held so gently. He had witnessed their tragic romance, a thing created purely from magic, accidentally by her passion for a man she could not have. In the end, after seeing the larger world hidden from most, she had been forced to abandon her former life.

"I can't very well remain a thief," she sniffed, "not after touching the mantle of God."

"No, cheri," whispered the weaponeer. "I suppose not."

"Well, if I'm stuck having to live in a world where I know angels and devils contest for the souls of men," she said, "then I'm throwing in with the angels—and you're not going to stop me."

Pa'sha held the woman for a few more minutes. Then he whispered something to the Pirate Queen which made her laugh. In less than half an hour, the pair and their driver were not only out of Washington, but halfway through Baltimore.

Now:

Along the way back to New York, Pa'sha planned their upcoming attack strategy. The intercepted memos had given them the location of the fragments, the name of the voodoo priest being brought in to use them, and even an idea of when the resurrection of their Donald Reynolds might take place. During the drive the weaponeer planned the upcoming assault—who he would take, what weapons and other supplies they might need, what vehicles, et cetera. The establishing of cover stories and alibis for all involved was immediately begun.

While Pa'sha was concerned thusly, Joan had taken the time on the drive back to Manhattan to do some research on the object of everyone's attention. After a few internet searches and several phone calls, she interrupted her friend's chain of thought, asking him;

"Would you like to know who Donald Reynolds was?" When the weaponeer responded positively, the woman told him, "Reynolds was an executive of the inner circle, but he seemed to have no job title. He started in the advertising department in the 1960s, but he was moved upstairs. Over the years his pay got higher and his job description got vaguer."

"And so, what does it mean?"

"It means we still don't have a guess as to why they're doing this. Maybe Reynolds knew something he never shared, never wrote down. Maybe he was the only one who knew the formula to Diet Quench—who knows?"

"We shall," answered Pa'sha, "and soon."

The weaponeer had made that statement while their car was on the New Jersey Turnpike, rapidly approaching the city. Getting a radio tip that the Hudson River tunnels were jammed, he had the driver cut across Staten Island, taking the Verrazano Narrows Bridge to Brooklyn, then cutting along its coast until reaching the Brooklyn-Battery Tunnel. Even though the roundabout route saved the trio at least a half an hour, all were tense within the limousine.

The tension did not disappear anytime soon. No sooner did the vehicle pull up to the warehouse Pa'sha had designated as their staging area, then those assigned to accompany him and Joan threw open the massive bolt-down doors and fired up the two trucks chosen for that night's mission. The weaponeer threw off his sports coat, accepting the combat vest being handed to him by one of his chiefs, even as Joan was taken to a room where she could change into the outfit she had requested be readied for her. In less than seven minutes after their arrival, the ten going out that night were on their way to the supposedly abandoned Quench bottling plant at the southeastern most tip of Roosevelt's Island.

The island was a long, thin stretch of land in the East River. The team took the trucks to a secluded dock they knew on the west side of Manhattan, then motored around the bottom of the larger island to the smaller one. It added some minutes, but the security of the launch space was essential. If anything went wrong, they needed a safe port to return to, and having it on the other side of Manhattan from where they would be conducting their small-scale invasion made everyone concerned more comfortable.

Both the launch and the docking at Roosevelt went extremely smoothly, as did their break-in at the old plant. Pa'sha would have been confident enough leading his own forces. But, with the expertise of the Pirate Queen folded in with his own, he was certain any and all security devices had been neutralized. Indeed, their entry into the plant was ridiculously easy.

"It's almost as if dey have no one watching."

"Dat make sense to you, daddy-man?"

"No," whispered Pa'sha back in response. "Not hardly."

"What if we're too late?" As all heads turned toward Joan save those on point, she asked;

"You said we didn't know when they were going to make their attempt. What if they've already tried it and it didn't work? What if they've all just left?"

"Or worse," volunteered one of Pa'sha's lieutenants. "What if dese white boys, dey fum-bo de mumbo? Could be one big lockdown full o'zombies, just waitin' fo us to open de wrong door."

And suddenly, everyone, including the speaker himself, knew he had gotten things exactly right. Slowly the members of the group all looked one to the other, eyes asking questions lips could not utter. Finally, rubbing his great meaty hands in and out of each other, the weaponeer said lowly;

"Doesn't matter. We come for de stones. We gonna take dem outta here. Dey ruin my daddy's sleep, help stain his name, make hell out of our homelands. And if dis idea be right, then we be de only t'ing what can save de world from goddamned zombies pourin' out over everything, don't cha know?"

And at that moment, the Hell all of them had just begun to imagine finally made itself known as around a corner before the nine came staggering a trio of zombies. Two wore coveralls, the other a dark, thin-striped business suit. The clothing of all three was shredded to one degree or another. The head of the one in the suit appeared to have been chewed upon. So did his arm. One of the pair in coveralls had but a single hand, his other sleeve almost covering a dripping stump.

At sight of the shambling creatures, the party froze for a moment. Most of them had never seen the walking dead, had never been looked upon by walking, moving beings as food. And yet, that was the glaze bubbling over the three pairs of eyes slowly fastening themselves to the raiding party. Hunger—greedy and mindless—turned their destinationless wandering into a thing with sudden and dramatic purpose. In their slow, steady gait, the trio of the walking dead made their way for Pa'sha and the others, hands grasping, throats muttering.

"W-What be de orders, d-daddy-man?"

"Orders?" The weaponeer targeted the head of the zombie in the lead and sent a burst through it. The creature's skull shattered, blood and brains exploding in all directions. As the other two kept moving forward, oblivious to their companions fate, their hands straining to reach, horrid, swollen tongues dancing in their mouths, Pa'sha finished;

"Put the filthy sons o'bitches back into de ground!"

So saying, the weaponeer fired again sending two more short bursts through the heads of the other approaching figures. The six bullets had the same effect on those zombies as the first three had on their companion. As their bodies crumpled to the ground, Pa'sha reminded his followers as well as Joan not to waste ammunition.

"Take off der heads," he commanded. "Break de brain and down dey go. Anyt'ing else, dey don't barely feel."

"Looks like we're goin' have our chance find out, big daddy."

All turned to see what Pa'sha's gunplay had attracted. From four different spots, streams of zombies were lumbering out of the darkness. Many of these, however, did not appear to be former Quench employees. Nervous speculation leapt from man to man like wildfire, legends of mass graves on Roosevelt from the old insane asylum, tales of mob killings, et cetera, were thrown out as possible explanations for the extra bodies.

Shouting out for all to pay attention, Pa'sha focused everyone's will, reminding them that where the zombies came from or who they were did not matter. Only keeping out of their clutches and recovering the crystals was important. Getting that across, the weaponeer divided his forces into three units, giving them all directions in which to head. Three men were sent to the left, three to the right. As usual, Pa'sha saved right-up-the-middle for himself.

All had the same instructions: fight their way clear of the large open area they were in and head for higher ground. Any executives in charge would be upstairs, as would any possible answers. On their way upstairs, they were to arm and plant the explosives they were carrying. Each of them had a bandolier containing thirteen compact but incredibly powerful bombs. Considering that they might have no alternative but to sterilize the Quench plant, the weaponeer had come prepared.

Roaring as he raced across the open floor, moving his three hundred and seventy-some pounds as fast as he could, Pa'sha continued to take out the approaching zombies one at a time with carefully aimed bursts. The man with him was not quite the shot the weaponeer was, but the Pirate Queen matched Pa'sha clip for clip.

The trio made their way upstairs with relative ease after their dash across the open area. Things might have been far worse if the Quench executives had staged their unholy rite in one of their fully-manned operational plants. But, the Roosevelt Island facility was an old one, watched over by not much more than a skeleton crew. Instead of hundreds upon hundreds of possible enemies, the group had been hoping for something around fifty or less. With the arrival of dead of unknown origins, however, the invaders had to adjust to the fact that all previous bets had suddenly been cancelled.

As each further stair revealed no more of the dead, though, Pa'sha was willing to consider that, then again, perhaps they had already seen the worst of things. Slowing his pace, the weaponeer's massive girth finally catching up with him, the Murder Dog at his side took point while Joan stepped closer.

"You shouldn't be running up stairs, *mon cheri*," she told him, a serious look of concern creasing her face. Pa'sha was just about to make a rude remark in return when the man before them screamed, then covered his cries in reckless gunfire.

Before the weaponeer could react, a pair of zombies which seemingly stepped directly out of the shadows caught hold of and tore open the Murder Dog's chest. Blood cascaded down the stairs, splashing Pa'sha and the Pirate Queen both. Each fired without hesitation, each killing the zombie at which they aimed, but it was too late; their companion was dead.

"Who's out there?"

"Who wants to know," responded Pa'sha with authority. "Show yourself, or die wit' de rest. Don't think I be carin'."

At the sound of the weaponeer's challenge, a door slid open in the side of the stairwell. From within came a frightened rustling, then the head of an older man nervously appeared, spouting;

"Please, please don't hurt me. Help me—save me! I can pay—a fortune—anything. Just get me out of here."

Pa'sha was frozen in between actions, hate and anger over the death of his man swamping common sense. Luckily, before he could act, the Pirate Queen stepped in between the two, demanding;

"Yes, everyone wants something. Who are you—now!"

"Johnson Edwards—"

"A name, a nothing to be lost on the wind," Joan spat back in the terrified man's face. Hoping to use that terror to gain the information they needed, she slapped Edwards, snarling;

"What are you? What happened? Where are the crystals? Speak—quickly. Or we'll kill you ourselves."

In rapid order the frightened man told the pair everything they needed to know. Edwards proved to be the CEO of Quench. He had greenlighted the stealing of the crystals after it was proved to his satisfaction they could be used to restore life to Donald Reynolds. The ritual had been performed the night before; it had been successful.

Reynolds' corpse, which had been stored at the Roosevelt facility for some time, had been given life before his very eyes. Upon opening its own eyes, however, the thing had immediately attacked its attendees, tearing the flesh from their faces and arms with its teeth and fingernails. Those so attacked were quickly slain by the mindless beast resurrected into their midst. Once dead, the slain rose rapidly to find their own fresh meat.

The building had been in total lockdown so those within could concentrate on the ritual without fear of interruption. Thus, with communications off-line for the ritual, those inside the facility only learned about the growing slaughter as it reached them. The CEO had been spared only by the fact he had chosen to watch the proceedings from above.

"Dis not what I want to know," growled Pa'sha suddenly. Grabbing Edwards, he yanked the older man off his feet, shaking him violently as he shouted in his face, "Why? Do you understand de question? Why did you do this?"

"We, we needed Donnie back," The older man's face became soft, his entire manner one of beseechment. Surely, his eyes pleaded, anyone would understand what they had been forced to do. His voice filled with a tone which implied that the words he was saying were as easy to understand as hymns, he added;

"Had to have him. Had to. He was the best jingler in the business."

"Jingler?" asked Pa'sha.

"Copy man, sloganeer," answered Edwards. "You know what I mean. He wrote all our best ones…'Quench yourself,' that was him. And, and 'Nothing does it like that what does…' Remember? That was him. All the great ones were him."

Pa'sha stood in the darkened stairwell, legs cold from the soaking feel of his man's blood dripping through his pants, mind focused on the terrible power of the crystals, knowing the answer to his last question even as he asked it.

"You had no idea what you were doin', did you? You didn't t'ink to ask if dere might be any danger—any consequences to your actions—did you?"

"The next quarter numbers were coming due," pleaded Edwards, as if the words vindicated any action. "The stockholders were whispering. Profits were in danger of dropping—further! They were already down—over one-eighteenth of a quarter of a percent, just over the rumors of Reynolds death. We were facing a crisis!"

"Here is your crisis, old man," growled Pa'sha. "Take us to the crystals or it is the end of your life."

Edwards pointed up the stairs, shaking some as he did so. As the weaponeer began upward once more, Joan moved the CEO into step behind him. As they walked, she said;

"You're all multi-millionaires; you could spend a half-million a day for the rest of your life and never see the bottom of your resources. What could it have mattered?"

"Market share." Edwards said the phrase as if delivering the final name of God. "It can't be allowed to slip. Each quarter has to generate higher than the last."

The CEO looked at the Pirate Queen exasperated, as if he simply could not find another way to explain to a dim-witted child that playing with fire is dangerous. His eyes going wide with the thought that she might not understand he said as they continued to climb the stairs;

"Our Clowntown restaurants, they only sell Quench beverages. If Quench falters, the chain suffers. That's millions of jobs on the line."

"Over one-eighteenth of a quarter of a percent? A drop that small, and only witnessed during a three month period?" Joan stared at the man for a moment, then sneered;

"And people call me a thief."

The trio continued upward uneventfully, reaching the top landing in only a few minutes. Finding a closed door, Pa'sha asked where it led, discovering they were outside the exhibition area where the resurrection had taken place. Opening the door cautiously, he peeked inside but saw no further zombies in the reduced lighting. Quietly, he slid the door open just far enough to slip inside. As Joan and Edwards followed, the weaponeer spotted the table where the ritual had been performed. Moving directly toward it, he found one of the crystals on the table where Donald Reynolds had been laid out the day before. Scooping it up, he stuffed it into one of his vest pockets, asking;

"Dat's one. Where's de other one?"

As if to answer, the far door opened, admitting another herd of zombies. The mix of workers and executives was much the same as those previously encountered, except for two figures. One, dressed in skins and feathers, looked to be the voodoo priest brought in to perform the ritual. The other, an executive-type, took on singular distinction because of something he carried.

"His hands," blurted Joan. "He's got the crystal."

"It's Donnie!"

Indeed, Donald Reynolds led the parade of twisting, muttering dead as they filed into the room, the second gemstone clutched to his chest. Seeing his one-time golden boy staggering into the room, Edwards suddenly pushed his way past the Pirate Queen and Pa'sha, shouting;

"Donnie, it's me—Johnson!" Walking carefully, cautiously, the CEO held his arms out in a universal gesture of trust and acceptance, saying;

"For God's sake, Donnie, calm down. All is forgiven. We can get past all this. We can still salvage the quarter. With your genius at the helm, we can keep Quench at the forefront—you know we can..."

Pa'sha and Joan watched as the approaching zombies slowed, following Reynolds' lead. The former ad man slowed, his head turning, eyes trying to focus. As Edwards continued to talk, begging his one-time employee to return to the way he once was, Joan whispered;

"I don't understand. Why is it listening at all? I thought they were all mindless?"

"Dey are," answered Pa'sha. "When de body die, de soul leaves. Dat's it—period. Dat be why zombies are just beasts. De walking dead, dey got no souls. It must be de stone's power, forcing somet'ing to work in de zombie's brain."

As the pair watched, Reynolds' corpse actually seemed to understand some of what Edwards was offering. Complete amnesty, safety and luxury for Reynolds and all the other zombies, if only he could return to the fold. The zombie stared at the CEO for a long moment, then amazingly, it opened its mouth and in a painful, laborious tongue, said;

"It…it…it's…quench-o-licious!"

"Hummmmmm, I don't know," said Edwards, placing his hand to his chin, "I wonder if it's pre-teen friendly enough."

Reynolds' only answer was to reach out and snag hold of the CEO's collar. Catching the man off-guard, the thing jerked his one-time employer forward, setting on him tooth and nail. As several others joined in, Pa'sha let loose a double burst, splitting Reynolds' head and neck down the center. As the zombie dropped the crystal, Joan raced forward to grab it up even as others of the slow-moving pack headed in her direction. Pulling out a length of cord from her belt, she whipped it before her and caught up the glowing gem, yanking it backward in her direction.

The pair turned and ran back the way they had come, only to then find zombies of all manner pouring out of the stairwell they had just used. Swerving off, the two charged down the only hall open to them. For a moment, they made good time, outdistancing their attackers with ease. Then they came up against a solid door, one with a highly complicated series of locks.

Pa'sha knew to shoot the lock would quite possibly only jam it. He also realized explosives could not be used for there was no place for Joan and himself to hide from the back blast except down the hall in the ranks of the zombies. Knowing they had no other choice, he set the Pirate Queen to getting the door open while he worked on keeping the zombie horde at bay. Once he had gone through most of his weaponry, he asked how close she was to success, only to be told,

"I need another minute."

Pa'sha groaned. Still, he knew his partner was doing the best she could. Choosing to be philosophical about their situation, he pulled the pin on his third to last grenade, counted off the correct amount of seconds, then let it fly. The following explosion erupted nicely, flinging burst wire and burning metal in all directions. Those closest were shredded—limbs torn away, faces ruined, legs shattered. All but two in the front line were knocked over, and those the large man sent staggering backward headless with two careful bursts of his automatic weapon. Each burst released three rounds—more than enough to splatter a brain and drop a walker.

The ranks continued on forward, those that had been broken still tried to rise, as always, even as those behind attempted to walk over top of them. Knowing he had but two grenades left, and possibly twenty rounds of ammunition, the weaponeer reached into an inner pocket of his vest and pulled forth a flask filled with coconut rum. Downing a hefty swig, he slid the flask back into his vest, then unconsciously made the sign of the cross as he prepared one of his two last grenades.

Just as he was about to throw it, however, a part of his brain forced him to listen carefully. Despite the ringing in his ears caused by setting off explosives and firing weapons indoors, he believed he could hear voices coming from somewhere. His eyes going wide as he suddenly understood what he was hearing, he began to say something about the phenomena when Joan shouted;

"We're through!"

Instantly the two got through the doorway, Pa'sha flinging the readied grenade into the center of those approaching. On the other side of the thick metal door, the pair found themselves at a bank of elevators. Joan stared working on restoring operating power while the weaponeer contacted his other two teams via his headset. Miraculously, only one other man had met his fate. Pa'sha called for immediate withdrawal, telling the other two teams to head for the dock, making certain to spread their remaining charges on their way out.

The Pirate Queen took control of the first elevator to arrive. Making certain it was clear of zombies, the pair took it straight to the ground floor, and then fled the building, locking the exit behind them. As soon as everyone was in one of their two boats, Pa'sha gave the command to shove off, and immediately thereafter triggered his detonator. The explosion that followed lit up the night sky with a dazzling violence that could be seen as far away as Staten Island and even the Bronx.

On their way around the bottom of Manhattan, the three teams filled each other in on what had happened to them. Pa'sha's telling of the reason for the resurrection attempt ended as he told the others;

"And de chanting, de voices I was hearin'...wouldn't you know it, it were de damn zombies, all o'dem mutterin', 'it's quench-o-licious, it's quench-o-licious.'"

Pa'sha's indignation over the zombie chorus brought laughter from his men, as well as one suggestion that they decide for themselves. When the weaponeer asked what the Murder Dog meant, he found that the man had grabbed a case of Quench on the way out. Tossing cans to everyone remaining, he said;

"Let's see how quench-o-licious dis stuff be."

Pouring a healthy slug of the soda into the water, the weaponeer poured an equal amount of rum from his flask into the can. Taking a taste, he responded;

"Hummmmmmm, maybe de old white boy was onto somet'ing."

Pa'sha passed his flask to Joan while the Murder Dogs broke out their own resources. While two fired up outrageously thick blunts, the Pirate Queen took a deep drink of rum, licked her lips, then mused;

"All of this death and destruction, just to sell cans of soda."

"Oh, don't be forgettin' protectin' de jobs of de Clowntown folk...apparently also important." The Pirate Queen nodded, adding,

"I remember something Marshall McLuhan said, that 'Advertising is the greatest art form of the twentieth century.' What do you think, Pa'sha?"

"I t'ink," answered the weaponeer, taking a long pull on his doctored can of soda, dat I agree more with Mr. Orwell, the '1984' fellow, when he said 'Advertising is the rattling of a stick inside a swill bucket.'"

Joan smiled, partly at Pa'sha's comment, partly at the Murder Dogs who had already begun to sing a steel drum-rhythmed song about the joys of their favorite quench-o-licious drink. Looking into each other's eyes, the weaponeer and the Pirate Queen saluted each other silently, then sat back to get as drunk as they could on what supplies they had available.

I turned down "Fast Eddie" for the original The Dead Walk! *because it only had a single zombie in it. Years later, I heard the story read aloud by its author and realized what a terrible, silly mistake I'd made. But, like Fast Eddie himself, I now have the chance to rectify that mistake.*

FAST EDDiE'S BiG NiGHT OUt

by John L. French

Safe: that's what he felt like when he finally became aware of himself. Safe and warm. He hadn't felt like this since, since—he didn't know. It didn't matter. Wherever he was, he was at peace.

He called himself "Fast Eddie." It wasn't his real name. That was Wallace—Wallace Cromwell. He'd hated that name, hated being called Wallace. Hated "Wally" more. Hated being asked how the Beaver was. Then one night he saw a movie on late night TV about some guys shooting pool, Paul Newman and a fat guy. Newman's name was Fast Eddie. He liked that and started using it as his.

By then he was mostly on his own. He still lived in his mother's house, but his bedroom was in the basement. He came and went as he pleased. Mostly he went home to eat, sleep and get clean laundry. Some days he didn't go home at all. There was too much happening on the street—people to see, stuff to do.

Some of the stuff involved drinking—beer, wine, whatever he could get. And some of it involved girls—those who gave it away, those who traded it. And some of it involved drugs—reefer, crack, whatever made him feel good and forget the boredom that was at the bottom of his life. And all of it involved money. Money he usually didn't have and always needed. Money his mother had stopped giving him. Money he had to get from somewhere, no matter what.

He tried street jobs, but that was low percentage. The guy you robbed might not have any more than you. Or he might be armed, and your payoff a knife in the side or a nine in the head. It was better to B&E. Less chance of getting caught, and VCR's, DVD's and computers always brought him enough to get by.

He went home less and less. One night he went back and didn't have his key. Hadn't had it for a long time. How long he didn't know. He pounded on the front door. No answer. He went around and pounded on the back. Still nothing. He broke the pane of the basement door, reached it and unlocked it.

Things were changed. None of his stuff was there. He didn't know the man standing in the basement. He did know the man had a gun. And he knew that the sirens in the distance were coming for him.

Nobody believed that he thought it was still his house. His mother hadn't lived there for months. What had happened to her he never found out. Without money for bail he sat in the Baltimore Detention Center for six months, awaiting trial. In that time his prints came back on six other burglaries. He got three on top of the half he'd served. Overcrowding forced him back on the street inside the year.

When Eddie came out he went back to the B&E, back to yoking tourists who went down the wrong street, back to jacking cars from the fools who came down from PA looking to buy drugs. He had to. Inside he had picked up the habit, and now it needed to be fed every day.

He went inside the second time because he got stung. The guy in the Honda looking to buy turned out to be a cop. When Eddie pulled his piece the cop pulled a bigger one. Without turning around, Eddie knew that there were two more big guns pointing at the back of his head.

Two years this time. Eddie's cell mate was a no-parole lifer who had found Jesus—or was it Allah? Whoever It was, the lifer always talked to Eddie about a better way. With nothing else to do, Eddie listened.

It didn't make sense until three months after Eddie was out. Out in the cold and rain, huddling in a doorway, the better way that the con had talked about seemed very good to Eddie. He'd change, Eddie told himself. He'd find a program and get clean, give up this half a life and start living again.

Getting clean was harder than scoring without cash. All the programs were full. The drug treatment centers had waiting lists. Despite his wanting it, no one was offering any help. Desperate and willing to do anything to escape the limbo he was in, Eddie did the one thing he never expected to do.

He called a cop.

"Yeah, I'm interested...Thought there might be, how much? Oh! That might take some doing...No, didn't say it couldn't be done, have to pull in a few that's all...Give me your cell...Thought everybody did...Pager then...Well then, call be back in two days...Yeah, this number. I'll work something out, get you clean."

Detective Dante Amberson hung up the phone.

"Who was that?" Andy Russell asked his partner.

"Some stoner called Fast Eddie," Amberson replied, turning to his computer. He logged on to the Citynet and searched "drug treatment centers—open beds." There weren't that many.

"I remember Eddie. We almost shot him, what, two years back?"

"That's why he called us, because we *didn't* shoot him when we could have. Thinks he can trust us." Amberson started copying names, numbers and email addresses into a document, highlighting the ones he'd try first.

"What's he want?"

"To give us Santos."

Russell's eyes widened. Antoine Santos wasn't a major drug dealer, but he was big enough that once arrested, he could be squeezed until he gave up a few people who were. "How's Eddie know Santos?"

"Used to work for him, still does some running." Amberson hit print. Two lists came out of the printer.

"And for Santos he gets...?"

"Placement in a drug treatment center. He wants out of the life."

"That's it, no money?" Russell was amazed: everybody wanted money.

"He wouldn't turn it down, but without treatment, no Santos."

"We better make some calls."

Amberson handed Russell one of the lists. "Tell me about it. Start calling, partner."

Two days later Eddie called back.

"All arranged, my man," Amberson told him. "Got a room at the McCulloh Treatment Facility with your name on it...That's right, where Church Home Hospital used to be...You're getting the works—detoxification, blood cleaning, counseling, job placement, everything. You be there tomorrow morning, eleven sharp. We'll get you settled, then you give us what we need on Santos…What's that?"

But Eddie hadn't been talking to Amberson. The detective heard him say something to somebody, his voice low as if turned away from the phone. There was a muffled reply, then three loud pops.

"Oh shit! Eddie! Eddie!" Amberson yelled into the receiver. To his partner, "Andy, call 2284. Get this line traced. Get an ambo started. Eddie!" he yelled again. No answer.

"Got it," Russell said calmly. "Units and medics are rolling. Anything on your end?" Amberson shook his head. "Damn. Well, let's get out there." Amberson looked at the admissions folder they'd gotten from McCulloh. "Damn," he said again, "and after all our hard work."

When the two detectives rolled up on the scene, they saw the ambulance pulling away.

"Follow that," Amberson told his partner. "Let the district guys and the Lab worry about witnesses and spent casings. If Eddie's still alive we'll get his statement."

Russell followed the ambulance down Wolfe St. He groaned when it turned right, bypassing Johns Hopkins.

"Taking him right to Shock Trauma," he said. "Must be bad."

Madison to Central. Central to Fayette. From Fayette straight to Shock Trauma and the best emergency care available. Russell knew the way, every detective did, and stayed close to the wagon. He wanted to be there when Eddie was pulled out, to hear him say who shot him, hoping the name was "Santos."

Lights flashing and siren screaming, the ambulance raced down Central. But when it turned on Fayette, it went silent and dark as its emergency system shut down. It slowed, now keeping pace with traffic rather than weaving in and out.

There could only be one reason for the sudden lack of urgency. "Damn," Amberson's fist hit the dash. "They lost him."

Still, Russell followed. From Fayette St. the wagon turned on to Penn St, and from there down the ramp that led to the Medical Examiner's Office.

Russell parked along side the ambulance. The detectives caught up to the paramedics just as they were wheeling Eddie into the receiving area.

"He say anything?" Amberson shouted as he ran into the room.

"Like?" asked the medic. He was on the twelfth hour of a sixteen-hour day. He'd had two "breaks"—once he stopped for a coffee and doughnut at a convenience store, both of which he gulped down rushing to yet another overdose call. An hour later at Hopkins he stopped briefly to call his wife and use the bathroom. Somehow he couldn't bring himself to get as excited about this dead junkie as the detective was.

"Like, did he say who shot him?"

The medic shrugged. "Maybe. I wasn't listening." In fact, the medic had stopped listening a year ago. He'd heard a dying declaration from a gunshot victim, reported it to the police. That lead to his going to court several times, spending hours waiting in a cold, dark hallway only to be told the case was once again postponed. When he finally did get to testify, he was on the stand three hours as a team of defense attorneys challenged his competency, questioned his hearing and subtly suggested that he'd let the victim die so the declaration could be used in court. When a "not guilty" verdict came back, the medic decided that from then on, he'd be deaf to anything not directly related to treating his patient.

Like a baby, Eddie felt himself being cradled in someone's arms. There was a gentle, rocking motion. Gradually, the arms became a hand, with Eddie cupped in its palm as if being weighed. He became aware of all the decisions, good or bad, he'd ever made in his life. He saw too all the decisions he'd failed to make. Every path his life could have taken was revealed to him. Some were worse than the one he had lived. Most were better.

From somewhere there was a voice. "A life mostly wasted. An effort at redemption towards the end." A light appeared—a golden light. Eddie was drawn toward it. But he knew without the voice telling him that despite his yearning, he'd get no closer to the light than where he was now.

"Can you make the ID?" the attending examiner asked Amberson and Russell.

The detectives looked down at the body. There wasn't much to see—a body ravaged by drugs, thin and dirty from too many months on the street.

"Yeah," Russell answered. "For your records, I identify this body as one Wallace Cromwell, a.k.a. Fast Eddie."

"And do you agree, sir?" the examiner asked Amberson. There was a slight lilt of the Caribbean in his voice.

Amberson nodded. "Well, Eddie," he said to the corpse, "I guess you won't be needing that treatment now. I just wish you'd held on long enough to give us Santos."

Now would be a good time, the examiner thought. In his six months in this country, five months doing this job, he'd seen too much of this tragedy, too many wasted lives. It was time to do something about it, if these men were willing.

"He still could."

Both detectives looked at the examiner, who had finished weighing the body and was now filling out a toe tag.

"Excuse me, Mr...?" Amberson asked

"Jones, Dominic Jones. I said that maybe he still could."

"And how, Mr. Amberson, could he do that?"

"I am from the Dominican Republic. My country, as you may or may not know, shares its island with Haiti. When I was in medical school, it was close enough to Haiti that, occasionally, myself and other students would slip across the border to study, shall we say, comparative medicine and religion."

"Voodoo," Amberson said softly.

"Vodou," Jones corrected, giving the word a slightly different pronunciation.

"Wait a minute," Russell said, almost shouting. "You're saying you can bring this guy back from the dead?"

Jones smiled.

"Not exactly. Rather, it may be possible to awaken a soul, as if from sleep, before it passes on. If so, one can ask what questions one needs to, before the soul is called away forever."

Russell gave a derisive laugh. Amberson, on the other hand, asked, "And you can do this?"

"I have seen it done. An old man, called back to tell where he had hidden his wealth. A woman, dead after childbirth, summoned from the dark to say which man in the village fathered her child. In each case, the priest performed the ritual. In each case, an answer came from the corpse."

Russell interrupted. "And there are guys in Vegas who stick their hands up dummies's butts who can do the same thing."

"Ventriloquism, Detective? Maybe. But the money was found where the old man's ghost said it would be. And the child grew up in the image of his announced father."

"Do you know the ceremony?" Amberson asked suddenly.

"This is crazy!"

At his partner's exclamation Amberson said, "And we haven't seen crazy before? Besides, it's not like we got anything to lose. Unless you've got a better idea?"

"I can do it, Detective. I have watched the priests and studied with them. One thing about this place—it's got everything I need, except...do you know where we can get a live chicken?"

Eddie drifted. Try as he might, he couldn't move closer to the glow. Then he felt himself being pulled away. He thought he heard someone call his name. And then—something else. There was something else he had to do. The golden light got fainter, smaller. Like the dot on an old TV, it faded away.

"Eddie, Eddie, can you hear me?" Amberson shouted, shaking the corpse. "Come back, Eddie! Give us Santos!"

"It's no good, partner." Russell drew Amberson away. "It was dumb idea to begin with."

"It should have worked," a despondent Jones said. He looked at the bodies of the dead pigeons in the biohazard waste bin. "We should have used chickens."

"Yeah," Russell turned on him, "and I should maybe run us all up to Mercy for an emergency commitment. Me searching the parking garage for those birds, catching them yet. I have to be crazy."

"The only other choice was regular or extra crispy," Amberson said. "Come on, we've already wasted two hours. Let's get some papers signed and get back to work. Mr. Jones, thanks for your effort, but let's not mention this to anyone."

"Agreed, detective. Now if you two will step into my office, we can get the paperwork out of the way."

It took Jones about ten minutes to find and fill out the forms. Amberson signed them and gave them back. Jones was just putting them into a folder when an alarm sounded.

"What's that?" Russell asked.

"The door to our vehicle bay," Jones explained. "Someone's coming in."

They went out into the receiving area to see who it was. Russell was the first to notice the empty gurney where Eddie's body had lain.

"Or someone left."

Beside him, Amberson swore quietly.

"You know," Jones said, staring at the empty place where Fast Eddie had been, "when you use a chicken they usually don't get up and leave."

Eddie woke up, sort of. Light and sound rushed back in. His chest hurt. He felt the cold steel of the gurney beneath him. Not knowing where he was or how he got there, Eddie got up and walked toward the door. It opened automatically, as did the gate of the vehicle bay when Eddie crossed the electric eye. Driven by a need he didn't understand, Fast Eddie walked out into the night.

He was confused. Memories of a warm, safe place where he was loved conflicted with other thoughts. He was talking to someone, someone who was helping him. He heard a noise. He turned. Talking, then more noise, louder this time. Pain. Eddie looked down at his chest. His shirt was open. He could see the holes the loud noise had put there. A clear liquid was seeping from them.

Eddie was still looking at the bullet wounds when he wandered into the street. There was a screeching of wheels, then Eddie was struck by steel, glass and steel again as he went up and over the car that hit him. Eddie stood up and, ignoring the curses of the driver, slowly walked away.

"Now what do we do?" Amberson asked no one in particular.

"I don't know about you two, but if he's not back by six a.m., I'm shredding everything and he was never here."

"We'll find him, Jones."

"We will?" asked Russell.

"Of course," Amberson assured him. "How far can a dead guy go?"

The detectives left the ME's and walked out on to an accident scene. A late-model sedan with pedestrian damage to the hood, windshield and roof. Two patrol cars blocking the street. A uniformed officer taking a statement from a distraught driver. No victim, no ambo.

"What happened?" Russell asked one of the officers standing by.

"Damnest thing," came the reply. "Driver here says some junkie walked out in front of him. He couldn't stop in time and the guy went up and over. Says he came down hard, then got up and walked away."

"Driver didn't try to stop him?" Amberson asked.

"Would you?" The officer shook his head. "You'd think the guy would be dead, wouldn't you?"

Amberson looked at Russell. Russell looked back. Neither said a word.

Eddie wandered, his thoughts a jumble. He sensed a need, but for what? Dimly he recalled the taste of food, of strong drink. He vaguely remembered the touch of a woman and how that made him felt. Then there was the needle, the high that had made him float and forget. It had taken the place of the others, but it was still not enough, not now, not tonight.

Brightness blinded him. His wanderings had taken him out of the dark streets and alleys and now he found himself on Greene Street. Street lights, stop lights, neon and the glow of the not-so-distant Oriole Park all hit his too sensitive eyes at once. It came back—he needed the light, the golden light he'd been denied earlier. But no, that light was gone, taken from him when he was called back. Its absence left a yearning, a hole to be filled. Instinct turned Eddie to the east, towards the one man who had always given him what he needed.

"We've been driving in circles for hours," Russell complained. "It's time to give it up."

"It's only been an hour, and we're not giving up," Amberson said in a flat, determined tone.

"Can't we at least put out a description?"

"And say what? Eastern CID looking for a walkaway from the Medical Examiner's. Suspect's a light-skinned black male, about five-nine and believed to be dead?"

"That would do it," Russell said after some thought. "Look, Danny, we are never going to find him this way. We turn right, he goes left and we miss him. We drive straight, he turns down an alley, he's gone.

"So we quit?"

"No, we start thinking like cops looking for a suspect. Eddie never was that bright, and I'm betting that whatever smarts he had died when he did and didn't come back. He's down to memory and habit. Let's hit the Eastside, check out his haunts. See if anybody saw a zombie tonight."

Nobody had. Russell and Amberson hit all the corners where Eddie hung out. They questioned some of the girls he saw when he had the stuff to trade for their favors. They braced the low-level dealers Eddie knew. Everywhere was the same story.

"Nope, ain't seen him."

"Guess you ain't heard—Eddie bought one tonight."

"Hasn't been around."

"Eddie gone, some fool done kilt him over a phone call."

"Eddie got wasted."

"I want a lawyer. This is police harassment."

"Fast Eddie who?"

"You guys don't talk to each other, do you?"

"Eddie wouldn't get off the phone. Junkie wouldn't wait. Blew him away."

"You 5-0, I don't talk to 5-0."

"Thought I saw him. But he be dead, so it wasn't him."

The two detectives questioned this last one more thoroughly. "Where'd you see him? Which way was he going? How long ago?" For answers they got "Around, down there, don't know."

"The good news is," Russell said as Amberson turned down yet another side street, "is that he's here somewhere."

"So says one lowlife out of ten. And what's the bad news? Other than we haven't found him yet."

"Who says there's bad news?"

"There's good news, gotta be bad news."

Russell thought for a moment. "I guess the bad news is that Santos didn't kill him. Just some crackhead who thought Eddie was taking too long on his phone."

Amberson gave a rueful smile. "Yeah, it would have been nice to pin this one on Santos. Murder one, killing a witness—you get the needle for that."

"Damn shame," agreed Russell. "Santos would have sung just to do twenty-to-life. Actually would have worked out better than if Eddie have stayed alive to give him up."

Amberson stopped the car, looked at his partner, an idea forming in his mind.

I got a good life, Antoine Santos told himself. Not great, but good. A decent house, plenty of food, a nice ride, women when I want them. It's not a mansion in Guilford, steak every night, a Mercedes and Playmates, but it's better than the slobs I deal with have.

Unlike his clients, the ones who bought and resold his product, Santos lived outside the drug area. His house was on the east end of Federal, close enough to the Eastern District police station that it was in a safer neighborhood than most. That's why he bought it: for the security. He also liked the idea of the police helping to keep him safe, that the same cops trying to put him away were, by their very presence, protecting him. Irony, he thought, remembering an old English lesson. It was what Miss Helens back in high school would have called irony.

And was irony, he wondered, about how it ended with that Fast Eddie guy? Word from the street was that Eddie was shopping him to the cops, that he'd worked some kind of deal to trade what he knew about the organization for cash and a ticket out. Santos was going to have the boy hit then he'd found out tonight that he wouldn't have to. Poor Eddie, guess he forgot that you didn't use the holy phone anytime St. Kevin was around. Hell, everybody knew that. Kevin thought that that phone was his direct line to God, that one day the savior would call him up and invite him to Heaven. He got very upset if anyone used it. God might call, and what if He got a busy signal? And who would have thought Kevin had a gun?

As Santos contemplated his life, he heard a pounding on his front door. Who the Hell is that, he wondered. Wasn't cops, they'd have broken down the door. Can't be clients, they knew he didn't sell direct. And his boys had the word not to come to the house. Always some fool didn't get the message. Well, he'd get the message tonight, Santos decided. Find out who that fool is, then fire him or cut him off. He'll be flipping burgers for his cash and going to the Westside for his stuff.

Santos moved to go downstairs. The banging got louder. Then the crashing of glass. Santos paused, got his nine from under the bed, made sure the clip was good and the chamber was hot. He tucked it in his dip, just in case.

More banging, more glass breaking. Santos got to his door just as the invader came through. "What the—?" he started as he saw who it was.

Fast Eddie stood in his doorway, his shirt bloody, clear fluid leaking from the wounds on his chest. His face and arms had a death pallor and he moved with the stiffness of the rigor that had come over him.

"*Saanntoooosss*," Eddie's voice creaked as he raised his pale hands towards the drug dealer. "*I neeeedddd...*"

Santos reached into his dip, pulled out his nine. "You're dead," he cried, recognizing the absurdity of his statement while realizing at the same time that it was true.

Eddie ignored the gun, kept coming one step at a time. Santos fired—once, twice, a third time. Eddie's body jerked with each impact, but he kept coming. Backing up, Santos emptied the clip. Eddie slowed, stopped, fell.

Relief washed through Santos. He had stopped the Eddie-thing. Then as he wondered what to do next, Eddie's left hand twitched, then clawed the carpet. His right hand moved, fingers clutched the carpet and pulled his body forward. Slowly, Eddie crawled toward Santos.

Russell and Amberson were just pulling on to Federal St when they heard the shots. They looked at each other. "I got the back," Russell said as they both bailed out of the unmarked car. Amberson gave his partner time to get around back before going through the open front door.

Russell got to the rear of the house just in time to see Santos run out the kitchen door. Both men had their guns out. Santos saw Russell, made him for a cop and dropped his piece. A good thing. A second later, Russell would have done Santos like the dealer had tried to do Eddie.

"You okay?" Russell heard his partner call form inside the house.

"Okay," Russell confirmed, snapping the cuffs on Santos. "You secure?"

"Under control. Come on in."

"Let's go," Russell urged Santos forward. The dealer balked.

"Not going back in there. Don't take me back," Santos pleaded.

Russell shoved the dealer into the doorframe—hard. "Walk or get dragged. Either way, you're going in."

Amberson looked up as Russell came in from the back, pushing Santos ahead of him. "Found him," he said, indicating the mostly lifeless body on the floor.

Eddie was still trying to get to Santos, hands and knees weakly moving him along. Hearing the detective's voice, a distant memory came back. He turned towards Amberson, raised an arm and pointed it towards the dealer. "*Saanntoooosss*," he croaked out. Then, his appointed task done, and with what could have been a smile, or maybe just the effects of rigor, Fast Eddie collapsed and was finally still.

The detectives were quick to seize the situation.

"Doesn't look good, Antoine. Dead man in your house, your bullets in him," Amberson told Santos.

"Why'd you steal him from the morgue? Going to dig the bullets out?" continued Russell.

"No, no," Santos protested. "He was dead when he came in and—"

"And nobody's going to believe that, Antoine." Amberson interrupted. "Except maybe me and my partner." The sound of sirens in the distant, getting closer. "You gonna deal, deal now, else you get you a manslaughter charge."

Men in blue uniforms rushing the house from front and back, Amberson and Russell, weapons holstered, holding up their hands and badges to stem the charge. "I'm yours," Santos shouting over the initial confusion of men and voices. District detectives then homicide men arriving. Amberson and Russell holding tight to their charge.

By morning Santos had given up his entire network, from suppliers down to runners. In exchange, he was charged as an accessory after the fact in the death of Wallace Cromwell, aka "Fast Eddie," with minimum sentencing guaranteed.

As for how the theft of Eddie's body was explained, Amberson and Cromwell referred anyone who asked to Dominic Jones. Jones, in turn, told the questioner to ask Santos. Santos, whose reputation was only enhanced by the belief that he had committed such an audacious crime, always denied it, but in such a way as to assure his listener that he had beyond doubt done the deed. The Medical Examiner's Office did get a new state-of-the art security system to keep whatever had happened from happening again.

With no one to claim it, Fast Eddie's body was turned over to the Anatomy Board. Unusually well-preserved for an unembalmed corpse, it was used for three weeks before it was cremated and the ashes disposed of.

Safe and warm, Eddie again felt the warm embrace of loving arms. He floated, bathing in the warmth of the golden light. It was not for him, not this time. He'd been judged and he acknowledged that the judgment was fair and just. He felt a tug. Somewhere a new life was being created. Consciousness faded as the soul that had once been Fast Eddie Cromwell sped off towards another chance at doing things right.

A tale of Millwood, one of the few scrappy remnants left alive in a vast, undead wasteland, and the subject of many of Nate Southard's post-apocalytic stories of survival horror. Although, to be honest, at this point in the town's history, things aren't looking so good...

OF CABBAGES AND KiNGS

by Nate Southard

Holly stumbled down the winding country road, her feet sore and her legs tired. She tried to remember how long she'd been walking, but she couldn't. It felt as though she'd been shuffling along forever. Her eyes drooped closed, and she forced them open again.

Jesus, she wanted to sleep.

But she knew that was a bad idea. She hadn't seen any dead since she'd escaped the bus, but that didn't mean anything. They were quick, and if one caught her off guard, she wouldn't stand a chance.

Just like those poor bastards in the bus.

Twenty-two souls, all that was left of Millwood. They'd barely made it five miles before the dead had swarmed them. She could still hear their shrieks of terror, smell the rot reek of the dead as they surged over the moving bus or crunched beneath its wheels. She felt the twist of her stomach as the vehicle lurched, spun, and finally rolled, sending the people inside this way and that.

And then the dead had come through the windows.

And Holly had run.

It was luck, dumb-fucking-luck. The wreck had knocked her off her feet, and she'd rolled down the aisle until she rested against the emergency exit. An instant after the bus had finally stopped, her wits had returned in full, and she'd thrown the exit open, setting off the bus's alarm. The sound had confused the dead for the briefest of moments, and in that time she'd leapt from the bus and bolted to the edge of the forest.

She'd been too scared to drag anyone else along with her.

Even now, more than a day later, or maybe it was closer to two, she felt a great weight of shame on her shoulders. There had been children on the bus, and elderly. They had been her responsibility because the escape plan had been hers.

Well, hadn't she escaped?

She almost cracked a weak smile at the thought, but another crushing wave of guilt fell on her, and she felt a fresh round of tears well up in her eyes. She blinked, and they spilled down her cheeks, cutting furrows in the grime that had built up there. She wanted to squeeze her eyes shut until the tears stopped, but every time she tried she heard the screams emanating from the bus, the cries to God and others, pleas for help or mercy that had gone unanswered as the dead tore everyone inside to pieces. She remembered how she had felt so powerless and scared standing just beyond the edge of the forest, knowing a braver person would try to help, would think of a way. She had only stood there, however, afraid to move and make any sound that might give her hiding spot away. She had watched for more than an hour, terrified and sickened, as the dead ate the people she cared about, not stopping until they had finished every last morsel. And then they had charged back up the road toward Millwood, no doubt hoping to find others who might not have made it out.

Holly turned to look behind her. In the distance, filtering the morning sunlight, rose a column of black smoke. She assumed it was from Millwood, but she couldn't tell with any certainty. She wasn't very good with direction or distance, never had been. Even now, she could only guess that she was somewhere between Versailles and Madison. She had probably walked more than twenty miles in the last day, but she couldn't be sure. She wasn't even positive she was heading toward Madison. She had to stay away from the main roads and towns. That's where the dead gathered. Then again, the bus had been on a country road yesterday, and it had still been attacked. Maybe the dead had been on their way to Millwood, coming from Milan or Dillsboro, and had just lucked into a meal.

She growled to herself, trying to push the thought out of her brain. She didn't want to think about the bus anymore, about the wreck or the screams or the dead surging through the windows and doors or how she could only—

—STOP IT!

She fell to her knees, shrieking with rage, and pounded both fists into the gravel. She hissed as the rocks bit into the flesh of her hands. She punished the ground again, crying out, and felt the warmth of her own blood as it trickled down her wrists. She cursed herself. The dead could smell blood, or at least she was pretty sure they could. She'd have to move faster now. If any were in the area, they'd have no trouble locating her.

She pushed herself to her feet and continued along the gravel road. Her hair fell in her eyes and she brushed it back with her fingertips. It was getting long again. She'd kept it so short over the last twenty months, ever since Blake had failed to return from Rundberg and she'd decided to take a more active roll in Millwood's welfare. The shorter hair had helped keep the others off balance, see her as something other that John Manton's daughter who used to work the counter at the Dairy Barn. The short hair had helped them see her as a leader, somebody to listen to. She had kept it short right up until things started to get bad, until the pressure began to weigh on her as she had to think first of the town's defense and then of escape. Now it was long enough to cling to her face and chin. Had it been months? Had it really been so long?

She wondered if it was really June. Had her people paid close attention to the days? The weather had been rainy recently, and that made her think she was in the ballpark, that she was deep in the middle of June, but she could only guess at the actual date. Eighteenth? Nineteenth? She didn't know.

She pushed herself to her feet and began to walk again.

A breeze fluttered down the road, cooling her dirt-smeared and sweat-soaked skin. She began to breathe deep, a reflex, but caught herself. She didn't like to breathe too deeply anymore, not since the dead had returned. Now, the air always carried a stench along with it, a smell like roadkill or a pig farm, just underneath the natural scents of the world. Holly could only imagine what the larger cities might smell like. She'd met a few people who'd made it out of Cincinnati, and they'd said the odor of rot had been unbearable, even in those early days.

She looked to the sun as it rose to her left, determining which direction was east. She figured she was east of Highway 421. Soon, she could turn right and head into the forest. If she was correct, and that was a big if, she would reach 421 where it ran alongside the Jefferson Proving Ground. The military base, a former testing area for bombs and other weapons, would be fortified. It had been their original destination when they'd made their escape from Millwood. The proving ground was huge, surrounded on all sides with a razor wire-topped fence and armed to the teeth. If any place had withstood the dead's rise, it was Jefferson. And even if it had fallen, maybe she could find a weapon, something she could defend herself with until she found a more permanent shelter.

Or maybe she'd just lower her arms and walk into the dead, give herself up and end the whole stupid thing.

Maybe that would be better.

Holly wiped the blood from her hands onto her jeans and listened to the shuffle and crunch of her boots over the gravel. The rhythm, slow and rumbling, did little to comfort her, but it took her mind off of other things. She listened to her own footsteps so closely, so intently, that she didn't hear the piano until the trees fell away to her right and she saw the church.

The structure was old, but then again, most of the buildings in this part of the state were. The white paint of its clapboard sides had faded to a dull gray, the wood beneath peeking through in more than one place. Its shingles still held on, but there was a sense of desperation to their grip, as if the next puff of breeze might strip the entire roof bare.

A single sign, built of sturdy wood, stood by the roadside. Holly could still make out the words Fellowship Baptist Church, but they had been painted over with a single coat of white. On top of this, the words New World Ministry had been written in uneven letters with blue spraypaint. Holly came to a halt, considering the words for a moment, and an uneasy fluttering passed through her belly. She couldn't quite understand it, but something about the words frightened her the slightest bit.

"How ya doin'?"

She jumped at the masculine voice, her breath catching in her chest and her hands drawing up defensively. She hadn't heard human speech in well over twenty-four hours, so the words, despite their friendly tone, startled her. Her eyes darted to the church, standing alone in the middle of the field with only an empty blacktop lot to keep it company. An upright piano sat on a small porch that surrounded the church's main entrance. A man in a white dress shirt and a green ballcap sat behind the keys, banging out hymns. He looked back at her as he played, and Holly could only assume this was the man who had greeted her.

As if to answer her suspicions, the man called out, "You okay?"

Holly nodded. It never occurred to her that the man might not be able to make out her weak movements.

"You gonna stand there all day?" the man asked. "Once that sun gets all the way up, it's gonna get pretty hot. Muggy, too. The rain we been getting lately's wreaking havoc on the weather, but I guess I don't need to tell you that. Come on over and rest your bones a second."

Holly smiled at the invitation. She could use a rest, no doubt about that. Her legs and feet practically begged for one. A sudden wave of exhaustion, more powerful than she was prepared for, rolled over her, and she knew she needed to sit down for awhile.

She let out a long sigh and left the road, shuffling across the grass toward the old, gray structure. The man continued his recital, the hymns taking on a more regal, buoyant quality, and Holly almost smiled as she realized he was giving her some marching music, announcing her arrival. Her trek across the field seemed to take forever, the grass cushioning her stride but slowing her pace. She glanced at the church and wandered if it was really getting closer, almost afraid to believe so until she finally placed her hand on the banister that ran alongside the four steps that led up to the porch and entrance.

"Good morning!" the man behind the piano called. His voice seemed to bounce alongside the chords he played.

"Hi," Holly managed. Her voice seemed little more than a croak compared to the piano player's.

"Come to rest your weary bones? Come to make peace with the Lord in these times of never-ending trouble? You have come to the right place, my friend. You have come to the right place."

He changed chords and began to sing, his voice deep and resonating.

"Then sings my soul, my Saviour, God, to thee. How great thou art. How great thou art!"

Holly eyed the man as he rocked back on the piano bench, his fingers shuddering over the keys and his eyes drawing closed even as his jaw dropped open to deliver his voice. His face was rugged but handsome, the skin tanned and rough, his jaw freshly shaven. His dress shirt shined in the early morning light, the cleanest thing she'd seen in well over a year. His hat displayed the John Deer logo with pride, though it was a bit more weathered than the shirt. A pair of light blue corduroys and some old loafers completed the outfit, conveying an image of trustworthiness and station despite its simple origins.

He hunched over the keys again, making the chords shiver, and Holly lowered her face into her hands, thankful for the opportunity to rest.

"Oh Lord my God, when I in awesome wonder..."

Though she could probably do without the singing. She wasn't so sure she believed in God anymore, not after what he had let happen to the world. Still, she couldn't deny that some people, in times of crisis, felt better with a little religion in their lives. If it helped them, where was the harm? Why should she give a damn?

Besides, the guy at the piano had a pretty good voice. He was no Elvis, but he wasn't half-bad.

She looked up at him, but he was bent low over the keys, his eyes squeezed shut and his face drawn in a long expression of emotion—something between joy and sorrow—as he sang. She decided to let him finish. There were worse ways to spend the time.

The man's voice rolled through the hymn, swelling with each chorus and falling to a reverent hush with each verse. He finished with a prolonged note, his vibrato perfect, and the piano fell still, ringing out one final note before leaving the church and the clearing in silence.

Holly opened her eyes at the sudden absence of sound, realizing for the first time just how loud the man and his song had been. Wasn't he afraid of the dead hearing him? That kind of racket could probably draw the walkers from more than a mile in any direction.

Maybe the dead had left the area, decided to head toward someplace more urban.

Or maybe this asshole didn't have a single goddamn lick of sense.

The man spun around on his bench, swinging his legs behind him. He stuck out his hand, his lips spreading into a wide, jubilant smile.

"Hi there! Name's Toby. Brother Toby, I guess. It's a great pleasure to see somebody come along this Sunday."

Holly reached up, took the man's hand. She was amazed at how soft the skin of his palm and fingers felt. It didn't seem to match his rough appearance.

"Is it Sunday?" she asked. She really didn't know.

"To the best of my knowledge. It's not like the TV Guide shows up every Monday anymore. I just marked the days off on an old calendar. Once we reached a year, I started marking 'em again. This isn't a leap year, is it? That would've thrown me off."

Holly shook her head, a little dumbfounded by the man's rapid speech.

"That's great! I've been worried about that for months. Don't want to go calling to worship on a Saturday, right? It's not like we're Catholics here."

She shook her head again. Her mouth tried to form words, but only a light click escaped her lips.

Brother Toby dropped her hand, and it fell back into her lap. She hadn't even realized they were still shaking. Something about Toby confused her, seemed to sap her intelligence and will. Maybe it was his rapid, boisterous way method of speech. Maybe it was that smile that seemed to grow wider and wider with each passing moment.

Maybe she had just grown paranoid over the past year. Billy Hudson's assassination attempt would have had that effect on anybody. It was possible that there were still good people in the world. Hell, until a few minutes ago, she hadn't been sure there were people of any kind left.

She took a deep breath and decided to give Toby the benefit of the doubt. At least he was still alive.

"So, sister. What should I call you?"

She blinked, hoping she hadn't been silent so long it was noticeable. Time had been slipping away for her so much over the past few months, and she'd spent the last day or so wandering if she'd ever have a conversation with anyone other than herself again.

"Holly," she said, and she gave him something she hoped looked like a smile.

"Sister Holly! It is a real pleasure."

"Please, Holly is fine. I was never anybody's sister."

Toby shrugged. "We're all brothers and sister to one degree or another. The Lord says so."

"He does?"

"Sure, he does. It's right there in the bible."

Holly wasn't about to argue with him. She was a lot of things, but a bible scholar had never been one of them. If Toby said it was in there, she was willing to take his word for it. It sounded biblical, at least.

She decided to change the subject.

"How long have you been here, Toby?"

A shadow crossed his face. "Since shortly after… well, I'm sure you know. I came from near Friendship."

"Really? I'm from Millwood."

"Millwood? That's marvelous! I've been through Millwood a time or two. Nice little place. What brings you my way?"

"Long story. We tried to get out. We didn't make it. I guess that's the short version."

One of Toby's eyebrows arched upward.

"We?"

"There were others. A busload, as a matter of fact. There was a wreck, though, and the dead got everybody else. I managed to escape and hide in the woods. Later on, I started walking."

He nodded. His face was a map of concern.

"I'm so sorry to hear that."

"It's okay." It was a lie, but she didn't feel like being the brunt of his condolences right now. She just didn't have the strength.

"So where were you headed? Were you just wandering, like Moses in the desert, or did you have a destination in mind?"

Moses? she thought. The guy was a little over the top. She'd thought the evangelicals and such stayed farther south. Was she going to hear about a plague of frogs next, or did he plan to jump right to the Second Coming?

"I'm headed toward the Jefferson Proving Ground," she said. "Thought it might be safe there."

He nodded, then shrugged. "Maybe. Then again, maybe not. Jefferson's a ways off, and I'm afraid I just can't tell you one way or the other."

She'd figured as much. The lines of communication had unraveled since the dead had risen. Even Millwood had only received news whenever a fresh crop of refugees arrived, and that hadn't happened in more than four months.

"Am I headed in the right direction at least?" she asked.

"I think so. You'll have to cut east eventually, but that shouldn't be so bad. You'll hit Route 62 if you keep along this road, and that'll take you to 421. It might not be the easiest path, though. I'd recommend you stay away."

"Really?"

"Sure. What place is safer than a house of the Lord?"

Holly fought the urge to roll her eyes.

"I'm sorry, Toby. I'm just not sure I believe that anyplace is safe nowadays."

"Belief is usually the problem."

She looked up. Toby's face had grown solemn, the lines in his dark skin deep and shadowed. He didn't look angry, though, just sad.

He shook it off.

"Look, I'm sorry," he said. "I'm not trying to freak you out or preach to you, okay? I'm just trying to offer some kind of... I don't know... stability in this big clusterfuck we've got going on now.

"I found this church about a year ago. The preacher and his wife were dead, so I got rid of them and set up shop. I'm not really a holy man or anything. I'm just feeling my way as I go. I pulled the piano out here, and I play every Sunday. Every now and then somebody hears it and wonders along. Most of the time they don't. I'm just trying to make a difference, Sis— Holly, give a little comfort to anybody who might happen along. I don't mean to creep anybody out."

Holly stared at the worn wooden steps for a moment, then nodded. "I'm sorry. Really. I didn't mean to come off like that. It's just, well, you know what's happened to the world. We all do, right? We've all got to be careful, and I guess I'm trying to be a little more cautious than most. Like I said, I'm sorry."

Toby dismissed her with a wave. "It's not a problem. I won't have you pretend that it is, okay? You stay if you want, or you go along your way when you feel you're ready. In the meantime, let me know if there's anything I can do to help."

The offer made Holly's throat burn, and she realized she had been without water for at least a day. She tried to swallow, but a scratchy dryness prevented it, and she almost coughed out a few rough notes before she managed to recover.

"You got any water?" she asked, and her voice sounded raspy, like old newspaper tumbling across hot concrete. She rubbed her throat with one hand, wincing at the pain the sentence had caused.

Toby's fingers leapt from the keyboard. He stood almost as quickly. "Water? Sure! I always keep a few jugs handy. It's not cold, of course, but it should help your thirst a little bit, regardless."

"Thanks."

He stepped to the church's double door and motioned for Holly to stand. "C'mon in, Holly. It'll do you good to get out of the hot sun, anyway."

She couldn't argue with that. Even this early in the morning, the heat and humidity seemed to press down on her from all sides. A few minutes inside, where she would at least be in the shade, would probably do wonders.

She grunted and pushed herself to her feet. She dusted her jeans off with her hands. "Sounds good, Toby. Lead the way."

Toby opened one of the doors wide. He gestured with a flourish. "After you."

She gave him a playful curtsy. His smiled turned into a chuckle. She laughed, as well, and then she stepped through the door and into the small church.

The smell hit her at once.

The dark church reeked of death. The rotting, clinging smell squeezed the air from every direction, forcing its way past Holly's nostrils and down her throat. She gagged, bending in half as her stomach fought to expel its meager contents. She bit the urge back, but her body convulsed once, twice, and then she fell to her knees, vomiting all over the church's carpet.

"Yeah," Toby said behind her, "I never really got used to the smell either."

She looked back over her shoulder, straining to see Toby through the darkness and her own tears. She saw his fist cock back, and she tried to move, but he was too fast. The hand struck her just behind the ear, and she collapsed into unconsciousness.

"Wake up, Sister Holly. Time to rise and shine!"

Something wet and cool splashed against her face, and Holly sputtered. She tried to blink the liquid—she hoped it was only water—from her eyes. She tried to wipe her face off, but her arms wouldn't budge. An instant later, she awoke enough to feel the ropes cutting into her wrists.

Toby had tricked her. She'd let down her guard for a single moment, and the bastard had gotten the drop on her. Now she was trapped in an isolated church in a world where nobody would hear her scream for help.

Helluva a mind you got there, Holly. You're a step ahead of everybody, a real thinker.

She left the thought to die and concentrated on her current problem. She was tied to a chair, and Toby stood over her. He grinned down at her, his face smug and frightening at the same time. A gleam that could only be considered malevolent blazed in his eyes.

She couldn't see much of the church. It was too dark, and Toby stood too close. She guessed she was at the front, near the altar or whatever you called it. She could catch a glimpse of sunlight filtering through the stained glass windows, bursting through in solid rays where the glass was broken. That clinging aroma of death and rot filled the room, and she could make out the rattling of chains somewhere beneath the ringing in her ears.

She glared up at Toby, wishing she could burn him with her hate.

"What the fuck is this, you piece of shit?"

"This?" he asked, spreading his arms wide and looking around. "This is my church." He pointed toward the door.

"Back there is the steeple."

He crouched in front of her, his face filling her vision.

"I brought you inside… "

He whirled away.

"...So you could see all the people!"

Molly screamed.

The pews were full of dead, their rotting bodies writhing and shaking. There were men and women, adults and children. They wore clothes of every type: suits and sundresses and T-shirts and shorts. Some had been dead longer than others, their flesh hanging from bones in dried strands and clumps, while others were fresh, their skin moist as it decayed.

A leather collar wrapped around the neck of each, a chain securing them to the pew. Their arms had been removed, the stumps raw and black and running. They hissed through their teeth, snapped their jaws, straining against their binds. The pews were heavy, though, made of sturdy wood, and they never even budged as the dead fought their trappings.

Holly stared in wonder, her mouth open and her voice dying to a rasp. The dead leaned toward her, their remaining teeth clacking uselessly as they ached for a meal. Holly shook her head violently, then looked to Toby with frantic eyes.

She could see now how insane he was. It was so obvious.

He patted her head.

"Okay. Maybe I wanted to freak you out a little."

She looked back out at the living corpses that filled the pews. There were at least two dozen, maybe three. How long had they been here? How long had Toby been keeping them, and why?

As if in answer, Toby slipped an arm around her shoulders.

"I know. It's hard to understand. I get that; believe me. I wasn't lying to you before, Sister Holly. I did live in Friendship. Lived there my whole life, as a matter of fact. Hell, I was there, sitting in my living room, when the first reports came over the tube.

"Like just about everybody, I guess, I watched the first week or so on television, wondering what to make of the whole thing. I mean, c'mon! Dead people were returning to life, eating the living people, and turning them into walking dead folk. That's not something you see everyday!

"So, I sat there, and I watched, and I searched my mind for an answer. There had to be one out there, some way to make sense of all of it. I just had to sit and ruminate on it long enough. Sooner or later, it was going to dawn on me.

"And it did."

Holly watched him, holding her breath. He leaned in close and whispered to her.

"Angels."

He took a step toward the first row of pews, swinging a single arm wide.

"Angels, Sister Holly! What else is going to make the dead rise from the grave? What else could possibly stop death in its very tracks and transform it into life? The angels have come down from heaven and taken root in the only form available to them, that of the dead and rotting.

"I realized they're trying to tell us something, Sister Holly, something important. All we have to do as a species is prove ourselves worthy of God's love. Once we've done that, the angels will deliver their message, and a new era of peace will greet the Earth!"

Holly let his words settle for a minute, then she replied, her eyes never leaving Toby's.

"You're fucking crazy."

His fist struck hard and fast, jolting her head back like a speed-bag. She let out a single groan and tried to shake the cobwebs loose.

"You think I'm crazy? Who the fuck are you, Sister? Miserable little shit, got her whole town massacred and ran away from it! You aren't holy, bitch, you're a Goddamned heathen! You just want to feed off the Earth, suck it dry! I want to learn, Sister Holly! I want God to bestow his blessings onto me so that I can heal this sick world!"

"By killing these people? You killed them, didn't you?"

He shook his head. "I did no such thing. I made vessels ready for the coming angels, and if I take good enough care of them—if I can prove myself worthy and ready—they'll deliver God's lesson."

"Take care of them? Is that what lobbing their fucking arms off is for?"

He frowned. "I'm not a fucking retard.

"Truth of the matter is, The Lord works in mysterious ways. These angels, they're one of those ways." He walked down the center aisle, and the dead on either side snapped at him, their chains keeping them at bay.

He patted one on the shoulder, snatching his hand away when the zombie tried to bite him. "See? They kill us, but they want to save us. It's all very Old Testament; I don't expect you to understand."

"So what do you expect me to do, Toby? You going to kill me, make me another member of your little flock?"

A hurt expression flashed across his face. He placed a hand to his heart, leaning back. "What? Why, no, Sister Holly! I have enough angels. Now, I just need to take care of them, bestow blessing unto them until they feel the desire to bestow their blessing unto me."

A chill raced down Holly's spine. She closed her eyes for a moment, opened them. She had an idea what was coming next.

When Toby drew the knife out of his waistband, she realized she was right.

He approached her slowly, letting her get a good look at the blade. When he drew close enough, her grabbed a fistful of her hair.

"It appears it's communion day!"

The knife sawed through her hair, yanking the roots from her scalp. She screamed, then bit down and rode out the pain.

The pressure suddenly eased, and Toby stepped away with a handful of her hair, the hair that she hadn't even realized had been growing so long.

He stepped toward a zombie seated directly across from her in the first pew. It wore a filth-smeared suit that might have once been a lighter shade of blue.

"This used to be the preacher here," Toby said. "I believe he told me his name was Michael, but I can't be too sure. It was a pretty long time ago."

He pulled a few strands of hair from the fistful he carried with him, dangled them over the dead man's head. The former preacher leaned back, his jaw opening and closing, black tongue flopping out like a dying fish.

"That's right, Padré. Little appetizer for ya." Toby lowered the hair into the corpse's mouth, and the preacher sucked it in like pasta, chewed it for a long moment.

Holly had to turn away when the creature swallowed.

She heard a crescendo of groans, heard Toby cheer the dead on as he fed them morsels of her hair. She tried to think. There had to be a way out of this, someway to break free. She pulled against her binds, but they held fast. The son of a bitch had tied her to a chair. She was his to play with until he felt differently.

She guessed that would be a long time coming.

She tried again, leaning forward as far as she could, opening her eyes to watch her captor as he fed his congregation. She eyed him so carefully that she almost didn't notice the chair's rear leg's lift from the ground.

Her eyes widened. She could move! She watched Toby, making sure he wasn't watching, and she checked her balance. She leaned forward, curling in half until the chair lifted completely off of the ground. She lowered it to the floor again, but continued to struggle. She had an idea, but she knew she would only have one chance, and that depended on catching the lunatic off-guard.

She glanced at the dead folk in the pew in front of her, watching as the former preacher and three others chewed on her hair, an expression like ecstasy filling their faces. They looked so anxious, so hungry. She knew the next thing Toby carved off of her wouldn't be hair, and she also knew she couldn't let that happen.

He'd have to kill her first.

"All gone!" he said, his voice almost child-like.

You can do this, Holly, she told herself. *You ran a town for almost a year. You can handle one religious psychopath.*

"What happens now?" she asked, putting an extra hint of terror in her voice.

He smiled. "Oh, I think you know, Sister Holly." He pointed the knife at her, twisting it in the air as he stepped closer. "I think you have a really good idea what I'm gonna do next."

He stepped past the first pew, stood directly in front of her.

"Do you have a good idea?"

"Yeah," she said. "I've got a fuckin' great one."

She screamed at the top of her lungs as she surged forward, lifting the chair behind her. She slammed her shoulder into Toby's gut, and she almost smiled when she felt him double over, the air whooshing from his lungs. She kept pushing, pumping her legs across the carpet, until she hit something solid.

Toby flew off of her, landing on the preacher and the rest. He tried to scramble away, but it was too late. Their teeth had already clamped down on him. The dead holy man had him by the throat, and with a great wrenching movement, ripped the flesh and tendons and veins away, spraying the area with blood.

Toby's scream died before it could even get started.

Holly staggered backward, then leapt into the air, leaning back. She landed with her full weight, and the chair cracked and splintered around her. She kept her eyes on Toby, watching the light drain from his eyes, as she struggled to her feet and managed to wrench her hands free of the rope coiled around her wrists.

"Is that the message you wanted?" she asked, but the only reply was the sound of teeth chewing meat.

Slowly, Holly walked down the center aisle, ignoring the dead as they leaned out, trying desperately to reach her with their jaws. She didn't bother to stop and look for water. She would find a creek in the forest. Instead, she stepped across the church's deserted lot and onto the country road beyond. She would walk until she found Route 62, and from their she'd make her way to the proving ground.

Maybe there she would find something worth believing in.

Though the author posits the following tale as the onset of a plague of the living dead, what he describes is, in fact, a typical day in the City That Never Sleeps. As well as rats, roaches, and street gangs, New York has a zombie problem that never seems to make it into the brochures...

LaUNdRY DAy

by Steven A. Roman

Josh Kosinski hadn't planned on going to the laundromat that night the world went total bugfuck crazy, but the stench from the pile of shit-streaked underpants and grimy work clothes in the bathroom hamper finally became too much for even him to ignore. Besides, he'd run out of air freshener.

Truth be told, it wasn't the nostril-singeing scent of ripening Fruit of the Loom that bothered Josh so much as the fact he'd run through his drawer of briefs and boxers and been forced to go commando the past couple of days. Not an altogether unpleasant experience under the right circumstances—he occasionally preferred his "boys" to have their freedom—but the crotches of the pants he wore as a mechanic at Triple G Auto Works over in Blissville always chafed him like a son of a bitch when he moved around. Underpants, therefore, were his only protection from a daily dose of friction burns.

The work clothes were another story. Most of the dark gray denim shirts and pants were so deeply stained with motor oil and grease and sweat, so stiff from coolant and antifreeze and wiper fluid spills he should've tossed them in the garbage a long time ago. But Josh liked to think of himself as the frugal type, pinching a penny here and there whenever possible. It was a polite way of admitting he was too cheap to buy replacements, but as long as the seams didn't split and the holes worn in them remained small, he didn't see any reason to throw away something he still considered usable. A little machine washing, he firmly believed, and they'd be good as new. Well, almost new. Of course, that would require he actually take them to be washed...

There was no way to put it off any longer, though. With nothing left to wear but a threadbare Knicks sweatshirt whose elbows had dissolved somewhere along the way, and a pair of corduroy pants he hadn't squeezed into since the late Nineties, his options were limited to either dragging his procrastinating ass around the corner to the Drip 'n' Dry Laundromat, or showing up for work on Monday morning in his birthday suit. And considering the donuts-and-beer "diet" he'd been on for the last five years, the latter was really no option at all. Not that he gave a fuck what the guys at the shop would say if he walked in all nude and shit. Even with his love handles and beer gut he was still thinner and better looking than all of them combined.

Okay, that wasn't saying a whole hell of a lot, but still...

It was the girls in the back office he'd be afraid of facing. Afraid of what they'd say, or how they'd laugh at his doughboy physique and hairy back (hairy everything, to be honest about it; he looked like a regular fuckin' Star Wars Wookie when he took his shirt off). Marisol the bookkeeper would be the one with the most disparaging comments to make. That chica was *muy caliente*, with an ass that would give J-Lo a run for her money, but she also had a tongue sharp as a knife. If anybody was capable of metaphorically cutting off his manhood with just a couple or three words, she was the one. And Josh figured he had enough low self-esteem problems without asking to get sliced up by Marisol's Ginsu-tongue—even in an uncomfortable scenario that was only playing out in his head.

Still, it took some effort to get off the living room couch. After working ten-hour shifts all week, all he wanted was to grab a couple bottles of Heineken and a few Entenmann mini chocolate donuts, and veg out in front of the TV for a late-night marathon of *I Love the Eighties* reruns on VH-1. But when the stench from the hamper drifted down the stairs, and he began breathing through his mouth so he didn't have to smell it, he knew that laundry day had finally arrived—although, truthfully, 2:30 on a Sunday morning wasn't exactly a daytime run.

With a soft groan, he sat up and swung his legs off the couch and onto the carpeted floor, then used his knuckles to push off from the cushions. Shuffling along in stockinged feet from the living room—giving the boys a good scratch as he went—he crossed the narrow main hallway of his house to enter the kitchen. Like the rest of the house, it served as a showcase for Josh's slovenly habits, the theme of this particular room apparently vintage Frat House, right down to the stacks of empty pizza boxes, Chinese takeout cartons, and beer bottles scattered across the counters. The formerly white tiles on the floor had faded to a dingy yellow, and the sky-blue paint on the ceiling had acquired a few greasy storm clouds, courtesy of the many hamburgers and Spam slices burnt on the stove in offering to the great god Hunger. If his parents, who'd moved down to Ft. Lauderdale back in '02, ever got a look at the current condition of their once immaculate home, Josh had no doubt they'd disown him.

Little chance of that coming to pass, though. Albert and Dora had become too comfortable in their retirees' paradise to bother visiting their only child, even on holidays. It's too far to drive, Josh, especially with my bad back, Albert told him once. And you know how your mother is about flying. Yeah, he knew; he knew it was a lot of bullshit. So if they'd abandoned him like they had the house, why should he give a fuck how clean it was?

The only part of the property he paid any real attention to was the rose garden in the backyard. Dora had planted the bushes years before Josh was born, but he had turned out to be the one with the green thumb. On those occasions when he was feeling particularly down on himself (which were often), Josh imagined he was supposed to be the punchline in one of God's cruel ideas for a joke, one in which he was allowed to grow and nurture just about anything organic—except a relationship. Because when it came to having a love life, he was pretty much Suck Master Numero Uno.

Well...at least he was good at something, even if it was just plants.

Josh opened the cabinet under the sink and rummaged around past the paper towels and bottles of cleaning solutions until his hand closed around the box of black garbage bags all the way in the back. He grabbed one, then fished out a box of laundry detergent and headed for the stairs. As he began the climb, he waved a hand in front of his face to dispel the noxious fumes that wafted down to meet him.

"Phew," he muttered. "Smells like somebody died in here..."

It was while he was transferring the odorous mound to the garbage bag that the ring tumbled out from the bottom of the hamper.

It wasn't an expensive one—hell, he would've pawned it long ago if it was—or even a "real" one, for that matter. It was thin and metal, its band painted a bright gold to bring out the color of its setting: a small blue "gem" made of plastic. A toy ring. A prize from one of the Laundromat's gumball machines, purchased for a couple of quarters last Valentine's Day as a token of his affection for—

"Siobhan," he murmured.

Josh sighed and shook his head forlornly. He'd really thought she'd be the one: the love of his life, his perfect match, his soul mate. And he was sure she'd felt the same way, although she never came right out and said it. But like the old saying went, some things were just never meant to be, and the possibility of Josh Kosinski settling down with Siobhan Tennant was apparently at the top of that list. Then again, he'd felt the same way about Cindy Speers and Angelica Crichton and Eugenia Rodriguez, and look how those had turned out—exactly the same.

He shrugged. What could he say? He was a fool for love, a hopeless romantic, setting himself up for a fall time and again and then starting the process all over, but he felt neither embarrassed nor frustrated by his numerous attempts to find for Ms. Right. No matter how many short-lived relationships he stumbled through, no matter how disastrous the break-up, he was certain that the right girl was still out there, waiting for her prince to sweep her off her feet...even if he was as hairy as the Wolfman.

But with Siobhan he'd tried, really tried to win her heart, to show her they could be happy together if she'd only give it a shot. Sure, there was a twenty-year gap between them. Sure, they didn't have a lot of the same things in common. Sure, her parents would have objected if they'd known he was her intended suitor. But none of that mattered to Josh. Age was irrelevant if the two people involved really loved each other. Hell, there were plenty of May/December romances that ultimately worked out, like Michael Douglas and Catherine Zeta-Jones or Donald Trump and any one of his trophy wives. What was wrong with one more?

It was the wavy auburn hair that first caught his eye four months back at the Drip 'n' Dry. He always had a weakness for redheads—natural ones, not the ones who got their color from a bottle of Pantene or whatever—and Siobhan was as natural and straight-out-of-Ireland as they came, right down to the fair complexion and the freckles that dotted her cheeks like sprinkles on a dish of vanilla ice cream. He'd been reading the sports section of the Daily News, catching up on all the details of the Knicks' latest ass-kicking courtesy of the Miami Heat—and wishing he hadn't made that fifty-dollar bet with Humberto at the shop on the outcome—when he saw a flash of red above the top edge of the paper. He glanced around the article in time to see her gliding toward the back of the laundromat, a pale green summer dress swirling around her knees. He tried to play it cool, though, nodding politely when she turned around to glance at him, but the thousand-watt smile she flashed in response took his breath away—literally. The air caught in his throat, and he fell into a brief coughing fit that made his eyes water and brought an even brighter smile to her lips.

So much for acting like Joe Cool. Still, his comical reaction gave him the opportunity to strike up a conversation when she walked over to see if he was all right. Things only got better after that...for awhile, at least.

It was all his fault; he eventually came to accept that after they broke up. He'd pushed too hard, tried to move things along too quickly before they'd had enough time to really get to know one another. A recurring problem of his, that boundless enthusiasm, one that had screwed up every relationship he'd been in going all the way back to junior high, yet one he'd never been able to solve. With Siobhan, though, he'd crossed the line. After being venomously rebuked, he'd grabbed her by the arm and given her a good shaking. She responded by kicking him in the sack. He slapped her back—hard—across the face. Matters quickly spiraled out of control after that.

But even after that dust-up he tried to make it up to her. The toy ring was an impulsive—in other words, desperate—last-ditch attempt to win back their relationship. A peace offering that wound up momentarily blinding him when she threw it back in his face and the sharp metal band glanced off his left eyeball.

"Fuckin' bitch," Josh muttered testily. "Who needed your kinda grief anyway...?"

He tossed the ring out through the open bathroom window, into the backyard. There was a faint pinging sound as the tiny prize bounced off the brick patio and tumbled into the garden, but he didn't bother to see where it landed.

Drip 'n' Dry was a little busier than Josh expected for a graveyard shift. On most late runs like this he usually had the place to himself—not counting Mrs. Alvarez, who owned the laundromat with her husband. She was always there, usually stationed behind the counter like she was tonight, making change for the customers so they could use the washers and dryers. Josh couldn't remember the last time he'd seen her old man put in an appearance; he probably only popped in when one of the machines was on the fritz. Not that it would kill him to pay a little more attention to the place. About fifteen or so ceiling tiles were heavily water-stained from the steam pipes above them, and had started sagging in the middle. The blue paint on the walls by the front windows had been scraped off at waist-level by customers constantly shifting around the plastic chairs—provided by the Alvarezes—that they sat in while waiting for loads to run their cycles. The strip of decorative wallpaper pasted just below the ceiling border—some kind of desert scene at sunset, with the sand painted a deep red against a pink-and-lavender sky—had peeled and flaked away in large swatches along the length of the entire laundromat. And in the six or seven years Josh had been coming to this place, nobody had ever bothered to correct the sun-faded, misspelled sign taped to the wall above the washers:

PLEASE NO DYING

Everybody knew what it meant, though: the Alvarezes didn't want customers dyeing their clothes in the washers, and have them end up ruining the next person's laundry or crapping up the machines. Of course, it could also mean they didn't want anybody croaking on the premises (might be bad for business, after all), so if they felt a sudden case of death coming on they should drag their ass somewhere else to deal with it. Josh had never bothered asking which one it was supposed to be.

About the only things that ever got some kind of regular maintenance were the arcade games in the right-hand corner at the back of the Laundromat, and the gumball machines next to them, and that was because the company that owned them had a guy come in every few months to empty the coin boxes and swap out the games and stale candy for new selections. The Mortal Kombat and driving games he'd seen the last time he stopped by were still around, but Josh noticed that the Superballs, Skittles, and toy jewelry had finally been replaced with *Homies* figures, *Bratz* stickers, and some kind of sweet-and-sour jawbreakers. There wasn't a metal-and-plastic ring to be found among the bunch, but that was probably for the best. After the trouble with Siobhan, he'd had his fill of cheap reconciliation gifts.

But Mrs. A apparently didn't need her husband around tonight, for work or companionship, not when she had a small black-and-white TV on the counter and four patrons of the laundry arts to keep her company. Along with Josh, there were a couple of twenty-something hipsters—the guy sporting a shaggy haircut parted in the center and a small soulpatch under his bottom lip, the girl a bottle-blonde with dark roots showing everywhere and a silver nose-ring pierced through her right nostril—and some black-haired Hispanic chick with painted-on blue jeans and a tight gray T-shirt knotted in the back to make it even tighter. He caught a flash of a black Playboy bunny logo printed on the front as she turned to dip into a red metal shopping cart for another armful of clothes.

Josh tilted his head to one side and stared hard at the woman. That mane of shoulder-length hair might be obscuring her face, but there was something awfully familiar about those major league boobs and that J-Lo-competitive ass…Then it hit him.

"Holy shit…" he croaked, his voice jumping an octave. "Marisol?"

She undoubtedly heard her name being called, even above the muffled roar of the washer next to her, and turned from the machine she'd been stuffing clothes into to face him. Her light hazel eyes grew wide, and she grinned. "Oh, hey, Josh! Wha'cha doin' here?" she said in that heavily accented Queens voice of hers. It always reminded him of that movie actress Rosie Perez, only nowhere near as gratingly nasal.

"I live around the block," he explained as he walked over to join her.

"Yeah? Me, too!" she said, clearly surprised. "Well, not around the block. Couple'a blocks over." She gave him a playful little push on his chest. "Shit, I din' know you was from 'round here! How come you never tol' me?"

Josh shrugged. "Never came up. 'Sides, you woulda known about where I live if you just looked at the payroll records. I mean, you're the one doin' the accountin', right?"

She frowned, clearly annoyed that he'd pointed out that oversight. "Yeah, well, guess I just never paid it no attention." She gave a little shrug. "No biggie. So, how long you been livin' in the 'hood?"

"The 'hood,' huh? Too fuckin' long," he said with a lopsided grin, and jerked a thumb over his shoulder toward the front door. "I'm over in my parents' house." He saw her eyebrows start to rise and quickly added, "I mean, I don't live with 'em. They moved out years ago. Down to Florida. I got the house to myself."

"*Pobrecito*," she cooed in Spanish. "So you all alone, then? Got nobody t'go home to?" The way she said it, though, and the dismissive look she flashed as she gave him the once-over, didn't add up to being any part of a seductive come-on. In fact, it seemed a hell of a lot more like she was mocking him.

"Don't worry, you ain't my type," he replied dryly, somehow managing to avoid gritting his teeth while he said it. "But don't get all choked up 'bout my situation, sweetheart. I know there's somebody out there for me. I ain't gonna be 'all alone' forever."

She poked him in the belly with a dark blue fingernail. "Yeah, well, try losin' this first an' maybe you'll get lucky. Girls don' go for fat guys 'less they got money"—she flashed a condescending grin—"and that's somethin' I know you ain't got." The grin widened. "I'm the one doin' the accountin', remember?"

Oh, here we go, Josh thought. *Didn't take long for her to start pullin' out that fuckin' Ginsu-tongue...*

But if Marisol had any plans of further pruning his manhood, they were interrupted by the loud bang of something hitting one of the big glass windows. She gasped, and pointed over Josh's shoulder. "Jesus Christ, what the fuck is that?"

Josh turned around. His first impression was that it was a couple of neighborhood teenagers horsing around in Halloween costumes. They were made up like zombies, with torn-up dirty clothes and piles of gunky, discolored makeup covering their faces and hands. One guy's head was tilted against his right shoulder as though his neck was broken, with a thick layer of fake blood crusted around his mouth. The other moron had his dingy blue denim shirt unbuttoned to show off the major gash that bisected his stomach—a gaping wound through which fake intestines were poking out. Both deadheads stared into the Laundromat with wide, unblinking eyes, and pawed at the glass like they wanted in.

"Ah, it's just a couple stupid kids," Josh explained to Marisol. He turned back to the walking dead. "Hey, Halloween's in October, ya fuckin' mooks!" he called out. "Come back when they start passin' out the candy corn!"

Instead of taking his advice, however, the jackasses continued pounding on the window, only now they added loud, melodramatically drawn-out moans to the act. Well, Josh thought, at least you gotta give the shitheads some credit for stickin' to their act. But after another thirty seconds or so of the constant groaning and banging, it stopped being amusing and became annoying as all hell.

It was more than just annoying to Marisol. After her initial shocked reaction, she'd quickly regained her composure and started brandishing that sharp tongue of hers again, obviously with the intention of slicing up a couple of window zombies. A blessing in disguise, as far as Josh was concerned. Now that she had somebody new to pick on, she'd completely forgotten her first target.

"*¡Hacete coger, putas!*" Marisol shouted at them with a sneer. "You *chaperos* are lucky I don' come out there an' kick your asses!" Josh noticed, however, that as angry as she was, as loud as she barked at the two kids, she made no move to run outside and carry out her threats. It was all talk and no action with Marisol Puente, apparently.

Or maybe it was because the zombie makeup was starting to freak her out; it sure looked like the other two customers were headed in that direction. The hipster couple was frozen in place, the guy having awkwardly positioned himself behind his girl—*Now there's one brave motherfucker*, Josh thought sarcastically—while the girl nervously chewed on her bright pink thumbnail and hugged herself for reassurance. Both of them looked about ready to shit a brick. But none of the prankster nonsense going on outside bothered Josh—he'd seen scarier, far more disgusting shit on medical shows that ran on the Discovery Channel, and that stuff was real. This was just a bunch of cheap makeup tricks and bad acting from teenagers with nothing better to do with their time. It wasn't anything to get all worked up about.

Mrs. Alvarez wasn't bothered by the spook show, either; in fact, she looked more pissed-off than Marisol. Probably afraid the dumbasses are gonna break the window with all that hammerin', Josh imagined. Slipping out from behind the counter with a broom in one hand and a ring holding the keys to the store in the other, she stomped up to the front door and flung it open.

"Stop that!" she ordered, pointing the broom handle at the kids. "Get away from there before I call the police!"

Immediately, the teenagers stopped their carrying on and slowly turned to face her. As Mrs. Alvarez and the potential vandals silently faced off, Josh suddenly heard the theme from that old Clint Eastwood Western, *The Good, the Bad, and the Ugly*, echo in his head. *Ah-ah-ah-ah-ah-wa-wa-waah…*

He couldn't help but smile.

"Oh, this oughtta be good," said a male voice to his left. He glanced over to see that the two hipsters had moved up next to him, no doubt wanting a better view of the argument to come. Apparently Mrs. Alvarez's charge had inspired Soul-Patch to grow a backbone and stop hiding behind his girlfriend. "Five bucks says she cracks that broom handle over Joey McGutsy's skull."

Beside him, Little Miss Nose-Ring giggled.

Josh frowned. "You know those two assholes?"

"Nuh-uh," Soul-patch said with a quick, worried shake of his head. Probably thought Josh would pop him in the face if he admitted to being their buddy. "I was just, y'know, makin' up a funny name for the guy with his guts hangin'—"

"Oh, shit!" Nose-Ring squeaked, her hands flying up to cover her mouth as she looked past Josh. "What're they doin'?"

Josh turned back to the window in time to see the zombie teens launching themselves at the old woman, arms outstretched and mouths hanging wide open. Now they're really goin' over the top with that shit, he thought.

Taken by surprise, Mrs. Alvarez stumbled back, her feet tangling around the broom's dirty, splintered bristles. Spinning a half-turn as she tried to right herself, she instead lost her balance and crashed onto the sidewalk. The teens pounced on her like starving lions bringing down a gazelle.

"H-help me!" she screamed. "Please somebody help me! They're—AAAHH!—they're biting me!"

It was more than just biting, though; even from fifteen feet away, Josh could see the blood—bright red under the store's florescent lighting, and anything but fake—on the teens' lips as their heads rose and dipped above the old woman's struggling body. Biting? Shit, they were chewing on her!

"Shouldn't we, like, do somethin'?" Miss Nose-Ring croaked. "Call the cops, maybe?"

Josh nodded mutely but, apparently like the others, he was too mesmerized by the violent act being carried out right in front of them to do anything more than stand and watch. It was a hell of a street show, too. For an overweight woman in her sixties, Mrs. Alvarez wasn't going down without a fight. She kicked and punched the teens, slamming their faces with her elbows, driving her knees into their balls. But none of the blows did anything to convince them to break off the attack; in fact, her struggles seemed to excite them.

And then the one with the exposed guts bit down hard on her left leg, viciously snapped back his head, and tore out a chunk of her calf. He gobbled it down hungrily and went back for seconds.

Mrs. Alvarez shrieked loud enough to rattle the windows; the sound was almost high-pitched enough to match the scream that leapt past Marisol's tonsils. Almost, but not quite. Josh winced, wondering if he'd ever hear clearly from his right ear again.

"Holy shit, they're real!" Soul-Patch yelled.

Yeah, they were real zombies, all right. And a lumbering movement under the streetlights on the corner of the block made Josh suddenly aware that the teens weren't the only ghouls out for a late night stroll. They had company—lots of company. It looked like the cemetery over on the next avenue had opened its gates so every goddamn stiff in the joint could run loose. Problem was, they had only one thing in mind right now: answering the ringing dinner bell formed by Mrs. A's vocal chords. Holy Christ, could that woman scream!

"Oh, God!" Marisol wailed, and hysterically clawed at Josh's shirt. "There's more of 'em!"

"I can see that!" he snapped, and pushed her away. "Get a fuckin' grip, wouldja?"

"Whatta we gonna do?" Soul-Patch asked. "When they're done with the old lady, you know they're gonna come in here for the main course!" He moved behind his girlfriend, what little backbone he'd developed in the past five minutes having oozed down his leg to join the trail of urine pooling at his feet.

"What about lockin' the door?" Nose-Ring asked.

"Yeah, like that's gonna keep 'em out," Josh replied with a sneer. "Besides, Mrs. A took the keys with 'er." He gestured to where the key ring lay on the sidewalk by her now fingerless right hand. Alvarez's screams died away to a soft moan that rose and fell, providing some unsettling dining music for the rotting duo as they ate their fill. "Joey McGutsy" had gnawed Mrs. A's left leg like a drumstick, right down to the bone, and was now working on the left arm. As for his buddy, the broken-neck corpse was bent low over the old lady's pelvis, his angled noggin wedged between her hips in such a way it looked like...

Jee-zus God, Josh thought. *Is he...actually eatin' her pussy?* He felt the mini-donuts and beers he'd had earlier start racing up his gullet, and clenched his teeth to keep them from spewing all over his last clean shirt. What he couldn't decide on, though, was which was more stomach-churning: having a mental image of the old lady's used-up snatch bouncing around in his head, or watching Junior there cuttin' himself a slice of poontang pie.

A big, hairy, wrinkly, blood-filled, clam-scented slice of poontang pie.

He felt his gorge rising again...

"Shit, let's jus' run out the back!" Marisol shouted, and pointed to the far end of the Laundromat. Just past the arcade games and gumball machines, an EXIT sign glowed dimly above a battered metal door with a pushbar set across its width.

"I like that plan," Josh said, nodding vigorously, grateful for anything that would take his mind off picturing Mrs. A's private parts. He began herding Marisol and the hipsters toward the door, taking care to avoid slipping in Soul-Patch's puddle. "Let's get the fuck outta here. If we're lucky, the two out front won't even know we're gone."

But luck, he realized, had very little to do with it as he glanced back over his shoulder. Truth of the matter was, the teen corpses were just too busy eating to pay the Drip 'n' Dry customers any mind—until, that is, Marisol gave a hard shove to the back door pushbar and set off the ear-piercing screech of the fire alarm. Then the zom-boys became all too aware that their future meals were making a run for it, and, stuffed though they were on Fillet of Senior Citizen, they didn't look happy about missing out on the next course.

Neither did the mob of walking dead that finally arrived on the scene. There must have been a couple dozen of Calvary's finest residents crowded together on the sidewalk, all of them looking into the laundromat like it was the display window for a butcher shop, all of them sizing up the cuts of meat to be found on the sides of beef standing on the other side of the glass. It reminded Josh of the time he'd been walking past an Ecuadoran bakery over on Queens Boulevard, and glanced in to see a couple of the workers carrying dead pigs into the back, the animals' bellies slit wide open and emptied of intestines. It had struck him as unusual to see hollowed-out porkers being stocked in a pastry shop of all places, but damn if his own gut hadn't rumbled hungrily in response. The sight of all that meat, coupled with the sweet aroma of pies and breads fresh from the oven, had made his mouth water like a goddamned faucet.

Kind of like the way the mouths of the starving corpses outside the Drip 'n' Dry were watering right now.

Josh raised his right hand and held up his middle finger. "Yeah, well, this wittle piggy says, 'Go fuck yerself,'" he said with a grin. Then he turned around to leave—only to find his three unwanted charges standing in the fire exit, frozen like the proverbial deer-meets-headlights scenario; Marisol's hands were even still on the release bar. You would have thought getting away from the noise of the fucking alarm would have been Priority One for them—after all, it was just another dinner bell calling the damned to supper—but apparently they were too stupid to figure that out for themselves.

"Jesus Christ, what're you doin'?" he bellowed. "Run, you stupid shits! Run!"

That got them moving. They bolted outside, with Josh bringing up the rear. He didn't bother to look back when he heard the front windows shatter.

When he stepped into the dead-end alley that ran the length of the block behind the stores and apartment buildings, he only found Marisol waiting for him. She pointed to the entrance before he could say anything.

"They jus' kept goin'," she explained.

Josh looked to the mouth of the alley, just in time to see the hipsters turn the left-hand corner. "Stupid fucks," he snorted. "That's just gonna take 'em back to the main street, where all the corpses are runnin' loose."

"Don' you think you oughtta go tell 'em that?" Marisol asked.

"I don' gotta tell 'em shit," Josh replied with a sneer. "Let 'em figure it out for themselves."

That didn't take too long—the high-pitched scream that echoed down the alley was proof enough. Josh wondered who'd voiced the nails-on-a-blackboard screech; might've been the girl, but for all he knew Soul-Patch could've had a set of pipes like Donna fuckin' Summer. The thought of piss-pants launching into a terrified rendition of "On the Radio" as zombies tore off his balls brought a wicked little smile to Josh's lips.

Marisol glared at him. "You're a piece'a shit," she snapped.

"Yeah, an' you're a real charmer," he replied dryly. "A mouth like that, it's no wonder every guy in the shop wants t'bone you." Before she could think of another four-letter comeback, he grabbed her hand and pulled her toward the entrance. "C'mon. Those things in the laundromat'll be bustin' out here any minute, an' I don't wanna be stuck between them and their buddies around the corner."

They raced past odorous piles of trash bags from the Golden Wok restaurant next door, scattering the swarm of flies and handful of stray cats that had gathered to share a late dinner; hopped over mounds of discarded fliers and leaflets advertising the 99-cent store abutting the Chinese takeout; stepped gingerly around smashed beer bottles and crushed soda cans and pieces of broken furniture dumped by people in the area for who-knew-what reasons. Along the way, Josh alternated between listening to his reedy, labored breathing—he really needed to lay off the goddamn donuts—and stealing glances at Marisol's Playboy-decorated funbags as they bounced up and down. If she noticed the attention they were getting, she wasn't saying; given the circumstances, she probably considered some guy from the shop oggling her bra-less titties the least of her worries. That didn't mean she wasn't making a mental note of every peek he took, however, and knowing her like he did, odds were better than good she'd give him shit about his Peeping Josh act the first opportunity she got.

He wheezed to a halt at the entrance to the alley and pulled her over to stand against the left-hand wall. He held up a hand for silence before she could object. "Lemme...lemme take a look first," he gasped. Marisol nodded, and Josh eased his head around the corner. He immediately wished he hadn't. "JesusMaryGod..." he croaked.

The street was filled with zombies. Shuffling and stumbling on twisted, atrophied legs, crawling on their ruptured bellies if they couldn't stand, they swarmed across both sides of the two-lane avenue in search of a living food. They smashed into a corner bodega and the front office of a private limousine service, forced their way into apartment buildings, battered down the front doors of the small homes lining the next side street. Screams and shrieks and cries for mercy echoed through the neighborhood; occasionally there was the firecracker-like pop of a handgun being fired as a few well-armed residents tried to defend themselves against the undead intruders. And farther back in the distance could be heard the wail of sirens—cop cars or ambulances or fire trucks on their way to answer the frantic 911 call somebody must have placed. Or maybe the Laundromat's fire alarm had alerted them—Josh could hear the damn thing continually blaring even from a half-block away.

As for the two hipsters, other than a quickly drying pool of blood and a few discarded body parts, there wasn't much left of them after they'd been ripped apart and passed around like a plate of buffalo chicken wings by the dozen or so zombies that were hunched over their remains. A snapped-off jawbone decorated with a small tuft of hair under the lower lip was proof enough of Soul-Patch's messy demise. As for his lady friend, evidence of her gastronomic fate came in the glint of street light bouncing off the silver nose-ring that lay on the pavement—a ring that still had part of her right nostril attached.

"What're we gonna do?" Marisol hissed in his ear, startling him.

"Get off the goddamn street, for one thing," he replied. He looked over her shoulder in time to see that the zombies crowded into the Laundromat had finally discovered the fire exit. Light spilled into the alley as the door flew open, and a trio of corpses led by "Joey McGutsy" staggered out. They swung around in small, confused circles, but it wouldn't take them long to figure out the direction in which their not-so-happy meals had run.

In spite of the danger, Marisol suddenly moved closer, pressing her right breast against Josh's arm; he could feel the hardened nipple through the taut fabric, and a pleasant chill crawled along his spine. He forced himself to ignore it. "Hey," she whispered huskily, "din' you say you lived right aroun' the block? Maybe we could hide out there, y'know?" Her right hand touched his thigh, then slid around toward his crotch. "Bet you got plenty room for me in that big house, huh...?"

He gave her a small push back. "Are you fuckin' comin' on to me?" he asked incredulously. "Right in the middle of all this shit?"

She sneered. "Well, I din' think you'd take my money, not the way you were starin' at my tits. So if it means I gotta blow some fat loser just t'get a place t'hide—"

"I said you ain't my type," Josh said.

"Oh, no?" Marisol flashed a wicked grin. "Then what is your type, Joshie? You like the boys instead of the girls, is that it?" She chuckled. "Yeah, I always thought there was somethin' freaky 'bout you." Her eyes widened, and she pursed her lips. "Or maybe you like the little boys—is that it? You can only get it up for the little—"

His hands tightened around her throat, and he slammed her against the brick wall. Struggling for breath, Marisol pulled at his wrists to break his grip; when that failed, she beat down on his arms, then reached out to scratch his face. Josh responded by squeezing even tighter. Her eyes bulged in terror while her mouth frantically opened and closed as she fought to pull in air.

"You fuckin' whores," he snarled. "You don't know nothin', do you? You think just 'cause you're pretty every guy in the world must wanna fuck you, an' if you run into one who don't then they gotta be a fag or somethin'—right?" He leaned forward, applying even greater pressure to her windpipe. Marisol's struggles began to lessen; her arms dropped limply to her sides. "Well, there's more t'life than just fuckin', sweetheart. There's a thing out there called 'true love.' There's a thing out there called 'findin' your soul mate.' An' I just happen t'be the kinda guy who believes in that shit, all right? Stuck-up whores like you always laugh when a guy like me says it, but I know the right girl is out there somewhere. An' one'a these days, so help me, Christ, I'm gonna find 'er."

He gave her neck one last powerful squeeze. Marisol's eyes rolled completely up in her head, until he was only looking at milky white orbs. "An' in case you ain't figured it out yet, bitch," he whispered in her ear, "you ain't the one."

He opened his hands and let her slide down along the wall to a sitting position. Whether she was dead or alive meant little to him; he was just happy to have finally dulled the edge on that sharp tongue of hers.

It took him a few seconds to regain his composure, and by then the laundromat zombies were starting to close in. He grabbed hold of Marisol's ankles and dragged her to the center of the alley, then rolled up her T-shirt to fully expose her stomach and breasts, to ensure the Carrion Crew would see all that fresh meat and stop for a quick bite instead of electing to pursue him. He thought again of the butchered pigs in the Ecuadoran bakery, and smiled as he gazed down at the woman sprawled at his feet.

"I bet this wittle piggy tastes like woast beef..." he said with a childish grin. Then he turned and ran, heading away from the zombie-choked avenue.

He was halfway down the block when he heard Marisol screaming. So he hadn't killed her after all, he realized, just choked her into unconsciousness. Well, he told himself, like the old saying went, some people were just too mean to die. Unless you fed them to a bunch of hungry corpses, that is.

"Enjoy your meal, boys," he whispered to the darkness. "There's a lotta meat on that ass." He laughed. "An' don't forget to try the Ginsu-tongue. It's extra spicy."

By the time he tumbled through his front door, the neighborhood had erupted into full-blown chaos. People ran through the streets, pursued by ravenous chowhounds. Panicked drivers plowed their cars through both living and dead, littering the asphalt with broken limbs, crushed organs, and unspooled intestines. A couple of avenues over, a fire had broken out in one of the apartment buildings; from the way it was raging, it looked as though it would consume the entire block before the Fire Department ever reached it. If they ever reached it.

Josh locked the dead bolt on the door and switched off the porch light, suddenly grateful that it had been the only lamp he'd left on when he headed off to the Drip 'n' Dry. A darkened house, he hoped, might increase the odds he'd be overlooked when the army of the dead came marching through his block. For good measure, though, he jammed a metal folding chair under the doorknob. Then he headed for the kitchen for a beer. Right now, he needed a drink—a big drink. Maybe a whole six-pack if the world was really coming to an end. And from what he'd experienced tonight, who's to say it wasn't?

He was all of two steps from the refrigerator when he heard the light footfalls on the brick patio in the rose garden.

Shit! he thought, unconsciously holding his breath as he stared at the back door. *Those fuckers can jump six-foot fences?*

The footsteps continued back and forth along the patio, as though whatever was out there was looking for something. They'd walk a few paces, stop, then move to another location.

After a minute or so of the constant shuffling, curiosity got the better of Josh. Maybe it wasn't a zombie, he thought. It could just be one of his neighbors hiding out from the massacre—but then why the hell didn't they just knock on the door and ask to be let in? And what could they be looking for?

Or, he suddenly realized, it could be a burglar, looking to take advantage of the situation and break into some houses while everybody was going nuts out on the streets. He grabbed a large carving knife from the utensil drawer as he eased up to the window that overlooked the rose garden. Just to be on the safe side.

It took him a few moments to recognize who was prowling around out there in the moonlight. The last time he'd seen her she'd been a hell of a lot more active than the shuffling, rotted flesh-bag she'd turned into—active enough to have kicked him hard in the balls when they had their falling out—but the red hair was a dead giveaway.

It was Siobhan Tennant. She was covered in dirt and clumps of fertilizer, there were rose petals and thorny stems tangled in her hair, and her creamy pale complexion had faded to an ugly, almost metallic gray, but the red-sprinkle freckles could still be seen on her sunken cheeks—if you looked hard enough.

And yet despite her appearance, even after spending a couple of months in the ground, goddamn if she still wasn't the sweetest, prettiest ten-year-old girl Josh had ever laid eyes on.

"Siobhan..." he whispered, and found himself smiling wistfully.

He really thought she'd be the one: the love of his life, his perfect match, his soul mate. That was why, even after she'd spurned him, even after he'd choked the life from her, he'd never had the heart to just dump her body into the Newtown Creek like he had with the other little girls: Cindy Speers and Angelica Crichton and Eugenia Rodriguez. Siobhan had been special, and a special girl needed a special resting place; that was why he'd dug her a small grave behind the rose bushes.

The green velvet nightshirt he'd buried her in—the same one she'd worn that night when he'd snatched her from her bed while her parents slept in the next room—hung in tatters on her small frame. Some of the rips looked new; probably from the cloth snagging on the rose thorns as Siobhan dug her way out. But it wasn't the gown that held his attention, so much as the glimmer of moonlight being reflected from a small metal band that encircled the third finger on her left hand.

She was wearing his ring.

The toy ring he'd bought from the gumball machine; the ring he'd thrown out of the bathroom window in a fit of anger just a few hours ago. That, he realized, was what she'd been searching for during her circuit of the backyard.

Josh smiled. He'd meant it as a token of affection, as a way of proving his sincerity—that, in spite of the terror he instilled in her, in spite of the things he did with her, the things he did to her, he truly loved her. And if he'd hurt her in any way while he'd tried to strengthen the bond between them...well, didn't being in love always involve some kind of pain?

She hadn't understood; none of the girls had. And that's what always made him so goddamned angry, what always loused him up: that no matter how much he opened his heart to them, they refused to see him as anything more than a monster. They'd scream at him, curse him, strike out at him, and then he'd eventually lose his temper and do something rash. Only later, after he'd disposed of their bodies, would he come to regret his actions. Like with Siobhan—ending their relationship had been just about the most difficult thing he'd ever done.

But none of that mattered now. She'd come back to him, was even wearing the ring he'd bought as a peace offering for her. Maybe she had loved him, although she'd never come right out and said it while she was alive. Just like he'd always believed. Just as he'd always hoped.

He placed the knife on the windowsill, opened the back door, and slowly stepped into the yard. Siobhan turned to face him. Her lips pulled back in a cold, feral smile, and she ran to him. He opened his arms wide to welcome her, and grunted contentedly as she slammed into his chest. And when her teeth began gnawing into his throat, he couldn't help but laugh and hold her even tighter.

What could he say? He was a fool for love.

And after all, didn't being in love always involve some kind of pain?

A moist and amusing slice of wedded, domestic hell, as well as the first published piece of zombie fiction from Mr. Kirkbride. It should give you pause to note that the following is inspired by a true story...

MaRRiED ALiVe

by D.J. Kirkbride

The truth of the matter was that Millie didn't really enjoy company coming over anymore. Oh, she used to. She used to be something of a social butterfly, especially when she and Charlie first got married. Now, since Charlie lost his job, she felt like a shut-in when she got home from work. She actually said as much to her friend once, but Cheryl was never one to listen.

The doorbell rang, and Charlie didn't even move. He just sat there, watching whatever was on the television, as he'd been doing for what seemed like weeks now. Millie was fixing dinner, steak. It was about the only food Charlie had any interest in of late, even though he never offered to make it. He used to at least like to grill, "manly cooking" he jokingly called it, but lately he just expected to be served. And while he used to be adamant about all the meat he ate being well done, almost burnt to Millie's tastes, he now preferred his steak rare; basically just slapped on the grill and browned on both sides. It nauseated her, to be blunt, and she refused to cook it that way due to health concerns. So, there she was, cooking a dinner that she was likely to be the only one to eat, the leftover scraps going to their cat Buggles, who seemed to be spending more time hiding and only coming out for food, occasionally letting Millie pet her, but steering clear of Charlie, whom she used to adore. Everyone in the house had been out of sorts lately.

The doorbell rang again.

"Charlie, can you get the door?"

Charlie looked at her blankly and said, "*Buuh-busy.*"

Sadly, this was pretty much the reaction Millie expected. Actual words were a bonus at this point.

When she saw it was Cheryl at the door, she was both embarrassed and relieved.

"Wanna go get a drink or something?" Cheryl asked, making a face at the odor emanating from her house.

No amount of Lysol spray could get rid of that smell. She thought maybe a small woodland creature, like a squirrel or beaver, had died under the porch. Or something. She couldn't find anything in the house, which she prided herself on keeping very clean.

"I'll tell you, Cheryl, I'd love to, but money's been pretty tight since..." she trailed off and looked to her husband, blankly staring at the television.

Her friend waved off this excuse. "I got this one."

In the face of such generosity, Millie took all of two seconds to consider this offer of getting a drink with her old friend. "Charlie, Cheryl and I are going to go out for a little bit."

"Buh-bye."

Millie had the foresight to turn off the oven before leaving.

They went to Chang Wok's for sweet, syrupy Americanized Chinese since neither had had dinner yet. Millie was loathe to go on and on about her woes, but Cheryl prodded her, sensing all was not well with her oldest friend.

"It didn't always used to be like this," Millie was saying.

"I know, I know. Some guys, you know, once they get you, you know, get you to marry them, they just, I dunno, you know, let themselves go."

"If only it were just that. Charlie...hasn't been himself lately."

Cheryl was really trying to be understanding and supportive. "Since he lost his job?"

"Oh, no. No. Before that. It's why he lost his job. Actually, I can't get a clear read on things. He might've just kind of stopped going to work. I'm starting to think that's why he got fired."

Cheryl took a sip of her martini. "Wasn't his company downsizing or something?"

"Not that I know of."

"I thought I read that."

Millie stirred her cosmo absently and looked around the huge restaurant. It felt like it'd been so long since she'd gone out or talked to someone other than at work. "He just seemed to lose interest."

"In work?"

"In *everything*."

Their wedding had been pretty much picture perfect. Exactly what Millie had always imagined it'd be. Both of her parents were there, with her father walking her down the aisle. The crowd, Cheryl among them, gasped at her beauty and the wonderment of the ceremony. Charlie, his mother in the pews and his father surely looking on approvingly from Heaven, awaited her, unable to stop smiling as he gazed at his bride to be. She'd never felt more beautiful. Their storybook romance, starting in college and continuation through first "real" jobs and a place of their own, was culminating to this moment. The moment when they'd become Mister and Missus. Millie could not have been happier, and she saw nothing but joy and true love in her future with this man. This man who so was so clearly enamored with her. Perfection.

Millie found it hard to believe that was only a year and a half ago as she stood in the kitchen, watching her Charlie sitting on the couch, blankly staring at the television before Cheryl had stopped by. He'd hardly moved all day and could be barely bothered to even look at the bride he'd once gazed upon so lovingly, offering only the occasional grunt, or one-syllable word if she was lucky, when she spoke directly at him.

Millie returned home from dinner and drinks to find that Charlie hadn't moved. She said "Hi" to him, and, after a pause, he slowly turned his head to her and just looked at her blankly. They'd lost their insurance with Charlie's job, but he had to see someone. Millie had been trying to figure out how to bring up the subject, but she was a little buzzed and didn't feel like it tonight.

Instead, she said, "Did you eat?"

Charlie didn't respond verbally, merely nodding.

She went into the kitchen with the small cardboard box containing the half of her meal she'd just been too stuffed to eat, noticing all the steak was gone, but there were no dishes. Maybe he did them, but" she hoped he'd cooked it at least somewhat thoroughly, though she had serious doubts.

Charlie stood slowly and mumbled, "Good…time?"

"Oh, sure. Yeah, Cheryl and I just talked some. You know, girl talk. Or whatever." She was so tired. "Did you just eat and watch TV?"

Without answering her, Charlie walked laboriously to their bedroom, almost tripping over Buggles, who viciously hissed at him.

"Buggles!" Millie scolded her, even though Charlie didn't seem to mind or even notice.

The cat merely ran under the couch.

Charlie was on his side, back turned to her when Millie made it to bed. She lie down next to her husband and tried spooning with him a bit. He was either sound asleep or upset over the whole dinner thing. When she kissed his neck and got no response, something that used to be unheard of, she had to go to the bathroom and just let herself cry. Her marriage was falling apart, and she had no idea why.

Just a few weeks ago, Charlie would get aroused by Millie sitting close to him, or even looking at him a certain way. That seemed like so long ago now. She had no idea what she was going to do. Insurance or no, she made the decision to look into some sort of therapy or counseling for him. She knew there were some clinics with sliding scales, so maybe he could talk to someone for cheap. She didn't know what to do at this point, as he clearly had no desire to talk to her.

Charlie didn't object to the therapist as much as Millie had expected. He didn't seem particularly interested, but he didn't object. Since she wasn't sure of his driving anymore, Millie took a long lunch the following Wednesday to drive Charlie to his first session.

In the waiting room, Millie almost gagged as she filled out the paperwork. "This place reeks, doesn't it" Charlie didn't respond to her, and she leaned over to him, taking a whiff. "Um...did you shower this morning, Charlie?"

Her former neat-freak of a husband looked at her for a moment, then simply shook his head.

Millie sniffed again. "Christ, when's the last time?"

Before he could give a monosyllabic answer, the receptionist informed them that the doctor was ready for Charlie.

Millie tried to occupy herself with the various outdated magazines that littered the waiting room. The latest celebrity scandal and dieting tips couldn't take her mind off of what was being said in that backroom. Was it her fault? Would Charlie cite something that she'd done to drive him over the edge? That made him just give up? That's what it seemed like to Millie. Like Charlie just gave up on life. And her. The giving up on her, whom she once thought he loved more than anything, hurt the most. She was a little ashamed to think that, as it seemed unbelievably selfish, but it was true.

When Charlie stumbled out fifty minutes on the dot later, Millie naturally asked him how it went.

"Uhhh..." Charlie groaned, which was the norm now, but in his eyes, it seemed like he was trying to get something out. But he couldn't.

Curious, Millie had Charlie wait for her and asked to see his new therapist.

Dr. Louridge was a slight, feisty older woman. She only had a few minutes before her next session, but she seemed eager to speak to Millie as well.

"I don't normally do this, but...I'm afraid that" you should know that your husband is seriously depressed. Deeply so."

Millie's heart sank, even though she knew it and said as much. "I knew it." She took a breath and tried to steady herself. "Well, why? Did he mention losing his job?"

Dr. Louridge shook her head, taking a sip of her iced tea through a straw. "No. We didn't talk about work at all, actually."

"Well, what then? Is it me? Is it something I'm doing?"

Trying to comfort her by slightly smiling, Dr. Louridge shook her head. "No one can make anyone else happy or sad. Your husband's issues are his. I can't really get into details, but...honestly, even if I could, there wouldn't be much to say."

"What do you mean?"

"He's a tight-lipped one, that fella of yours. It was almost twenty minutes of awkward silence, and when anyone talked, it was usually me, though he nodded and seemed to at least try to speak up occasionally. It was as if he didn't even have it in him for anymore than that."

Millie had hoped Charlie might open up to an objective third party, someone trained to help in these matters. "Is that...Is that normal? For depressives or whatever?"

Dr. Louridge shrugged, checking the wall clock next to her jam packed bookshelf. "Everyone's different. Though we didn't get much talking done, your husband's overall demeanor and body language do suggest a very, very depressed individual. I advised him that, in addition to the therapy, he see a psychiatrist."

"Wait—aren't you a psychiatrist?"

"Psychologist. Means I talk a lot but can't prescribe medicine."

Millie was embarrassed. She knew the difference between psychiatrists and psychologists. "I'm...that's right. Right. I'm just really exhausted. Not much sleeping lately."

"Perhaps you should come in, as well."

"Couples counseling?"

"By yourself. For yourself."

Millie was about to go into how they couldn't afford for both of them to go, and it seemed to her that Charlie was the depressed one and that once he was feeling better, she would, too; but Dr. Louridge sited the time and how she really had to go as she didn't want to keep her next patient waiting too long.

During the next couple of days, Millie wondered what she should do. Should she make a psychiatrist appointment for Charlie? Could they afford that on her librarian's salary? She bet the pills were very expensive. Maybe she'd get an idea of the price ranges from the internet at work, even though web browsing was frowned upon there. This was important, though. Still, she knew the medicine would be too expensive. She was worried about Charlie, but she was becoming equally as worried about how they were going to afford rent and groceries, let alone all of this other stuff.

There had to be something else she could do to bring him out of this. Maybe she could do something that he wouldn't be able to ignore. Something to really get his attention that might snap him out of this depression, if only briefly. Just a moment of seeing her old Charlie would be enough at this point.

On Friday night, knowing she wouldn't have to work the following day, Millie was determined to get some reaction other than an empty-eyed look and grunt from her husband. Opening the contents of the pink bag from the store, almost embarrassed, Millie put on the skimpy, lacey things. She felt absurd in them, but it wasn't as if she thought she was completely unattractive. Maybe she'd gained a few pounds that showed here and there, but her body didn't look too different form when she was in high school. A little droopier in some key spots, but she was kind of surprised to find herself almost pleased looking in the mirror, trying to determine if her hair should be up or down.

Lighting several candles newly-purchased for just this occasion, she posed as seductively as she could and called for her husband. When there was no response, she called again—a little louder this time—and finally heard him laboriously get up from the couch and plod down the hall. She hoped he'd showered this morning.

The door opened slowly, and he looked upon his wife, trying her best to turn him on and be sexy for him, with the same indifference he looked upon everything else. Her heart sank for a second, but then she reminded herself that he was severely depressed, and she was trying to give him some pleasure. Pleasure nothing else, not even talking to a therapist or "happy pills," could give him.

She motioned for him to approach her, and he did so, as if hypnotized. He just stood there, breathing through his mouth, looking down at her. She suddenly noticed how pale he'd gotten. Almost sickly. He'd probably not been going outside much. Anyway, he made no move, so she shifted around and approached him, on her knees, her face right by his crotch. She looked up at him with a smile, and, even though he wasn't reacting, she unbuttoned his jeans and slowly unzipped his pants.

"It's been a long time, hasn't it?" she said, reaching into his boxers.

Much to her chagrin, it smelled as if he hadn't bothered to bathe again. Soldiering on, Millie took him in her hands, deciding to convince herself that he smelled like a man. Musky. Manly. Strong.

And, to her surprise, he was rock hard.

"Well, at least that's something," she said, putting him into her mouth.

He only grunted, but it sounded to her like a pleased grunt.

Though he moved stiffly and rarely looked into her eyes like he used to, Millie found the lovemaking to be far more pleasurable that she'd initially feared. Were they even really making love, though? She used to find it so intimate, but this...this felt like *fucking*. Which, honestly, was very enjoyable in its own way, too.

Charlie was more forceful and sure of what he wanted than the timid lover he used to be. He almost seemed stronger to her as well, pinning her down and powerfully thrusting himself into her. No, it wasn't as romantic as she'd wished it might be, and there was nothing interesting about the position, he on top of her, but he kept hitting her spot like Robin Hood hitting a bull's eye. Mille was close to orgasm, something Charlie usually couldn't do without going down on her. She wished she could just lose herself in it and enjoy it more, beyond the physical pleasure, but she kept looking for some sign, some spark of life in his eyes.

Suddenly, his eyes lit up and looked at her, almost savagely. She felt herself close to coming as he shot into her with a moan. She felt alive and sexy and loved for a moment as Charlie moved his head in closer to her, moaning in orgasm, and, she thought, preparing to kiss her.

Millie hoped the shoulder wound didn't require any stitches, because she didn't think she could pay for an emergency room visit. Millie hadn't been able to say a word to Charlie, who didn't apologize, just slumped over on his back and fell asleep as she ran to the bathroom to clean and bandage her ravaged shoulder. She was shaking. There might have actually been some blood on his mouth as he slept soundly. Maybe it was just some of her lipstick. It troubled her, his breathing quiet and shallow but steady, when she returned to their room. She was scared and felt violated. Charlie had never been rough before, and, even if he had, it was safe and within reason, usually at her suggestion. But that—that was barbaric. And sick. How could this be related to depression? What kind of depression caused a man to nearly bite his wife's shoulder off when coming?

Unable to lie in the bed she and Charlie had purchased when they first moved in together, when they had started building their life, Millie went to the living room. Buggles was on the couch. She gently picked her up and was going to pet the cat as she tried to relax, but Buggles hissed like she'd never hissed at Millie before. "Bad!" The cat bit her. "Damn, Buggles!" Millie tossed her to the floor in anger, and she scurried away.

Millie didn't feel like staying home the next day. Without saying a word to Charlie, who didn't seem to mind, she fed Buggles, who seemed to keep her distance, and left the house. Not sure where to go, she called Cheryl, and they met at an Apollo's coffee shop.

"Are you okay, Millie?"

She swallowed her strong, piping hot coffee, wanting to touch at her shoulder but trying not to. "I...no." Millie felt her eyes tearing up. "Oh, god...Cheryl, I don't know what I'm going to do."

Cheryl seemed concerned but also a bit uncomfortable, like she wasn't sure what to say or was choosing her words extremely carefully. "Have...have you and Charlie been getting along at all?"

Millie looked up at her, eyes red and wet.

"Dumb question," Cheryl retreated, picking up her coffee and sipping it absently.

"I don't know if I can do this...I can't." Cheryl put her hand on Millie's arm but said nothing, letting Millie talk. "Charlie...he's the only man I ever loved, but he's not himself anymore. He..."

"He hasn't been for a long time," Cheryl finished for her.

Millie wiped her eyes and had to look away from her friend. "No." She hugged herself absently. "He hasn't."

"You've done all you can, Millie," Cheryl said. "You can't force him to get help or snap out of this or whatever it is he needs to do. Maybe...maybe you need some space. Maybe he does, too."

Millie protested, "I don't want to leave my husband. I'm not going to give up, I just..." She paused as she touched her shoulder. "There has to be something I can do."

Cheryl finished her coffee and sighed. She picked up her purse from beside her chair and started to rise but hesitated. "Millie, I—If there's anything I can do…if you change your mind, you know you can always stay at my place."

Millie nodded mechanically. This wasn't what she wanted to hear, but Cheryl was a good friend.

"I have to get back to the office, but call me if you need anything. Seriously."

Millie managed a weak smile and remained seated as Cheryl left.

The following couple of days, Millie couldn't bring herself to look Charlie in the eye. She let him fend for himself and doubted he'd made it to his second therapy session. She was planning on leaving after a couple days. He was looking so sickly, almost gray, but he refused to speak to her. Even Buggles ran from her. She was hissing on a regular basis, too, which kind of broke Millie's already shattered heart even more. This was a kitty she'd found too young to be without her mother, sickly and alone in the parking lot at her work. She'd taken care of this kitty, and they always used to be friends. Now Buggles seemed to hate Millie. First Charlie, now Buggles. It was a dumb thought, but it was how she felt. Millie was becoming more and more miserable.

At work, she found herself just zoning out. She couldn't keep her thoughts clear. Sometimes, it felt like she didn't even have any. When she got home, Charlie would be on the couch, often in the same clothes for days, smelling worse and worse, just staring at the TV. Lately Millie found herself just plopping on the chair next to the couch and just staring at the TV as well, not caring what was on.

Cheryl called a couple of times, but Millie found it harder and harder to follow what her friend was saying. When she tried to speak, her words started coming out more and more slowly. Cheryl kept asking if she was "okay," and Millie couldn't wrap her mind around how to respond.

That night after work, unable to figure out how to get her car started, Millie merely left the vehicle, keys in the ignition, and stumbled home. She felt drunk or high or something. She couldn't muster up the mental power to be concerned, though. She just instinctively walked home.

Their front door was unlocked, which was lucky, because Millie had left her house key on the chain with her car keys. It didn't bother her, though.

Inside, Charlie was sitting on the couch, as usual, but Buggles was on his lap. This surprised Millie at first, as the cat had started hissing and scratching at him long before she began doing the same to her. She noticed Buggles wasn't moving. Then she noticed that it looked like she'd been hurt, a large gash in her side. Millie remembered that she should be concerned, but when she noticed the blood, meat, and fur on Charlie's mouth, she merely grunted and went to the kitchen, pulling out one of those old steaks from the fridge. She reached for the oven to turn it on, but instead decided just to eat the meat, as red, wet, and squishy seemed so much more appetizing.

On one particularly boring, empty day at work, Millie slowly realized her boss was sternly talking to her, almost yelling, about some work that hadn't been done or about ignoring patrons, or something. Her boss said Millie "smelled," but Millie couldn't smell anything. She wasn't even sure how she got there or how long she'd been there, to be honest. Millie couldn't keep any of it straight and just stared at her boss, whose name she couldn't place. When her boss stopped talking, likely waiting for Millie to say something, Millie merely stood up and lumbered out of the library, unlikely to return.

On the walk home, Millie's cell phone rang. She reached into her purse clumsily, pulling out the tiny plastic thing, but fumbling the purse itself, which she let drop on the sidewalk. She managed, while hitting all the buttons, to hit "talk." It was Cheryl. Millie remembered that she should say something.

"Huuh...huhhh...lo?"

"Millie?" came Cheryl's concerned, tinny voice. "Is that you?"

"Yuh...yusss."

"What's wrong? What's going on? I've been calling and calling..."

Not sure what to say, Millie just let the phone fall from her hand and continued home. She thought she heard Cheryl's small voice say from behind her, "I'm coming over."

It took Millie a long time to get home. It was about a mile, and she was going very slowly. This was in the back of her mind, but she couldn't bring herself to move any faster. She looked side to side occasionally, noticing people moving very quickly around her, some staring. How rude. Millie thought she should tell them so, but all that came out was, "*Ruuuuuhhh...*"

At home, she noticed a car in the driveway. It was not hers. She didn't realize it at first, but it was Cheryl's. Cheryl was her...friend? Her friend. Her friend that was worried about her. She did not know why.

When she made it to the front door, she reached to open it, but it was already open. She walked in, hungry and hoping there was more steak in the fridge, even though she hadn't been shopping in some time. She heard noises. Was someone talking? Buggles didn't meow or hiss anymore, so it wasn't her. Looking to the couch, expecting to find Charlie alone on the couch, watching the glowing box, she noticed Cheryl was with him. They were moving around, and Cheryl was making a lot of noise. There was that tasty red stuff everywhere.

She wondered what was going on and decided to ask. "Wh-whu-uuuuh...?"

Charlie looked up at her, mouth full, then to Cheryl, whose struggling and noises were becoming weaker and more faint. Charlie scooted over some and brushed Buggles's little bones aside. He patted on the now empty space next to him.

Timidly, Millie sat down beside him. He tore a long part of Cheryl off, either an arm or a leg, and handed it to Millie. Millie smiled. This was the first time in a long time, longer than she could remember, that he'd made dinner for her.

I didn't know it at the time but "Flesh Wounds," which appeared in the original The Dead Walk! *was Mr. Knave's first published piece of fiction, zombie or otherwise. Since then, he's written numerous other shorts, a serial novel, and much more. I am prepared to accept full responsibility for this.*

HiGH NOON of the LIVING DEAD

by Adam P. Knave

Now this was back in the early days of the dead west. Back then it didn't have a name or anything, it was just where man was losing the fight to survive. The desert was bad enough on its own, but add the Brainers and their mounts to the mix and, well, to be blunt we were gettin' real bad. Most civilized areas had already collapsed, and the future wasn't lookin' none too bright.

By then, this was only ten or so years after the Brainers had come, in you understand, the whole of what used to be called Texas and most points west of it clear to the ocean had already fallen. The Brainers moved fast, faster than anyone thought they could. The disease they spread with them affected mammals of all sorts and made 'em hunger. It made 'em kinda stupid too, at first, but they got smarter as they adapted. That was our mistake in the first days, we showed 'em all what we could do and they learnt from it like children.

They swept clean across the land, legend has it they came right out of the sparkling ocean in old California and just started marching east one day. They hit the rest of the globe too, the same way, walking at first. Damn them anyway, they learned. They started riding horses again, Brainer horses to be sure, and training dogs and everything. They couldn't eat no Brainer steer but then they didn't eat anything but the brains of the living anyway so what did they rightfully care? Still they were kinda smart, even if they didn't talk except to grumble and growl like old men arguing without teeth.

We stopped 'em around the Mississippi for a while, superior firepower still meant something even if we hadn't learned some of the tricks to killing them that we know now. Most of us had given up on the west. When the Brainers came across California they started to bunch up in the west, see, and what with us holding them back from moving much further the west became their stronghold. Not that I would credit them with enough smarts to think in terms of conquering strategy, their natural movements just gave them the appearance of it. They were smart, yeah, but they weren't that smart. Some higher brain functions would always be lost to them, and they only had crude hand signals and gestures to coordinate themselves.

Once they had a natural stronghold growing though, they learnt to use it. Hand signals increased and patterns started to form up out there in the harsh sun. You gotta understand, it wasn't as if they had killed every living person in their path. They needed the food source, but they also needed the fine control labor.

With memories came wants and with wants came the problem: the Brainers couldn't rebuild things. They could tear a house down just fine, but they couldn't work together well enough to build one. So they took living men and women and forced them to do the hard work. At first, to be sure, work was refused. Then again how many people around you do you have to watch die for refusing to lift a hammer and work some nails before you find that same hammer in your hand a-swinging?

We all gave the west up for good. There wasn't a good clear choice otherwise, that we saw. Two folks found it in themselves to disagree. Franklin Cleaver and Edward Bones was what they called themselves, if pressed. Most folk called 'em simply Cleaver and Bones but they always called themselves Frank and Eddie.

This is where a lot of historians, if I can use the word to describe myself, disagree. Some say the two men were assassins until the Brainers came, fingering their expertise and willingness to kill as explanation. Some point to evidence, namely Bones' crockery collection, that they were just chefs in some lowly military outfit. Still others like to claim, and Lord knows what they base this one on, that the two men were sports players who got separated from their team and struck out on their own. They certainly didn't play any sports that I ever saw.

Yeah, I saw 'em. I was with 'em when they... but that's later on. The rest, including how they came to the point that they considered their plan, I heard tell from others in town, like I'm tellin' you now.

They came into what was left of Logansport, Louisiana early one Saturday. Thing was, they came from the west. No one, by then, came in from the west unless they were a Brainer looking for a snack. The sentries on the town wall, a hastily constructed thing of wood and mud, almost shot 'em. Bones and Cleaver were covered in sand and dust and they looked for all the world like statues come to life.

The sentries shouted warnings to each other and readied their guns, hoping for a clean shot, when Franklin shouted right back at them. Brainers didn't shout, even the guys dumb enough to land sentry duty knew that.

"Hey, buddy, open the damned gate, will ya?" Franklin asked.

The sentries were too shocked to do any opening of anything besides their mouths at that point, so they stood there, jaw-dropped at the two men. Edward sighed and took a rifle out from under the sand colored poncho he had draped over his small frame.

"Frank here asked you to do us a favor," he said cheerily, "think maybe you could get to doing it? Today?"

The sight of the obviously well kept gun shook the sentries into action. Two of them rushed down the rickety old hand-lashed ladder and started to work at getting the gate open. The other two sentries stayed where they were, taking in the sight of men. Men from the west.

"We'll get it open, it's just," the first sentry stammered, "we don't use it, see."

"Yeah it... no one comes from this direction. No one that's still talkin' at least," the second explained.

"We gathered," Franklin said mysteriously. He yanked his bandana off his head and his scarf off his face and started to wipe the grime clear from his skin. Franklin had the ability to loom over people even while the people he was loomin' over stood twenty feet above him on a wall.

Edward pulled out a bent and broken cigarette, hand rolled but crushed in the folds of his poncho. He shook his head sadly and looked at it, turning it this way and that in his fingers. "Hey, Frank?"

"Yeah, Eddie?" the bigger man answered without looking, spitting into his scarf and trying to wipe his face somewhat clear.

"This ain't right," Edward Bones said sadly to his partner, "I didn't even get to smoke the fucking thing." He presented the broken smoke to Cleaver like a child handing over a broken toy.

"And what," Cleaver asked, "am I supposed to do with this?"

Still, Cleaver took the broken thing and studied it for a second before muttering under his breath, breaking it in two and handing half to Edward. Then he stuck the remaining half in the corner of his own mouth and started to dig out a match.

They went on like that, smoking and talking as if nothing was unusual while they waited for the gate to work its way open. The sentries on the wall fell silent, out of awe or fear depending on who you asked later. The two sentries who couldn't see any of this, but only hear the mutterings on the other side of the thick and stuck gate figured the two men on the other side to be insane.

Either way, the gate got opened with a bit of teamwork and, more importantly, closed and firmly locked again once Cleaver and Bones were through. Edward waved at the sentries and the two men just walked on past, uncaring, aiming right for the bar. They had no way of knowing where it was, but somehow their feet took them right to it with only a stop at a horse through to finish washing off the dust from their faces.

The air in the bar was hot and unmoving, like the beer, but that didn't stop Cleaver and Bones. They ordered up two mugs of the local swill and found a cracked and leaning table to sit at, Franklin Cleaver putting his feet up on the edge of the table and causing it to sway.

Sammy Burns, the bartender in the Last Drop, swore till the day he died that they looked right at home from minute one, never stopping to give pause or consideration that they were somewhere new. They had a sense, Sammy would say, that everywhere they stopped to sit was their home and you were welcome to share it with them so long as you played by their rules.

No one wanted to ask the two strangers any questions at first. They didn't exactly go out of their way to hunt down people to interview 'em, either. A week passed. Then two. The town got used to them, as much as they could, lettin' them go about their business, which seemed to consist of drinking and talking to each other and no one else. They always had money for their drink and never seemed to do nothin' to earn it. Which is what eventually broke the mutual silences, I'd say.

It happened late one night, out back of the bar. Edward was setting up his cook pots and slicing roots into a bucket. Franklin was busy starting a roaring fire. The men had taken to cooking late nights, Edward seemed to insist, and feeding whomever was still awake. It didn't invite conversation much other than thanks, but it warmed some of the locals to the two.

Johnny Boots saw it different. He felt that his woman, Betsy

Klein, was paying that Bones man far too much attention. Betsy didn't see it that way at all, but then she also didn't see herself as Johnny Boots' woman, either.

Boots was out back watching the fire grow along with his ire. He shot Edward a look, trying to warn the man off through sheer force of will. None of us knew, then, that battle was a losing proposition. Johnny Boots learned it soon enough though, and learned it for all of us.

"Hungry?" Edward asked Johnny, gesturing him closer to the cooking pots that were warming up over the fire. The night was dry and hot and the fire's heat warmed men that didn't need warming. Edward's face was coated with a fine sweat but, like his partner, he still wore fine clothing and layers of it regardless of the heat.

Johnny shook his head at Edwards question, stopping his head shake to spit. "Naw, I jus' don't think you oughta be paying so much attention to my woman," Johnny said slowly and then jerked a thumb over towards Betsy. She rolled her eyes and started walking towards the fire.

Edward held a hand up to stop her and smiled warmly at Johnny Boots. "Hey, man, I have no interest in her," he told Johnny as easy as discussing the weather, "I mean, no offense... uhh... Betsy, right? But yeah, guy, I'm sorry if I gave you some sort of impression there. Whatdda ya say you have a plate with me when I'm done, we can call it the past?"

Johnny turned to look at Betsy, who was smiling, and looked back at Edward, turning his full attention on the slender man. Edward's green eyes fairly twinkled in the firelight and his short black hair shone with beads of sweat. Somehow that managed to rile Johnny even more.

"How'sabout you stop lookin' at her and I won't have to deal with you myself," he said, putting as much menace as he could into the sentence.

Edward laughed easily and gave Johnny another smile. Franklin didn't even perk up at the exchange, bent over and busy with stoking the fire as he was. Both men looked as if nothing at all was going on, except making dinner.

"Hey, Frank?" Edward asked, his voice light and uncaring.

"Yeah, Eddie?" his partner answered, still not looking up.

"Do we have any oil, and perhaps another turning fork would come in handy, if we could spare one for a few hours."

Franklin reached over and passed Bones an old glass bottle half full of oil. The makeshift wooden stopper was jammed into the bottle at an odd angle and it took Edward a second to pry it loose with his teeth.

"Yeah, we should have another turning fork," Franklin added, glancing over at the large bag of cooking supplies they lumped out back every night. He stood up and walked over to the bag, undoing the flaps slowly and rummaging inside.

Johnny Boots stood there, confused for a moment. He wasn't sure what was going on except that it seemed like he was being ignored. Growling deep in his throat Johnny took a step towards Edward, raising a fist.

Edward Bones threw the contents of the oil bottle at Johnny's face without seeming to move, stopping the man mid-swing. Johnny stood there, sputtering, and reached a hand up to wipe at his eyes.

Bones grabbed a small stick from the fire and flicked it at Boots casually, turning to look at Cleaver before it even struck home.

"You know, I could really do with some potatoes, Frank," he said as Johnny Boot's face caught fire. Boots screamed and stumbled backwards, losing his balance and falling on his ass near the cook pot, upsetting it. Franklin was already moving, putting out a hand to steady the pot and then thrusting down with the fork. It caught Johnny Boots in the neck and he sputtered and gurgled, trying hard to figure out the trick of breathing blood. He died pretty fast, between the injuries, but not a second of it was anything but hellishly painful.

Edward walked back to his favorite standing spot, looking into the pot and considering the temperature before dumping out his bucket right into it. A sweet sizzle erupted from the pot, smoke puffing upwards tinged with the smell of fresh cooking vegetables.

"We don't have any more potatoes," Franklin said, handing Edward the fresh turning fork, "but that smells good there."

"Thanks, Frank." Edward looked up at the people who stood around. They were gaping, to a body, rooted to the spot in fear. "So who wants a plate?" Edward asked, sticking his hand into the pot to stir.

It only took one moment like that to convince everyone with a lick of sense to steer as clear of Cleaver and Bones as possible. Sadly some of the other folk in town didn't have a lick of sense. They crossed paths with the men and ended up much the same as Johnny Boots, sometimes their deaths were simple and sometimes they were full of complex and strange plans of action, but they always ended up dead. Not once did Cleaver or Bones seem to care about killing a man.

The days continued to pass and the town grew used to Cleaver and Bones, ignoring them where possible and being respectful where they could. Everyone in town was respectful of the pair, except the men themselves. They berated each other and gave one another enough grief that some expected it to erupt into violence, which it never did. Outside of them though, the only other things which didn't learn to respect both men were the Brainers and the weather.

The sun beat down on the town like never before, causing even the weeds to shrivel up and die. Food got scarce and men went hungry. No one knew what to do. There was hardly ever even a wind to help cool off a man's skin and the nights were just as hot as the days, heat radiating back off of the ground in uncomfortable waves.

The Brainers, they made occasional attempts at the wall. None got through, but with the heat and hunger depressing and addling so many hopes dropped and a general feeling rose up in its place: the Brainers would get through and overrun the town.

Hadn't, some asked, the government left the west for dead in the first place? Hadn't they pulled out and then left places like the very town they stood in to defend themselves? Why wouldn't the Brainers over run things, they reasoned. The idea spread and grew and overtook the sense of the town as a whole.

Except, of course, for the minds of two people.

Cleaver and Bones seemed to be having a perfectly fine time of it. Hell, they almost seemed to be expecting and awaiting the mood of the town to shift downward. Franklin smiled more and the both of them conferred in hushed tones, not giving a damn who noticed them whisper to each other.

About a month after they showed up, Cleaver and Bones walked to the center of town and stood in the middle of the street, looking around and catching as many eyes as possible.

"Listen up, if you wouldn't mind," Edward said with his customary friendliness, "we have something that we think you might all want to hear."

"We," Franklin said with the mean, hard grin of a man thinks he can move boulders with his bare hands, "have a plan."

It was the sentence that was to change everything, and even as it was said, the whole town knew it.

People gathered up inside the church, filtering in as word spread like wildfire. Cleaver and Bones stood near the altar, but not directly on it. They watched the crowd in the room grow and conferred between themselves in quiet tones. Eventually they had to figure the mass of people was as big as it would get and Franklin nodded at Edward and then at the crowd, starting to speak.

"In case you all didn't notice, the current situation won't hold for long," he said matter-of-factly, "and when it gives this town will fall. When it falls, the Brainers will move in, take down the wall and inch further across the land. That needs to stop."

"But it's more than that," Edward cut in.

"Not yet, Eddie," Franklin said with a glance over his shoulder. "One thing at a time."

Barbara Haines stood up and looked around the church. "What can we..." she started to say, before she was cut off by a sweep of Franklin's hand.

"Hold off for now. Let us tell you about where we were."

"We've spent the last few years in the west, and it was..." Edward grinned slowly and tapped his partner on the shoulder. "Hey Frank, it was kinda like that time when we..."

"Don't start, Eddie, just tell them what we discussed."

A murmur spread out along the crowd. I had just gotten to town myself a few days ago and learned all about the two strange men, so when I found out about a gathering you can bet I ran there as fast as I could. Still, at the idea, the simple thought, that these two had spent time out west in with the Brainers made us all wonder. How did they survive, what were they doing, what could they want now?

"Right. Well, settle down some, folks." We fell silent at Edward's words, all attention on the front of the church again. "We were curious, you know how it is. So we traveled west and then came back east. We came back north of here, of course, but we've been going back and forth for a while. At first it was a job, don't worry about that. But the second time we wanted to see what was really up."

People were rooted to their seats. Edward stopped talking for a second to root in his pockets for what turned out to be a smoke and you could've cut the tension with a knife. He took his time lighting the cigarette and then took a long drag off of it, holding the smoke deep.

"The Brainers were a curiosity." Edward exhaled and waved a hand around a bit in thought. "They weren't at all like the old Vodoun ideas of a zombie, but they also didn't seem to fit any other popular mythology concerning the concept. It was confusing. Myth is, I mean, it's an engine and like Joseph Campbell said..."

"Eddie," Franklin broke in, "the facts?"

Edward nodded and shrugged, the cigarette in the corner of his mouth. Something in his eyes though, something deep in there had flicked back on. We could all see it, even Franklin.

"Sorry, Frank. But yeah, we wandered a while. Looking. It was just like that time Frank and I had to deal with Freddie Six-Fingers..."

"Except for the fact that Freddie had otters."

"We dealt with the otters, though didn't we?"

"At the cost of my car. Again."

"Still wasn't my fault. But the Brainers were just like him. They were showing one hand and playing another. We all know they don't kill everyone they meet. Who does, right?" Edward shrugged and then smiled. The both of them seemed to be warming up somehow, breaking out of a shell.

"Bennie."

"Yeah, all right, Frank. Bennie. But the Brainers don't. Some people they take with them. Now from what we heard when we got back the last time they were supposed to be taking them somewhere and using them for labor. What no one knew was how."

They didn't pace and didn't move their arms a whole lot, standing as still as possible while they spoke, but something about the *way* they started to speak was different. More alive. They seemed younger as they went on, instead of the fifty-odd years of life that had weathered and etched into each man.

"Eddie's right. Everyone had a theory, but no one had seen it in action. So we went and looked. They tie them up and march them out across the desert. The Brainers ride some Brainer horses and corral them, like so many cattle."

"Although traditionally you don't tie cattle when you go on a cattle drive. Then again, I suppose that cattle don't often want to escape. They might, granted, but they seem to be fine just walking."

"Yes. Thank you, Eddie, for that brief, yet fascinating, look into cattle herding," Franklin said with a roll of his eyes. "When we saw that we realized we couldn't ignore it. Humans suffer, they die and they do what they need to in order to survive. We get that, better than a lot of people, probably. This is different."

"Besides, we've seen you all," Edward dropped and stubbed out his cigarette, his eyes scanning all of us slowly as he did.

"We have. You're breaking. There's no fighting back going on. No anything. You are all now sitting here waiting to die. That's it, that's all you have left for yourselves. You'll slowly sink further and further down and the wall over there will get a weak point, but you won't care. Then another. Then it'll fall down."

"Walls fall but they don't have to. If this wall falls, do you think other people north or here, or south, will hold their lines forever, either? What man, my grandfather once asked me..."

"No he didn't, Eddie. Why do you have to attribute bad sayings to this man who, I might add, you never even met?"

"Not the point, Frank. The point is that he was right."

"He couldn't have been right, he never even...why do I bother?"

"I couldn't tell you. But I can tell you that the point is that if you don't hold why should you expect any one else to?"

"But what can we *do*?" James Higgins, the town butcher, asked.

"We're getting there," Edward told him, "see we would've tried this ourselves but we needed supplies and we needed a few extra hands to help."

"To help with what?" I asked, unable to hold my tongue. The mood of the crowd was shifting slowly. We grew restless.

"Getting there," Edward Bones said with a smile. "We also needed to make sure there would be a town to come back to."

"We intend to bring the fight to the Brainers and disrupt their little herding plan," Franklin said, the glint in his eye unmistakable, "even just one, just to start working out how we can do it again and again and hold the walls and eventually push them back."

"Trust me," Edward put in, "it surprised us to think of this, too. We're not normally your public servant type. Though I did once work collecting garbage."

"You also sold rugs. Let's not push it."

"I wasn't really selling... oh well, no, I mean I really was paid to collect garbage, Frank."

"I couldn't imagine caring any less. Can we get on with this?"

"Sure," Bones said and straightened his shirt a bit. "We need about four guys who can deal with camping out and fucked up conditions and death. Four guys who aren't so afraid of the Brainers that they'll be useless."

"They should also," put in Franklin, "be able to follow orders."

"Are you saying that I can't?" Edward asked, with a hurt look on his face.

"History speaks for itself, Eddie. Still. That ain't all we'll need. We also need supplies."

"Yeah, let's see," Edward thought for a moment, recalling a list the two had obviously spent time thinking over, "we need twenty or forty feet of chain link fence, an equal footage of two-by-four beams, enough so the width of the beams adds up to the length of fence, see? About a hundred feet of solid steel wire, a staple gun, ten or so four by eight wood beams, a few tents, some padlocks and some styrofoam, you can't get rid of the stuff so I'm sure there's a bunch somewhere around here. What else, Frank?"

"Mmm, let's see now, Eddie. As much razor wire as you can find, bolt cutters, rope. Good strong rope, none of that twine shit."

"I hate that stuff, the nylon?"

"Cuts your fingers. About six pounds of raw mint leaves, if possible."

"Don't forget the make-up. We need make-up, women's stuff will do."

"Right. A bunch of wax, enough water for six people to last about a week and dried food to last the same. Heavy duty rubber bands, if any still exist, a few bags of flour, extra boots for everyone involved, heavy gloves, gasoline or the like, and maybe some tennis balls if you can find any."

"See," Edward said with his customary smile growing even bigger. "Simple."

It wasn't nearly as easy as Edward Bones claimed, of course. Some of the stuff they wanted could be managed without too much hassle. Jerry Smitts agreed to give up a section of his chain link fence for the cause without too much bitchin' and moanin', for example.

The wood beams were likewise simply a matter of talking someone into helpin' out. People wanted to help, any way they could, unless it meant personal hardship. That was understandable, to a point, but only to a point. It felt like the town's survival or a few people who had needed goods. In that sorta situation, when the person won't give up what's needed, it gets taken. It gets taken right quick, too, to be honest about it.

Deidre Fontaine had herself a few tents that she never really used. Still, she saw a potential use for 'em in the future and wanted us to find something else to use. We woulda, except for the fact that hers were the best tents around. They were on the list. One night Deidre put her foot down, firmly, by slamming her door in the faces of some of us other townsfolk.

Well, she mighta' slept well right after, but the very next night she was woken up to the sound of her front door coming down in splinters. The tents were bundled up with the other equipment and when Deidre asked about them, screamed about them, why no one had any clue what tents she was talking about.

While the stuff was being gathered, as best it could be, Cleaver and Bones picked their team of companions. They needed four men and found themselves facing down fourteen volunteers. Both men smiled at that, but they went down the list, asking questions and watching the eyes of the men and women answerin'.

In the end Sally Teekin, a widow who had bigger arms than most men, Otto van Potts, who also supplied all the rope and steel wire needed, Billy McDougal, a damn fine shot, and myself, were chosen. I ain't sure why I was picked above some of the others. I guess they liked the look of my eyes and my steady hands.

It only took a few days to get everything together, the gasoline and tennis balls being the only item we couldn't locate any of. High octane moonshine was used for the gas and Edward Bones gathered up a bunch of avocado saying they'd do as well as tennis balls. The styrofoam packing, which I thought would be a problem, was actually in use as insulation up in the barber's house.

Cleaver and Bones lashed all the equipment into bundles and arranged straps for each bundle, handing them out to us and taking a fair share themselves.

"Ain't we gonna use horses or something? A mule at least to carry this stuff, maybe?" Billy asked, shuffling his pack onto his shoulders and frowning.

"Horses and mules generally are not smart enough to avoid smaller mammals," Franklin said, "and they don't think of them as threats. But everything out there that is not the six of us is a threat to us. Beasts of burden would only cause us problems. We carry the load."

The West Gate was a horrible thing to see, then. It was suddenly all that stood between being brave and being dead. I could read it in the faces of my fellow travelers, all except for Cleaver and Bones. Their faces were neutral, for them this was just another day. But for us, well we hadn't been out west since things started to settle. I knew I was new to town and all, but it wasn't as if I spent the time before that wandering in the wasteland like our two tour guides had.

The west wasn't something you went back to. It was hard enough scratching out a living on the safer side of the gate. The sentries didn't want to open it, looking around for someone to tell them to stop even as they started to pull the thick, heavy barrier wide. Some of their fellow sentries stood on the wall, making sure nothing was in view that could leap out and burst through the gate before they could react.

Once the gate was open wide enough for us to walk, well, we started walking. Ahead of us lay nothing. Sand, the occasional tree and low sitting bush, and the awful power of the sun. It seemed hotter on the other side of the gate, even though that was stupid to think. That was it. Not a Brainer in sight. No animals of any sort. Not even a bird in the sky. We could see nothing worth seeing, but we could see one hell of a lot of it.

The sound of the West Gate closing behind us caused a pit of fear to swell in my belly and I looked around. Otto nodded at me, letting me know that he shared my fear, but wouldn't let it stop him. I nodded back and adjusted my pack. Where we were now we were only gonna come back from one way. If we passed back through the gate into town it meant we were successful. If not, we were dead.

We walked on in silence, the punishing sun doing its level best to stop us. If we kept covered we wouldn't burn but keeping covered enough made most of us feel too hot to move. Damned either way, we would remind each other that the burns weren't going to be worth the temporary relief of removing any protective covering. The guarded friendship that seemed to blossom instantly made the walk a little easier at least. We were watching out for each other the best way we knew how then.

By the time the sun started to dip low in the sky we were well out of sight of town. The wall was behind us, we knew in our minds, but glancing back showed the same featureless expanse as looking forward did. It didn't exactly help our state of mind.

Of course whenever I'm sayin' "we" here, I refer to the four of us that came along with Cleaver and Bones. The two men themselves I wouldn't really wanna guess about. Their minds were their own, and though we traveled with them they weren't in the same space as we were. We were being led, they were leading. They said nothing, so we said not much of anything. They walked so we trudged behind. When Franklin held a hand up and stopped cold, we all froze in our tracks and tried not to look too worried.

"Eddie," Franklin asked, "do you see that?"

"Yeah, Frank," Edward answered, neither men looking at us, "what do you think?"

"I think we keep moving for a while longer, then set up camp." Franklin looked back at us. "That good for you guys, too?"

We nodded and shrugged and made other motions of acceptance and agreement. What could we do, say no? How would that have gone, I wonder? It didn't matter and so we pressed on.

Otto nudged me a few feet later and pointed out to where Franklin and Edward had been staring. I looked off the point of his hand and then slowly turned to look at the man himself.

"I don't see it either, Otto."

"No, I *do* see it," he told me in a whisper, "and I'll tell the others. It's something moving. You *really* can't see it?"

I shook my head and tried to look in that general direction again. If I tried really hard I thought maybe I could see something moving towards us, but it could've been heat waves off the ground or any other damned thing for all I knew.

The sun set and the temperature started to drop. We marched on, regardless, for a while. Our feet hurt from walking all day, our backs shared the pain lugging the packs and our very skin crawled with sweat and grit. When Edward discussed something with Franklin, they were far enough ahead that I couldn't hear 'em. When they turned and gestured to us that we were stopping for the night Sally puffed a gust of relieved air from her cheeks.

"All right, drop the packs and let us get set for the night," Franklin said, "unroll the fence and get out the wood and wire and staples, will you?"

We did as asked, as quickly as we could, which wasn't half as fast as they wanted us to I'm sure. Everything got laid out of the ground in front of us. Edward and Franklin walked around the supplies, nodding. Travel and packing hadn't seemed to have damaged a thing.

"All right," Edward said, grabbing the fence and starting to wrestle it upright, "get this up." Sally and Billy moved to help him and together they strung the fence in a big circle around us. Franklin locked the fence in place and pocketed the keys in silence.

Then he took the two by fours and started to staple wire to them, weaving it in and out of the fence as he did. When he was done, and he asked for no help at all doing it, we were locked into a metal and wood barrier. The four by eights were laid down on the ground inside the circle, causing us to dance a bit as we tried to put boards under our feet.

It was getting cold by then and even with the gloves on I wanted to cram my hands into my pockets for warmth. After the bristling heat of the day the wasteland's night chill burrowed into my bones. In town, at least, there were fires, other people, buildings. Civilization that kept us all warmed, not only in body but spirit. Out here we had ourselves and it was too bad if that wasn't enough insulation.

Otto and Billy got the tents up, cramped though they were, and we huddled into them for a few. Our leaders stayed outside, watching the darkness. Without planning it, Billy, Otto, Sally and I all huddled in the tents facing the still open flaps, watching our watchers.

"Can we maybe light a fire?" Billy asked hopefully.

"What? Light the ground you sit on, now how does that sound good?" Otto asked in response before Franklin could say anything. Instead of speaking, Cleaver just nodded at Otto and went back to watching the land. Both of them slowly turned, taking in everything around us.

It fell silent. The silence of the waste, of death. In that silence I could hear something though, something muffled and out of place.

"What *is* that?" I asked no one in particular.

"Rabbit," Franklin said over his shoulder, but it didn't sound like no rabbit I had ever heard.

"Brainer rabbit," Edward corrected.

At that we scurried out of the tents at speed. Suddenly we were all standing around looking out into the darkness. Now, even I could see it. See it and hear it.

The Brainer rabbit was trying to hop with back legs that didn't work quite right any more. Moonlight cast irregular shadows on it as it came shuffling on. It would try to hop, back legs coiling and then extending, but the muscles weren't connected right anymore and each hop turned into a horrible shuffling limp that sent the rabbit's ass into the air and then back down a few inches further on.

One of its front paws was totally missing and the other didn't look like it was doing so well, so each hop also shoved its body forward, scraping the front of its body along the ground. Fur and flesh was sloughing off in strips and chunks. Still it came on. Otto let fly with a ragged panicked laugh. Sally cuffed him for it, shutting him up quickly.

"Should we shoot it, maybe?" Billy asked before I could.

"You are a smart one," Franklin said with his back to us, "neither one of us mentioned even having a gun, this whole time."

"Not that we would travel without one. It's like going for a trip without stopping to go to the bathroom first, isn't it? You should always know better than to do that, too," Edward added, turning to us with a shrug and smirk.

"But, to answer your question, no we should not shoot it. It's bad enough we're talking. Let's not make more loud noises than necessary."

We nodded and went back to watching the rabbit shove itself onward, ever closer to us. Yeah, it was just a rabbit. Not a very big one, even. But even a Brainer rabbit could kill us if we were stupid. We all knew that and none of us took its existence lightly.

"Hey, Frank?"

"Yeah, Eddie?"

"I did not think they were out this far, yet," Edward said, stoking his chin and reaching for a cigarette.

"It's just a rabbit," his partner pointed out. Franklin then gave

Edward a warning look and Franklin put the match he had taken out back in his pocket, leaving the cigarette dangling from his lips unlit.

"I do realize that, Frank. I just mean where there is smoke there is also fire."

"We would have noticed them by now. Tomorrow." Both men just nodded at that, but blanched. They had to be talking about Brainers. That we would see them was the whole point of the trip, but the idea that there were Brainers not two days march out of town was sobering.

"The rabbit then?" Edward worked the cigarette in his mouth, rolling it from one corner to the other with his lips.

"Would you? Thanks," Franklin moved over and dug the keys out of his pocket, unlocking the padlocks until he could yank open enough of a gap in the fence for Edward to slip between.

Edward slid a knife out from under his poncho and crouched low, running straight for the rabbit. The rabbit saw him coming, or sensed him or something, and perked up, lifting its head sluggishly. It bared teeth and waited for the man to get close enough to kill.

Edward didn't change course of speed, heading right for the rabbit. His knife flashed in the moonlight and the sound of it burying into the rabbit's head was loud enough to feel like it was happening right next to us. He picked up the Brainer hare by the ear and worked his knife free from its skull. Then he flung it far away from us and walked back toward our camp, stopping to clean his knife on a low sitting bush.

"Smaller things are easy," Edward told us, "they can move fast but they also get hurt quicker, which slows them down considerably. Don't think a Brainer will be this easy. Hell, I wish they were. But they aren't, and don't forget it."

We let Edward back into the camp and then locked the fence again.

"They are not much of a threat, when you can stalk them like that," Edward said, "it's when you don't see them that you have to worry." Then he sat down and put his back against one of the tent's support poles and closed his eyes.

We went back into the tents, ourselves, and tried to force ourselves to sleep. It didn't work and when the sun rose we were, all four of us, already watching its first rays brush the land. I poked my head out of the tent and saw that Edward was up, watching the land, and Franklin was asleep where Edward had been.

I didn't say anything to him, I just watched the man in profile. Him and his partner were so different. They were both obviously in their fifties but Franklin looked like he was on the later side of them compared to Edward. Edward was a smaller man, built for speed and sureness, where his partner was made for strength. They fit each other perfectly and I wondered how they had met, originally.

In the spreading daylight I could see a splotch of black tar-like goo where the rabbit had been. I remembered as a little kid hunting rabbits with my father in the woods. They were fast creatures, but more scared of you then you could ever be of them. Hell, you had to rile one to get it to bite, most times. They weren't considered sporting fare, except for their speed. That thing out there last night hadn't been remotely close to what I would have called a rabbit.

If whatever happened to Brainers did that to a rabbit what had it done to men? We'd heard stories but I didn't know many who had seen 'em, and most of *those* wouldn't talk about it in detail. I wondered, yet again, what we were up against and what our chances were.

Breakfast was a solemn affair of dried meat and bread washed down with a few gulps of water. That shook me out of my revery. Brainer rabbits, Brainer men even, loomed in our near future, but running out of food or water would do us in just as fast. Whose side was the planet on, to give us such miserable hunting grounds. Maybe, just maybe, it was somehow as bad for them as it was for us. Maybe the Earth was an impartial third party to the life and death going on along its surface. Maybe.

We packed up the encampment and put it all back onto our shoulders. Otto nudged me as we started to walk and bent his head close to mine.

"Hey, man, if we have to take all these protections to keep alive out here at night, how the hell did those two do it by themselves without any gear? They didn't have any of this stuff when they came into town, I swear."

"You think it isn't needed, that they're trying to, what, scare us?"

"No, but then, how the fuck did they do it?"

"Ask them."

"No way, you do it."

We bantered like that for a few hours, taunting each other in quiet voices, trying to get the other to ask Franklin and Edward about their own survival skills. Neither of us did though. It'd be real easy, right now, to tell you that we didn't do it because we feared them, or because we felt the answer would make us look soft and incapable of the inhuman feats that Bones and Cleaver seemed to live and breathe.

It wouldn't be true though. No, we didn't ask because any answer had the potential to reduce our guides to being simply human again, and without the reassurance that we walked with people who were somehow far more than we could ever be I don't know if we would have gone on.

Around mid-afternoon we heard a low pitched keening sound. A banshee with laryngitis, maybe. Edward glanced back at us and grinned. Our pace sped up, which felt backwards to me. At the arrival of that sound I wanted to go faster—the other way.

"See, Frank, I told you he'd still be here."

"Well of course he's still here," Franklin said, "where else could he go?"

"Exactly my point."

"No," Franklin corrected his partner, "your point was that I had somehow doubted the idea. Which, for the record, I did not."

"Either way, he's still here, just like I said."

On the ground a twitching lump came into sight. The heat waves off the ground made it difficult to figure out what it was supposed to be that twitched, apparently left here by the men now returning to it.

As we got closer we could all make out what the shuddering heap was. A Brainer. It didn't look like Brainers were supposed to, not by anything I had ever heard. Sure, there was the gray skin and the cold black eyes that shone in the sunlight at a distance. The swollen tongue lolled around like I had heard and the howls and grunts matched up. This Brainer left the garden of the known at that point. He was curled into a fetal position and looked like old leather, cracked and dried. When he tried to move he simply twitched a bit, his skin too stiff and shrunken in to allow for the movement his brain fought for.

Franklin turned to us and nodded. "Yeah, Brainer. The sun doesn't treat them too well. Which is what we figured. We staked this one out last time as a marker, partly to prove a point. He can't grab you unless you get real close. So don't."

With that little speech our march resumed. We gave the Brainer a wide berth, probably wider than necessary, but why take chances with a thing like that? The going was slower after spotting their twisted marker. Off in the distance we could all see a dark shape slowly moving. Cleaver and Bones started to move around it, positioning us directly behind the column ahead.

"There they are," Edward said over his shoulder. "They don't move too fast, and slower still when they have captives, but there are at least three of them for each of us. I am reminded of Custer, except he wasn't on the move and the Brainers don't have arrows. Also, we'll win."

"That is the general idea, Eddie," Franklin said and then turned to face us, stopping our walk. "Here's the thing. The captives won't be much help to us. They'll want to be but they're weak and hungry by now. Which makes them a threat to themselves, really."

"So we should separate them and get them clear," Edward put in, "except that leaves us down a few men, doesn't it?"

"It does. So here's what we were thinking. If we can break their circle and round up the captives then…"

"But they can't run, so we'll be slow getting clear. Which gives the Brainers a good chance to surround us all."

"Which is why we brought the rest of that stuff," Franklin finished and unslung his pack.

The Brainer herding party got themselves a good sight farther from us as we hunkered down and got to work. Work was trying to dissolve the styrofoam in the alcohol and making it a good slush, before we filled some hollowed out avocados with it. Supposedly the rubber bands would hold the avocado together without too much slop.

While Otto, Sally and I made makeshift napalm avocado grenades, Billy helped Franklin and Edward mash some of the mint leaves. The paste of it was then handed around.

"Smear this under your arms and across the back of your necks," Edward told us as Billy passed the glop around, "then apply a handful to your heads."

"They hunt by scent," Franklin said with an evil grin, "their eyes are all right, but nothing special and the mix-up in scent will slow down their reactions."

"As will being on fire," Edward added with a childish smirk.

"One would think," Franklin Cleaver said and nodded.

"Also don't forget, the make-up will make a nice thing to stripe and prevent glares from hitting your eyes some. Use it, but don't use it up, we may need some to help get away," Edward said as he got back to work.

When we finished up our chores and packed the resulting goodies carefully it was turning towards dusk. Edward and Franklin told us that we'd be on a fast march from then on in and started off. I carried the half avocados with Billy lugging the other half. We lagged a bit behind, trying to hurry without sloshing the stuff around and making the avocados nothing more than useless. The sheer amount of nervousness might have had something to do with it, too.

"We have to get close," Franklin said just loud enough to be heard, "and break their line before we set any fires. We don't want to risk them just tightening their circle while on fire. So first we distract them. Then we get folks clear. After that we douse them as we retreat."

"Then," Edward finished, "we come back for them and finish them off."

"Of course we do," Edward said with a nod, "I figured that went without saying."

"I said it anyway."

"You always do, Eddie."

"Thanks, Frank."

"That wasn't a com—you know what? Never mind. You're very welcome."

We drew ever closer, hunched down and moving as quietly as possible. The column ahead didn't seem to notice us, but we could see them clearer all the time. The Brainers seemed to all be riding horses. The horses moved all right, a bit of a lumber, but not slow for horses. That worried me.

"When we get there, Eddie and I will break the rear guard and them move up to start distracting the rest. I want you guys to circle the humans and get them free. We'll retreat as one unit and then go back for more." Franklin looked at us over his shoulder, "Remember, take out the head on the Brainers. And don't get bitten."

We nodded nervously and looked up at how close the Brainers seemed to be. I realized that we were doin' the hunting here, they were our prey, but it sure felt like we were just a take-out meal waitin' to happen.

Cleaver and Bones didn't give us another sign, or impart anymore advice, they just moved. Suddenly they were ten feet ahead of the rest of us. Really, I guess them breakin' away and startin' towards the goal was a sign for us, so maybe they did give us one after all.

Whichever, we picked up our own pace and stayed as close behind as we could. Moving at that speed we closed with the Brainers in no time at all. We could see them clear as night now, the Brainers in long coats and wide brimmed hats, clearly dressing as they remembered they had when they were alive, or perhaps simply still in the clothes they died in. The sight truly made me wonder if maybe we hadn't picked the wrong group and these were just cowboys on an old style cattle drive.

The sounds they made washed that thought right out of my being, and quick like. It was the same keening and moaning we heard from the staked Brainer back a ways, except there were human moans added in along with an almost barking sound from the Brainers, a dry coughing expulsion of air that felt like someone trying to fake being able to talk. It was all so utterly not human that it sent chills along my spine and I tightened my grip on the straps of my pack until my fingers hurt from the pressure.

Still, we got nearer and nearer until we had fully closed with the herd.

Edward and Franklin were, of course, in front. They came up behind the rear Brainers and even as they were noticed both men drew knives and hamstrung the Brainer horses, sending them toppling. A quick thrust deep into the base of the skull and both horses stopped twitching.

Their riders, on the other hand, were already up and moving. Edward went in close with his knife, slicing and confusing the Brainer until it couldn't keep up. Then he went in for the kill, leaving his knife in the chest of the thing and pulling a gun. Franklin pulled a gun, too, seemingly out of nowhere. They fired a few seconds shy of together and the twin reports sounded like two sharp cracks of thunder pounding across the sky.

It might not have been the best move. All of the Brainers turned to see what was going on, as did the humans in the center of the circle. The gun shots caused too much confusion, on both sides. Not that it stopped Cleaver and Bones. With all the Brainers looking at them, they skirted the inside of the circle, trying to break the line.

We moved in, pushing past the downed Brainers and their horses to start grabbing the humans and tugging, cajoling and forcing them towards freedom. Otto noticed that one of the downed Brainer horses had a sword in a scabbard along the saddle. He grabbed it free and stuck it in his own belt—it was either a prize or hopeful advantage and I didn't know which he was going for.

The humans didn't want to come with us. Their minds seemed destroyed and I wondered if we would have to kill them just to help them. Flames whoomphed to sudden powerful life towards the front of the line and I knew that the mixture worked at the very least decently. Brainers howled and started to leave the humans alone, moving to rid themselves of their biggest distress.

Edward and Franklin shot a few times, and lit a bunch more fires, causing the Brainers to start to hang back. They pulled back and started to go around the fires. Their mounts were ditched as soon as they became a problem to ride.

The humans were panicked and unresponsive, having no idea

what was going on. their hands hadn't even been tied. They weren't being held by anything other than fear and exhaustion. Neither were things we could fix right off, but we hadda push 'em as hard as we could, regardless.

Two Brainers broke free and came at us from the right. Otto stabbed one in the head with that new sword of his and I chopped another in the side with my knife. I meant to aim higher but I was in a rush. Looking back I could see that the Brainers couldn't locate us easily what with the brightness of the fire hurting their eyes and the mint distracting their sense of smell. Still, we weren't exactly quiet by then.

Time seemed to slow. The fires blazed and moved, Brainer horses and men shambling along the ground, casting hellish light on anything near by. The moaned and howled their pain and frustration to the heights of heaven. It was a sound that would stick with me, clawed into my brain for all time. The sound was animal, sub-animal even, but also oddly human. I hoped like hell there wasn't a live human in the mix, burning alive.

We pushed at the humans, moving around them as we did, screaming at them and growing desperate at their lack of focus. These were broken men and women and I wondered if they could even be brought back to even an approximation of sanity after what they had gone through. I doubted it, but that didn't mean they weren't worth saving.

Eventually, we had the humans moving, somehow I had moved to the back of the mass as we went, next to Billy. Sally and Otto had the front, leading us out. Edward and Franklin were still doing what they did best. Killing things, that is.

But just as suddenly as the sun breaking through a cloud they were right between Billy and I, helping us force the humans out to safety. A few of he Brainers were coming after us, on foot. I felt something sharp tear at my ankle, right through my boot, and cursed. I was sure I had been snake bit until Franklin started barking orders.

"Otto! I saw you grab that sword. Get it here fast," he bellowed. Otto was next to me quickly. I wasn't sure what was going on as time seemed to slide in and out of focus. I looked down, trying to see what kind of snake it was and saw a Brainer with blood on its mouth in a trail that led to my ankle.

I was dead, and I knew it. Franklin didn't seem to agree.

"It's a god damned infection. We have to stop it before it spreads," he said tightly, grabbing the sword Otto offered him.

"Frank, we haven't proven this," Edward started to say.

"Then we will now, Eddie."

I saw the blade rise and then it swam in my vision. The pain didn't swim though. No, it bit down hard and sharp. I blacked out as soon as I started to feel it though, so that was all right.

I woke up a bit later and looked around, confused. I was inside the chain link barrier, but it didn't seem to have been set up right, or at least fully. My leg hurt, the left one where I had been bit. It throbbed with pain, a harsh constant thing that felt almost alive in its intensity.

I looked down and saw that my left leg ended just above the knee.

"He's awake," I heard Sally say.

"Yeah," I managed, "what happened?"

"It looks like they saved you. You haven't turned," she said, mopping my brow with a cloth gently.

"My leg?"

"Small price to pay for living."

She was right. I had to thank Otto for being dumb enough to take the sword in the first place and Franklin for deciding to try his theory. It made me wonder though, if Brainer infections could be stopped that easily.

"Not always," Franklin said, kneeling down next to me and seeming to read my mind. "Sorry, I know what you're thinking, it's obvious. No, I just had to try it. The infection *acts* like an infection, even if we are not sure if it really is one. You were bitten low enough it was worth a try, but it spreads fast."

"Are we done, then?"

"Not quite. Eddie and I need to discourage anything from following us. There are still ten or so Brainers out there, coming after us. You guys are done. Get back to your town, with the guys we saved."

"See you soon, then?" I asked him. The pain broke down any reluctance I held towards talking to Franklin with my usual deference and respect. He was just another man to me now.

"Sure will," he said and nodded at someone I couldn't see, "Otto, finish this and move them back towards town, we'll catch up."

Otto came into sight holding an avocado. He broke it open and poured some of the contents onto my stump. Oh lord the pain, the stinging wretched pain. I threw up and realized from the taste of my mouth it wasn't the first time I had vomited from pain.

"Otto?" I managed weakly.

"Sorry, man, we have to cauterize this. It's gonna hurt as bad as the amputation. But it's the only way."

"Sounds good," I interrupted, "just do it before I think about it."

He nodded at me and lit a match.

I woke up to the swaying motion of being carried. I turned my head to try and see what was going on, where we were, but the motion of my head combined with the gentle sway of whatever I was being carried on made me feel sick. I closed my eyes again and lost more time.

I didn't really come to until the West Gate was being opened for us. The cheering woke me up. We had done it, we were heroes. I couldn't figure out, at first, why Otto and Sally, who were both in my line of sight, looked so grim. Yeah it had been a slice of hell but it was done and we all made it. My left leg was a small enough price for that, Sally was right.

When we got into town and settled some I found myself in a small cabin with Sally Billy and Otto. That's when I noticed the problem and why they all looked so down, despite our victory. It wasn't quite a victory after all.

As for exactly what happened, well there were a few different stories on that. They all agreed that Cleaver and Bones went back out to kill the remaining Brainers. That much was certain as anything. Sally thought she heard Franklin scream in pain, but Billy was sure it was Edward. Otto said he didn't hear any screaming at all, just some gun fire. The gunfire was the other thing they agreed on.

Did Franklin die, or did Edward? Neither? Both? We didn't know. Otto and Sally wanted to turn back and help 'em but Billy had pointed out that the hostages were the more critical of the two groups just then. So they had gotten us all back to town. Sally demanded that the three of them go out and look for Franklin and Edward. Billy waffled on the point, sure they would come back of their own accord before too long. Otto just wasn't sure. Me? Well, shit, I wanted to go look for 'em. They had saved my life.

No, more than that they had given us a burst of hope that we all needed to survive. It was the start of things. The first Brainer raid, but not the last. How could we not go find them, or their bodies, and pay them the tribute they deserved?

Well, in the end the three of 'em went off on a recon to see what they could find while I sat watch on the gate for them. Those were the worst three days of my life, possibly. Just waiting, unable to do anything to help.

In the middle of the third day they came back, though. They found a lot of spent shells and dead Brainers and a lot of blood. It didn't tell us anything and they didn't see any sign of Franklin or Edward.

A month or so later when I had learned to use a crutch almost as well as I had used my leg, Sally and I went on another hunt for the two. No Brainer men in the area, just some rabbits and a possum. No live men either. Nothing. The west had reclaimed them as utterly as it did everything else.

Well you know what happened after that. Brainer hunts started to form up and Otto trained a lot of 'em. Sally and Billy became leads with him and they made a bunch of difference between 'em. I took over guarding the West Gate for a bunch of years, keeping my eyes peeled, every dammed day, for two men in dusty clothing sauntering up to the wall.

The desert was still bad enough on its own, but adding the Brainers and their mounts to the mix didn't seem quite as bas as before. We were still losing the fight but now we could see a way to hold it where it was if not turn it, eventually. Civilized areas started to slowly, very slowly, come back. The future didn't look bright, but it wasn't all blackness neither. All because of two strangers who got fed up with everyone feeling defeated.

They paid some kinda price for it, too. Or maybe they were just still out there, fighting. No one knew, and no one ever reported finding so much as a clue to what really happened that day.

Some days, I still sit up on the wall, looking and waiting.

From Bruce Gehweiler comes a tale of his cryptozoological/parapsychological investigator heroes, Blakely & Boles, as they delve deeply into Pogo Possum and Albert Aligator's old haunt, looking for—and finding!—signs of the living dead.

RaGGED BONES

by Bruce Gehweiler

Okefenokee National Wildlife Refuge, Georgia

Cattails stirred as something moved in the dark waters of the swamp. Tiny waves blossomed on the surface as decaying plants, fresh leaves, and mud were disturbed from the bottom. Only the impersonal gaze of the full moon witnessed the event. Blue reflected light cut through the twisted branches of cypress trees, speckling the area as the form rose from the murky waters. Dripping, broken and ragged, it staggered into the humid air and the redemption of dry earth so long denied. Torn clothing hanging from yellowed bones and the remains of flesh preserved in the moist mud of the swamp, a single bulging eye swivelled as the new-risen thing surveyed the area. Then finally, responding to some siren call heard only by it, the creaking form began walking one sodden boot step at a time.

Pink flesh simmered, crisping in a frying pan as its conquerors sat in small aluminum and canvas chairs before their roaring fire. The chubby one spoke excitedly;

"You'd never catch a largemouth that big up north, Fred. I was right to drag your Yankee butt down here for some decent southern fishin'!" The very sunburned Fred laughed.

"I've got to hand it to you, Tom," he admitted, still grinning, "today was the best fishing I've ever seen anywhere. If I could stand the heat and the bugs, I'd move here just for the fishing. And, of course, if there was some way for me to make a living in the middle of nowhere."

"By the way, Fred," Tom tossed a plastic bottle to his friend, telling him, "you may want to discover a southern secret called sun block tomorrow. You're so burned, you're glowin'!"

"Very funny...it does kind of hurt though."

"Dinner's just about done," said the third of them. "Cookin' over an open flame is a lot faster than usin' an electric stove." Glancing at Fred, he added, "I've got some Aloe lotion in my back pack I can give you for that burn."

"Thanks Skip, I'm going to need it tonight. Thank God you think of everything. Are you the simply the best fishing guide around here, or are they all as good as you?"

"I wouldn't want to seem prejudiced, but I might be." As the others chuckled, Skip admitted, "I grew up in Waycross, and the town and the swamp have always helped each other survive. Hunting, fishing, and farming are the main industries in this area. I guess everybody here grows up learnin' their way around a rod and reel. Of course, we have all the big city amenities these days—even Wal-Mart!" Fred nodded and smiled at Skip;

"Well, I guess that does put Waycross on the map then."

"Listen, Fred," started Tom. He was about to say something about the what he considered to be the destructive business practices of Wal-Mart, as well as Home Depot, Starbucks and all the mega-convenience stores, when something caught his attention. He listened for a moment, then asked, "Hey, did you guys hear something?" Fred shook his head.

"Don't try any of that Snipe hunting prank stuff on me you two—just because I'm not an outdoors man doesn't mean you can fool me."

"I can't hear a damn thing over all the toads and crickets," offered Skip.

"I thought I heard a twig snap over there." All three men squinted to see past the light of the camp fire, but nothing moved within their fields of vision.

"Must've been my imagination. Sorry, guys," Tom apologized, asking immediately, "This place always been this spooky?"

Skip dished up the fish and some fried corn for everyone, a thoughtful look on his face. As they all began to eat, Skip spoke between mouthfuls.

"The Okefenokee was the home of runaway slaves and the

Seminoles for centuries. You can get lost back in the swamp easy without a guide. But you'll have plenty of company—panthers, wild pigs, cotton mouth snakes, black widow spiders, giant, fresh water clams that can take your leg off, and giant snapping turtles, among others."

Fred perked up, "Why would a wild pig be considered dangerous?"

Skip almost choked on a piece of corn, "Cause full-growed they outweigh any of us. Add their sharp teeth and mean temper, you've got a critter you don't want to tangle with."

"You think we're safe camping here so near the swamp?"

"We'll keep the fire goin' all night to scare off any animals, plus I brought my huntin' rifle. You never know when a big buck deer will walk by—"

Skip stopped abruptly and put down his plate, grabbing his rifle. The two city-dwellers froze, turning in the direction of Skip's eyes, mouths hanging open, food clinging to their teeth unchewed. A group of small pine trees at the edge of the firelight moved as something pushed at them, seemingly moving in the direction of the camp. Skip rose quietly, taking the safety off his rifle. A bony hand parted the last of the pines, revealing its owner. The sight made fish and corn fly from the tourists' mouths.

"What the hell is that?" exclaimed Tom.

Fred's mouth moved but no sound came out. Bringing his rifle up to his shoulder, Skip took aim at the approaching figure, asking in a strong voice;

"Who are you and what do you want?"

Slowly but steadily, the man-like thing continued on toward the camp, mindless of the deer rifle aimed at his disease ruptured chest. Flickering flames danced the dim light across the rag-covered body, revealing bones protruding from hanging flesh. A hole where the end of the thing's nose should be made its face resemble a living skull. One eye socket looked sucked-in and empty while the other had no flesh around a single bulbous eye. Scraps of black and white hair sprang up from paper-thin skin stretched across the head. As the seconds ticked by, the men realize the rags draping the approaching figure had once been the uniform of a Confederate soldier.

A loud gunshot rang out making Fred and Tom jump to their feet. Fred managed to vocalize a hoarse sounding scream while Tom grabbed Skip's arm like a frightened child seeking a parent's protection. A rib on the right side of the thing's chest caved-in as the bullet entered and left the thing's chest, but the wound did not halt its approach. Skip fired once more as Tom pawed at him, lost in abject fear, making the guide miss his target.

Fred, frozen in place, still screaming, stopped abruptly as a bony hand closed around his throat. The tourist's face went red, then purple, as skeletal fingers snapped the bones in his neck. With its free hand, the thing grabbed Skip's rifle and jerked it away from its own who had just managed to shake Tom from his back. Feeling the strength of the shambling figure in that motion, Skip yelled;

"Run!"

Tom obeyed immediately, spinning off into the dark tangle of trees and underbrush beyond the firelight's reach. Skip pulled his hunting knife and rammed it into the thing's stomach. The well-maintained blade tore easily through tissue-thin skin, but lodged in the back bone. Skip tried to disengage his weapon as thin, ivory arms wrap around his lower back. As he wrenched his blade back and forth, the shrunken lips of the Confederate soldier bit cleanly through Skip's nose. The glob of bloody flesh was spit out, then the snapping teeth returned for a second bite. The guide's cheek split under the teeth even as a cracking sound emanated from his lower back. Blood sluiced down Skip's face as he felt his spine separate and felt his world go mercifully black.

Waycross, Georgia

People were drifting through their day in the usual manner when the phone rang in the small front office of the downtown Waycross jailhouse. The officer who answered it listened with customary politeness, then asked in a tense voice;

"You saw a what last night?" Deputy Dan Worthington could not believe his ears.

"Mr. Field, you said you saw a Confederate soldier outside your barn last night?" Another pause. Then, "Listen Mr. Field, we've got three people missing in the Okefenokee—we don't have time for pranksters right now." Dan hung up.

"Mr. Field saw a what?"

The questioner was Sheriff Donna Fargo. Massaging the back of her neck under her shoulder length auburn hair, she felt the tension she had been trying so hard to work out returning as her deputy replied in an exasperated voice;

"He says he saw a man dressed as a Confederate soldier out by his barn last night. Saw the guy from his bedroom window."

"What a day. Is everyone going nuts in this town?" The sheriff knew better, but said the words anyway. After what had happened in the swamp near Field's only a month previous—the murderous

Skunk Ape, the witch controlling it—Donna Fargo just wanted things to settle back into their normal, boring routine. After all, that was the point of being the sheriff of a small town. If she had wanted excitement, she could have joined the Atlanta Police Department.

Rookie Deputy Carlos Reaguez hung up his telephone and said, "We've got Mr. Perelli and Jessie Montgomery bringing their hunting dogs to the westside logging entrance of the park in an hour."

"Good, let's get ready to go, guys. If you want to bring your own hunting rifles feel free. Hopefully, our tourists just got lost, but if it's an animal attack we'll need to be ready to track whatever it is and kill it."

Dan shook his head, "I can't imagine Skip getting lost in the Okefenokee. The man grew up in that swamp—calls his ma from it every day just to keep her from worrying. I'll tell it, when she called to say Skip hadn't called in this morning, that's enough to get me worrying."

Carlos chimed in, "Maybe he lost his cell phone or the battery went dead. Cell phone batteries do wear out ya know."

"Good point," Donna grabbed thigh high waders out of the closet, adding, "I hope that's all it is.

Okefenokee National Wildlife Refuge

An official Park Services vehicle was parked at the logging entrance along with two pick-up trucks with dog cages in the bed. As Donna pulled the department Chevrolet Tahoe SUV onto the side of the road, the National Park Ranger got out of his truck and walked across the road to join the new arrival. He wore his dark brown hair in a crew cut under his government issued baseball cap with the National Park Ranger logo on the front. The sheriff had never seen him before, but he looked ex-military and all business which she appreciated. Donna got out with her two deputies, grabbing her waders from the middle of the front seat.

"Hi, I'm Paul Vanaport, new westside Ranger. You must be Sheriff Fargo." Paul offered a tanned hand. Donna gave him a firm handshake, saying;

"Nice to meet you, Mr. Vanaport. Usually the new Park Rangers stop by the office and introduce themselves when they start. Why haven't we seen you yet?"

"I...I," Paul stammered, caught off guard. "I just started this week, Sheriff. My first day off's Monday and I was planning on stopping by then to say 'hello.'"

Donna watched Vanaport's eyes carefully as he spoke—a habit she had cultivated over the years. Vanaport seemed to be telling the truth, "It definitely helps to know who's on your team, especially when something like this comes up. It wouldn't look too good for you to have three people lose their lives in your area of the park during your first week, would it?"

"You're right there, Sheriff," bright white teeth appeared as Vanaport smiled. "That doesn't sound much like a career booster."

Donna introduced her deputies to the ranger, then suggested they get started before they lost their daylight. Dogs bayed impatiently as Donna put on her waders, then checked the clip in her 9mm Beretta pistol.

"You doing all right, Mr. Perelli?"

"Sure am, Miss Donna." The fifty-five year old man pulled shyly at his denim overalls, nearly blushing as he reported, "The soybean crop is doing just fine this summer and Miss Lilly's egg house has been real productive as well." Mr. Perelli was a traditional southern gentleman, referring to all women as "Miss So and So" including his wife of thirty-six years.

"How about you, Mr. Montgomery? You doin' all right," Donna asked an elderly black man as he let down the tail gate of his ancient Ford pickup truck.

"Can't complain none, Miss Donna—even though I'm real good at it." Jessie Montgomery grinned and chuckled at his own joke. "Glad I can help out my ol' neighbor."

Mr. Montgomery had owned the farm next to the Fargo's spread for at least as long as her family had owned their farm. Donna had spent half her days at the Montgomery's during her childhood, playing with their daughter Theresa. Theresa had joined the military after the September 11th, 2001 terrorist attack. The two friends had not seen each other much since.

"I got an email from Theresa the other day," Donna told the elder, "said she was shipping out to Iraq next week. I'll keep her in my prayers, Mr. Montgomery."

"Thank you Miss Donna, I know she'll appreciate that. Theresa is a good girl and a good soldier. Lord willin' she'll make me even prouder than I already is."

"Could that be possible, Mr. Montgomery?" Donna teased the old man, but he answered her as if he had not noticed, smiling as he said;

"Maybe not, Miss Donna."

The dogs were out of the trucks by then and Worthington brought them a shirt worn by Skip just two days previous. Once the hounds had the scent, Mr. Perelli and Mr. Montgomery started them down the dirt logging road. Fargo, her deputies and Vanaport followed behind. Sweat was already beginning to make the sheriff's uniform stick to her—it was going to be a long day tromping around the swamp.

It'll be worth it if we find those boys.

Fargo pursed her lips at the thought, a grim whisper in her mind telling her they were already too late.

Heat blanketed the swamp. Even the shaded areas seemed oppressively hot on the windless afternoon. A six foot long alligator hung from a tree branch on the shore of the swamp as a tall man split the stomach open with a large hunting knife. Red cotton pants and suede leather boots were all the black-maned man wore with the exception of a small black vest that looked about two times too small for his deep and powerful chest. No hair covered the muscular red skinned upper body.

Suddenly, the big man heard something crashing through the forest. As he stood beside his scaly catch, a stranger erupted into view, gasping for breath. The man stopped short at the sight of the alligator's dead body ejecting its intestines from its slit belly, slipping in the mud and screamed hoarsely.

"Who are you," asked the big man with a menacing voice.

"T-T-Tom..."

"You are trespassing, Tom—on Seminole land."

Tom's eyes rolled wildly as he scanned the trees and bushes behind him, "S-Seminole...", he managed to croak out through his dry throat. "Thing...out there. Help me."

"Why should I help a white man?"

Abject fear made Tom shake like one with Parkinson's disease. "He just kept coming at us...Skip shot him...didn't stop him."

"Skip? The guide?"

"Yes...he had a rifle...", Tom coughed dryly.

The big Seminole reached into a small backpack nearby and retrieved a canteen. "Drink this, Tom, then I'll take you back to the nearest highway."

Donna had to fight back the urge to vomit as she stood over the bodies. Two murders. Two. In her town! Just a month earlier a string of weird slayings had turned out to be connected to the supernatural. In horror she heard herself hoping the deaths at her feet were not linked to supernatural forces.

God, I'm sick, she thought. I'm praying for normal murders when I should be praying for no murders at all.

Whatever had killed the men at her feet, they were not accidental deaths. The purple faces showed strangulation and suffocation. A nearby campfire was nothing more than gray ashes. The four-man tent nearby stood quietly, its front flap trembling on the breeze. Mr. Montgomery confirmed that the small clearing was one used often by Skip on his hunting and fishing tours.

While her deputies sectioned off the crime scene with their standard yellow tape, the sheriff used her cell phone to call the County Coroner. She turned away from the corpses as she spoke.

"Dr. Ossaka, we've got some work for you in Okefenokee National. Two victims, one with a broken neck and one with a broken back."

The pair talked a moment longer, then Donna said she would send Reaguez to meet the coroner at the entrance to the logging road. She also informed him that she would be bringing in the Georgia Bureau of Investigation to provide them with a crime scene investigator. As she finished, Mr. Montgomery walked over to Donna, letting her know that the dogs had picked up something leading away from the camp. When he asked;

"Do you want us to follow it?" Donna turned to her deputies, ordering;

"Carlos, head back to the highway and bring Dr. Ossaka back here, please. Dan, I'm going to ask you to stay here—guard the bodies from animals or any intruders. I'm going to keep searching for the third man with Mr. Perelli, Mr. Montgomery and the dogs." As the two men nodded in sober agreement, she added;

"Both of you keep in mind that whoever our third man is, he may be our killer, and if he isn't, then we've got someone else running around these woods. So stay sharp, and keep your weapons ready."

"Okay, Sheriff, will do," replied Dan.

"No problem, Sheriff," said Carlos. "And I'll be back in no time with the Coroner." Donna nodded to her men, then turned her attention to the hunters.

"I've got to call the GBI," she told them. "Get those hounds pacing. I'm right behind you. And, let's keep a good grip on your hunting rifles—just in case we run into trouble."

Both men released their dogs. Donna dialed the number for the GBI and, once she got the proper office, outlined her situation. They agreed to send out a Lieutenant Murphy whom they promised would be at the sheriff's office at 8AM the next morning. Donna thanked them, then cut the call abruptly as somewhere up ahead the dogs suddenly went wild.

As the sheriff and the hunters moved through the swamp, Donna held her pistol in front of her. Mr. Perelli and Mr. Montgomery kept their rifles to their shoulders. From the distance, two voices shouted from the trees.

"Call off the dogs!" The hunters recalled their animals who obeyed immediately while Donna shouted;

"Come toward us with your hands above your heads. We are armed and will fire if attacked!"

Two men came walking out of the shadows through the trees and thick brush. While still at a distance, the taller of them called out;

"It's Longwalker, Sheriff Fargo. I found this guy wandering around the woods. He's in shock and pretty much scared to death."

Donna was relieved to see Longwalker, the local Seminole Shaman, and a disheveled man that certainly did not appear dangerous. Longwalker was not the most pleasant person the sheriff had ever met, but at least he was a known quantity. As the pair approached, she left the tourist to Mr. Montgomery and Mr. Perelli as she asked Longwalker;

"What happened?"

The Seminole Shaman spoke in concise sentences as if the English language was distasteful. Donna was familiar with Longwalker's views on white people and the fact that after three Seminole Indian Wars, the tribe had never surrendered to the United States. Swamps like the Okefenokee and the Florida Everglades became the Seminole Nation's last refuge. Longwalker was a fanatic and a hothead, but he had yet to cause her any trouble. After the shaman had told the sheriff what little he knew, she turned to Tom.

"What happened to your friend and Skip?"

Tom's eyes looked haunted. His head continually moving, eyes scanning, he said in a shattered whisper;

"He just kept coming… wouldn't stop. Skip shot him right in the chest, but he kept coming at us. Grabbed Fred… choked him 'til he broke his neck. I heard it." The man drifted off for a moment, as if remembering, or trying to forget. Then, without warning, he started shouting.

"It was, it was, it was so sick—I'll never forget it. When he dropped Fred, and he grabbed Skip, grabbed him around the waist and bit him. And squeezed. Squeezed the life right out of him. I ran then—I had to. I had to! I couldn't stay—not there. Not with that thing. I couldn't!"

Ignoring the obvious, Donna asked, "Who killed them? One man? Was he a big man, like a football player?"

"No, he was skinny… starved looking… he only had one eye… but he was so strong… and he killed them!" Tom began sobbing uncontrollably. No one made to stop him. Then, without warning he went quiet. Turning to the sheriff, his voice taking on a tone which told her he was falling deeper into shock, he said;

"He was dressed funny…holes in his clothes…old…"

"What kind of clothes?"

"Old, military. Like, like a…a…Confederate soldier."

Lieutenant Murphy of the GBI was a short man with absolutely no body fat. Donna was sure the little man could wear boy's sizes. She watched as his dark eyes scanned the crime scene for clues, standing quietly out of the way while he did his job. Camera flashes made her blink as he photographed everything.

The intense man rose to his feet, his hands holding several plastic bags containing possible evidence of the crime. A deep frown line split his forehead as he spoke.

"Sheriff, I've found two different blood samples, probably from our victims, on some leaves and pine needles. I found a bone fragment, but it's not fresh—more than likely an old pig bone that came back up to the surface of the ground after the last rain. I'll verify that back at our lab. The tent poles, plates, utensils, and rifle all had numerous fingerprints—it'll take about twenty-four hours to check them against our files. I also found a piece of cloth near the bone fragment that doesn't match anything from the camp or the clothing of any of the victims."

Donna replied, "Thank you, for coming out here so quickly. My town just got through a bizarre string of murders. I can't believe less than a month later we've got two more. It just doesn't seem possible."

"Did you catch the killer of the first crime spree yet?"

"Yes, we even got a confession from her. She's locked away in Blachard Mental in a straight jacket," Donna swatted at a mosquito as she spoke.

The GBI man mopped his sweat-covered brow with a handkerchief, "Maybe this is an accomplice to the earlier murders, or a copycat killer." He paused thinking deeply, "At any rate, I'll get these back to our lab and analyze them for you. I'll email you a report on each sample collected from the crime scene. The coroner will also be copied."

"Thanks again Lieutenant." Donna and the GBI man began the long walk back to the Tahoe. She had already sent Dan home to get some sleep. Carlos was stubbornly napping at the office in between phone calls. The Sheriff's mind was not on sleep, however. It was, instead, concentrating on the question of what was loose in Waycross now.

She would not be comforted when, several hours later she would receive a call from the coroner, Dr. Ossaka. First he confirmed her guesses. Fred Dunkirk, he agreed, had died from extreme trauma to his neck which resulted in partial strangulation as well as a broken neck. Stanley "Skip" Carlson spinal column had been severed. The killer had also partially bitten off Skip's nose, as well as his cheek. The teeth marks reveal the killer has broken front teeth, which Ossaka was certain he could match.

Pleased with the report, the sheriff asked if the coroner had found anything else. The man hesitated, then said, "Yes—there was one other thing...odd, really. Both victims had substantial traces of decaying skin on them."

"You mean like from a corpse?"

"Yes. At least one hundred years worth."

Wind whipped through the barn, making the old structure creak and groan. The five horses within sensed the coming storm would be a bad one and began stamping their hooves and snorting, trying to gain the attention of Brian McCrarey, their owner.

"It's all right ladies, I'll close the barn doors so you can get a good night's sleep." McCrarey moved with a severe limp in his left leg, the result of a childhood horseback riding accident. He pulled the barn doors closed at one end of the barn and then made his slow way to the other end, speaking to the horses as he moved between them.

"You don't think the McCrarey Plantation would let any harm come to its finest mares now do ya'll?"

As the horse trainer pulled at the last barn door, it suddenly stopped as if jammed. The plantation patriarch pulled harder at the door, grunting with the effort. It made no difference. McCrarey mumbled to himself as he peered around the edge of the barn door;

"What are you stuck on?"

A single bulging eye stared back at him from the face of a corpse.

McCrarey cried out as he back peddled away, his bad leg threatening to send him off balance. The door released, the thing threw it open and stalked inside. Knowing the advancing shambler meant him harm, McCrarey craned his head searching for a weapon. Spying his pitchfork atop a bale of hay, he hobbled as quickly as he could toward it. Barely able to stay in front of the grasping hands of the animated corpse, he screamed;

"What are you? What do you want with me?"

One of the thing's hands caught McCrarey's shirt, tearing the back out, leaving bloody scratches running down his skin. Pain searing from the wound, McCrarey cursed his game leg as he finally grabbed hold of the pitchfork. Spinning around on his good right leg, the horseman thrust his weapon into the grasping thing with all his strength, managing to knock the skeletal figure backward to the ground. The lunge threw McCrarey off balance, however, sending him falling across the thing's legs.

Scrambling to regain his feet, McCrarey moved in the wrong direction, suddenly finding bony legs locked around his head and neck. As the horseman screamed, yellowed bones wrenched the pitchfork from its chest. Then, again and again, long dead fingers sent the fork through McCrarey's body. Blood splattered hay, wooden beams, and the horse stalls, the smell of it sending the nearby mares into a frenzy.

Kicking McCrarey's body away from its legs, the murderous thing regained its feet. The horses neighed wildly, kicking and stamping in their stalls, wide-eyes transfixed with fear. Oblivious to the mares, the thing shambled past the stalls, the blood of its kill staining every step as it made its way back into the moonlight and the solitude of the woods beyond the field.

Sheriff Fargo looked at the large, dried scarlet pool and the bloody foot prints leading out of the barn. "Sorry to have to call you back again so soon, Mr. Murphy." The small GBI man smiled politely, offering;

"No one plans on murder, Sheriff, except of course, maybe the killer, but I did have the reports from the first two murders to bring you anyways." The GBI man pulled latex gloves onto his hands. "Do you mind if I examine this crime scene before we go over them?"

"No, of course not," Donna shook her head. "Please proceed." As the CSI man went about his trade, the woman clasped her hands in front of her and stood still, thinking;

I can't believe this is happening again—so soon. The voters are going to throw me out of office, they'll think I'm bad luck or something. And who's to say they're not right? First female sheriff in the history of Waycross, not a single murder here in twenty years, now all of a sudden we're keeping pace with Atlanta.

Donna's instinct told her that the murders were not "normal." Dr. Ossaka had hinted as much, but she had tried to deny it—at first.

Maybe I'm just a magnet for these things. Maybe I should accept that job offer from those two professors...Duke University does have a beautiful campus after all...

Impulsively Donna asked Lt. Murphy if he had heard of Dr. Blakely and Dr. Boles of Duke University. Without ceasing his movements, the officer answered, "I believe I've heard of a Dr. William Boles. Parapsychologist, isn't he?"

"Yes."

"Registered with the GBI as a crime scene psychic. Yeah, I've heard of him—heard he's good." Still studying the ground before him, the CSI man added, I remember; he helped us solve the Williams murders over in Atlanta... so who's this Blakely?"

"Dr. Hugh Blakely... crypto-zoologist; he studies the world's hidden and unknown animal species. It's an obscure branch of zoology. Duke recently received a whopping endowment from the Kirowan Estate, but with the condition those two had to team up and help each other with investigations. They don't seem to like the arrangement, but they do make a good team."

Murphy turned from his work and raised an eyebrow at Donna. "You seem to know more about them than I do; so why'd you ask me about them?"

"Guess I wanted a second opinion. They helped me solve the last string of murders. Afterwards they asked me to join their team. I've been thinking it over, but my Mama lives here in Waycross. Since my Pa died, it's been just the two of us. I don't know if she could handle being alone."

The lieutenant used the moment to free his cigarettes from his shirt pocket. Shaking one free, he asked, "Why couldn't you take your mother with you to North Carolina? I'm sure she'd be very proud of her daughter, working at such a well respected university as Duke."

Donna nodded, "You may have a point, Lieutenant. Duke is known as the Harvard of the South. I just hope I can handle hunting monsters and ghosts for a living."

"Speaking of which," Murphy said slowly as he lit his cigarette, "when I tell you what I've found at the site of the first two murders, and this one, you just may want to call your two academic friends again."

Donna looked hard at the blood stains in the hay, "I was afraid you might think that…"

Duke University, Durham, North Carolina

The beautiful stonework of the chapel bell tower stood far above the serene gothic architecture of Duke campus. Students and professors moved about between dorms and the academic halls under clear blue skies. In front of one building, a knot of students surrounded their professor, throwing questions at him like a gaggle of reporters.

"Professor Blakely, are you going to need assistants for your next expedition?"

"I always need assistants for my expeditions, but I have to get clearance from the university's administration before I can begin accepting volunteers."

"Where are you going next?"

"Sometimes field research opportunities come up on their own. At other times, it seems, the Kirowan Foundation will be planning expeditions. Unknown animals don't live by a daily planner, if one is seen, sometimes I scramble to a sighting location very quickly, before the trail grows cold. In those instances, we don't have time to ask for volunteers and go through the approval process." Blakely wiped at the sweat on his forehead, then continued.

"For instance, I've been trying to put together an expedition to what they used to call 'the Congo.' The natives believe a type of dinosaur still exists there which they call Mkele Mbembe. Just for things like that I've already asked the university for a full-time assistant, someone who could accompany Dr. Boles and I into the field on a moments notice."

I wish Donna had taken our offer, he thought. Aloud, however, he merely said;

"We haven't made a final decision yet on any candidates for that position. I'm sure we'll take a look at some more soon, though."

Another student asked, "What qualifications are you looking for?" Blakely paused for a moment, then answered;

"High grade point averages in Biology, Zoology, and Psychology for starters. Physically fit, long distance runners, some rock climbing experience wouldn't hurt, either. Good knot tying skills, familiarity with weapons, computer skills, especially relating to Internet Research…"

As Blakely continued, a rotund, balding man in a three piece suit walked up to the tightly knit group. "Excuse me students, I need a word with your professor."

The professor added, "Okay kids, see you in class Thursday. I'll be in my office for student conferences Wednesday afternoon, if, that is, you've made an appointment. Thanks for your enthusiasm." As the students drifted off, the newcomer spoke in an excited whisper.

"Sheriff Donna Fargo placed a call to you and Dr. Boles." Blakely smiled broadly at his boss.

"Ah good, Chancellor, she's reconsidered the job offer!"

"Much better," answered Chancellor Gordon S. Pimms with ill-suppressed glee. "I'm afraid that's not why she called you—she needs your help again. There seems to be a new string of murders occurring in Waycross and the Okefenokee Swamp."

Blakely's positive attitude changed to one of worry. "I'd better go get Dr. Boles…we've, *ah*, got a long drive ahead of us."

Pimms watched the professor walk off quickly, thinking, yes, my boy, I thought that might be your reaction.

Okefenokee National Wildlife Refuge, Georgia

Almost silently the dugout skimmed the surface of the dark swamp water. The heavy air swarmed with mosquitoes and flies. It was a warm day, and both were biting. Longwalker moved his single paddle from side to side, cutting silently through the water. The shaman was accustomed to life in the swamp, which meant he did not relax his guard even for a moment—ever.

It had been six months since Longwalker had been to this side of the swamp. The "guardian" of this area had become his friend, had given the Seminole something he desired more than life itself—hope for revenge. Hatred of the white man burned in both of them. Revenge for the humiliations heaped upon them by the United States of America provided them both with purpose.

Longwalker directed his dugout into the heavily overgrown cove. Pushing branches aside to make room for his passage, the shaman disappeared into the dense undergrowth. When the craft could go no further, Longwalker secured it, then stepped into the shallow water and walked to shore. Coming to a patchwork shack hidden from sight by a gigantic and warped cypress tree, he stood outside the door and called;

"I thought we were allies. Why did you attack them now? I am not yet ready to begin my part in our plan." A stirring was heard from within the hut, followed by a woman's voice.

"I simply released an old curse upon the white man. It is a small test of our powerful magic. Let us discover if blue eyes can see a way to stop it." Longwalker sighed in frustration.

"You've brought them swarming into the swamp. I had to slide into my Tonto-skin to keep them from stumbling over my own preparations for the coming conflict."

"And what would they know if they found them? If they found me, even—how would they know it was I who unleashed the horror? The white man knows nothing. Believes nothing. Their only religion is the worship of money, a faith whose god is the most fickle whore of all." The old woman cackled, slapping herself on the arms and chest with a frenzied glee for several seconds. Finally calming once more, she added;

"They do not understand my religion or my powers. We will be safe."

"You are able to fight while hiding in the swamp, but soon I must go forth into the white man's world to begin my battle."

"And famous shall you be for so doing—I have seen this in my visions. Now calm yourself," the woman commanded. "Go back to your people, and prepare to meet your great destiny."

Longwalker made his way back to his dugout. His war with the white man would become his only focus now. Soon his people's enemies would pay.

Waycross, Georgia

Dusk turned the Georgian sky above the Waycross Sheriff's Department building a spectacular reddish-orange. Despite the latitude, the night already held a hint of the coming Fall. A lean, wiry man shook Donna Fargo's hand briefly, saying, "Good to see you again, Sheriff. After I spoke to you during our trip down from Durham, I did some research on the Internet. I made several interesting discoveries, and may have the beginnings of a theory about your murders."

A muscular man got out of the driver's side of the Ford Explorer and walked over to Donna interrupting the other man in mid-sentence. Embracing her in a strong bear hug, Dr. Hugh Blakely whispered, "He's been babbling like this for hours."

"Really, Doctor, and I use the title only because you keep insisting the diplomas hanging in your office are legitimate—I've been attempting to carry on an academic discussion with you throughout our journey… perhaps my predilection for words of more than one syllable has left you stupefied to where—"

Donna interrupted Dr. Boles, asking diplomatically, "How about some fresh coffee to get rid of the cobwebs of the road?"

"Lead on," said Blakely.

"Warmed insides solve all disputes," sniped Boles. "You'll make a excellent haus frau some day, Ms. Fargo."

He's as charming as ever, thought the sheriff. Grinning through her irritation, however, Donna simply shepherded the two academics inside, announcing;

"Hey, gather round, troops. Let me introduce everyone. Dr. Hugh Blakely, world's leading cryptozoologist and Dr. William Boles, world's leading parapsychologist, both of Duke University. These two gentlemen were instrumental in helping me stop the last murderer we had in these parts."

Donna then introduced the two professors to her deputies, Reaguez and Worthington, Dr. Ossaka, Lt. Murphy. After that, she pointed them to the coffee. The coroner gave his report on what he had found first. Murphy followed, briefing everyone on the scientific evidence gathered so far. The professors took it all in, Blakely sitting with one arm draped over the desk next to him holding his coffee. Boles sat to his right, taking notes the entire time without looking up. When both men had finished, Blakely said;

"Humph—sounds like the killer has a serious skin disease or something." The bigger man turned to his partner, asking, "Make any sense to you?"

Rubbing his salt and pepper goatee, Boles did not respond at first. Then, after a moment, he said, "Three thoughts; possibly someone with a longevity serum needs human blood and brain fluid to create more, it's some simple, free-ranging beastman, or, and this seems most likely, it's a reaminated corpse."

"I think I follow you on the first two, but the last one—a reanimated corpse—are you saying we have a Frankenstein running around Waycross?" The parapsychologist looked into Donna's green eyes.

"In layman's terms, I meant to imply it may be a zombie."

Blinking rapidly as her mind raced, Donna asked, "And that's the theory you believe is correct?"

"Yes, the two people in town who sighted a confederate soldier live near the Okefenokee—yes? Swamps and bogs have a tendency to preserve bodies far longer than regular burial… something to do with moisture combining with the mud…" A phone's blaring ring interrupted Boles' explanation. As Worthington answered it, Donna asked;

"But why would it come back to life?" Boles shook his head, answering;

"Zombies don't come back to life—someone has to call them back."

"Why would somebody call back the body of a Confederate soldier?"

"Maybe," Blakely offered with a smile, "to kill all the damn Yankees that decided to stay in Georgia?"

"Excuse me Sheriff," Worthington broke in, "but Louise Cunningham says she saw a man dressed in rags crossing highway 10, heading towards the old Barton Plantation."

The words electrified the room. In a terrible moment of slow motion, the sheriff watched as all heads in the room turned in her direction. Within her brain, scores of ideas screeched at one another, all demanding attention.

Damn, she thought, fear and frustration throttling her, freezing her in panic. Damnit, damnit, damnit! Not again—not a goddamned monster—not again! I do not need this—I do not deserve this…I…I…

Iron control racing past her frenzy, Donna found the will to shove aside the terror gripping her. The flood of images of what had happened to her and her men the last time something had come crawling into her town from the swamps beyond were shoved aside, cancelled, banished as she took charge, commanding;

"All right, by the book, gentlemen. Everybody grab a radio in case you get separated. Dr. Ossaka, would you like to be issued a sidearm?"

"Yes, please," the coroner nodded, his usual calm unraveling slightly. As a spare pistol was found for the doctor, Blakely interjected;

"Do you have some fire axes we could take along, Sheriff?"

"Good thinking, we'll stop by the fire department on the way. Dr. Ossaka you're with Deputy Worthington in his truck. Lt. Murphy, accompany Deputy Reaguez and myself, please," Donna commanded. As everyone began to move, Boles spoke up absently;

"Might I suggest we all carry salt?"

Donna frowned, "Salt?

"Zombies hate it—trust me."

"Okay, we stop by the grocery store, too—now, if no one thinks we need to rewatch 'Night of the Living Dead' for pointers, let's move!"

Barton Plantation

The moon had not yet risen. Utter darkness swallowed the Barton spread as an unusual silence pervaded the gently rolling hills leading to the old plantation house. No crickets chirped; no toads croaked; no animals called out to the night. Indeed, the only noise on the air was that made by the shambling footfalls of a solitary figure moving between the giant magnolias lining the long driveway that connected Highway 10 to the historically registered Barton mansion.

Within, Robert Barton III sat in his favorite chair, in his favorite of the house's many rooms, the trophy room. One wall displayed a massive glass case filled with athletic trophies, testament to the Barton family habit of producing great athletes. The remaining three walls were covered with British hunting green wall paper and paintings of various sporting events. As Barton sat watching the evening news broadcast one of the servants knocked on the door, opened it, and asked;

"Can I get you anything, sir?"

"Yes, a glass of bourbon, please, Margaret."

Before the woman could respond the window behind Barton exploded, fragments of glass and wood scattering inward. Margaret screamed as something climbed in through the devastation. Barton rose to his feet quickly, turning to see an intruder both deformed and decaying. The plantation owner gasped as the approaching thing's single eye swivelled in its socket, staring at him unblinking. As Barton motioned his servant toward him, bony hands grabbed the winged-tip chair they stood behind and hurled it aside.

"Run, Margaret!"

Hoping to give the woman some time, Barton sucked down a great lungful of wind, then threw a balled fist as hard as he could at the thing's head. His fingers flattened and cracked as if they had hit a bowling ball. Agony shot through Barton's hand and arm, more as the horror reacted by wrenching his arm out of the socket. More pressure brought the plantation owner screaming to his knees. The bones in his right arm snapped as the silent thing viciously twisted it with tremendous force. Barton's shirt sleeve ripped, then his flesh—muscles, cartilage and bones separating at the shoulder, pain and blood spraying across the room.

As Barton slumped to the floor in shock, the thing threw the man's arm aside, reaching for his neck. Margaret screamed for help while picking up a heavy marble ash tray to throw at the attacker. Movement at the window caught her eye. The servant spotted a form outside, racing toward the house. It was another woman, dressed in a uniform, one who threw herself in through the broken window aiming a gun with two hands!

"Freeze!"

Margaret continued to scream as Donna drew a bead on the dead-smelling thing leaning over Robert Barton. The plantation owner's face turning purple, Donna stepped closer, ordering, "Release him, now! I will shoot—you have 'til the count of three—one..."

A cracking sound emanating from Barton's neck forced Donna to fire. Bone fragments and tufts of hair exploded as the 9mm bullet slammed into its target. The assailant stood up, unperturbed, then turned and swivelled its single eye towards Donna. Seemingly no longer interested in Barton, the dead man took a step toward her. Behind Donna, Doctors Blakely and Boles stepped through the empty window frame. Donna backed up, asking;

"Is this your goddamned zombie, Boles? Is it?! I shot the son of a bitch in the head—in the head!" Far less excited, the thin man craned his neck forward to get a better look at the approaching thing, saying;

"Yes, I do think this is the genuine article."

Her hands shaking slightly, teeth beginning to chatter, Donna reached inside herself and slapped away her fear. She had come close to a breakdown the last time, but had pulled through mainly by telling herself it could never happen again.

Well, here you are, girl. Again. Goddamned monsters—again!

Before she could fire, however, she heard Blakely ask his partner, "Okay, so you were right—now what?"

The wiry little man moved around the shambler to pick up a bone fragment it had left behind. "I've got an idea. Let the thing leave. I'm thinking it might be quite advantageous if we follow it."

The zombie moved away from them then, headed towards the opening it had smashed through earlier. Across the room, the sheriff knelt over Robert Barton. His neck was twisted and swollen, his tongue hanging limply from his mouth while his empty shoulder socket continued to leak blood.

No pulse, thought Donna. Another murder in my town. Worse, another monster murder in my town. Shit—why me? Aloud, she said merely;

"Barton's dead."

The zombie had already exited the room. Blakely, ax in hand, kept an eye on it. While he did so, Boles cupped the bone fragment he had recovered in both hands and closed his eyes. The sheriff holstered her pistol, turning to her radio.

"Worthington and Reaguez, assailant is leaving the mansion—do not intercept. We are following subject and will maintain contact. Send Ossaka and Murphy inside for crime scene work and victim recovery." Glancing over at Margaret, Donna added, "A woman at the crime scene needs treatment for shock. Secure the area."

"Roger that," said Worthington.

Margaret sank to her knees and slumped onto the carpet, losing consciousness. As Donna crossed the room to attend to her, Blakely followed the thing out into the darkness. In a moment, the sheriff had made the woman comfortable. As she rose, Ossaka and Murphy entered through the broken window. The lieutenant pointed at Boles asking;

"What's with him?" Donna stopped for a moment and stared at the professor. After a second, she realized what he was doing, remembered seeing him do it previously. Just as she made to answer, however, Boles' eyes came open sharply. The thin man gasped, shaking as if an electric charge was running through his body. Catching the parapsychologist as he fell, Donna asked frantically;

"What's wrong?"

Air hissing between clenched teeth, Boles' eyes rolled back in his head. Then, his breath returning slowly, he gasped again, wincing as if in pain.

"I know who he is..."

"Who?"

"The zombie," Boles scrambled to his feet, seemingly fully recovered from his momentary ordeal. "We must catch up with Blakely. That thing is returning to the one who resurrected it for new orders."

Donna and the professor moved outside. Eyes adjusting to the darkness, the sheriff spotted the bulky shadow of Blakely just moving beyond the plantation's edge. The pair ran to catch up to him. Ahead, moving stiffly, the zombie continued onward, in no way acknowledging their existence. The three were able to keep pace with it easily as it moved across Highway 10, back toward the western edge of the Okefenokee swamp. Boles spoke excitedly;

"The skull fragment brought me a vision—a confederate soldier being chased by a platoon of Yankees. Sherman had already burned Atlanta, was marching on Savannah, when private Benjamin Evans deserted his company with five others. They ran South, ended up in Waycross."

Boles found himself gasping, his vision having drained him more thoroughly than he had first thought. Trying to both catch his breath and not fall behind, he continued speaking in short bites.

"It was just a tiny farming community then, much smaller than today. The confederate soldiers, didn't realized they were being hunted, not until the Yankees caught up to them. It ended in the swamp... terrible—an ungodly slaughter."

Blakely stopped the party because the zombie had stopped, its boot tops covered in murky water.

"What now, Boles?" asked Blakely.

"Ironic, isn't it?"

Startled by the new voice, the trio looked around, but could not find anyone. "Show yourself," Donna commanded.

"Certainly." An elderly black woman with short-cropped white hair came from behind a tree. Hunched over by age, she wore filthy overalls and a wool shirt. Her bare feet, like her hands and face, were wrinkled and cracked.

"Who are you?" asked the sheriff.

"I'm nobody. Don't exist in your world, white woman. My mother gave birth to me here in this swamp. Forgotten by the town that spurned her."

Boles noted that Blakely was keeping a firm grip on his ax with both hands. Keeping his eyes on the bedraggled woman, he asked, "You're the one who called this poor soul back from the dead—correct?"

"Yes." A crooked smile revealed both rotting and missing teeth. "And I say again, it's ironic, wouldn't you agree? Dead Confederate thing, serving me, a black woman. Someone his kind considered sub-human. But I know secrets greater than any white man's ever known. Power to bring the white race to its knees—to make slaves of the masters."

Keeping his eye on the still immobile zombie, Blakely broke his silence, asking;

"You been living under a rock, lady? Seems you missed a few things—Lincoln, the Emancipation Proclamation, the Civil Rights Act, Martin Luther King, Jr. Any of this ringing a bell?"

The bent and twisted woman directed hate-filled eyes at Blakely. While the sheriff quietly pulled her 9mm free, the gnarled figure hissed;

"What do you know about slavery, white boy? About racism? Your kind killed the Indians, stole their land. Brought blacks here by the millions to slave in your fields and make you rich. Hateful, disgusting white devil bastards—you owe us, and I will make you and yours pay for what you've done! My zombie has killed the descendants of slave owners, and he will kill all their descendants—justice will be done!"

"Oh, my God," laughed Blakely. "The zombie queen wants reparations." While the professor chuckled, the sheriff said quietly;

"Ma'am, I do believe this is over now. Justice is not served by vigilantes—black or white. Not anymore. At least, not in my town. So drop the white devil spiel, because from where I stand, the only racist here is you!"

Enraged, the swamp priestess lifted her arms. Moving them in a near-hypnotic pattern, she shouted, "Benjamin Evans, I command you—kill them all!"

Ragged bones swung into action as the zombie abruptly turned on Blakely. The sudden speed of the undead soldier surprised the muscular man, catching him in the shoulder and knocking him off his feet. Taking advantage of the moment, the zombie leaped at the fallen professor. Donna searched for a clear shot but could not find one in the darkness. Blakely managed to use his ax to fend off the thing's snapping teeth, but its clawing hands were a different matter. Tearing through shirt, then skin, the zombie elicited a bellow of pain from the crypto-zoologist. Reflexively thrashing, a lucky kick sent the zombie sprawling at Donna's feet.

Instantly leveling her gun at the thing's skull, the sheriff squeezed the trigger repeatedly. Bullet after bullet blasted into the thing's head—driving splinters of yellowed bone into the asphalt of Highway 10. Unfortunately, it was not enough to stop the now headless body of Benjamin Evans from crawling forward towards Donna.

"Boles, for Christ's sake, how do you kill a zombie?"

Back on his feet, Blakely began hacking at the thing, bone fragments flying in every direction. Even dismembered, however, the individual pieces of the long dead deserter continued onward. Bones vibrated on the roadway. Skeletal hands pulled themselves forward, inch after inch. As Blakely did his best to smash the severed hands, Boles said;

"Salt has been known to send zombies back to the grave…that's why I suggested we bring some." Reaching into his jacket pocket, he pulled out a baggy and began sprinkling pinches onto each piece of the zombie.

"You see," he said, preening just a bit. "They're not moving. The salt is breaking the bond between them and their master."

"Very good, white boy." A peel of laughter rang out from the small black woman, "But, if you're thinking you've got a chance, then you'd better have a whole heap more salt!"

Nearby, the swamp began to boil. Violent rings spread into boiling waves across the dark water of the swamp. As the voodoo priestess chanted in a long-forgotten African tongue, scores of forms began to break the muddy surface. As the sheriff and the professors began to back up, glances to the left and right let them see there was no where to run. Up and down both sides of Highway 10, skeletal hands shoved aside dirt and weeds, dragging their long decaying bodies upward into the starlight.

Grimly, Blakely brought his ax to a ready position, backing up slowly to form a defensive triangle with Donna and Boles. The sheriff pulled two baggies of salt from her pockets, as did Boles. Delighted at her enemy's resistance, the priestess sent her warriors forth one at a time. Broken teeth snapped, clawed hands tore. Blakely continued to knock each one down with his ax, growing more tired with each assault. Handfuls of salt were thrown over each zombie as it fell, until finally, Donna yelled;

"Blakely, we're out of salt!"

"What do you want me to do about it?" The big man, panting hard, swung at the next zombie approaching. He missed it, allowing the thing to get close enough to grab his ax. Laughing hysterically, the old woman screeched;

"And now, white devils, this ends!"

With a gesture the priestess sent all the zombies moving forward. As Blakely struggled with the moldering thing clinging to his ax, all about the trio, hundreds of the dead stumbled forward, arms grasping, teeth grinding. The smell of the grave drawing ever closer, the sheriff slapped a fresh magazine into her gun. She took aim at the closest zombie and then, as a sudden burst of mathematics rushed through her head, she swung her arm in a different direction and fired, her gunfire echoing throughout the swamp, and through the ears of the Civil War dead all about her.

Waycross General Hospital

"Sheriff Fargo, how good of you to come." Boles tried to suppress a rare smile.

"I see you gentlemen haven't talked them into letting you have your pants back yet."

"Nope, just hospital gowns and bandages." Looking around first to see if there was anyone else who might hear them, Blakely asked, "How'd your plan work?"

Donna shut the door, all humor as well as her initial smile leaving her face. "The official verdict, thanks to the planting of a stolen weapon, was self-defense." When her green eyes went sad and dropped to the spotless floor, Boles offered;

"You did the right thing, Sheriff, and if I might add, you were very brave. You saved our lives." Nodding in agreement, Blakely sat up slowly, adjusting his hospital gown carefully as he added;

"You know, we're just a pair of academics. We keep getting mixed up in this stuff, but we don't have the training you do...or your composure in a stressful situation. Have you thought about our offer?"

Before Donna could answer, Boles added;

"Yes, I think you've proven that we need you on our team. Besides, you'd make a much finer partner, all things considered, than Dr. Blakely here, Sheriff."

"Ex-Sheriff." When both men registered shock, the woman told them, "That was part of the deal. Ossaka and Murphy aren't fools, you know. They know a planted gun when they see one. They went along with the self-defense story on one condition...I had to resign. Dan Worthington was sworn in as acting Sheriff today, until a special election can be held."

Blakely sputtered a moment, and was about to make a further comment when Boles pointed at the television mounted on the wall opposite the hospital beds and asked;

"Isn't that the Seminole Shaman you mentioned Ms. Fargo?" asked Boles. "There...on C-Span." As the woman turned, she read the line running along the bottom of the screen.

"'The speaker at Florida State University is Longwalker, a Seminole Indian Shaman'..." Stunned, Donna murmured, "What the hell...?"

As they all watched, Boles adjusted the controls on his bed rail. Instantly the television filled the room with a deep and angry voice.

"The Seminole nation has never surrendered to the government of the United States. Now as the spokesman for my tribe I am demanding the immediate withdrawal of U.S. citizens from Seminole tribal land. Historically speaking that stretches from Waycross, Georgia to Miami, Florida. If the U.S. government does not agree to our demands, the Seminole Nation will declare war again on the U.S. and expel all non-Seminoles from our lands."

Playing to his audience, Longwalker looked hard into the camera lens. "I am also calling on the leaders of the five hundred Native American nations to join me in this war. The Great Spirit has shown us the way to victory. Send your leaders to Waycross, to meet with me, and to be shown the warrior's path. My brothers and sisters, our time has come." Longwalker backed away from the podium at that point, turned, and left the stage.

As Boles shut the television off, Donna commented, "Great—another hate peddler. Just what America needs right now."

"He certifiable, but harmless," said Blakely. "I mean, what can the Seminoles do against the greatest army on the planet?"

"You forget about 9/11 already," asked Donna.

"Nicely put," said Boles with a sly grin. "And a nice attempt at changing the subject, Ms. Fargo, but you never have answered our question."

Donna Fargo shuddered slightly. Her mind raced, a voice from deep within her, whispering;

Skunk apes, witches, zombies—*zombies!*—for Christ's sake. And that was just here in Waycross. And these two yokels want to take you around the world hunting this stuff.

Aloud, however, she said only, "Oh, you mean about coming to work with you two?"

"Yes, really Ms. Fargo," responded Boles, his tone close to desperate, "if I'm to continue to risk my life with…" pointing at Blakely, the professor considered the phrase 'this buffoon,' but opted for discretion as he finished, "this fellow, well, we really need to know."

Her green eyes flashed at the two academics. As the phrase "around the world" repeated in her mind, she headed for the door, responding teasingly, "I'll think about it, boys," knowing her answer already.

And now, the esteemed Mr. Xalieri introduces to us a most novel and scientific method of raising the dead, for both fun and profit...

THE SPaRE

by Laszlo Xalieri

It bubbled in the oversize beaker with a color and odor akin to afternoon urine. It looked septic and vile, though Bud knew for a fact that any lifeforms in it had already done their worst to the concoction and given up, poisoned to death by their own foul metabolic by-products.

Bud poured himself a full glass. He poked with a cautious finger at the thin layer of scummy foam that formed on top of the liquid. He took a sip, reminding himself that it was medicine. He grimaced.

Behind him there was a sudden loud clattering cacophony like someone dropping a tray of clarinets from shoulder-height. Bud didn't even twitch. He was expecting it.

Boy, was he expecting it.

He gulped his medicine. A meaty paw slapped down hard on his shoulder and squeezed, threatening to dent clavicle and scapula and everything between. To Bud's credit, he sloshed nothing and kept gulping.

"Your turn," the paw said. "Don't let us down. Again."

Bud left the glass a third full and stood, rotating his shoulder in the socket to pop the dents out. He faced the owner and supposed controller of the hand that had landed on his shoulder. He decided to say nothing to Matt. Probably wise.

Without looking, Bud pictured Matt in his head. Matt stood nearly seven feet tall and nearly half that wide. He looked more like a parody of a large man than like a normal human being scaled up.

Matt looked like Kodiak bear and mountain gorilla had figured prominently in his recent ancestry. And possibly a pair of stilts.

When Matt was upset with his own bowling performance, he would glom his sixteen-pounder with one palm, completely disregarding his custom-drilled holes, and fling it down the lane. He'd bowled entire games like that with little detriment to his score.

How far away and on which side of your lane Matt stood changed your lane's characteristic tilt. Everyone treated him like his presence also warped space and time.

Bud, on the other hand, was ordinary-sized, brown-haired, brown-eyed, and slightly pudgy. The ordinary icing on the ordinary cake was faded jeans and a checked flannel shirt loose over a tucked-in undershirt. And rented red-and-blue bowling shoes.

He's smarter than me, too, thought Bud. *It's just not fair.*

He wobbled his way around Matt to the ball return and poked the balls around until he found his nondescript thirteen-pounder. Beer sloshed in him a little. He made his little run up to the foul line and released. Not much loft this time, too straight, too little english, and he left the four, nine, and ten pins standing. Bud sighed.

As he waited for his ball to return, he sneaked a glance at the competition. Twelve guys counting a handful of spectators, a complete mixed-bag of races and shapes and sizes, except Bud was sure that if he added all their ages together he'd come up with a number on the wrong side of a thousand. They all wore lame light-blue polo shirts with the legend "Clancyville Stonecutting and Bricklaying" covering up most of their backs in frayed cursive embroidery. With gold sequins.

Bud and Matt and Dan and Dan and Grayson and Daniel had no spectators. The Southside Irregulars had no matching shirts, and especially no sequins, with the possible exception of one of the Dans, who rumor had it had strange tastes in undergarments. So did the other Dan, but he was Mormon, and that was expected.

The Irregulars were getting their asses kicked by six of the wrinklier of the geezers.

Bud shifted leftwards and slung his ball fairly straight at the four-pin. It dutifully swung around and took out the nine and ten.

He heard a grunt and a quiet exclamation in what he swore was Chinese. As he looked around he saw a fiver change hands from the shriveled brown guy to the shriveled Asian guy. Olduvai George had apparently been betting against Bud picking up the spare.

Bud tried to ignore them and rolled his next frame. He left the one-pin standing on his first roll, then grazed it and made it wobble on the next, but left the frame open. He could feel the weight of Matt's displeasure behind him, tilting the entire alley backwards. Bud slunk back to his seat, facing a third of a pint of warming beer. Matt sulked at the scoring table. Dan, Dan, and Daniel bickered goodnaturedly while Grayson polished his ball with his do-rag, which possibly wasn't quite legal. The German geezer in the tight leather pants bowled two strikes, one after another. On his turn, Olduvai George picked up a spare seven-pin with a two-handed between-the-legs granny roll and capered afterwards like a chimpanzee.

Bud drank another two glasses of medicine. Matt drank the better part of Bud's second pitcher mainly to keep Bud from doing so.

The Southside Irregulars' asses remained firmly kicked throughout. Mormon Dan and Daniel drove off back to the hospital where they were interning, Fruity Dan and Grayson got on bikes and headed to an all-night diner. Matt, shaking his head, trudged out the door to go push buses over or scare children or eat puppies or whatever he did to feel better after an evening of abject humiliation by a team of decrepit old bastards that each individually could make Keith Richards look like a rosy-cheeked schoolboy.

Bud negotiated with the bartender until she allowed him another half-pitcher. He took it back to his table and set it next to his basket of hot wings—the condition under which Bud was allowed his final half-pitcher. He found a few weird old geezers sitting at his high-top table. He gave them his best kicked-spaniel look. The Asian poured himself a glass out of Bud's half-pitcher, watching Bud carefully the whole time as if daring him to object. The one he'd been thinking of as Olduvai George plucked a wing from the basket and played with it. They and Bud exchanged stares.

"Well, what?" Bud blurted. The Asian guy elbowed Leather Pants and said something harsh filled with Xs and nasals. George pulled the wing off the table, hiding it in his lap. The German cleared his throat.

"I'd, *erm*, I'd like to talk to you for a few minutes about your work with stem cells and bacterial hybrids. *You* know. Your *extracurricular* work." His English was good, if hesitant. His accent was somewhere between French and German, but not very pronounced. His expression crinkled at the eyes and he shrank back almost imperceptibly, as if expecting Bud to explode.

Bud sat a moment without saying anything, or even moving. "What do you know about that? Who are you people?" The words came out in a single uninflected stream.

"I'm St. Germain. This is Lung, and this is Enoch. We're just... concerned."

"*Lung* means dragon," Bud tendered.

The Asian leered, exposing a mouthful of uneven, if healthy, teeth, and grabbed at an exaggerated bulge in his crotch. The German rolled his eyes.

Bud glared at the Asian, then at the rest of them in turn. "I don't know who you are, but stay away from me. I'm pretty sure you shouldn't be spying on me either, and the school's already arrested two people for prowling around the grad student biology labs. You can read about what I'm doing in there the second I publish. Fuck off."

"We know you're a little, *erm*, stuck...Maybe we can help there, too." The German crumpled a napkin nervously.

"I'm doing fine. I said fuck off."

They all stared at each other over Bud's nearly empty pitcher.

"Really," Bud added. "I mean it. Go away."

The Asian frowned, St. Germain sighed, and George hopped down off of his stool, tossing the wing back on the table. Bud waved them away with a shooing motion, and they turned and left, waiting until they were most of the way to the door before muttering to each other. Bud drained his glass as they disappeared into the night.

He picked up the discarded wing, meaning to drop it in the paper basket he'd been given for the bones. His hand twitched and he dropped it a bit early on the red-checked plastic tablecloth. As he went to pick it up again, he realized that it wasn't his hand that had twitched.

Bud used a table knife to pull the wing toward him across the table.

It had been a complete wing, not pulled apart into sections before frying. Now it was, well, played with. The ulna had been pulled free from the skinny end and was waving a little from side to side. The wing tip had been split at the end, and that split was now opening and closing like the beak of a chick that had hatched too early. In fact, farther up along the wingtip was a shiny black dot, like a tiny beady eye.

Bud used the knife to push the wing back across the table to precisely where George had tossed it.

He gingerly lifted another wing out of the basket. It was folded up, deep fried, sauce-covered, and completely inert. He held it for a moment to make sure, then pulled it apart and ate it.

Matt's chair creaked as he trundled it over to Bud's desk. "Werstheimer's being a real bitch today. Thought you ought to know," he growled.

Bud lay his head down on the stack of closed books next to the open one and shut his eyes.

"What's the bug up her ass today?" Bud kept his eyes closed. "I gave her my progress report. That she makes you double-check."

"Increase in funding got denied. Our place is messy. No one wants to pay for sloppy results."

Bud groaned. "Oh, fuck that. You could lick one of our lab tables and survive for at least a month. We're the only lab in the building that washes the outsides of our test tubes."

"Not the labs, man. Here. Our place."

Bud thought for a moment and pictured their shared office in his head. Piles of hardbacks, composition books, and immorally mating spiral-bound notebooks. Take-out and delivery boxes stacked up in and on top of the trash cans at their desks. Styrofoam and waxed paper cups here and there, and occasional mysterious constellation of sticky spots on the floors and desks and tables. Dusty computer monitors. Keyboards that if you licked them you would probably not survive a month. Somewhere, under the piles, a telephone that had probably gone pale and blind like a cave fish.

"They're worried that the journals'll publish the coffee rings on our manuscripts? Hell. Never mind that. We'll e-mail 'em in."

For response, Matt remained silent.

"There's nothing in here, man, but a thousand pounds of evidence that we work too hard and never go home. They'll get their money's worth."

"Werstheimer told them that, of course. She's not all bitch. She tried to stick up for us. She asked them to come back tomorrow and told them they'd find the place spotless."

"Spotless like my hairy ass is spotless. This place hasn't been spotless since 1948. This place has the ground-in grime of a million beleaguered grad students. Their stultified psyches have seeped into the linoleum and cinderblock and acoustic tiles. You can hear their crushed spirits moaning with the ballast in the fluorescent light fixtures."

Matt's chair creaked, but he said nothing.

Bud continued. "Great God, man. June Fucking Cleaver couldn't clean this room in twenty-four hours."

"More like twelve since it's already close to midnight. And Werstheimer said start with your illicit mold collection." Bud felt him, through the spatial distortion Matt's presence wielded, pointing at a neat stack of Petri dishes on the desk near his head.

Bud groaned again.

"Illicit like my hairy ass is illicit. Those dishes and the Jell-O in them might be 'borrowed', but there's nothing in there from the labs. Those pets of mine have grown from nothing that doesn't occur naturally in this room. As long as you consider that Chernobyl-red sauce in the General Tsu's Chicken natural..."

"They go, Bud. File whatever environmental impact statement you have to and tip 'em in the dumpster. *Fungata non gratis.* Give 'em their walking papers." Matt's chair creaked dangerously.

Bud's eyes snapped open and he swatted at Matt's reaching hand. "Piss off, you goon. I'll find someplace else to hide the fun-guys until the coast is clear."

Matt kicked a paper carry-out box over to Bud's desk, sliding it across the floor. "Take 'em home, Dr. Moreau. But keep 'em in your fuckin' room. And for the sake of future funding—you know, the stuff that pays for our drugs and booze and women—you leave 'em there."

Bud moped, unmoving. "I'll miss their widdle voices singing their inspirational hymns in the middle of the night whilst I'm working through the wee hours. Their cheery yet reverent praises keep me going when I'm tired."

"You'll have to drink coffee like the rest of us, you freak. They go. As soon as you've come down from whatever the hell it is you're on, we're carting a few sacks of garbage out and raiding the janitorial closet."

Bud closed his eyes again and wondered how he'd keep his little project going.

A crashing noise woke Bud up. It sounded like a bookshelf falling over. Maybe it even was a bookshelf falling over. Bud looked around, and, lo, there were books all over the floor, and a tipped-over bookshelf. Behind the bookshelf was a wrinkled old Asian man, shirtless, in jeans and a pair of cowboy boots. Behind him was a wrinkled-old-Asian-man-shaped hole in the gypsum-board wall, with a few joists and studs and wires and such-like poking out uncomfortably. Some gypsum-board dust floated around in the air. Behind the hole was the living room, and on the opposite wall in the living room was a similar hole in the exterior wall. Bud could see that the sofa had been knocked askew and there were bricks on the floor in the living room.

Bud sat up on his bed. The shirtless old wrinkled Asian man coughed up some wallboard dust. It was less than threatening.

Bud bleared into the half-light. "What? Lung, right?"

Lung, folded over with his hands on his knees, coughed miserably and nodded.

Bud leaned over and looked out through the consecutive holes in the walls. A damp breeze stirred the odor of last week's socks.

"Don't have doors where you come from? What the fuck is your problem?"

Lung put a hand up, still coughing. He lurched closer to Bud's bed, grinned between spastic suppressed attempts to clear his chest of dust, grabbed Bud by the front of his pajama shirt, and flung him in a single graceful movement upside-down through the far wall, smashing through the window and attendant wooden framing.

Bud twitched and groaned on his back on the sparse grass of the backyard. He watched, stunned, as Lung hopped through the hole he had just used Bud to make and lumbered over until he was near enough to kneel on the dirt near Bud's head.

Lung leaned over until his upside-down head, silhouetted against the city-lit clouded night sky, filled Bud's nauseously spinning view. Bud smelled his strange old Asian man sweat and chalky breath. Bud didn't see Lung's lips move but he heard him croak awkwardly, "Thousand ways to do it right. Thousand thousand ways to do it wrong. Sometimes even the right way is wrong. Use your head. Think. What do you want from forever?"

Lung put a closed fist on Bud's chest and pushed himself upright. He chuckled and coughed again gently, sauntered over to the chainlink fence, ripped an enormous twanging hole in it, and strode away into the darkness.

Bud blinked for about ten minutes, and the next upside-down face in his view was Matt's.

"You never told me you sleepwalked. You should pay a bigger share of the rent."

Bud, wrapped in a blanket on the sofa, listened to the ringing in his ears and the pungent beeping of the microwave. Momentarily Matt emerged from the kitchen and took a seat in the Salvation Army reject armchair he had shoved up against the closet door that was blocking the hole in the living room wall. Matt had a microwaved burrito on a paper plate and a can of something. Bud could hear the quiet fizzing of the can even though his ears were still ringing.

Matt cleared his throat. Bud twisted around until he could see him sitting in the nearby chair. They stared at each other for a few long moments.

Matt waved at some of the remaining debris. "You tell me what's going on right fucking now, or no burrito."

Bud gurgled a bit and groaned. "I got beat up by an old Asian pig-fucker."

"So did the house. And a bit of the yard. And my Playstation. And your L. Ron Hubbard collection. Tell me more." Matt took a bite of the burrito.

"One of the guys from the league game. Sore winner, maybe? Fucked if I know."

Matt took another bite. The burrito was two-thirds gone. "Took a bit of talking to convince the cops we weren't building bombs."

"What did you tell them?" Bud rubbed the side of his head where he had hit the window andor the turf.

"Hit-and-run motorcycle accident. You jumped through the window to keep from getting run down." Matt finished the burrito. "Your turn. Talk, or I'll take you to the infirmary."

"What's wrong with that? They're good for hydrocodone. Besides, I could probably use a few thousand x-rays."

"You're fine, bastard. For now. You walked all the way here from the backyard. Besides, you think I'd let you keep a bottleful of M357s? Talk, or I'll eat another burrito at you."

"Lemme think."

"Suit yourself." Matt got up and reentered the kitchen. There was a freezer-opening sound, and then more microwave-y-beepy noises.

Matt returned to find Bud asleep. He kicked the leg of the sofa, and Bud said, "I've been thinking."

"Good for you. Tell me what you've been thinking."

"I think I'm onto something."

"I think you're on something."

"Goes without saying. But I think, I really and truly think, that the old bowling buggers want my pet bugs."

"The fun guys? You're nucking futz."

"There's no way I'm Canadian. Now listen. I've been working on something."

Around a bite of burrito, Matt mumbled, "So you've been telling me. So you've been telling Werstheimer. Spill it. What have you not been telling me about the bugs, and realize that telling me now won't save you from a beating."

"Another beating."

"Fine. Another beating. As many beatings as you like." Matt finished off the second burrito. After a moment, he added, "When you think too long, you're making shit up. Out with it."

"They live forever."

"Duh. Sure they live forever. Somewhere around here is the original ameba. When stuff multiplies by mitosis, you get two identical copies. If you declare one to be the original, then the original of them all is still alive. Sophomoric nonsense, but literally true."

The room was quiet except for nearby road noises and a distant train.

"Some of those molds and fungi and bacterial cultures are actually tissue cultures. *Um.* Mine."

Matt stood up. "Can't risk the bullshit, Bud. You talk more while I get the scope. If we need to get back to the school for the high-powered shit, then I hope you feel well enough to travel."

Bud creaked himself into a sitting position while Matt found a low-end microscope from his bedroom. Matt said, from outside the room, "I'm fetching your little buddies from your desk drawer. Pardon me for wanting to prep some slides myself..."

Bud wriggled his shoulders and stretched his neck. "Do what you gotta, man. I'm getting something for the pain."

A few minutes later they were both at the dining room table.

Matt opened, "You stopped talking some time ago."

Bud yawned. "Letting the bugs speak for me. Tell me what you see."

"Skin cells. Maybe. I'm not sure I like what I'm seeing if they are..."

"You see a couple of partially differentiated stem cells, right?"

"Yep. A few more than I'd expect to see in a sample this small, but yeah."

"Discovered a tiny little enzyme."

"Telomerase? Dead end, man. Extending the telomeres on a differentiated cell just gets you lots and lots of copyability..."

"Sure. But it's a tad more complicated than that. When cells are feeling lonely, they make more, right? Well, when they're feeling low on stem cells, they want to revert, and occasionally one of them does."

Matt looked up from the scope. "So I've heard it claimed. Peer review is iffy on that."

Bud sighed. "It's like neural cell division. Very rare. And it usually involves a partially differentiated neural stem cell. For neural cells, anyway. But it happens. The cells want it to happen, but they're typically missing a little sumpin'-sumpin'. And when that protein shows up, they revert and then, quite, quite soon, you get partially differentiated stem cells that make more neural cells."

Matt put his eye back to the scope. "You found that something?"

"Lots of people have. I just found a gene-combo that creates it."

"Not all of these look like skin cells, Bud. How bad did you stab yourself getting this sample?"

"Scraped the inside of my mouth, man. Fetched out a single epithelial stem cell. All the stuff in tray four is his younguns."

"Striated muscle tissue? I think?"

"Yeah. That's growth. Not original."

"What the fuck have you done, Bud?"

"Detects the lack of stem-ish cells and makes 'em. No muscle tissue nearby when there ought to be some? Undifferentiates back far enough to be able to make both. Whoops! Now we seem to be short on bone tissue, and maybe a nerve nearby would be kind of cool... Soon, the differentiated stuff dies off in favor of the less differentiated until it really gets cookin'... and I drop the tray in the incinerator when it starts to look too much like a blastocyst."

"Keep going, Bud."

"It's context-based. If the stem cells are in a bunch of differentiated tissue, they tend to stay there and be happy. But if the tissue is under stress, then a new stem cell gets made, weakens the adhesion proteins somewhat, then wanders off to where it thinks it might be needed..."

"Metastasizes. Right. Did you just drop this gene in, or is it spliced...?"

"Right at the end, right before the telomeres. Like, maybe, apparently, *umm*, where it used to be. Like that gene we used to have that synthesized vitamin C. Which this seems to do, too. Doesn't seem much like an accident."

"You don't say."

There was plenty of silence while they brooded.

Matt cleared his throat. "You can't publish this. You can't even say you found it while you were fucking around and send it through the right channels. You know what happens to you when people hear you've been fucking around with human tissue without oversight?"

"Bad shit."

"No shit bad shit. I should kill you now out of mercy, but, for some reason, I don't feel too much like being merciful. Even though every researcher between Werstheimer and God Himself will grill me to my dying day about why I let you live. How'd you splice this in?"

"I just about told you. Stripped off the telomeres, glued it to the end, telomerased a few kilotelomeres to the end..."

"No sequencer?"

"No sequencer."

"You're telling me you did this with fucking chemistry?"

"Yup."

"You bastard."

"Yup."

Matt stood up and stretched. "But this stuff doesn't live forever. You can kill it, or starve it, or poison it, or any of a number of things. Immune system rejection even, maybe."

"Sure. But it doesn't seem to age. Or rather, doesn't seem to undergo any of the effects we'd normally associate with the aging process. Older, malfunctioning, underfed cells hit apoptosis, no problem, but then the stem cells make replacements for them. Everything stays young and fresh. Shows all the signs of regeneration, too."

"What happens when you take a modified cell and put it in a culture of normal tissues?"

"The usual. The original cells die off when it's time and the new cell, unless it gets damaged or killed somehow, makes cells to replace them, and then they make new cells to replace each other, etcetera, etcetera. The new tissue eventually takes over. Just like you'd think."

Bud drank more of his painkiller. Matt loomed over the back of his chair.

"You haven't done the stupid thing yet, have you?"

Bud swallowed. He pretty much heard Matt behind him draw back a fist.

"Not yet. I figured it should take some thought, you know?"

Matt went back to his chair and sat back down heavily in front of the scope. "And the bowling geezers know about this?"

"Seems so. There've been some break-ins at the labs, right? I guess that was how it got out. You know. Through chinks in the walls."

Clancyville's Finest, accompanied by a representative of the state bureau of investigation, came by yet again to ask a number of pointed questions. They brought an explosives-sniffing dog that for some reason kept barking at the hall toilet, which was then professionally removed and bagged for further forensic investigation off-site. The lack of motorcycle tracks interior and exterior to the building was duly noted.

No charges were filed.

As soon as they were given permission by the cops and the landlord, the loose closet door was moved to cover the interior ruptured wall. Matt and Bud collected displaced bricks and brick fragments and carefully jigsawed them back together. In the manner of inventive college students worldwide who have to jury-rig exterior walls in their homes, they duct-taped them into place. An old stained futon took the place of fiberglass insulation and a layer of gypsum board and was duly staple-gunned between the studs, the irregular gypsum board chunk having been earlier hijacked to cover Bud's broken window. More duct tape sealed the edges of the wall's wound, and Bud took the opportunity to paint the duct tape and futon to more-or-less match the wall with a can of latex paint he found in a linen closet.

The wall bulged comfortably at the bottom, lapping over the mysteriously intact baseboard like an architectural beer-gut over a wooden belt. Bud sighed the sigh of a job well done.

Matt spoke. "See? I told you padded walls were in your future."

"It's a start," Bud replied. "Shy on the leather straps and the Thorazine."

"We can get Thorazine from our normal supplier. Leather straps you're gonna have to get online just like everything else. The vaguely Midwest is still occupied and overseen by invading Puritan forces."

Matt and Bud had the Playstation taken to pieces and arranged artfully on the dining room table before the knocking on the front door started. Bud nursed another can of painkiller and turned his best puppy-dog eyes on Matt, who huffed mildly and headed for the living room. He returned leading St. Germain and Enoch. They were in their Clancyville Stonecutting and Bricklaying bowling shirts. Enoch leered unsteadily, rubbernecking around to take in the place. If St. Germain had had a hat, he would have been twisting it in his hands.

Bud rubbed his can across his forehead in greeting. "Whut up, Saint, George? Need a can of beverage? Lemme getcha sumpin'. Sit a bit. Fix the Playstation. Be right back."

Bud went to the kitchen. There were fridge-opening noises. Matt waved at the other two liberated diner chairs at the table and took a seat himself. Bud returned with three opened cans, handing them out to everyone and regaining his own. Enoch was sitting already, peering intently at the game machine carnage. St. Germain was just in the act of reluctantly taking a seat. Silence levitated over the middle of the table like the suspicion of a fart.

St. Germain stared at the opened can in front of him on the table. He looked up at Bud briefly then cast his eyes back at the Formica table. "*Umm.* As little as it is our right to decide, we have decided that you need to learn the value of death." He looked up at Bud again, who paused in mid-sip.

St. Germain then stood, rolled his shoulders in a typically old-man stretch, and then stabbed an icepick neatly into the back of Matt's neck. Matt slumped onto the table and three cans of beer tipped over, lubricating the Playstation parts and the dining room linoleum. Enoch casually got up, caught St. Germain companionably by the hand, and led him to the front door.

Bud, frozen, watched them close the door gently behind them.

"I did do the stupid thing, Matt," Bud whispered to his pithed roommate and best friend on Earth. "Tray four was from *your* cells. I also forgot to mention the anaerobic mitochondrial replacements. Get well soon. Fucker."

Amusement at the police station ensued.

"Why did you kill your roommate?"

"God, I hate the smart ones."

"Did you and Matthew fight much? What about?"

"What was your last disagreement about? Were there witnesses?"

"Tell me again what happened to wreck the house you're renting."

"Tell me how the drugs fit in."

"If it wasn't you, tell me who you're protecting. Why protect someone when you'll be going down for this if you do?"

"You know what I think? I think you promised someone a buncha drugs for a buncha money, then you tried to screw whoever it was, got beat up, got your house wrecked, then you and your buddy got in a fight about it. And you killed him."

"This was all about drugs, wasn't it?"

"Piss in this cup."

"A lawyer from the county DA's office? I'll take my chances on my own, thanks."

"I didn't kill my roommate."

"Why the hell would I even own an icepick? I get cubed and crushed from the door of the fridge. What year is this? 1910?"

"Matt threatened to take my life every day. We're roommates, for Chrissakes. We're on the same lab team. We share an office. It's impossible not to get up someone's nose when you're in their face eighteen hours a day."

"I don't waste beer. Ask anyone. How many cans were at the table?"

"Given all the dangerous crap I work with, poisons and scalpels and all kinds of shit, why would I attack a man three times my size with a tiny pokey thingy? I thought you said I was one of the hated smart ones. Make up your mind."

"Wow, that's good. You guys watch far too much fucking television. Except for *CSI*. Not enough *CSI*."

"How could this possibly be about drugs? We're *med* students. Drugs are *free*. What we can't score from the dispensary with fake scrips we can cook up in the lab at school."

"This isn't about drugs."

"Jesus. Go back and look at the house again. If we were selling drugs, what were we doing with the money? Check the fridge again and see what brands of beer we've been reduced to."

"If I do are you going to drink it? You won't come down for weeks."

"How about I ask you a question? If you guys thought, perhaps, that the break-in at our house was somewhat suspicious, why weren't you watching it? If you had been, you'd be three-quarters done with this case by now. Schmucks."

"On second thought, I'd like to see that lawyer now. Because I'm done now and I'm going home, and apparently you need a lawyer to tell you that."

Bud. Bowling alley. Beer. One entered another and ordered a pitcher of the third. Then the third entered the first. Bud drank until his head was on the table. The bartender came over to make sure he was still breathing, then went away again.

News travels quickly in small towns.

In between ten-minute blinks, St. Germain, Lung and Enoch arrived and took seats at Bud's table. Upon noticing them at the table, Bud said, "You're late. Too late."

St. Germain replied, "Too late for what, my man. To save your friend?"

Bud groaned and sat up. "No, you insufferable prick. Too late to kill him."

Enoch elbowed St. Germain and tapped a few fingers on the table in a complicated rhythm. St. Germain looked sharply at Enoch, and Lung merely looked puzzled at the both of them.

"By all that's holy. You *didn't*."

"You bet your clavicle I did, Saint. You mind if I call you Saint? Like I care? Anyway, more than a month ago. I just hope we can bust him out of the morgue before the autopsy. 'Cuz that would suck, an autopsy on a living man. They do those, you know, when they suspect foul play. They'll probably take out his brain to weigh it or some shit, and that would, like, totally suck for everybody. Mostly Matt, though. And me. I need his brain to get through my thesis defense."

St. Germain and Enoch and Lung exchanged looks.

Bud continued, "He's smarter than me, 's'what I'm sayin'."

Lung spoke up. "Saner, too, I trow."

"You don't trow anything in the twenty-first century, pal," Bud countered. Lung looked suitably baffled.

"I can't break him out on my own. I can get into the building, but, for various reasons that make plenty of sense, they keep the cold room locked and guarded."

Lung nodded. "Aye. Resurrectionists?"

Bud shook his head blearily. "Nah. Pranksters. The morgue's at the university hospital."

St. Germain spoke up again. "See here, *erm*... Bud. We are not inclined to..."

"What if the autopsy doesn't kill him, either?" Bud interrupted. "He—I mean, it could take years, maybe, even, but he might be able to get better from that. Or he could drag out the actual dying for years. One way or the other we have to intervene."

Enoch shook his head vigorously.

"You guys haven't exactly explained crap. Who are you and why did you stab Matt in the head? I'm really angry about that."

"I thought we'd given you enough hints, my man. We're immortal, and we're trying to warn you off." St. Germain fiddled with the lapels of his bowling shirt.

"Exclusive club, eh? Or is this just hazing?"

"Nothing of the sort. Well, possibly something of the sort. It's complicated, but not too complicated. It's just that... eternal life is *tricky*."

"If Matt were here right now, he'd be much more capable than me of explaining, in Latin if necessary, how moronic you sound."

St. Germain sighed. "An example, then. What if you turn someone—or yourself—into a giant, ever-growing cancerous lump that eventually devours its own brain from the inside yet remains largely unkillable? What if the methodology you use to make tissue more resilient turns out to be, in some fashion, infectious? Viruses quite frequently incorporate some of their host's genetic material when they replicate. It's why some mutate so rapidly. What if you accidentally combine both of the above? How about infectious, unkillable, all-consuming cancers?"

Bud thought for a moment. "Would they name it after me?"

"Almost certainly. At least."

"You guys seem to be doing fine."

"Perhaps right now. Sometimes it takes effort. Take Lung for example. He has incorporated the… the attributes, the genetic material of several different animals into his own physiology. These attributes constantly vie for supremacy. If we lose track of him for a length of time, sometimes as short as a month, even, we may find him again as some kind of ravening monster—unkillable ravening monster—that we then have to heal and recondition until he is once more recognizable as our friend, and once more recognizes us."

Bud frowned intelligently. "And you? How does yours work?"

"I haven't the foggiest. But once about every ten or fifteen years I fall asleep for a fortnight and wake up with a fairly thorough case of amnesia. I have to spend a couple of months reading to get caught up to the present date, and I have to spend a couple of hours each day on my diary for when it happens next time."

"And George?" Bud asked, gesturing across the table.

St. Germain wobbled his head. "No one knows. We call her Enoch as a kind of a joke. She's not even our species. I'm no mean scientist, but she's as close to magic as anything I've ever seen. She exudes life into anything she touches."

Lung poured himself a glass from the remains of Bud's pitcher.

Bud sat back in his chair. "What do we do about Matt, then?"

"Who says we do anything, Bud? Matt should, by all rights, be a simple murder victim for whom nothing more needs be done. The fact that something remains, so to speak, is your fault, your responsibility, and your problem."

"You killed him, you bastard! How is none of this your responsibility?"

"Simple, my man. I choose to take no responsibility. I choose to offer no assistance. It's as simple as that. If you want to play with these powers, you must learn to handle the consequences."

Enoch reached across the table and patted Bud's hand. Then they all left him with his empty pitcher.

"Pricks," Bud muttered, face down on the table.

The cold room's attendant emerged into the hallway to find Bud slumped on the linoleum in front of the metal door. With a mumbled profanity, he rolled Bud onto his back and put his ear to Bud's mouth to check for breathing. Bud chose this moment to belch gently. The attendant stood up quickly.

"You pathetic booze-smelling motherfucker. That isn't funny. I ought to crack your skull just so I can have the CPR practice." He gave Bud a half-hearted kick in the ribs.

Bud moaned. He dragged himself over to the wall and halfway sat up. "Nonononono," he said. "No mouth-to-mouth, no CPR. Jus' need someplace quiet to lie down for a few minutes."

"You're drunk off your ass, man. This is the morgue. Two, three floors up, that's where the living people lie down. Come back when you're dead."

"Can't do that. I'm an intern up there. They'd put my ass back to work. You've been there. I can see the scars. Hide me. I'm already pickled, just like you said. Embalmed. Just give me a drawer."

"Put you back to work my ass. They'd pump your stomach and give you a room, if not a three-day psych eval on the fifth floor for attempted suicide."

"Not that drunk, really, man. Had a beer or two and then got paged. Forgot I'd switched shifts. It's the first dead time we've had in twelve hours. Hide me."

"Dead time." Bud got another half-hearted kick. He subjected his lab-jacketed tormentor to his best puppydog gaze.

"Fuck it," the attendant grumped. "Prove to me you can stand and you can watch the place for half an hour while I smoke an entire pack of cigarettes. There's a body in there that's marked Exhibit A and we're not supposed to leave it unguarded. My relief still hasn't shown up tonight."

"Deal." Bud coughed and got to his feet.

The attendant punched a combination into the fiddly buttons underneath the doorknob and held it open, already rooting in his pockets for cigs and a lighter. "You know the program. Kill anybody who busts through the door. From either side."

It only took a few minutes for Bud to find the keyring with the key for the padlock on the only locked drawer in the wall-fridge. Mostly out of habit he found a labcoat, a mask, and gloves, and put them on before sliding the tray out reverently and unzipping the black body bag. Matt's body, gray and at rest, seemed even more enormous than usual.

Dead people grow a foot. Dead people put on fifty pounds. Dead people lay there with their eyes open, dull and dry. Dead people ought to be stiff as a board eight hours after death, but Matt was not.

Matt's eye nearest to Bud rotated to point at him accusingly.

"On the assumption you can hear me, let me tell you that you're paralyzed due to some spinal damage. Axis, atlas, or above. Typically this affects autonomic systems, like breathing and heartbeat and all kinds of fatal shit, and I believe your case is no exception. Except you're not dead, I think. After a fashion. And yeah, that's my fault."

Bud lifted Matt's arm and looked at the underside. "Lividity. But not extreme. Your blood has pooled, but... not exactly coagulated. All in all, man, for a dead guy, you're looking pretty fresh. And don't worry about the breathing and the heartbeat thing. Not sure how long you've been functionally anaerobic, but you probably haven't really needed to breathe for a week or two." He tapped the top of Matt's forearm and watched the goosebumps form and the hairs stand up. "Oh, hell, that must tingle. Don't know how long it'll take for you to heal enough to stand up and walk out of here, but we should probably get you out before they cut you open. Just on the off chance that'll actually hurt or maybe kill you and shit."

Matt's eye stayed fixed on Bud as he poked and prodded.

"You're too heavy to carry, man. I really wish you'd get up. And put some goddamn clothes on."

Bud simply waited for the attendant to return. After twenty minutes or so of looking through magazines and journals and the odd textbook, there was some noisy clicking and the door opened.

The attendant entered, saw Bud in mask and labcoat, and began to freak out when he saw the padlock on the desk and Matt's drawer open.

"You just cost me my job, if not my career, you fucking bastard. I'm going to kill you now so at least it'll look like there was a struggle."

Bud waved at the camera in the corner of the room. "Nobody's watching, friend, but it's all on tape somewhere. We're all already fucked. Kinda. So chill a second and have a look at this." Bud tossed the attendant a box. The attendant pulled a couple of latex gloves out of it and tugged them on awkwardly, working around his trembling rage. He ripped one, tore it off, and got another out of the box to try again.

Keeping an eye on Bud the whole time, he edged toward Matt.

As he got closer, he noticed the goosebumps on Matt's arm, and then saw Matt's eyes move jerkily to track him.

"*Rrrr-rrr*," Matt said.

"That's right," Bud quipped. "You go, big guy."

"Fuck!" shouted the attendant, who quickly checked for a pulse at his neck and for signs of breathing. He stiff-armed Bud to the floor to get him out of the way, and after duly checking Matt's mouth for obstructions, started mouth-to-mouth and chest massage.

From the floor, Bud muttered, "Sorry I didn't think of it, big guy. Sure as hell can't hurt."

After a moment or two, Matt's color began to return to something resembling normal, if still a little pale and bluish. Between breaths, the attendant muttered, "You could make yourself a bit more useful by calling down to the emergency room or something. Jesus! You useless fuck!"

"I'm not worried. He's doing fine. I'm just waiting for him to sit up so we can walk out of here. Maybe if you gave him a blowjob... He's been asking for one for weeks."

The attendant snapped his head around to look at Bud, who was still lounging on the floor. Matt clubbed him gracelessly in the back of the head with a backhand, and he collapsed to the painted concrete, moaning.

Bud got to his feet. "Dude. You should have waited. I'm absolutely sure he was considering the blowjob."

"*Rrrr-rrr*," Matt said.

"Yeah, sure, I'll help you up."

Bud grabbed Matt's hand to pull him upright. Matt swatted him across the temple, knocking him to the ground. Bud got back up slowly, rubbing his face.

"Okay, yeah, sure, I deserved that. But dude, we should get the fuck out of here. This place is cold enough to cause permanent shrinkage. That's obviously what happened to fuckwit here to make him so uptight."

Fuckwit, still facedown on the floor, moaned again.

With tugging and cajoling, Matt was sitting upright inside ten minutes. It was another twenty minutes before he could throw his legs over the rolled edge of the drawer, and shortly around then he was hindered by a bout of uncontrollable shivering.

By that time Bud had discovered that Fuckwit's name was really Earl and that he had no interest at all in either bowling or drinking as a hobby. Earl, in fact, seemed to be interested mostly in sitting under his desk and studying for an upcoming test while he waited for Bud and Matt to get out of his hair so he could get busy with pretending it all never happened.

There were a few more snags.

"Don't look at me like that, man. You can't fit into my clothes. Or even his," Bud critiqued. "You'll have to make do with the lab-coat. I'm sorry they don't seem to come in 'behemoth' unless you special-order. Earl, do us a favor and hit the laundry. Isn't it on this floor? See if they have any scrubs in 'behemoth', will you?"

"Fuck you," drifted out from under the desk.

"We'll be out of here sooner...," sang Bud.

Earl spouted more curses, skittered out from under his desk, and hit the door.

"He's not going for scrubs, man. He's gonna bring back some orderlies. You can probably wear some of their clothes after you eat their heads or whatever it is you feel like doing. Hey, what is it you feel like doing, big guy?"

"*...hurts...*," grunted Matt.

"Well, duh, morphine. Lemme see what Earl packs with his lunch." After a few minutes of scrounging, Bud remarked, "No such luck. No pills, no booze... Fucking Earl is straightedge. He's not coming back with orderlies. He's bringing cops."

"Oh, shit," he added after glancing at Matt. "Keep breathing, dude, even if it's a lot of work. You're turning blue again, and it'll probably make it hurt less."

"*...why not...why not...auto...*"

"I told you, man. Spinal damage. Fucker stabbed you in the back of the neck with an icepick. He was going for your medulla, I'm sure. Might have nicked it, even."

"*...who...?*"

"St. Germain. Another one of the old bowling geezers. They came over when we were wrapping up painting and shit."

"*...don't...remember...*"

"Not surprised, man. You never saw it coming. Also, you know, you lost consciousness kinda suddenly. You tend to lose ten or twenty minutes that way."

"*...kill...you...*"

"Sure. Sure."

"*...you...this...you...?*"

"Nah, man. Not yet. I told you. Just you. You're fucking perfect, man. You're brilliant, you're strong, you're beautiful, you're at your motherfuckin' peak. I love you, man." Bud's voice choked up. "Stay like that forever."

"*...kill...you...*"

"Do what you gotta, man."

There was nothing but quiet, labored breathing for a few minutes.

"*...blow...*"

"Still no blowjob, man. I don't swing like that. Go fish."

Bud wrapped the insufficient labcoat around Matt a little tighter and chafed his arms and shoulders in an attempt to warm him up.

And then the door burst open.

"Whaddya know, Matt? Cops and orderlies. Earl must be the mother of all pussies." Bud put up his hands. After a moment, and somewhat jerkily, so did Matt.

"Get down on the floor! Put your hands on the floor! Now!"

Bud slid down to the floor and lay flat, palms down on the concrete, his head tilted sideways and upward so he could watch. Matt slid off his drawer unsteadily, dragging his body bag onto the floor behind him. In a couple of haphazard motions he was prone as well. The police rushed in and one hopped onto Matt's back, handcuffs in hand.

"The fuck are you doing, you stupid pig? Can't you see the man needs medical attention?" Bud got a clip across the back of his skull for that, but he couldn't tell from what.

Matt pulled his knees up under himself and started to stand, ignoring the weight of the cop on his back, who slung an arm around Matt's throat for a choke hold. Matt finished standing and lurched backwards, pinning the man between his bulk and the edge of the drawer he'd been lying on. There was an awful sound of bones popping and metal bending, and then Bud heard four shots fired from right near his head.

He struggled to roll onto his side so he could see and what he saw was Matt grab a brown-sleeved arm and a hand with a gun clenched in it, and then he saw Matt wrench them apart with a spray of blood. Half-deaf from the gunfire, he more felt than heard the sickening sound of tearing flesh, just like he more felt than heard himself screaming.

The mangled cop fell sideways and crabbed away a few steps before wrapping himself around his arm and rocking. The other cop was folded backward over the side of the bent drawer and wasn't moving. Matt was on his hands and knees on the concrete, covered in gore. Bud saw a couple of gobby holes had been punched in the back of the labcoat, and his stomach heaved. There was no sign of the orderlies or Earl.

Matt moaned quietly, or so Bud guessed since it didn't shake the building. He scuttled over to Matt to check him over and was forcefully shoved away. Bud slid sideways in the gore and righted himself. He crawled back to Matt.

Shouting over the ringing in his ears, Bud squeaked, "We have to get out of here, man! Can you get up?!"

On the fourth try, Matt, oozing blood down his naked front, got to his feet and lurched through the door. Bud scrabbled after him, trailing bloody footprints. On the other side of the door, crouched next to the wall, was Earl, holding his head in his hands.

Bud kicked him in the shoulder with a bloody sneaker as he went past, sneering, "Asshole."

Bud risked zipping quickly by the house to clean Matt up, bandage his chest a bit, and stuff him into jeans and a flannel shirt. Matt was moving more gracefully and talking, or perhaps wheezing, a bit more coherently by the time Bud was dragging him back to the car. A SWAT team had failed to show up and surround the house. Bud found this hopeful.

"Fuck this, man. We need somewhere to go. Let's go bowling."

Matt wheezed, "Nucking futz, man. Our lives are over. Why do you"—he coughed—"want to go bowling?"

Bud didn't answer.

A few minutes later they were in the bowling alley. They staggered over to Bud's usual high-top near the bar. Matt reached into his shirt, dug around a bit, and dropped a small but heavy metallic lump on the table.

Bud stared at the lump for a few minutes, then vanished to the bar to come back with a pitcher and a handful of glasses.

"I can't drink that, Bud. Shit'll come dribbling out of my chest. For all that I'm not dead, man, I'm not at all well."

"I hear you. We're just waiting for the geezers."

They sat in silence. Bud sipped slowly. Matt practiced breathing.

Eventually, Lung walked up to the table. Except for the cowboy boots, he was dressed exactly like Matt. It made Bud snicker.

Lung tugged a small tape cartridge out of his shirt pocket and dropped it on the table next to Matt's discarded bullet.

"Security camera tape," he grunted, by way of explanation.

Bud frowned thoughtfully. Matt shrugged.

"How much does that help?" Bud queried. "Matt's got an official document on file at the official courthouse that says that he's dead.

Officially. And I'm sure there's some kind of open case file that mentions a murder at my house and a corpse in desperate need of autopsy and some shit. And there are two dead cops."

"Who cares?" croaked Lung. "There is no body. Enoch has taken care of the police men." He said it as two separate words.

Bud was somewhat curious as to what Enoch had done to "take care of the police men" but he held his tongue.

"You want life to go on as usual?" This was from St. Germain, coming out of the nearby men's room. He caught himself tucking his shiny bowling shirt into his leather pants and pulled it awkwardly back out again. "You should have left things alone."

"Whatever. What happens now?"

Matt was staring at St. Germain, who was staring intently back at Matt. Matt slumped and his head bounced noisily on the table, jostling the beer. Bud scrambled to his feet but froze when he felt Lung's hand on his shoulder.

"The same thing that has already happened, my man. Your friend was murdered by hoodlums. You go home. You mourn. You throw away your toys. You finish your degree. You get a job doing supervised research. Life goes on. For *you*. Matt stays dead. *Officially*."

Lung casually hefted Matt over a shoulder in a fireman's carry. Bud noticed that Matt was still breathing. Occasionally.

St. Germain placed a friendlier hand on Bud's shoulder. "Go home," he counseled. "Forget Matt."

Bud refused to look at him. St. Germain sighed.

"We'll keep an eye on you," he sighed, and then he followed Lung out the front door.

Back at the house, Bud put the bullet Matt had left on the table back in his shirt pocket.

He picked up a Petri dish with "4" written neatly on a scrap of masking tape. "Hello, Matt," he greeted it cheerfully. "If that's who you really are. Let's check, shall we?"

Two hours later, having prepared six different slides and having spent some time examining each one in detail under his microscope, he spoke softly. "Looks like it is you. Hot damn. Good thing. You still owe me thirty-eight bucks for the cable bill."

Bud unwrapped a tiny syringe from a sterile packet like the kind adhesive bandages come in. He uncapped the needle and clamped the thing into a cast-iron-footed device covered in knobs and thumbscrews. After spending a patient half hour making adjustments, he then used the fine-control knobs to prod the tip of the needle around in the droplet under the scope while he watched through the eyepiece.

"That thirty-eight bucks is as good as mine, you big bastard."

He slowly rotated a knob on top of the stand and watched as a promising group of cells entered the syringe. He repeated the process four more times.

He unclamped the syringe from the device with all the knobs on it. Holding it up to the light, he said, "Should I worry? I shouldn't worry. You're the strong one. Stronger than me in pretty much every way, right?"

He inserted the needle as far as it would go into the top of his right thigh and gently pushed the plunger.

"When I'm you in a month or two, I'm sure I'll pay me back."

From the irrepressible Mr. Jack Dolphin, author of incisve introductions to several of C.J. Henderson's works, and a savvy, talented storyteller in his own right. What follows is a vintage tale of the living dead that reveals exactly how they dealt with them boogers back in the day.

ZoMBIEs ON BROADWaY

by Jack Dolphin

It is well known to one and all around and about Broadway that there is no oath more honored, no promise more carefully kept, no marker more certain to convert into genuine coin of the realm than that tenacious tenet of the theater: *The Show Must Go On!*

It seems the parties who involve themselves in show business see this pledge as more than a simple slogan one bandies about to promote the good will of the citizenry; to them it is a sacred trust. And the lengths some parties will go to in order to fulfill that commitment makes for an interesting set of circumstances, at that.

It is the end of last summer that I am standing out in front of Windy's Restaurant finishing a Perfecto-Perfecto which is furnished to me by a grateful citizen who overhears my bet on Shark Bait in the third at Belmont and, feeling inspired, places a pound note of his own on same. The horse proceeds to skate home in a halo and I add no small amount of potatoes to my kick as I catch him going off at 9 to 2. But I also profit to the tune of that one reasonably expensive cigar which I am enjoying to the very end before proceeding inside for a brisket on rye, when I am bowled over by a party known as Cyclone Murphy, who leaves Windy's as if they shoot him out the door from a cannon.

Our collision, the likes of which is a frequent occurrence around Murphy, who does not come by the handle Cyclone dishonestly unlike most other things he comes by, dislodges both Murphy's derby and my remaining quartersmoke, but no apology is forthcoming. He simply mumbles, "The show must go on!" as he stoops to recover his kady and strides off, crushing the remains of my stogie under his boot heel as a curtain call.

On that somewhat discouraging note, I see no reason to delay my meal any further. My Perfecto-Perfecto is so much shredded leaf on the sidewalk and standing around in public is nothing more than an open invitation to one and all who might have heard of my afternoon's good fortune to attempt to put the bite on me for a few bobs. So, I push through the two sets of doors and into the dining area, where I spot Broadway impresario The Great Schupbach alone at the largest table in the joint, waving me over to join him.

"Murphy leave any tread marks on you?" he asks. "As he is temporarily in my employ, I wish to make certain he does not leave me liable for any injuries or other ill effects related to his mission."

The Great Schupbach, being a producer of plays, gets his name somewhat sideways from the fact that he never once has a hit and, in fact, never comes close to having a hit and is somewhat renowned for persevering in his profession despite his considerable lack of success, but he manages anyway to chuck quite a swell and appear in the chips more than somewhat. How he is able to maintain this charade is a mystery to one and all, but he is well liked, especially as he has a habit of picking up the check. There is never a whiff of dishonesty or scandal attached to him so what use he can find for a party of Murphy's dubious talents I would not care to speculate. Neither can I ask him because asking questions is an activity that gets you known as a guy who asks questions, which is almost never a healthy reputation to promote. So, I tell him only that the extent of the damage is one nearly-smoked Perfecto-Perfecto, for which he offers a reasonable replacement from his pocket that I gratefully tuck away for later.

"You have heard of my Great misfortune?" he inquires, waving me to sit down and signaling for a waiter in one expansive gesture.

I do not say "Which Great misfortune is that?" for while I know of one or two already and hear rumors about any number of others, I do not wish to be known as a guy who dredges up the past, especially to a party who has a past as filled up with Great misfortunes as The Great Schupbach, so I mumble a no as I peruse the specials for the evening line on brisket.

I wish to point out that, despite being typecast by prematurely distinguished looks in his salad days as an actor to always play the banker, the lawyer or the politician, The Great Schupbach is a right guy who does not deserve the hoodoo he keeps harvesting. So, it is a more than somewhat sympathetic ear I lend as he proceeds to tell me about his new play, which is performing out-of-town tryouts in the City of Brotherly Love, and is, by all accounts, knocking them dead. In fact, the general consensus seems to be that The Great Schupbach has finally got a bona-fide hit on his hands and it appears it is in no small way due to the astoundingly lively performance of his lead actor, one Fenton Appleby, a perennial Broadway juvenile who comes into his own in this show in ways never imagined by the critics who fill their reviews in the Philly blats with a great deal of praise and general good will about this "marvel of charm and chutzpah", to the point where The Great Schupbach fears this Appleby will seek a raise.

"I am at a loss to see the Great misfortune in this situation," I say to The Great. "It would seem you are about to get onboard the gravy train in a very big way at last and even if it means you must cut this Appleby in on a few extra potatoes, there will surely be more than enough to go around, especially if he continues to pack them in on the home field."

"One is forgiven for thinking so," says The Great with no small amount of sadness in his face and voice. "But I am nothing if not consistent in my unparalleled ability to be on the receiving end of what I can only term buzzard luck."

He goes on to explain at some length the events of the previous evening which begins well enough with another fine performance of the show, continues smooth through a small gathering of the cast to celebrate their triumph before packing up for the trip back to the grandest of Broadway openings but ends most distressingly when Fenton Appleby keels over at the bar in The Mystic Room and croaks from an undisclosed ailment in the ambulance before reaching the hospital.

"I am born under a black cloud," bemoans The Great Schupbach. "Here I finally have the hit I am waiting my whole career for and fate yanks it out from under me like the tablecloth at a magician's dinner party."

"This is indeed a catastrophe of the first order," I say and I continue to commiserate with him all during my brisket.

Finally, I cannot prevent myself from remarking, "I am curious as to how Cyclone is going to be of assistance to you in this very grave matter, as he is not the sort I would generally suspect of being theatrically minded."

He explains that Murphy, hearing of The Great's misfortune, approaches him with an offer to connect him with some parties who might have a solution to this most inopportune incident.

"Murphy is somewhat vague on the details, saying only that it is a most unusual solution, no doubt, and once I make certain he is not shining me up to hire some third-rate, out-of-work actor pal of his, I allow as how I am willing to entertain any proposition whatsoever that prevents me from having to cancel the opening or open with the understudy, either of which means the same thing - a line of unhappy citizens demanding I refund their cocoanuts for so many sold-out duckets they stretch from here to Saratoga."

I agree any proposition that prevents this most dire turn of events is worth listening to at the least and I no sooner finish said statement that Murphy reappears to say the parties in question will acquaint The Great Schupbach with their solution around the corner in a private conference room back of Jimmy The Gent's Alibi Room. Schupbach dukes me a farewell with assurances he is most gratified by my compassion and my council and he further exhibits the qualities of a gentleman by taking the check, which is a very mensch thing to do, indeed.

So I sit back to enjoy my new cigar with a cup of Windy's genuine Jamaican java and an untouched bankroll when I hear a voice familiar enough to cause me some momentary worry that word finally spreads of my win and some enterprising citizen is preparing to put the bite on me. I am, therefore, considerably relieved when I realize it is only my friend Archer Mallot, the newspaper scribe, who is well-known to one and all as a guy who never puts the bite on any citizen whatsoever, which is an item of no small astonishment in my circles.

He gives me a big hello, sits down and lights a lantern wick of his own, which stinks like a burning mattress, a smell many a furnished room dweller knows by heart, and he gives me his disinterested gaze, which means he is fishing for info.

"So, what is the fresh dope on The Great?" Mallot asks, being both the columnist in charge of reviewing Broadway shows for one of the morning blats and a guy who always wishes to know bad news as soon as possible so he can slip it in under deadline. "Is he crazy enough to think the honking of some giddy Philly hackamores is going to be enough to bring him home in triumph? I give the new gasp five performances tops before it folds like a gypsy's tent and I do not even see it yet."

This is most typical of Mallot, who is roundly reviled on Broadway by any number of producers, actors and such that he carves up like Christmas turkeys in his column, for it seems Mallot never sees a play he likes even a little bit and he says so quite often in language most insulting indeed. I am witness to at least three separate occasions when a disillusioned dramatist takes a swing at Archer Mallot and they connect soundly one and all, since Mallot judges punches even worse than he judges plays.

Now, news that Schupbach's leading man is preparing for a long run doing the sod snooze is exactly the kind of fresh dope Mallot would give his left ear for. However, I am not inclined to pass such information along, for while Mallot fronts me any number of steak dinners in the past, he does not stand me the one I am just digesting and I decide to honor the confidences of the party who does, not to mention that I would have practically no use at all for another left ear, at that. Clamming up, however, is a significant risk, as Mallot is an unforgiving sort, but a brisket is no small matter in my book and honor is paramount, particularly when you can afford it.

"He tells me they open tomorrow night and he seems confident enough," I allow and I am searching for another suitably plausible comment when Windy himself stops at the table to tell me I have a phone call up by the cashier. I excuse myself from Mallot and grab up the talking stick, wondering if I can use the call as an excuse to get clear of my friend before I get myself in Dutch, so I am more than somewhat surprised to find myself conversing once more with The Great Schupbach. It seems he meets with the parties recommended to him by Murphy and they have a most unusual solution in mind, at that, and he wonders if I could see my way clear to dropping by The Alibi Room for a cocktail to hear this solution for myself and tell him what I think.

I do not ever expect to find myself being consulted in such a manner but a cocktail would go well with the rest of my cigar, so I agree, stopping on my way out to make my excuses to Mallot, who has zeroed in on a chorus doll making short work of a plate of goulash at the next table and is mostly indifferent to my exit.

I step around to The Alibi Room which is a narrow little joint in the middle of the block owned by Jimmy The Gent, a most prominent citizen in the beer business with a sideline in genuine pre-war Scotch, which is manufactured in the back of a Jersey collision shop and is a splendid substitute for formaldehyde, I am told. Of course, the booze racket is no longer the Wild West Show it is when Prohibition first commences but it does still attract the occasional exuberant yahoo, so Jimmy long ago builds himself a private conference room in the back of his joint with lead-lined walls, bulletproof windows and other luxuries designed to put a peaceful slant on any and all business proceedings within.

I make my way back to this inner sanctum, passing several of

Jimmy's fine collection of gorillas on the way, and find myself in a brightly-lit office with one big table in the middle and five parties sitting at chairs all around. It is a source of some concern to me when I see who the parties are, for in addition to The Great Schupbach and Cyclone Murphy the room contains a very prominent citizen known as Frank The Hat and his associates Mutter McCrea and Rocks Maybie, who are all formerly prosperous practitioners of "The Big Store" and "The Cincinnati Turnaround" and other vintage varieties of the old ackamarackus, but are lately suffering no small amount because of the hard times making it tougher and tougher to find some loaded Chester who is just sharp enough to get separated from his long green. Frank motions me over, dukes me a hello and says as follows:

"I am delighted to see you, friend, for when The Great allows as how he has an associate he wishes to hear our plan for his salvation, I am no little put out that some unknown quantity is coming in to pronounce judgment on us, but when he tells me who it is he wishes to invite I am greatly relieved as you are well-known around and about as a guy who always is most cautious and honorable in his dealings and I personally hold your marker on at least two occasions I remember and you always make good in a timely fashion, so welcome and grab yourself some support while we lay out the particulars."

Of course, I am smart enough to realize that all this palaver is so much bathhouse soap and the real message is I best not queer the pitch or Frank will look most unkindly upon me. Since parties whom Frank looks unkindly upon are prone to accidents of one kind and another, I park myself in the only empty chair at the table, the one with no view of the entrance, and forego my instinct for remaining loyal to The Great, conceding in my heart that survival is one thing that always trumps a brisket. Then I give out with some remarks about how I am naturally interested in hearing what is to be proposed and that I will try to be as neutral as I can in forming an opinion, which Frank smiles at, so it is clear he understands I am getting in line as quick as possible and he goes on to explain.

He tells us of an acquaintance of his who is very prominent up in Harlem in the policy dodge and how this party once introduces him to a woman of uncommon abilities in a religion that comes from a tropical island a short hop across the pond where the practitioners are able to bring the dead back to life. Frank says that for a modest fee, he can arrange for this woman to perform her magic and, with any luck at all, restore Fenton Appleby to his former status of breathing and thus rescue The Great Schupbach from a fate worse than death, namely refund. To say I am nonplussed is to describe the scene with much restraint.

I cannot figure how The Hat expects me to go along with him on such an unusual idea and I am trying to think of something I can say that won't get me in trouble with anybody. Before I come up with anything, Frank goes on to say:

"I understand the very idea is going to take some getting used to. Although, there is a very notable incident some years ago, where this woman enjoys a lot of regular employment from a single customer, which you might have heard about. There is, at that time, a rather frisky young fellow around and about the beer business who is prone to taking other people's beer, and the trucks it travels in too, at the point of a John Roscoe and naturally this does not sit well with some of the more prominent citizens in that business who consider it unsportsmanlike conduct and who make it a point to try and ventilate the lad. Now, this young chap, who originally goes by the name Jack O'Clubs, quickly becomes known as Bullseye because he is the target of so many eager marksmen. In fact, it is this very problem that starts the tradition of bringing in out-of-town talent to accomplish these tasks because the promoters of this action soon go through all the local sharpshooters with very unsatisfactory results. It is no time at all before Bullseye is well known around and about the entire country because it seems that regardless how many plugs are put into him, he continues to live and breathe and it is a matter of no little embarrassment to many of these parties as they are not accustomed to being shown up in this way, being parties of considerable reputation in the towns they hail from."

But to hear Frank tell it, many of these shooters do indeed turn Bullseye off, except that he has a secret weapon, this conjure woman who regular as post time turns him back on again. Everyone believes Bullseye to be possessed of superhuman luck, never suspecting that luck has nothing to do with it, and he gains no small legend as a guy what can dodge bullets. This goes on for quite a spell before finally one of these parties, exasperated beyond all endurance, puts three pills in Bullseye's pimple and with that Bullseye is turned off permanently, as even island magic can do only so much.

I am, of course, in awe of Frank's skill, taking a well-known local legend and finding a way to shade it to support a proposition as daffy as any I ever hear (and I wish to say I hear quite a few daffy propositions in my time) but above all I recognize my position is dicey, so I speak as follows:

"This is a most interesting and astounding proposition and from anyone else I would not give it a moment's thought before dismissing it entirely, but Frank is known to me as a most serious and studious guy who never brings up any malarkey as I ever hear of, so I am inclined to say it might be worth a try, especially as there is no other proposition on the table that looks to produce the desired result. It is a desperate measure but these are desperate times."

This seems to satisfy The Great Schupbach who says, "My thinking exactly but I am glad you concur as I am so distraught by the Great misfortune, I cannot be certain of my own instincts." With that he draws his checkbook from an inside pocket and, gold fountain pen in hand, scribbles furiously within.

After removing the check from the checkbook and waving it dry with a Great flourish, he hands the check to Frank The Hat, who gives it a quick glance and calls for a round of Undertakers, which he specifies are not to be concocted from Jimmy's regular Scotch but should contain the "Real MacNeil", at which everybody breathes a little easier. We nibble a few as a discussion of details ensues and part in the wee hours with the understanding that we are to reconvene in the morning, when the resurrection of Fenton Appleby will occur. The Great Schupbach already makes arrangements for Appleby's body to return from Philly by refrigerated freight car and will further specify delivery via Jimmy The Gent's specially cooled hearses which do double duty as deliverers of both booze for his speaks and stiffs for the funeral parlor he runs as a sideline, which some might think of as a conflict of interest but most citizens agree is a splendid display of business savvy.

After The Great Schupbach pours himself into a short for the ride uptown to his Fifth Avenue digs, Frank The Hat and his pals invite me to accompany them to Windy's. In most cases I would at least attempt to beg off, but as I am more than somewhat curious about the next day's festivities, I follow along. Once inside, Frank chooses a table at the back, sits facing the entrance and waves Mutter and Rocks into the surrounding chairs.

I hesitate because, again, I am left with my back to the door, which proves unhealthy to any number of gees throughout the years, but since these are generally peaceful times, when Frank suggests I sit down, I do so.

"We already dine," says Frank, "but there is no reason we cannot allow you to stand us to some coffees as I feel it might be a good idea to explain a few things to you." And right there you see the genius of the man, turning an invitation to join him into a round for the boys on you so quick you cannot hardly see his lips move.

"I hope and trust that my somewhat skeptical attitude does not lead you to believe I wish to be uncooperative in this matter," I say, "but I am no little confused by what you propose to The Great Schupbach, especially as it seems to go against your own code, which you one time explain to me some years back."

"I imagine you refer to the part about the mark being a guy of no little personal greed and general shiftiness in order to get him in line with the idea of putting something over on someone who he has no idea is him," Frank allows.

"Well, that, too, as far as it goes," I reply, "but I am more specifically referring to the part about never sending them to the river as it is a dirty trick when all is said and done to make a mark consider suicide a better alternative than the state in which you leave him. And things being how they are, it strikes me The Great Schupbach might not be able to stand another Great misfortune, particularly one that certain citizens might view as a dirty trick."

Frank and Mutter both chuckle at this, Rocks never being such a guy as to chuckle at anything, and when they regain their composure, Frank explains why they are amused.

"You are thinking we are on the grift here, but I can assure you that nothing is further than the truth. We are one hundred percent on the level with this." He sees this is a hard piece for me to swallow, so he explains that the "conjure woman" is as real as a Tiffany ring and, what is more, Frank sees her in action some years earlier, during one of her Bullseye sessions.

"Okay," I say with no little caution, having nearly as much trouble digesting this news as I would an undercooked spud.

Frank looks me over and says, "I can tell you still have something wedged sideways in your craw and I think I know what it is. You wonder why I set The Great Schupbach up with this secret weapon, when it is a resource a party might be forgiven for keeping to himself." Without waiting for me to acknowledge this most correct assessment, he goes on:

Many years ago (says Frank) I come to this town from a little burg out west. I am sure in my heart I am a world beater and figure this town is the only town for me. I am here only a few hours before I get myself into a three day crap game run by a most prominent citizen known as Moe Toledo. The Great Schupbach is also in this game although he is not yet known as The Great as he is just starting out in the producing dodge. But he flings some mean bones in his day and, along with a couple of other large players, I am soon skinned of all my bankroll. It is then The Great does one of the things that, by and by, causes him to get his nickname. Instead of making small of me in front of the other players by sliding a finnif across the floor to front me some breakfast, as it is coming on dawn, The Great Schupbach takes me aside and escorts me out of the police station backroom and across the avenue to his own personal tailor, who he has make me up a new suit more in keeping with the look of the day on The Main Stem and, when it is being fitted, he slides a fresh C note into the breast pocket in lieu of a display handkerchief. This is a kindness I never forget and am only too happy to be able to slightly repay it with this courtesy.

In fact (Frank continues), the only reason I make The Great pull out his checkbook in this matter is that I am momentarily financially indisposed and I need the cocoanuts to cover the conjure woman's fee and the tax on using Jimmy The Gent's stiff wagon and corpse clinic.

Well, this is an entirely different pailful of pike and I tell Frank as much, all the while congratulating him on his loyalty to an old pal and explaining how relieved I am not to have to continue wracking my brain to figure out how they figure to give The Great Schupbach The Send, which is the part of the scam where they get him to leave quietly after parting with his mazoom for a whole lot of not very much at all.

"Think nothing of it," says Frank. "I understand how you might come to a different conclusion, being in possession of only some of the facts. But we are somewhat loaded down with preparations of one kind and another and it would be most helpful if you would carry out a small errand on our behalf. It involves nothing more than a short cab ride to pick up this doll and then to deliver her to Sam and Eddie's Funeral Home over on Tenth Avenue."

I inform Frank that it will please me no little to assist him in this matter and, as the sun is already wide awake, I take the note with the doll's name and address, pick up the check and head uptown in a Yellow to fetch one Madame Grimm.

Madame Grimm, it turns out, is a tiny doll with a wrinkled face the color of bonded bourbon and she dresses all in black except for a pair of big gold dangling earrings and a pendent of unusual design and many colors. When I show up at her shop on East 145th Street, she is all ready to go with a bag full of I-don't-know-what at her side and a large, ebony-skinned fellow in a pinstriped suit following behind her with several boxes of supplies under his arms.

They say nothing at all to me the whole ride down to Jimmy The Gent's funeral facility and I am feeling no little apprehension but do not wish to appear ungracious or offer any offense, so I mumble a few pleasantries then clam up myself.

We arrive at the undertaking parlor, which is close enough to the docks to smell of old fish, and upon being shown to the basement by Jimmy The Gent's personal mortician, we enter a small white room filled with all manner of chrome-plated equipment, where we find The Great Schupbach, Cyclone Murphy, Frank The Hat, Mutter and Rocks all gathered around a large table which holds a form much like a body. A sheet covers this form and one and all are very quiet and solemn as Madame Grimm reaches the table and, without so much as a How-do-you-do, whisks the cloth off the corpse of Fenton Appleby. Now I wish to state that corpses are never a breed I spend much time in the company of, but I am well aware they exude no little odor and it is a surprise to me that the smell coming off Appleby barely makes a dent in the fish stench, so I judge that The Great's foresight in chartering a refrigerated freight car is no small inspiration at that.

Madame Grimm motions us back from the table and begins pulling things out of her bag and her companion starts emptying out the boxes. I see an upside down cross and a small wooden platform that appears to be an altar of some sort and jars of different colored powders and packets of things and all manner of small cryptic figures carved from wood and I look over at my fellow witnesses and see that we are all most impressed at the array of provisions Madame Grimm bears.

After a few minutes of arranging things here and there, she has her majordomo light up a number of crooked looking black candles and she drapes an ornamental shawl round her and begins chanting in a most unfamiliar sounding tongue that seems mostly made up of growls, grunts and general throat clearing.

She rubs some powder on Appleby's feet and sprinkles a little glittery substance on his eyelids and it all goes along easy enough until she gets to the part where she disembowels a live frog and at that everyone ducks out but Jimmy The Gent's undertaker, who seems quite fascinated with the whole process and can be seen scribbling occasional notes on the sleeve of his lab coat.

Out in the hallway, lighting up cigars passed around by The Great, we commence to wipe the sweat from our brows and nervously stroll back and forth awaiting word from within. After some fifteen minutes, her man appears at the door and motions us in where we are no little astonished to see Fenton Appleby sitting up and, save a small bit of pallor around the gills, generally looking no worse for wear. Well, there is no shortage of shouting and glad handing and all manner of carrying on as The Great Schupbach gives Appleby an abbreviated account of his recent premature demise and resurrection. To everyone's general amazement, Appleby seems to have suffered no ill effects from his short deceasement and indeed, save a little stiffness of limb which he immediately begins working out by performing a quick buck and wing across the embalming room floor, looks like he can take the stage as promised for the evening's performance.

It is at that moment that Jimmy The Gent's mortician's assistant shows up, a somewhat dumpy doll with sad eyes and bad teeth, and tells us we must clear out as an argument in one of Jimmy's speaks ends badly for one participant and the room will soon be needed for an actual dead customer.

Madame Grimm, who packs her supplies during the hullabaloo and sends her manservant out with them to whistle up a cab, turns to Frank The Hat and says, "Remember what I tell you about his diet." and the words are barely out of her mouth when Fenton Appleby turns and takes a large bite out of the mortician's assistant's shoulder. Well, the dumpy doll commences to screaming no little and the blood starts spurting out of the silver dollar-sized hole in her wing and Appleby stands there calmly munching on a mouthful of her flesh with the smile of a gee savoring his first forkful of an onion slathered sirloin at Windy's.

The scene for the next few minutes is somewhat chaotic but the result is we strap Appleby to a gurney, however, before we can do anything for the dumpy doll, she up and croaks from shock and loss of blood, all of which is most embarrassing because now we must tell Jimmy The Gent we allow Appleby to use his employee as chow which Jimmy will undoubtedly view as taking no small liberty.

It turns out the conjure doll tells Frank earlier about the peculiar eating habits of reanimated corpses but he neglects to mention it beforehand figuring such news will be easier to digest once the miracle is performed. But the long and the short of it is that in order to remain resurrected, Appleby will need to feed regularly on human flesh. Without it, he will go gray and listless and, the conjure doll assures us, his performance on stage will no doubt suffer considerably.

The Great Schupbach is a bit put out at this news but after a few minutes says he reckons this is not the end of the world as Appleby's hunger for humans is probably a cheaper proposition than his hunger for a piece of the profits, so maybe this works out in The Great's favor anyway. Jimmy The Gent, who by this time arrives to sort out the situation with his munched-on mortician's assistant, agrees to supply The Great's newest star with an ample supply of fine dining as he is about to commence a rather large argument with some parties in Brooklyn and meat figures to be plentiful. Frank The Hat apologizes most profusely for the damage to Jimmy's employee, but Jimmy finds the prospect of immediate and complete body disposal to be a business advantage of no small value and he does not even fine Frank the price of a new lab coat.

Frank remembers Madame Grimm once explains that already dead flesh, so long as it is fresh, is an acceptable meal for the most part but that Appleby will require live food from time to time and Jimmy agrees to see what he can do in that regard and, at last, everyone parts blood-splattered friends.

This would be the end of the happy tale were it not for a couple of somewhat upsetting developments that occur. First, some hours later, while Fenton Appleby is slaying them in the aisles of the Booth Theater, Jimmy The Gent is helping his mortician chop up the argument victim into a variety of choice cuts, when the bitten assistant wakes up as a reanimated corpse herself and chews more than somewhat on the mortician's left leg. A series of quick phone calls establishes that once bitten, a party will return as a flesh-eating member of the living dead, or what the conjure doll refers to as a "zombie", and sure enough, before their third performance, Appleby takes a chomp out of his leading lady and by show time, she, too, is eyeing every living being backstage with a look on her pan like a starving hobo taking a hinge at a lunch wagon. It is quickly apparent that an epidemic is a very definite possibility and, despite his initial enthusiasm for the whole idea, The Great is unable to accept the situation he sees unfolding before him. So, being a civic-minded individual, The Great Schupbach calls a meeting of the Broadway Producers Association to announce that it is his sad duty to put these two actors in the ground before they infect anyone else.

I run into the Great himself a week later and he fills me in on the doings of the meeting. It seems that despite The Great Schupbach's disgust with the circumstances he has created, the rest of the impresarios listen with no little interest to the state of the affair and decide that the murder of innocent victims is indeed a small price to pay if it means an end to outrageous salary demands from actors. The Great argues against this most ferociously, but he is overruled and threatened with taking all of the heat if he does not get in line. In no time at all, a plan is put in place. As Broadway is always most full of aspiring thespians, it is decided that talented hopefuls will be infected and thus controlled, while annoying talentless bums and schleps will be devoured completely. Tourists are also marked as fair game for feasting providing their wallets have been emptied beforehand.

In order to enforce these standards, it is seen as necessary to have a squad of rough and readies to keep the zombies in line and, as it happens, this is a requirement of most fortuitous timing as the recent announcement of the coming end to Prohibition threatens to leave a good many likely lads without gainful employment. So the Broadway Producer's Association recruits a group of ex-rumrunners and the zombies are handled accordingly and, despite allowing them to munch on a copper now and then (strictly by accident the ex-leggers are quick to assure), the plan works quite well.

Unfortunately for The Great Schupbach, the despair he feels over loosing this pestilence upon his beloved Broadway makes it impossible for him to enjoy the Great success he has with his show. He commences to looking more haggard by the day and can be seen quite frequently skulking along Broadway muttering under his breath, "The horror, the horror is too Great!"

Of course, the situation requires some adjustment on the part of the Broadway regulars, as an accidental zombie attack is always a possibility but it takes very little time for the guys and dolls to come to terms with this fact just as they adapt to all of the many hazards of life in The Big Town. I later hear that some of the bookies are laying 6 to 5 that, with the way urban horrors keep piling up day in, day out, it will be ten years tops before most folks completely forget there are zombies on Broadway.

In fact, the only thing I notice personally is the feeling I get now when I hear that there is someone on Broadway looking to put the bite on me.

In some ancient South Pacific cultures, it was considered the finest of romantic gestures for a man to raise the dead of his bride-to-be. However, this practise has not updated well in our fast-paced modern world, as is illustrated in the following piece...

ZoMBIE and SPiCE

by Patrick Thomas

It's rare that the Department of Mystic Affairs gets called in on a stalker case. I hate to call enduring the attentions of someone off in the head mundane, but it usually was. Folks with mystic power tend to skip obsessive fantasies in favor of making their sick dreams a reality. The perp in this one just hadn't managed to make that jump yet. Hopefully we'd catch him before he could.

What makes this case a little odder is not only did I ask for it, I threatened to quit if I didn't get it. The woman at the center of the depraved attention had never met me, but I owed her. I took away something from her life that could never be replaced.

When my partner and I arrived at Lucy Paxton's home, she invited Mandi and I in for coffee. If the DMA hadn't given me a new face when they recruited me, she would have never let us in the front door.

"I have to say I'm surprised that Federal agents were sent in to help me. Before this, I could barely get the cops to take me seriously," Lucy said.

"This was a little bit out of their realm of expertise, but falls squarely in ours," I said. Every night for the past week, someone had sent Lucy a gift. The last three were zombies. The first was a rat, the second a squirrel, and the last a raccoon. It took two animal control officers and four cops to take down the raccoon. When we stopped by the morgue on our way here its dismembered body was still moving. At least the locals were smart enough to separate the body parts into stainless steel containers. Three of the men were bit by the living dead rodent and were terrified they were going to become zombies. When I explained to them it didn't work like that, one of them offered to name his first born child after me. I declined. Karver was a bad enough name for me to bear, let alone an innocent kid.

"I have to admit, I'd never even heard of the Department of Mystic Affairs before," Lucy said.

"Most people don't hear about us until they need us," said Mandi. It wasn't like we were a secret agency, but most of the cases we deal with seem to only be reported on in the tabloids.

"Do you have any idea who has been stalking you?" I asked.

"I've been over this with the police. I have no idea of his name, but I have seen him a few times. He's got a medium build with dark short hair."

"That's not much to go on," Mandi said.

"I know," she said. "How did he send those animals after me?"

"There are different ways of raising the dead," I said. Not all of them were limited to zombies, but Lucy didn't need to hear that. If this guy was a necromancer, the danger for this poor woman was enormous. "We're going to stake out your house and see if we can catch him or his next present. We'll get a better idea of what he can do then."

"Wouldn't it be better to find that out before then?" she asked.

"Of course, but life's rarely that easy," answered my partner. Lucy wrapped her arms around both her shoulders and shuttered. Mandi's an empath and it was obvious she was confused by the emotions coming off our victim. "Are you okay?"

"No," Lucy admitted honestly. "I want to kill this guy."

"Normal enough feelings," said Mandi.

"No, not for doing this to me. Not entirely anyway. For using a raccoon. Raccoons were Winnie's favorite. She had more than a dozen stuffed ones."

"Winnie?" asked Mandi.

"She was my daughter."

Mandi glared at me as the name Winnie Paxton clicked in her head.

"She was killed by the serial killer Carver," said Lucy. The lady was tough. Her eyes got runny but she didn't let a single tear escape. "It must be rough for you, Agent Karver, to have to go through life with the same name."

I didn't point out the difference in spelling. It was the only way they'd let me use the name.

"It's a burden." But one I choose to bear so I never forget what that demon forced me to do.

"When they gave him the death penalty, I thought it would help. I even went and witnessed the execution." I stopped myself from saying I know. I wasn't there, but I saw the video of my supposed death and all the faces of those who came to watch. "But killing him didn't bring back my little girl. And now this stalker is messing with the only thing I have left of my little girl—my memories."

"I won't let him hurt you. I promise," I said.

"Ms. Paxton, will you excuse us? We need to examine the perimeter of your house to determine to best way to secure the area," said Mandi.

"Of course," she said.

I followed Mandi outside. I didn't need to be an empath to know she was pissed.

"You volunteered us for a case involving the mother of one of your victims? And didn't mention it to me?"

"I took away her daughter. She's in danger. I owe her that much," I said.

"The seriál demon killed her."

"Using my body," I said.

"It wasn't your fault," said Mandi. I remained silent. I had been told that, time and time again, after the DMA had pulled me off death row and exorcised the demon. Logically what they said made sense. Logic only goes so far. There was no way for me to fully explain that to anyone, even Mandi. My only answer was silence. "How'd you get Sarge to agree?" Deputy Director Winston of the DMA had started out his career as an army sergeant in WWI and somewhere along the way Sarge replaced his real name. Then again, Carver was the name the media gave me in my old life. It's my only name in my new one, with the one minor spelling change.

"I can be very persuasive," I said. Mandi tilted her head. "I used guilt and when that didn't work, I begged."

"You?" Mandi said. "I've never seen you beg for anything."

"Been saving it," I said. "Too bad the same can't be said for you."

Mandi raised an eyebrow and glared at me. "Begging?"

"No, saving yourself. I mean, you're the only woman I know that sailors follow from port to port instead of the other way around," I teased.

"Anything to support our troops. Now that you've started begging, don't stop. It might actually help you get a date that you don't have to inflate."

"Say what you will about Belinda Blowup, but she has the most amazing pair of balloons. And when I fill her with helium and take some out of the nozzle, I can make noises for the both of us," I said.

We did a perimeter check. Typical suburban house, a small lawn in front, a little yard in back. We set up infrared alarms along her fence line so we'd know if anything came through the back. We gave Lucy a radio that tied directly into the earsets we both wore and parked our car a couple houses away. Her home was at a T-intersection, so we had three blocks to watch.

We had thermoses filled with coffee, soup, plus the traditional box of doughnuts. Nothing happened for the first several hours except our food supply got low. Around nine o'clock in the evening Mandi pointed to a little girl in a dress coming down the bottom of the T. "Something's wrong."

"Not all kids have a curfew," I said.

"That's not it. I'm getting no emotions off of her," said Mandi.

Then I felt the slightest tingle on the back of my neck. My time as a possessed left me will the ability to sense different types of magic. Those involving Hell or demons I'm most sensitive to. If the girl was a demon or possessed herself, I would have known she was coming long before we could see her.

"I think it's a dead girl walking," I said.

The demon also enhanced my eyesight. As soon as the girl in the pink dress passed beneath a streetlight, my heart skipped a beat.

"It's Winnie. The bastard raised her daughter," I said, getting out of the car. A rage that wasn't entirely this sicko's fault took me over.

"Karver, get back in here. The raiser could be anywhere. We don't want to give away our position," said Mandi.

I was beyond listening. One of my dead was walking and I had to stop Winnie before her mother saw her or the emotional damage on Lucy would be something I couldn't imagine.

When I got close enough to the zombie child, I realized I didn't have a plan. Protocol dictates the best way to stop a zombie is to dismember them and separate the pieces. I had already sliced up this little girl once. Even though I carried two blades under the back of my coat, I couldn't bring myself to use them on her. Not again.

I needed another option. There was a sedan between me and the girl. I used my gun to smash open the driver's window and pull the trunk release. It popped and I opened it all the way. Zombies are not terribly creative. If Winnie's raiser had just told her to go to her mother's house, she'd only attack me if I tried to stop her. The magic used to raise and hold zombies together makes them very strong. There was a very good chance Winnie was stronger than me, so I had to be careful. I waited until she was near the trunk and grabbed her around the waist, spun her and threw her into the trunk, slamming the lid down hard.

The metal wouldn't hold her long. I could already hear her pounding against it.

Which is when the sensor alarm went off.

"Karver, he's heading in the back. I'm going after him," said Mandi.

I ran back toward the house, pulling out my gun in one hand and one of my knives with the other. I could hear Mandi shooting at something in the backyard. I assumed it was similar to what greeted me in the front.

A zombie pit-bull ran to intercept me. I swung my blade at the canine neck and sliced the undead head clean off. Each of my blades was covered with some pretty powerful runes, which made slicing and dicing much easier. I picked the head up and threw it up into a tree. I got lucky—it stuck on the first throw, but wouldn't stay up there long. The jaws were moving, trying to knock itself free. The body tried to run away from me, so I shot out two legs. That slowed it down enough for me to slice off the other two. I threw the pieces onto nearby roofs where three of them landed in rain gutters. I picked the body up and impaled it high up on Lucy's fence post. I hoped that would make it harder for the parts to reunite.

I charged the front door, smashing it in. The enhanced strength and durability the demon had given my body for its dark deeds did come in handy.

The stalker had already reached Lucy, who had curled up in the fetal position on her kitchen floor. The man who thought zombies were a sign of love was cradling her head on his lap and petting her head like she was a dog. He had a long slim, knife with a black hilt and carvings of its own pressed against her throat. Her eyeglasses lay thrown to the side of the floor.

Mandi had already gotten in. My partner had her gun drawn, but neither of us had a shot, especially since a mystic knife might not even have to cut Lucy to kill her.

I could feel the calming emotions Mandi was sending out at the stalker, but the propathic stuff didn't always work so well with the crazies.

"You two can leave us. My girlfriend and I would like to spend some quality time together," said the stalker.

"Can't do that," said Mandi. "Federal agents."

"Let go of the knife and move away from Lucy," I ordered.

"We just want to be alone. Why can't you see that?" the stalker said.

"I'm not sure Lucy is with you on that," I said.

"That's why I brought this." Stalker was indicating his knife. "One stab into the dead and they rise to obey me. If I use it on the living, they become a zombie too. Lucy will have to love me then. I'll make her."

"Actually, I think Lucy really does like you," said Mandy. Stalker looked at Lucy, wanting to believe her, but not able to take trembling in terror as a sign of affection. "It's just all the dead animals scared her. We girls are kind of frightened of dead things, you know how it is."

"I guess," conceded the stalker, distracted enough by the conversation to let me get behind an appliance island. He couldn't pick up that Mandi was putting out enough trust to let a known crooked politician get re-elected,

"I'm sure Lucy would be interested if you'd just take it slower," suggested Mandi. "Wouldn't you, Lucy?"

Lucy was terrified but she wasn't dumb. "I might be." The words might have been more convincing if she hadn't stammered.

"Most woman want traditional courting. Poetry, flowers, that kind of thing," hinted Mandi, her eyes subtly darting to a nearby counter.

Stalker looked up to see the flowers my partner had stolen a look at. He got a half smile and reached up for them, loosening his grip on his hostage. I leapt over the counter, landing with my knees on the stalker's chest. I had holstered my gun while I hid and used my free hand to grab his wrist. This loser had normal human strength so it wasn't hard to pull the knife away from Lucy's throat.

"Move!" I yelled. Lucy did. I smashed the hilt of my blade into the stalker's nose. There was a satisfying crunch as the cartilage broke and I was able to pull the zombifying blade free.

"You're under arrest. You have the right to remain silent"" I started to say but was distracted.

"Winnie?" said Lucy. The zombie that once was her daughter stood in the smashed in doorway.

"I thought you might want to start a family again sweetheart," said the stalker with a very nasal tone from his crushed nose. Lucy's eyes were so clouded with grief, hope, and the sight of her fondest wish come true that she hadn't noticed the traces of degeneration around her daughter's face and the open wounds on her knuckles from punching her way out of the trunk. The lack of eyeglasses probably didn't hurt either.

"Let me go or I'll order her own daughter to kill her," said the stalker.

"Not a chance," I said. "Besides I'm the one with the knife now." This clown had no magic of his own that I could sense. Everything came from the knife. Without it, there was a good chance he was powerless and I could control her since I had the blade.

"The one who used the blade has the power, not the one who holds it," he said. "Winnie, kill Mommy, honey. We'll raise her like you later."

The little girl moved toward her mother. So much for my neutering theory.

I put my knife against the stalker's throat. "Tell her to stop or I'll kill you."

"A fed kill a suspect in cold blood? Right," he said.

I already had too many dead and it might not stop him. Plus, spilling blood when necromancy was in progress was never the best of ideas. If he did succeed in making Winnie kill her mother, my principles might just go out the window.

Mandi was lining up an explosive round aimed right at Winnie's chest.

"No!" I shouted and put myself between mother and zombie daughter. "Winnie, don't do this. This bad man wants to hurt your mommy. You don't want that, do you?" I knew Winnie's spirit had long since moved on, but the body held some of those memories. Hopefully it would be enough. Lucy didn't need to endure the sight of us blowing up or slicing her daughter's body to pieces. It is a memory that would never fade and made the ones I had forced her to carry that much worse.

I made a foolish mistake. In my efforts to protect Lucy, I had taken my eyes off her stalker. So had Mandi. He used our distraction to grab a kitchen knife and then use it to again grab Lucy.

"Winnie, get them and rip their limbs off," he ordered.

I was no mage, but I held the zombie-making blade in front of me and focused every once of will I had into it. "Winnie, don't."

The little zombie girl in the pink dress stopped. I felt a surge of power from the black blade. Something was happening.

"Kill them, I said!" the stalker screamed.

"Winnie, do the right thing," I said.

The little zombie girl turned and moved toward her raiser who was her mother's stalker. With a burst of speed that even I had trouble following, she broke the man's arm that held the knife as she flipped him down to the ground. With a stomp of her left foot she crushed the stalker's right knee. With both hands she grabbed his left shin and twisted, ripping the hip asunder as easy as if it were the leg on a baked chicken. The stalker's screams were loud, shrill and inspired absolutely no pity in me.

"Winnie, that's enough," I said, whispering into the hilt of the zombifying blade as if it were a microphone. The little girl zombie looked up at me. Looking in those dead eyes, one of my victim's eyes, made me more nauseous than I've ever been in my new life.

Lucy had watched everything as if in shock, but she finally started to move, her eyes blinking. "Winnie, is that you?"

I spoke softly into the hilt: "Nod"

Winnie shook her head.

"I've missed you so much," said Lucy, opening her arms.

"Gently hug your mother," I whispered.

Winnie complied. Lucy held her little zombie daughter and wept. "I love you so much, Winnie."

"Kiss your mommy goodbye and then go wait outside," I said. Winnie complied.

"Baby, wait! Come back!" Lucy pleaded.

Mandi stepped in. "Ms. Paxton, your stalker raised your daughter as a zombie, planning to use her to hurt you. We were just lucky—"

"—That your daughter's love for you was so strong that she was able to disobey the evil man who did this to her," I said. Mandi gave me a look and a smile.

"Can't I see her again? Can't she stay with me a little while?" begged Lucy.

"I'm sorry, Ms. Paxton, but there is no telling when the magic animating her will wear off. She'll collapse back into how she was before. You've been through enough. You don't need to see that." No parent should ever have to see their child die once, let alone twice.

"Her love was really strong enough to break the evil spell?" asked Lucy, looking to Mandi for reassurance.

"Yes. I've never seen anything like it. You have one very special daughter," said Mandi.

Lucy began weeping, a mix of joy, grief, and pride with a smattering of hope that her daughter lived on in a world beyond, then collapsed into Mandi's arms.

We called an ambulance for the stalker, whose name was Horace

Cuomo. He had to undergo twelve hours of surgery to get his hip turned back around. The doctors would later tell us he'd never walk right again. However he refused to give up to us who had given him the zombifying blade. He was more afraid of them than he was of us. We gathered the animal zombie pieces I had cut off and the ones Mandi had shot up and put them in canisters for the locals to cart off. The dog head I put in the tree had fallen and managed to crawl to the fence where the torso was impaled, but wasn't able to climb the pickets to reattach itself. Danté Amato, a necromancer from the D.C. office of the DMA, was coming in to de-animate them.

We told Lucy I was going to lay her daughter back down to rest. She ran into her daughter's room and came out with a stuffed raccoon. "Please give this to her in case that bastard took the one she was buried with. Winnie could never sleep well without at least one of her racoons."

"I will," I said and walked outside. My partner followed.

"I'm going to stay with the victim a little while," said Mandi. Her powers were helpful when it came to cleaning up the emotional wreckage. "Do you think Winnie's spirit really saved her mother?"

I shrugged.

"You don't, do you?"

"I'd like to, but no," I said.

"Then what did it? It wasn't because you were holding the blade." Mandi had tested the theory by trying to tell the little zombie to go around the side of the house so her mother wouldn't see her again. Winnie ignored her.

"Necromancy was used to bring her back. Who would have more power over a zombie—the one who raised her or…?"

"The one who killed her," finished my partner with a sigh. Mandi knew I wasn't much for physical contact. It brought back too many of the bad things I did because of my demonic hitchhiker. Yet, she leaned forward and kissed me on the cheek.

"Why'd you do that?" I asked. I wasn't complaining. Mandi's the only real friend I had in the world these days. It felt good.

"You could have stopped the zombie, but instead risked your own neck to help give the mother closure," said Mandi.

"I risked yours, too," I said.

"It was worth the risk," she said.

"No insult or dig?" I said.

"Not this time, partner. I'm too damn proud of you," Mandi said. "You want company taking Winnie back? At least until Danté gets there to de-animate her?"

I shook my head. "I need to do it myself." Mandi handed me the car keys. "Don't need them."

Mandi looked confused. "You never even asked the mother where they buried her daughter. You don't know, do you?"

"Sure I do." I pointed. "About a mile and a half that way. I know where all my dead are buried." After I got a new chance at life, I visited the graves of each one of my dead. It didn't begin to make amends, but it was something I had to do.

Mandi nodded. The sun wouldn't rise for a few hours. I walked around to where Winnie stood waiting in the bushes and put out my hand. The zombie took it.

"This is from your mother. She loves you very much." I handed the dead girl the stuffed animal. "I'm very sorry for what I did. I'd give my own life to undo it."

The little girl zombie looked at me unblinking. I wasn't really expecting an answer or forgiveness. I wasn't worthy of either. All I could do was go on and do the best I could and, after Danté turned her back into a corpse again, bury the little girl I had killed for a second time.

Aside from providing the valuable service of reducing the population to a more manageable size, do the cannibalistic walking dead serve a higher purpose? In this stand-alone sequel to his "The Dead Bear Witness," Mr. Chambers sets out to explore this and other biting questions!

THE DEAD IN THEiR MASSeS

by James Chambers

1.

TURNED OUT LOHATCHIE was a long way off and the road there a hard bastard with a chip on its shoulder. Took us damn near two months to reach Florida, and by then the drive in my mind that had been so clear in the days after we broke out of prison had gone dormant. The longer we wandered silent roads inhabited only by the rotting undead, the more I felt like a helpless pariah caught between a killing field and an infinite and hating sky. The total absence of aerial clutter and mechanical noise of any kind—and of any human life other than our own—hammered home the isolation and loneliness.

Thing was we had a place to go, a safe place to call home, dig in, and weather the worst to come in a world lurching toward perfect desolation—if only we could get there.

I felt pretty good about our chances, at least up until the morning Della almost died and we detoured down that road west of Jacksonville, that ribbon of snakeskin pavement looking for all the world like a place where not even the slitbacks bothered roaming. The desolation should've tipped us off right away, because no matter where you go, they're always there, least a few of them, and it never takes much time for more to come shambling along once they catch wind of you. Nowhere is ever really clean of the living dead.

That fact kept us moving even on those bone-weary nights when all we wanted was to curl up in our fatigue and sleep a day all the way through. But stick around one place too long and the slitbacks always root you out, and before you know it they drum up a hungry mob with an appetite for living flesh. So we stopped mostly during daylight, a few hours at a time to forage for supplies, food, fuel, whatever, before lighting out again. We lived like nomads, a trio of warm-blooded ghosts haunting a dead world. Everywhere we faced mazes of streets and highways clogged with ruined vehicles; we traveled through burnt-out ghost towns populated by hordes of the dead that forced us to double back sometimes hundreds of miles looking for another way.

Mason's car held up well despite the beating it took from bad roads and slitback assaults, and I was grateful for it. Della and I owed Mason for his kindness, and knowing we could never repay him ate away at me. In the long run, could be life would've gone easier with Mason still around, but then again maybe not. He and I got along fine toward the end, but that bond was born of friction from back when he was a guard and I was a prisoner. An uneasy trust at best. No telling what might've come of a rivalry for Della stoking those old coals, but probably she and I never would have fallen for each other, not with Mason there, rugged and all-star handsome, a man with a clean record and a gentle touch, and fearlessness burning in his eyes.

That's all looking back, mind you. None of it crossed my mind before Mason died. Did my honest best to save him that morning, but sometimes luck just breaks yours balls.

I tried hard to find meaning in Mason's death, some silver lining for the dark cloud losing him brought, but in the end there wasn't any. Mason had been a good man and he deserved a better death, but then the dead are supposed to stay that way when they die, too. These days what *should be* and what *is* are like a pair of bitter ex-lovers. They haven't been on speaking terms since before I did thirty days in solitary courtesy of the late Warden Lane Grove and emerged to a world filled by reanimated corpses.

The night Mason, Della, and I escaped Grove's prison, we crossed the woods to Mason's bungalow on a cul-de-sac about twenty miles west. Took about six hours and along the way we dodged or cut down more than a couple dozen of the walking dead. Mason proved as good as his word, though. He put us up, fed us, supplied us with weapons and a car, and we spent a couple of weeks there, planning our trip to my Lohatchie hideaway, a cabin deep in the Everglades, far and away from anything resembling society.

By the time we rolled out a few slitbacks had taken up watch in the neighboring yards. They sensed us nearby but they couldn't find us, not as long as we stayed careful about keeping hidden. We waited as long as was safe before hitting the road, and then with the roar of the engine thundering in the quiet, out we drove, running down the new American dream: living long enough to reach a three-room swamp shack where no one was likely to ever come knocking on the door. We just wanted to live, pass the time as we liked, and not be smothered by the crush of the damned masses.

I used to rob banks and Mason used to herd convicts; neither one of us had much purpose in the new world. Only Della had anything worthwhile to offer; she was a nurse, a good one. She bandaged me up once after I sliced open my forearm smashing the back window of a gun shop; she soothed Mason through three nights of burning fever and back onto his feet after a leg wound he got climbing through a wrecked storefront became infected.

Four days later, he died.

It happened at a gas station in some pisswater town where the post office and the firehouse shared a building. We were a day's drive off our route, skirting a slitback-infested toll plaza on the main road. The town should've been empty of both the dead and the living, but like I said, no place is every really free of the slitbacks. Mason went scavenging for guns and tools in the trunk of a police cruiser and found a hungry corpse instead. The blind, legless thing propelled itself on its hands, dripping a trail of ripe intestines and tacky viscera, dropping its liver like a black, bloated egg. It latched onto Mason's face, dug its cracked teeth into his cheek, and gnawed. Mason yelled for help and fired his gun. Five or six rounds punched craters of putrid flesh and blood out the thing's back, but it held tight.

Della and I, thirty yards away at the gas pumps, saw it all and came running, while Mason staggered in circles and struggled to break free. Della tugged on the corpse by the ragged end of its filthy shirt, and I planted my shotgun between Mason's chest and the slitback's neck and fired. Mason flinched and howled through the blast. The dead body tore away, hit concrete, and then hopped around blind on its flapping arms, launching gobs of bloody sludge from the stump of its neck. The fucking head held fast, though, and way too close to Mason to risk another shot from the scattergun, so instead I pounded it with the stock, hoping to rupture it like a rotten pumpkin. A patch of bone the size of coffee can lid cracked loose and pinwheeled away, exposing an oil slick of rotten gray matter.

That's when the eye popped open and glared at me past the jagged edges of the busted skull. Pure white with an iris the color of desert sand, an eye where none should be. It blinked twice from between folds of necrotic brain tissue, watching me like a wounded fox watches a wolf. The heat of its gaze crawled over me with palpable attention, repulsive beyond anything I'd yet experienced among the living the dead. I poked the barrel of my automatic into the eye and fired, bursting the head in a splash of black and red.

Mason swatted at the remains and clawed at his face, sweeping away chunks of fetid meat and putrescence. He dropped to his knees, threw up, and when his stomach hit empty, he fell over on his back, his chest heaving, blood dribbling from his wounded cheek.

Della knelt beside him and stemmed the bleeding with a clean cloth from her kit; she sanitized it and packed it with gauze. Bad as it looked, the wound was superficial, and it certainly didn't dampen Mason's spirit. He shouted some mighty colorful phrases whenever Della's ministrations stung him the way good doctoring often does.

I found a stick lying in the grass and used it to sift through the quivering remnants of the head. The largest chunk of brain splattered there on the pavement shimmied for a second, rippled, and then sprouted another cold eye. It blinked once and looked right at me, its gaze hitting me like a cold breath, leaving me feeling sick and poisoned, until I drove the tip of the stick into the pupil, popped it, and then I flicked the whole mess into the tall weeds beyond the edge of the parking lot.

Della's screams snapped me back to the matter at hand. It shouldn't have happened the way it did. Mason would've survived his wound, but weeks of fear and running day and night had taken their toll on all of us. That, and the sight of those crazy eyes, one of which Della had glimpsed just before I destroyed it, had shaken us up.

No excuses, though. We got sloppy.

It was too late before I even turned around.

We'd forgotten to destroy the torso. Attracted by Mason's blood it crept up beside Della and shoved her aside. With its ribcage leaking a tail of dead organs, the thing clamped fly-like onto Mason and drove one of its splintery hands into his chest. It dug in hard, ripping up cords of flesh as it excavated Mason's heart and raised it toward a phantom head, driven by instinct to feed though the act was now impossible. I managed half a dozen running strides, my eyes fixed on the living organ, crimson and fat, pumping uselessly in the slitback's gray, dead fingers and glistening in the morning sun as it washed the concrete with steaming blood. Mason screamed and then his voice died in a heartbeat.

I gathered Della and her kit and rushed her back to the car. Nothing more we could do for Mason, and we already had enough gas loaded to reach the next town. Best thing was to get clear before more slitbacks turned up looking for fresh meat. It was the right move, the only move, but that didn't stop Della from swearing me up and down and calling me a coward for it or from punching me hard enough to leave bruises. I weathered her storm until we made it outside of town, and then afraid to lose control of the car, I pulled over on the grassy shoulder.

Della jumped out and slammed the door.

Let her work it out, get her thoughts together, and see how it is when she comes back, I thought. This little hard patch could get tricky fast. What if Della didn't see things as they'd been? What if she harbored some delusion that we could've saved Mason if we'd stayed? It would put a fine and irreparable crack in the bond between us, her waiting for the moment I might abandon her to save my own skin and no way for me to persuade her otherwise. I waited out Della's rage in the car, kept watch for slitbacks, and rubbed the aches Della had planted in my arm and chest.

She cried awhile, and her body shook with sobs. I saw her in the rearview mirror, one hand planted on the trunk holding herself up, her tangled, black hair draping her face. She spun around, screamed some more, kicked at something in the road, and then after awhile she rubbed the tears away and came back to the car. The stark redness in her eyes frightened me.

"I'm sorry," she said.

"Yeah. Me, too."

"It's just that we both know that didn't have to happen," she said.

"No, it didn't. We fucked up. We let Mason down, and now he's gone," I said. "Ain't gonna do us any good to break down over it. Not saying we shouldn't mourn him. He was our friend and a good one. But let's take this little experience as an object lesson about letting circumstances get the best of us."

Della looked wired, ready to fly off the handle again, to hit me some more and go on working out her anger, but instead she sucked down a few deep breaths, settled into her seat, and said, "Fuck it, you're right. Let's get away from here. Far away. Fast."

I gunned the engine and we drove in silence.

The barren road rolled away under our wheels and a burning sun marked our passage.

Couple miles later, Della said, "Shit, Cornell, we have to go back and burn him. I can't stand the idea of him becoming a slitback."

"We go back, we'll be just as dead as Mason," I said. "All that commotion and spilled blood probably pricked up the senses of every hungry corpse in a five-mile radius. Besides it's not Mason getting up, just his body. Mason's dead and gone now and free of all this bullshit."

Della sniffled and asked, "You think that's true? Like our souls go free when we die?"

That wasn't exactly what I'd said so I didn't answer. I'd never wasted much thought on whether or not souls even existed let alone what happened to them now that the dead walked the earth. Figured we all got the answer to that question sooner or later, so why waste time on idle speculation? Better to live in the moment, do what you needed to get by. Whatever the answer, I didn't want to think there could be any human part left in those shambling nightmares that plagued us.

"I'm gonna miss him," Della said.

"Yeah, me too," I told her.

Neither of us mentioned Mason again for several days, giving the wound time to scab over a bit, and as cold as it may seem to be thinking of such things only minutes after losing a good friend, I knew the moment when Della got back in the car that she and I were going to wind up much closer than we ever would have if Mason had lived. Didn't feel quite right to me then but I knew it would later. Maybe if I'd saved Mason nothing would've ever sparked up between us, and we might've avoided that lonely detour from the road home and into some of the worst business I've ever witnessed among the living or the dead.

So much for learning our lesson.

2.

MY FEAR OF losing Della tripped us up.

Time was I had a good woman at my side, but that was back when the world was still a place for the living. Evelyn had been one of a kind, and in no way was Della a substitute for a past love. Had Evelyn and my child growing inside her lived, we would've married, maybe even gone straight, and my life would've followed a very different path—but then I might never have become the kind of man who could survive in a world ruled by death. Whatever. I'd made my peace with Evelyn's ghost and we were square, and aside from a passing resemblance in the right light, Della and Evelyn had nothing in common. What I grew to feel for her was a different creature altogether than what I'd felt for Evelyn.

I'd never once felt an urge to shelter Evelyn from the violence and danger around us. Hell, half the time she was the one looking out for me on a job, making our relationship a true marriage of equals. With Della, we were equals in a different way, because there was something in her character that made me want to shield her. Not that she needed it. She was smart, tough, and dangerous when she needed to be, but that didn't change how I felt. And it didn't help that Della went along with it, maybe to humor me, or because it made her feel good to have a protector, or maybe because it made her feel just a little bit normal again to be playing boy-meets-girl like in the old days.

Whatever the explanation, that feeling was why I made her wait in the car while I raided the police station in that suburb west of Jacksonville. I was hunting ammunition or equipment, expecting little since that part of the place was blackened by fire and the rest looked pretty well looted. Figured I'd be in and out, fifteen minutes tops. Della and I had foraged together like that dozens of times, and there was no real reason to keep her out of it that morning—except for what had happened the night before.

About a week and a half after Mason died, things flared up between us. The night before Della and I reached Baker County we camped out in a highway rest stop, nesting in a back office with cinderblock walls, high small windows, and a solid, metal door, a place we could secure long enough to get some shut-eye. Sleep had been our plan, but sitting there in the silver moonlight, letting the tension flow out of us for the first time in days, we tumbled together as if driven by gravity. Our lips grasped in long kisses that sent shivers through our bodies. We spread out some blankets, stripped, and placed our clothes on top of them to pad the icy tile floor, and then eased into the furnace of each other's heat.

Della felt firm and smooth and I relished her touch. There was something extraordinary in the pure silence that surrounded us, broken only by the delicate sounds we made, the gentle susurrus of our breaths, the whispers of our skin rubbing together, and our little half-voiced moans of joy. It lasted quite awhile with each of us sparking the other through the ebb and flow of desire as we sought out tiny, hidden pleasures and catalyzed a strange chemistry that blended the nervous excitement of our first time with the unexpected comfort of familiarity. Knowing death waited on just about every inch of ground we had to cover, in every second we had to live, bred intensity. All that, of course, plus our conviction that we might genuinely be the last living man and woman in the world. I hadn't expected to ever experience something like that and I don't think Della had either. If that had marked our last night alive, I suspect neither one of us would have been wholly dissatisfied.

The affect was powerful. It opened my eyes to the prospect of something more than an endless struggle to take another breath, to travel another mile, to see another sunrise. I viewed Della in a different light after that, and the singular dread of the slitbacks I had lived with for so long now had company: my fear of losing Della, of letting her down like I had Mason.

That's why I made her wait in the car.

That's why the breath whooshed out of me and my blood froze when I came back empty-handed from the police station and saw she was gone.

3.

IN THE FIRST few days after we escaped prison Della kept to herself. She did her fair share of work and lobbed occasional bursts of sarcasm at me or Mason or toward men in general, but primarily she passed the time in restless contemplation. None of us felt like talking much, but to stave off boredom Mason and I got to know one another over nightly card games. Mason pretty much knew all there was to know about me, that I was a bank robber and a smartass, so it worked out he did most of the talking.

He'd been a high school athlete banking on a college scholarship until he destroyed his knee senior year. Wound up working odd jobs for a few years until he fell in love with a woman who made him want a better life. Except the only steady work he could get was at the prison, and as much as he hated it, he took the job because he had to.

Ironic, that. Mason's prison job made possible the life he wanted, but when the time came the prison could've saved his family, it didn't. Mason never forgave Warden Grove for turning away a busload of survivors who begged for shelter at the prison gates, a group that included Mason's wife and the rest of his family.

That was the difference between me and Mason.

He'd bought into the game, played by the rules, and worked hard for everything he had, but when it mattered most the rules changed and stole everything he valued. On the other hand, I'd never given a good goddamn for all that; everything I'd ever had, I'd taken for myself, and when I lost it all, I lost it on my own. And that, I believe, is why despite the fact that Mason and I became fair friends in the short time we knew each other, deep down he never completely trusted me. Considering how I let him die, maybe he'd been right.

Della had her saga, too. Morning we left for Lohatchie she caught Mason and me off guard when she opened up from the back seat and gave us forty miles worth of personal history. She finally let on why she'd been so skittish around us. She'd been married twice and divorced twice before the dead rose, and she hadn't known many honorable men along the way. Just her father and her brother, both killed in accidents years ago. She'd been waiting to see what kind of price she'd have to pay for living in Mason's house, for the protection he and I provided. Would it be me or Mason first to steal into her room in the dead of night and demand a pound of her flesh? When days passed and neither one of us laid a finger on her it confused her until she saw that whatever darkness Mason and I might have buried inside us, none of it was the kind that worried her. She talked about how she'd grown up dreaming of being a doctor, plans derailed by her father's death, and how both her husbands had abused and cheated her, and how she'd finally beaten her second husband into a coma with a tire iron the last time he came after her with that warning gleam in his eyes and a leather belt in his hands. She moved in with a girlfriend after that and worked her way through nursing school before she wound up at the prison.

No small irony there, either, Della working to heal a bunch of men no better and many of them far worse than the men who had damaged her so harshly. It was a living, though, and she'd planned to stay there only until she could get work at one of the local hospitals.

"And now I think I hope we might live through this," she said at the end. "Which is something I didn't back at the prison when I wished every single one of you crazy bastards playing your power games and mind-fucking each other would be wiped off the face of the earth along with the goddamned, stinking slitbacks."

Mason and I took that as a compliment. In fact, we started laughing so hard at the idea that the two of us had restored Della's faith in the future of humanity that Mason had to pull the car over. The three of us got out by the side of the road and gasped for air until the uproar died down to a quiet chuckle. Della saw the humor in what she had said as clear as we did, and that was the first time I felt like we were all together, all three of us moving in the same direction, and I felt pretty good about it, kind of like the old days of me and Evelyn blazing a trail of robbery from state to state, making headlines and scribing a big *fuck you* to the law.

Miles further down the road, though, embraced in the kind of quiet that often chases such a moment, I considered Della's time trapped in the prison after the dead began to walk, one of only three women among hundreds of men, and I wondered what she went through. Had Warden Grove lived up to his high and mighty ideals, warped as they were, and seen to the safety of Della and the other ladies? Even if he had, could he have protected them every hour of every day they were there trapped inside? Knowing all that, letting the weight of it sink into me during the days when Della, Mason, and I grew comfortable enough to stand one another's company day and night with barely enough privacy to take a piss was just another part of what made the thing that happened between me and her so overwhelming.

The empty passenger seat in Mason's car ran me through like a pike. I sprinted across the street and shouted for Della. The car looked clean. The doors were closed. Della's shotgun was gone. Hope flickered inside me. I clambered onto the front hood for a better view of the street, searched in every direction, called Della's name.

Nothing.

A dry breeze swept trash and debris along the vacant street. I waited for it to die down and then listened.

Voices and the grumbling of a car engine came from the distance. My heart raced. Then a shotgun blast reverberated among the abandoned streets, booming and declarative as if its echoes alone might bring the buildings crumbling down.

I leapt from the car and bolted toward the nearest intersection, in the direction of the gunshot. Around the corner and halfway down the next block Della stood on the steps of a cathedral, her shotgun raised to her shoulder, a patch of silver smoke spreading from its barrels. The shadow of a high steeple obscured her face and cloaked her target, but as I ran closer the two bodies took shape—one dead and unmoving sprawled atop another twitching slowly beneath it, the two of them clasped in a foul embrace on the granite steps of the cathedral. The top one had been alive before Della shot him. Blood gushed from his neck, making islands of the scattered bits of his head on the gray tablet of the church stairs. The dead man had his pants down around his ankles, the pale flesh of his rear stuck up in the air. Somehow he'd managed to strap a gag around the mouth of the armless slitback beneath him so he could tend to his business.

"Sick, fucking bastard," I hissed.

Della snapped alert at the sound of my voice and waved her gun before she recognized me and lowered it.

"You all right?" I asked.

"I heard him howling," she said, shaking a little, her voice rising to a shriek. "Kind of cheering, whooping it up. It's been so long since we saw anyone living I thought I should check it out. And this is what I find. Goddamn it all, months go by and we don't see another living soul, and then this is the shit I have to come out here and see!"

She cried. I wrapped my arm around her shoulder and pressed her face to my neck. We held each other and started walking, as I steered us away from the cathedral.

"You did the right thing," I told her. "If he'd seen you, no telling what he might've done. Man like that can't be right in the head. You know what I mean? He's better off dead. You did him a favor."

Halfway down the block, I looked back to see the dead man jolt upright, the skin of his face hanging inside out over his chest like a soiled bib. His slitback partner got up, too, and then they played out a pitiful bump and grind before they cleared each other and started shuffling after us, their desires of the flesh finally aligned.

"Time to go," I said, picking up the pace. "There was nothing left in the police station."

We hustled back to the car, eager to be done and on our way, and I was thinking it might be best if we avoided any other living people who might be nearby and possibly like-minded with the dead man. That's when something sharp and fast gouged a chunk of pavement out of the road three feet ahead of us and a gunshot cracked out through the air. Della and I crouched and dashed for the car as another shot buzzed between us and chipped the curb outside the police station. A third grazed Della across the shoulder, tearing her shirt and streaking a line of blood along her skin.

I spun and fired five shots in the direction of the sniper, hitting nothing but buying us time to reach the car. Faint static crackled on a distant walkie-talkie. Somebody laughed through the heavy stillness that followed and a second voice joined in, maybe two more after that.

Della and I scrambled into the car and blasted off along the road. Our planned route called for us to double back toward the highway, but that way was closed by the sniper, so we sped toward the other side of town, relieved when we left the buildings behind us and hopeful when we turned down that broken, desolate road, thinking it would lead faraway from the madness we fled. Mile or two along it, though, we reached the blockade, a jumble of wrecked cars shoved into the road and crushed together under a telephone pole. From a hundred yards away I saw the shadows of men with guns moving on the other side of it. I hit the brakes, cut the wheel, and spun the car around, driving hard, and we made it a quarter mile back the way we came before the pick-up trucks rolled into view, two of them, side-by-side, blocking the road, and each one bearing an armed man mounted behind the cab.

Right then I felt the presence of a nasty old friend of mine slinking back to my side, an unwelcome harbinger with its dank, familiar breath burning against the back of my neck, the hot, carrion air of the jackal I'd thought I'd left behind with memories of Evelyn and the madness of men who would kill to rule over an empire of rot and dust.

4.

I'M NOT A SOCIAL PERSON. People are too easy to manipulate, too ready to be misled, taken advantage of, and ridden herd, content so long as their basic needs are met and willing to pay much more than they need to for the privilege. Thus the arrival of armed, organized men who had been tracking us, probably since the moment we drove into town, discouraged me more than a little. Della and I held our guns out of sight on our laps and wondered if it might be better to hold tight and see what developed or burst out shooting and end this thing fast and clean.

Roadside pines swayed in the fast wind and dead leaves tumbled across the pavement. Horsehair clouds drifted above us, and for a moment we felt frozen in time. Cold sweat dripped down my back. The faint aroma of the woods filled my nose.

A barrel-chested man jumped down from one of the trucks, paused to adjust his belt, and then strolled halfway to our car. There he knelt and set his rifle down on the double yellow line, showed us a handgun he pulled from the back of his belt, and then placed it beside the first weapon. He walked forward. I rolled down my window.

"That'll do," I called. "We can talk from here."

He stopped and smiled under the silhouette of his Marlins cap. His eyes lurked behind mirrored shades.

"Well, listen to you giving orders," he said. "In case you hadn't noticed, friend, armed or not, my men and I got the upper hand here."

"Is that how you see it?" I asked.

His smiled faltered.

"Look, we don't want any trouble with you and we don't intend to hurt you. Fact is we're kind of happy to see some other living folks. Been too long staring at the same faces down at our camp. We thought everyone else hereabouts was dead and gone, that we were the only ones who survived."

"Oh, yeah? So, what, you and your snipers aimed to keep it that way I suppose?"

"No, no. It's not like that at all. We're real sorry about that. The shooting was uncalled for. See, that was one of ours, fellow named Cutter, your girlfriend dusted back by St. Pete's," he said.

"You saw what he was doing with that slitback?"

The man nodded. His jaw tightened into a grimace.

"I did, indeed. That's why you two ain't dead. Probably would've done the same myself if I'd found him first. Knew Cutter wasn't right in the head, but he was cagey about hiding it. We're better off not to have him poisoning the rest of us."

I held my tongue, which the man took for comment.

"Look, it's a harder world now than it's ever been, and sometimes it's necessary to kill the corruption before it spreads," he said. "I apologize for the shooting. Couple of my guys got a little overexcited before word got round just who it was your woman shot and why. That's why they were laughing afterward. Boys had a pool on how long that maggot would last."

"What do you want with us?"

"Seeing as how we got off on the wrong foot here, let me introduce myself," he said. "My name is Tom Weichert, and despite what this looks like, I'm pleased to meet you."

"All right, then, Mr. Weichert. Let's chalk this one up to a misunderstanding. Apology accepted. Been nice knowing you. Now, if you'll pull your trucks aside, we'll head back the way we came and be on our way," I said.

"Well, now, I wouldn't recommend that."

"And why's that?"

"You're heading south, planning to take the interstate part of the way, right?" he said.

"What difference does it make to you?"

"Not much. But, see, I know you didn't come up from the south, so I figure that's the way you're traveling. And about fifty miles along that way here there's a cluster of zombies, got to be something like a hundred thousand or more crammed together around a little town down there called Baxton. They're all gathered up like it's some kind of party. Been there about six weeks or so, not doing much of anything as far as we can tell but standing around decaying. Waiting for fresh meat to show up, I guess. So, that's what you're heading into if you keep on going."

I saw in Della's eyes that she believed Weichert's story. And for some reason, so did I. We had no reason to trust the man, but there was an honest resonance in his voice, his stance, his unwavering eyes, and the prospect of what he said chilled me. I'd never seen that many dead in one place. They tended to spread out unless there were live humans to attract them. A lot of them rotted out and stopped walking altogether due to weather damage and injuries that never healed, which kept their numbers down, but some of them seemed never to decompose at all and that could mean they were getting tougher, more dangerous.

"Tell you what, here's what I'm offering," Weichert said. "We got a place down the end of this road, hidden, fortified pretty well, about a hundred and sixty of us living there, and we keep the surrounding area clean by hunting scarecrows every day. That's what we call the dead ones, 'scarecrows.' That slitback gag's getting a little tired, don't you think? Anyway you want to come down and spend some time with us, you're welcome. You prefer to take your chances on the road, that's your call and it's been nice chatting with you."

Weichert gestured to the men behind him. Engines coughed to life and each truck pulled forward and off to the shoulder, leaving the route clear.

I didn't hesitate in slamming my foot down on the gas, rocketing by so fast that Weichert flinched and leapt backwards. We shot between the trucks and blazed up the road, and no one fired a shot or so much as made a move to follow us. In the rearview mirror I glimpsed the veil of shock on Weichert's face and the puzzled expressions of his men. Would've been easy enough for them to squeeze off a few potshots at us, try to cripple our car, but not one of them lifted a gun. No one tried to chase us. They just stood there and watched.

I eased up on the accelerator and rolled to a stop.

"What's wrong?" asked Della.

"Think for a minute," I said. "If what he says is true, then maybe we ought to hole up here awhile and figure out the best way to get south."

"Cornell, we don't need them," she said.

"No, we don't, I suppose, but we could use them for awhile to catch our breath, see if anyone knows what the hell is going on out there," I said. "If we have to wade through an army of slitbacks to make it home, I'd like to have as much information as possible ahead of time."

Della thought it over. Reluctance and apprehension steeled her eyes.

"Thing is, Della, we need some real rest. We lost Mason because of a stupid mistake. I almost lost you this morning because of another one, leaving you alone like that, and then we drove down this dead-end road and got ourselves trapped," I said. "I'm no more excited than you are to meet the fucking neighbors, but we've got to sleep more than a few hours here and there so we can get our heads together, recuperate a little. Otherwise we got no chance at all getting through that many slitbacks."

"All right," Della said. She didn't like it but she couldn't argue. "But we don't tell them where we're going or where we've been or who we are. This is a way-stop for us, nothing long term. We're just visiting."

"Agreed," I said.

I turned the car around and crept forward, noting the confused faces of the men as we rolled back between the pick-up trucks, and then pulled up to a stop beside Weichert. I cut the motor and got out.

"What the hell was that about?" he asked.

"Making sure your offer was sincere," I said and extended my hand. "We'd like to take you up on it. Name's Cornell and this is my wife, Della."

I don't know why I called her my wife. Instinct took over and the words came out, but the moment I saw the subtle shift in Weichert's expression and felt his grip tighten around my fingers, I knew I'd done the right thing at least on that count. Up close and exposed, something didn't feel right to me now. Della's warning jangled in my head. We'd been doing just fine without these losers, I told myself, but it wasn't entirely true. We were on the edge and needed a respite, and this was the only way we were going to get it. Still, that didn't stop that hard rocky feeling in my gut from telling me I'd just made my third dumb mistake that day, and that this just might be the big one.

5.

WEICHERT'S PICK-UP LED us down the road, me and Della following, and the other truck bringing up the rear. The land around us was thick with overgrown honeysuckle twisting amidst sugar maple and blackhaw trees and tall pines, all of it shielded by waist-high grass growing along the shoulder. Here and there bits of glass and metal sparkled in the sunlight, the remnants of debris where wrecked cars had probably been hauled away to clear the road and hide any sign that people lived in the area.

Out this way was wilderness. No stores or houses, no gas stations or farms, nothing but sun-hardened concrete and unchecked vegetation, probably infested with mosquitoes by the billions, and I wondered what kind of encampment waited at the end of the road. The further we drove from town, the quieter Della got. I knew how she felt. We were weak prey if Weichert's men decided to jump us, but I didn't think that would happen. They could have done it right where they first stopped us, and Weichert seemed too straightlaced for that kind of shit.

Man liked his rules and kept his word. Saw that much in his eyes. No doubt that's how he got to be head of the pack with this simmering bunch that included a freak like Cutter. Weichert's men were all clean-shaven, wearing fresh clothes without stains or tears, good shoes, and carrying well-maintained weapons. They put on a good, civilized show, but I wondered what might be hiding beneath the surface here, what kind of secrets Tom Weichert kept hushed up and queued, waiting for a chance to air out.

The pavement ended at a three-foot drop down to soft ground, but Weichert's pick-up cut right and moved along a gravel trail hidden by brush. I followed. The car lurched and the tires spun when we hit a sharp incline, but then the treads caught and trundled us upward into a hollow of high pines and mottled shade. Six armed men alongside the path watched us with blank faces. Della shrunk down in her seat.

"You think we did the right thing?" she asked.

I didn't know, so I kept quiet.

Around a crook in the road stood a twelve-foot black bear carved out of a pinewood trunk but looking fierce and alive in the dusty shaft of sunlight angling down onto it. Twice the size any black bear ought to be and sporting a mean snarl, it startled me. A sign mounted at its feet read "Cady's Indian Museum and Nature Outpost."

We crested a hill and a cluster of buildings came into sight, six in total: a sprawling brick mansion flanked by a cottage, a long garage, two large cinderblock and cement longhouse structures at the rear, and a brick station at the edge of a weed-pocked parking lot. About fifteen cars cooked in the sun, lined up in spaces, all of them clean and looking ready to roll. People roamed the grounds out in the open like there was nothing to fear, as if the dead of the world couldn't just walk up and take a bite out of them at any moment. Seeing that disturbed me for reasons I couldn't fathom right away. Maybe it was the arrogance and foolishness of it. Maybe it was my subconscious pissing on the first rays of hope I'd felt in a long time.

I pulled in beside Weichert's truck, and then Della and I got out. The noontime breeze chilled my back where sweat had matted my T-shirt to my skin.

"Welcome to Camp Cady," Weichert said as he stepped down to the pavement. "Not much, but it's home."

He laughed and slapped me on the back, flashing a smile better suited to an insurance salesman or cocaine dealer.

"You folks are awful lax about moving around in the open," I said.

Grinning, Weichert shook his head.

"Naw, we're safe here," he said. "We got hunting parties out daily to pick off any scarecrow comes within a few miles of the place. Long as they don't make it down here to the complex, they don't know we're here, and that keeps their numbers down and manageable. They're kind of like ants. Kill the scouts and they others will go elsewhere looking for food.

"Being off the beaten path works in our favor in more ways than one. About four months ago, an army troop came through town, burning and foraging, mowing down scarecrows like twelve-year-olds at a shooting gallery. Fine enough, except when they came across about a dozen or so living folks hiding out in an apartment complex, they cleared them out. Killed half the men, took all of the women, and kept on their way like a pack of coyotes on the carrion trail. We watched from a distance, and they never knew we were here. We took in a couple of the survivors afterward."

"And Cady don't mind you setting up camp here?"

"If he does, he's not going to say much about it. Cady died about a month before the dead rose up. Used to be a friend of mine, which is how I knew about his place. He was fixing to turn this into a tourist attraction. Group of developers were planning a major shopping mall and hotel complex about two miles back up the road. Cady's family owned this land going back more than a hundred-and-fifty years, and he figured the time had come to cash in. Built those longhouses and started up his collection of genuine Indian artifacts and museum quality taxidermy displays. Got a hundred acres of nature trails out there, too. I'll give you and your wife the dollar tour later. Right now, though, we ought to get you checked in."

We crossed the parking lot with Weichert. Della stuck close to me and held my hand. We entered the squat building on the edge of the blacktop, and though in there out of the sun the air was cooler, the whole set-up left me with a clammy feeling. Three men sat behind desks piled with stacks of papers. They looked up in unison as we entered and Weichert introduced us.

"Figure on them being with us more than a few days," he said, and then he glanced at me over his shoulder, and asked, "Right?"

"Don't know," I said. "We're not looking to impose."

"No imposition," he said. "This isn't a free ride. We'll get files started for each of you, get you in the registry, and then interview you about what kind of skills you have. Then, depending on what we need done, these men will assign you work detail. Once that's set, they'll fix you up with quarters and you can start working tomorrow. Earn your keep fair and square and take your turns in the hunting rotation. That's how we do things around here."

"What kind of work?" Della asked.

Weichert winked at her. "Well, that's up to you, isn't it? What kind of skills you got, ma'am?"

Della glanced at me, waited for my sleight nod.

"I'm a nurse," she said.

"Well, that sure is welcome news. You'll be working over in the infirmary," explained Weichert. "See how easy that is? This is no tent city down here. The world we knew may be ending, but we're not savages. Got to keep the building blocks of society alive, or else how will we rebuild? What will we have to go back to when this all up and ends?"

"What makes you think it ever will?" I asked.

"The dead got to rot away to nothing sooner or later, don't they?"

"We've seen plenty of them look like they stopped decaying and started toughening up. If you're planning to wait this out, you may be getting back to society from behind a walker."

"Heard rumors about that, reports from the hunting parties," said Weichert. "Well, we'll see, won't we? We're working on it. Meantime, you get yourselves all official and then get acquainted with some of the folks. You're permitted one weapon apiece in case any of the dead ones find their way down here. Whatever else you're carrying goes in the armory."

"Fuck that," I said. "You're not taking our guns or anything else we own."

Weichert's expression underwent a sea change and radiated with the flush of challenged authority.

"Excuse me, Mr. Cornell, but I doubt you actually own any single item you're carrying. If you got receipts to prove it then fine, you can keep it. I understand people need to do what they can to survive, but that doesn't mean stealing and looting is condoned. Just a necessary evil. Like I said we got a civilized community here and you're going to follow our laws. Someday the world is going to get back on track and one way or another we're all going to have reckon for what we've done and taken. You got that?"

Two of Weichert's men dropped hands beneath their desks, and I didn't have to ponder much to know their fingers were wrapped around guns. I nodded, slow and deliberate, feigning resignation.

"Your camp, your laws," I said.

"Good. Mind you something else. Got a good number of kids running around here, so we don't allow swearing in public. Do it again and you'll spend some time in the 'swear jar,' a small, dark place you won't like very much," he said. "Well, I'm happy to have helped you out today. I want us to be friends, but for the time being you'd do better to think of me like the others do. I'm not some high-minded volunteer. I'm a duly authorized officer of the law for the great state of Florida, and until we get to know each other better, you can call me 'sheriff.'"

Weichert flipped back his jacket and revealed a small bronze badge pinned to his shirt. Fuck my stupidity and fear and lack of confidence in finding a way for Della and I to weather whatever Hell waited for us further down the road. I'd had enough of lawmen to last me until my hair turned white and my balls shriveled up back inside my body. Took a lot of willpower not to shoot Weichert dead and run, but I knew we'd never make it down that winding gravel road, never reach the highway or the barricade before somebody squeezed off that lucky round and sent bits of my skull flying in a hundred different directions. And then there would be whatever happened to Della if she survived.

Della and I exchanged a quick glance. We both realized we'd have to bide our time, and both of us already hated every fucking second of it.

6.

THEY GAVE US a room on the third floor of the mansion, a tiny one, but clean and bright when the morning sun streamed in the windows. Married couples stayed together, which made me grateful for my spontaneous lie. Otherwise single women got the second floor and one of the longhouses, where Cady's museum displays had been cleared out and cubicles and cots had been set up, and men took the other longhouse or roughed it in tents or under open sky. Weichert asked once about our absent wedding rings, and I told him a group that jumped us back in Georgia had stolen them. That seemed to satisfy his curiosity.

Della's work in the infirmary made her feel good, and she telegraphed it in her face, in her walk, in how she smiled once in a while now after going so long without smiling at all. Having a routine helped. So did getting a good night's sleep when we needed it and having a safe place to be alone together. Mostly though I think that helping the injured nurtured Della's spirit; it gave her a way to fight back against the death and horror around us and reminded her that good things could still be done in the world and she could be part of them.

Weichert kept his word. He took everything we had and put it into "community ownership," to be used as needed for the good of everyone at Camp Cady. They took our guns, some of our camping equipment and other supplies, but left us our clothes and personal belongings. I managed at least to hide the spare set of keys for the car. After that first day Weichert left us alone, and we became two more faces among the crowd, two more names on a roster he was charged with feeding, sheltering, and protecting, of no immediate concern to him so long as we played by his rules.

Few folks we met liked Weichert, but no one argued with his success in keeping Camp Cady organized and secure. The ones who rankled against the rules vented their frustration on the daily scarecrow-hunting expeditions. I appreciated Weichert's cunning in giving folks a way to work out their anger by putting it to good use. Have to admit the man had a knack for leading the sheep and what he did wasn't all bad, either.

Della and I actually enjoyed ourselves for the first time since before we left the prison. We ate good meals together like normal people and went hiking along the trails around camp in our off time. At night, cozy in our little room with the door locked and the windows open to the breeze, we made love, moving together like we had that first time, rediscovering all the energy and passion that had impelled us toward each other. The way our bodies fit together was like we'd been tailor-made for one another, designed by fate to journey together through spiraling sensations of pleasure that drove us into deeper and deeper intimacy. I came to cherish the scent of Della's hair, the texture of her skin, the taste of her on my lips, and the secret desires she whispered in my ears. Even when we lay together sated and spent with the dawn creaking through the trees, we clung to each other like parting would be a form of amputation.

Those first few days felt wonderful, I admit, but at the same time it chafed to remember what living—really living and not just concentrating on not dying—was all about, because I knew one day the time would come for it to end.

Most mornings Della woke before me, and I stayed in bed and watched her dress, savoring the way her taut body moved through the hazy sunlight in a muscular perfection of lines, curves, and shadows. Her skin gleamed, and when she breathed her chest rose and fell in measured time that hinted at her growing confidence. She became more meticulous in her habits, more reserved in her choice of clothing as she slipped back into a professional state of mind. The changes worried me a little when I wondered if maybe she liked things at Camp Cady too much, but she always put my mind at ease without even trying, just the way she said things like "when we leave here" or "down at your place in Lohatchie will be different." She said those things often and I took them to heart.

At the infirmary they mostly dealt with injuries—cuts and scrapes and sprains and the like. Nothing too serious. Almost no one came in ill. Della attributed it to the environment, crediting the good weather, hard work, and the absence of pollutants spilling into the air for keeping people healthy. The other infirmary workers told her they hadn't seen a patient with a cough or a cold or an infection in months.

"I do feel bad for this one boy, though," Della said one morning.

She sat brushing her hair in the mirror, dressed in northing but a pair of faded blue panties with her back half-turned to me while I reclined propped up on pillows and listened.

"He's mostly been in a bed since he got here about two months ago," she told me. "Twelve years old and he's on his own, lost his family and everyone he had to slitbacks. He got away but he broke his leg jumping out of a moving truck. Lucky someone found him out on the road and brought him here, but it was bad break. He ought to be able to start walking again any day now, though. His name's Christopher. You can see in his eyes what he's been through, and the way he stares off into space sometimes makes me think maybe it's even worse than the things you and I've seen, like it aged him terribly and there's an old man living inside him now."

I thought about the eyes growing from the brain of the slitback that had killed Mason and wondered what worse things Christopher could've possibly witnessed.

"Good thing, then, he's got you to care for him," I said. "You wait and see, get him up on his feet again and he'll be running around like a normal, healthy boy in no time, playing football and dreaming about girls. I promise."

"You should come visit him sometime," Della suggested. "Not a lot of men come by the infirmary unless they're hurt, and I think he's getting tired of being mothered."

"Stuck in bed with a bunch of sympathetic women to tend him? Boy doesn't know how good he's got it," I said. "Give him another two years, he'll change his tune."

"Still," Della said. "Couldn't hurt."

"No, it couldn't," I said. "Mainly cause it'll give me an excuse to come by and harass your sexy ass. Drop by this afternoon, all right?"

Della smiled and put her brush down, then rose and crawled back into bed and kissed my neck. Another minute and she was under the covers with me, and we were back where we'd left off just a few hours ago.

That's how it went most days, the two of us doing what was required, indulging in the luxury of not having to look over our shoulders every minute, enjoying throwing our energies into something other than keeping alive, and cementing the bond between us. Got so goddamn comfortable sometimes I started worrying I might be the one who'd want to stay at Camp Cady.

Lucky me, though, I had some balance in my life to make sure I never forgot what was going on in the world around us and just where was the safest place for me and Della to wind up and plant our roots. I had Weichert and his men to thank for that. They were the ones who assigned me to the greenhouse to work with a man named Birch, a military scientist no one liked and no one wanted be around. As a new guy with no special skills I pulled duty as his assistant, but they expected me to last no more than a day or two.

Birch's lab stood in a meadow a short hike through the woods, fixed up in a greenhouse, an oblong structure of glass and steel hidden by orchards from the compound's main grounds. The botanical supplies had been trashed and discarded, replaced with Birch's equipment. My first day there I learned why everyone else avoided him.

Birch's eyes flickered like Christmas lights in the rain and a scrub of gray hair clung to his skull like dried heather. He moved in fits and starts, standing stock still and lost in thought for minutes at a time before rushing to one part of his lab or another, fumbling with some inexplicable mechanism or assortment of glass containers filled with sloshing fluids. Being around him made me jumpy. I never knew what he was going to do or say and I could never tell what his experiments amounted to if anything. The day we met he saw me coming through the woods and stepped out the front door to greet me by flipping me the bird.

"Hey, asshole, did Weichert send you down here to keep tabs on me?" he said. "Where does that hollow-headed mouth-breather think I'm going to run off to?"

"I'm supposed to assist you," I said.

"Well, fuck off, I don't need assistance."

"Not that simple. Got a job to do, and I guess I ought to do it or risk the wrath of Sheriff Shithead," I said. I pushed past him into the greenhouse, looked around, and said, "Where do I start?"

Birch and I sized each other up. I noticed the tattoo on his forearm, a dusty Marine Corps insignia, ample warning for me to not pick a stupid fight. Besides, we seemed to share an opinion of Weichert, and I hoped that would give us some common ground to get along. If Birch's grating personality had been the only thing driving others away from him, it would've been easy for me to tough it out at the greenhouse, but of course, that wasn't the whole story. There was the wall, too, and that was something that did get under my skin.

Birch gave me no warning. I put in a good half-day's work cleaning up and getting piles of supplies organized before I got to that part of the greenhouse, where the body parts hung mixed in with thick ivy in the shadows of the back corner. Legs and arms; hands; a pair of lungs; several hearts; a head with no eyes, ears, or nose; six loose eyeballs, wide and staring; and an array of decomposing organs beyond identification—all pinned up like a butterfly collection. When they weren't moving you hardly saw them, but then a brisk wind carrying the scent of the living might cut through the shattered panes of the greenhouse and set them stirring so the wall looked like a swarm of moths was wriggling over it.

Worst part was the eyes. Not the ones staked up there for observation, but the ones sprouting from the other specimens. They peered out from lung tissue, rolled and blinked amidst withered cardiac muscle; eyes peered at me from the severed stump of a hand, tracked my every move from beneath the oily film coating lumps of unidentifiable putrescence. Birch and I worked in the lab, and the eyes observed our progress, silent and accusatory, their gaze palpable even to my turned back. That's the real reason no one wanted to work with Birch, that sensation of constant surveillance, the way your skin never stopped crawling in the greenhouse, the strange jerks and tics of the specimens. No one wanted the dead watching them all day long.

I told Birch about the eyes I'd seen in the brain of the slitback that killed Mason and it didn't surprise him. It was happening more often of late, though not to all of the dead, he told me. He hoped it might lead to some new insight as to what caused the dead to walk. The hunting parties kept him supplied with test subjects, and he kept the bits and pieces that grew eyes around the longest. The rest he burned when he finished with them. Weichert thought Birch was working on "a cure for not dying when you die," but he wasn't. He'd given up the search weeks ago and turned to studying the living dead, documenting everything he could about them and how they functioned. It wasn't much.

"There's no cure," he said. "See, Weichert is a man whose mind works in two modes: black and white. His world is cut and dried. There's a reason for everything, and I don't mean that in a pussy 'oh, it was meant to be' kind of way. With Weichert, there's a bump in the night, it means someone knocked. Get what I'm saying?"

"Yeah, he's the original problem solver," I said. "No mysteries. Find the cause and you find the cure."

"Catch is, there's no cause," Birch said. "At least nothing scientific like Weichert thinks. There ought to be, sure. He's right as far as that goes. But I've been working the problem for months and if an answer was there to be found, I'd at least have a few good working theories. Used to be chief researcher for a biotech company with a shitload of military contracts, and I've never seen anything like this. Best I can describe what's happening is time stands still for the dead on a cellular level. The putrefaction slows down almost to the point of cessation. As for what's keeping them moving, making them feed off the living, I'm stumped."

"Does it matter?" I said. "By now the undead must outnumber the living. The world is more theirs than ours."

This conversation occurred after I'd lasted a week of Birch giving me nothing but shit work and hitting me with the silent treatment. I stuck it out because I enjoyed the solitude of the greenhouse, and I figured that if anyone at Camp Cady could tell me something I didn't already know it was Birch. Eventually we got down to serious work, and we got to know each other pretty quick after that. Found we had common taste in books ranging from William Faulkner to Jim Thompson, and Birch started loaning me stuff out of his personal library.

On my week anniversary, he told me no one had worked with him that long for almost three months and then declared it time for a celebration. He slapped me on the back and steered me toward a cabinet on the far side of the greenhouse. He produced a bottle of Johnnie Walker Black and two glasses, and we sat in wide-backed wicker chairs.

"Glad to have you around," he said then threw back half his drink.

"Nice to be wanted," I said, following suit.

"Tell me," said Birch. "Weichert pick you up on the road? Near town?"

I told him the story of how Della and I came to Camp Cady and what Weichert had said.

"Well, everyone knew Cutter would need putting down sooner or later," he said. "But listen. Don't get too comfortable here if you value your principles or your sanity. This isn't 'Cady's Indian Museum and Nature Outpost' anymore. It's 'Tom Town.' At least that's what I call it since Tom Weichert's started running it like a tin tyrant. You got anyplace else to go, do yourself a favor and go there. Clean sheets and hot food have their appeal, but leaving here will make your life a lot easier in the long run, especially if you can look out for yourself out there."

"Trouble is I'm not sure Weichert is ready to lose us. My wife's a hell of a nurse and word is she's been a godsend at the infirmary. Besides, only place we got to go is south," I said.

Birch frowned.

"The first problem I might be able to help you with, but if you're heading south, well, then maybe you don't have anywhere else to go. Forty, fifty miles south is where the dead are gathering. Something big brewing down there at Baxton. A real Deadtown. They're shambling in by the thousands."

"What's it all about?"

"Fucked if I know, but don't tell Weichert that. He thinks I'm working it all out so I can hand him a big fat report someday."

We drank again, and I enjoyed the soft burn of good liquor, a welcome change from the cheap stuff I'd found on the road. A light drizzle began to fall, pattering against the glass and leaves overhead and turning the air damp and chilly. Whiskey heat infiltrated my body, and I didn't object when Birch filled our glasses once more and then put the bottle away. Leaning back, I stared up through the glass ceiling where smoky, furrowed clouds swept above the swaying treetops. The greenhouse was quiet and lonely, a sanctuary amidst the overpopulated compound, a shunned and haunted place. Birch and I could get up to just about anything down here and no one would likely find out.

"What's with the eyes?" I asked.

Birch cleared his throat. "What do you mean?"

I straightened up and studied his craggy face, its lines deepened by the afternoon gloom, and I saw he knew more than he was telling. He hid it well, but I used to make a living off snap judgments of people's disposition. It helped to know whether or not an assistant manager could really open a bank vault before you pushed a gun in his face and tried to persuade him to do so.

"I mean, what makes those eyes pop up like that?"

Darkness crept into Birch's expression and his gaze drifted toward the trails of rainwater snaking down the outside walls.

"Magic," he said.

"That so?"

I rose and walked over to the specimen wall. It bothered me the way Birch had everything strung up and mounted and spread out over an eight-foot span. The limbs and bits of flesh were like a man pulled apart alive, only I knew there was nothing living there, just mute and mindless scraps of what had once been life.

"Acid works," Birch said. "To destroy them, I mean. Fire. Lye. Anything that causes irreparable cellular damage. Microwaves would work nicely. Shooting them or cutting them slows them down, makes it hard for them to function. Told Weichert what he needs are flamethrowers or some pesticide tanks filled with acid, but he's holding out for a panacea. Thinks he can get his hands on some crop dusters and spray a miracle cure far and wide. Man's got visions of reclaiming the state and running it like his own little kingdom."

The specimen wall repulsed me, yeah, but something about it drew me in, too, and I stared at the random constellations of eyes, noticing their glistening pupils move, and watching dead flesh strain to blink. I couldn't imagine how they could see without a brain to process the image, but I sure as hell felt seen.

Birch laughed. "You got some balls getting that close, my friend."

"Don't worry. I'm well acquainted with this sort of bullshit," I said. "Tell me about magic."

A dense chuckle rolled up from Birch's throat.

"I mean it," I said. "What? Like ghosts? Voodoo?"

Birch's face changed and adopted the bone-weariness that until then had only been apparent in the cast of his shoulders and the tepid resignation in his voice.

"Nothing like that. Got some theories, but none that'll solve Weichert's problem. I've worked on the why long and hard and I've come to the conclusion that it's a matter beyond science," he said. "That is, unless you want to believe that the basic laws of physics and biology can be broken or made to change on an individual basis."

"I don't follow," I said.

"It's like I told you. Time is standing still for the dead, so they're not rotting. You've heard of relativity? Imagine ten seconds go by. Ten seconds pass in the world while maybe one, or one-tenth, or one-one-hundredth, or one-one-thousandth of a second passes for these dead fuckers up walking around and making our lives miserable," Birch told me. "Can you explain that? I sure as hell can't. And that doesn't even touch on why they're ambulatory or need to eat live flesh. I'm trained to see the world in a rational way and look for the underlying reason things are they way they are, the mechanisms that drive reality. But as far as I can tell, what's happening out there is a cosmic whim or the result of some fundamental alteration in the nature of existence."

"You can tell all that from this little kitchen chemistry set you got here," I said.

"You haven't seen what I have downstairs," Birch said. "Trust me—I've got all the equipment we need plus two generators Weichert endlessly bitches about keeping fuel to run it all. Took most of it from my old lab. Before the dead rose up I was working on the highest profile stuff, my friend. Things the mainstream would say were fifty, sixty years out, all top secret, all rather dire and revolutionary, and a few patently illegal under international law. Before that, there was the work I did and the things I saw in the Marines before I went back to school and got into the lab. That all gave me a rather finely tuned set of instincts for sorting fact from horseshit.

"If there's a biological reason for the dead to be walking, I'm the man who would've found it. In fact, I was working on it back in my old digs before I decided I'd be safer outside the arms of the military and struck out this way. You think you've ever seen crazy, you should've met the two-star general who took over our complex during the crisis. Interesting story, that, but I'll save it for another time."

"So what's the sticking point? You said you had some theories. That mean you think you have some of the answers?" I said.

Birch scowled and hunched forward.

"You really want to know what I think? Fine. There's no scientific reason. The dead come back to life because God—whatever he, she, or it may be—willed it so. The universe, my friend, is dying on the vine, and this is all part of a great, necromantic wave sweeping the cosmos. You and I, Mr. Cornell, are nothing but pall bearers who have overstayed our welcome at the funeral, nothing but dung beetles looking for an easy meal. We're corpse fauna, and if we're lucky maybe the Almighty won't forsake us altogether when he's done with his killing and resurrecting."

The scientist sipped from his glass and sank back into his chair. I set my drink on the table and rubbed my eyes.

"How do you know you're right? Take it on faith?"

"I don't have any faith," he said. "I've seen this—out there in the ranks of the dead, in here when I look into their eyes. And in my dreams where I see and hear things I don't think any man was ever intended to know. Maybe I'm wrong. Maybe I'm fucking nuts, but if I'm not, then about fifty miles south of here, where the dead are gathering in their masses, they're getting ready to write the epitaph for an entire world and maybe countless others beyond. It's some fucked-up shit, believe me, and now you know why I'm just leading Weichert along and keeping this all to myself."

Damn civilization, I thought. No matter where I go, I got the law to my left and God to my right, and, as usual, neither side playing nice with the other. And so there I was, once more caught in the slavering jaws of the same beast that I'd thought I'd left behind in prison. I pined for the road, to be alone with Della, barreling down the ruins of highways no one cared about anymore, the sky and the earth our own to do with as we pleased, and no one to get in our way. Birch said the earth was dead; I said it was the Garden of Eden. Right then I started planning how Della and I were going to make our way back to it.

7.

WEICHERT VOLUNTEERED ME for a hunting party. All the men took turns in rotation, so he bumped me to the head of the list after I lasted two weeks with Birch. Maybe the scientist and me hitting it off made him uncomfortable, and he wanted to remind me who was in charge. Della hated the idea of me out in the wilderness with a bunch of Weichert's men. She didn't trust them, didn't trust Weichert, and worried I might never come back.

Losing me would strand her in Camp Cady. We'd been talking about leaving in another week, maybe two, but our plans had gotten more complicated. Della wanted to bring Christopher. The kid reminded her of her dead brother, and whatever he had been through gave Della and him something in common. He talked to her and no one else about his experiences, and she wouldn't tell me what he said. I didn't press it.

I met with Christopher several times and shot the breeze about rock music, and the walking dead, and how he had wanted to grow up and race cars. He was a skinny, picture-perfect kid with fine, unruly hair, the kind of boy I could picture swinging off a long rope into a cool lake on a July afternoon. He was smart, too, and I liked him, but I didn't know what benefit there would be in him hitting the road with Della and me. Chances were good not all of us would live to see Lohatchie, and Christopher would probably stand a better chance staying put. I was enough of a realist to accept that, but Della clung to her high hopes, except where Weichert and his crew were concerned. But despite her concerns there was no way out of my going on the hunt.

I tried to ease her mind by pointing out that sending me off to the woods to be killed wasn't Weichert's style. He wanted to break me as an example for the others. Everyone at Cady's lived in Weichert's shadow, and it showed in their guarded expressions and furtive conversations, in their efficiency and conformity calculated to keep them off Weichert's radar. I saw how unhappy everyone was, except Weichert's inner circle of "trusted deputies." That's what he called the men who kept the rest of us in line. Camp Cady was so orderly and well mannered, folks hardly hollered when they stubbed a toe, and Weichert had to know that with the strings pulled that tight, a revolt could erupt any time.

So I didn't expect him to pull something clumsy like staging a hunting accident to get rid of me. I hadn't challenged him openly, but he was smart enough to see what kind of threat I could be and how some of the others had started to look up to Della and me. Weichert probably knew I'd be getting ready to deal with him one way or another—and he was right. I didn't mean to leave Camp Cady without leaving Weichert a clear message as to what I thought of him.

The morning of the hunt, sun poured down from a pristine sky and baked my skin. Three days of rain had broken and passed in the night, leaving the ground soft and the air damp with the perfume of pines and wet loam, but the heat would dry it soon enough. Six of us went out, led by a deputy named Wrigley, driving a pick-up as far into woods as the terrain permitted; it was on foot from there. We each carried a handgun and a rifle, extra ammunition, a machete, and a day's worth of food and water. One man led two mutts on long leashes, a security system of sorts: canine noses would smell the slit-backs long before we could and dogs got skittish around the dead.

Trudging single file through the mud we marched for a couple of hours, moving over grassy slopes and planes until we reached the bank of a marsh. An odor of rot wafted off the stagnant water, and the air buzzed with a haze of flies and gnats. We circled around to the far side, swatting insects the whole way, picked up the trail, narrower and rougher on the other side, and continued on. By then we'd traveled twelve, fifteen miles from the compound, moving in burdensome silence, sweating under the high sun. All our concentration turned to watching for signs of movement in the brush, listening for the dogs to bark, sniffing for that telltale stink of the dead. When it came, it hit like a gale coming off a landfill.

The mutts dug in and wouldn't take another step down the trail. Bared their teeth and growled so loud their keeper trotted them back before they gave away our position. The rest of us crept forward to where the path widened through a stand of pines and led toward cottony brightness. Through the shadows of the tree trunks we saw movement.

"There's a meadow the other side of those pines," Wrigley whispered. "We scatter, move up, weapons ready. Hunker down just this side of the trees. Fire on my order. Cripple them and then we go in close for the hack-and-burn work. Everyone got it?"

We crept through the dead stench that billowed around us thick as smoke from a rubber fire. A chorus of moans cried out from necrotic throats, rising and falling in a way that reminded me of the losing teams fans at a football game, and it under it ran a current of white noise like electrical lines humming on a rainy day. The men swapped anxious glances, all of them thinking the same thing I was but too frightened to speak up. Good thing I wasn't.

I gripped Wrigley's shoulder and said, "Wait."

The deputy snapped his head around, surprised, nervous. He glared at me, and I dropped my hand, gave him some distance.

"Cut the crap, Cornell. You got your orders."

"Use your head," I said. "Smell that? Hear that? That's not a few strays wandering by. Got to be a mob of them: dozens, if not more. You want to walk right into that?"

"Can't be a mob. We never get that many scarecrows back here. No reason for them to come this way," he said.

A man named Farmer inched forward and spoke. "You're right, Deputy, but so is Cornell. Okay? We've all been on enough of these hunts to know something's wrong here, something's different. Damn stink is making my eyes water. And you ever see the dogs tense up like that before?"

Wrigley flashed me a "see what you started?" kind of look, but then he wandered a few feet further down the trail, dropped to his haunches, and listened. Languid wind shook the pine needles and a bird called from somewhere far away, gentle contrast to the steady groaning of the gathered dead.

Wrigley returned with a hard expression, and said, "Best be right, Cornell, or Weichert will hear about this insubordination."

The threat rang hollow, words a trusted deputy had to say to keep face even if he knew they were bullshit.

"I can live with that," I said.

"All right, then, here's how we do it," Wrigley said. "We creep up to the tree line, stick to the shadows, hang fire, and see what we're dealing with. Y'all can handle that? Y'all feel better this way? Bunch of tired, fucking pussies I got backing me up."

I smirked and said, "Language, Deputy. What would Sheriff Weichert think hearing you swear like that?"

Wrigley sneered at me before he led us down to the edge of the trail. We crouched on hands and knees, nestled into the high grass encroaching from the field, concealed behind a jumble of deadfall. Past the pines the dirt trail cut into a deep, concave meadow. Grass bleached pale by sunlight practically glowed as it swayed in the breeze, flitting back and forth like the golden tongues of a hundred thousand snakes. Through it shambled an unbroken line of corpses, their rag clothing flapping from their decomposing bodies, their flesh black and purple in the searing daylight, their wounds that would never heal rippling and wet with maggots and flies. The noise of a million carrion crawlers buzzed under the dead's constant moaning. The fresher corpses still looked like men and women, but most of them had deteriorated beyond the point of possessing distinguishing features although the filthy ruins of a necktie or a bra strap provided an occasional clue. Children were the easiest to pick out, but nobody wanted to look at them. The line shuffled along, a trajectory of guided chaos, eight or ten bodies wide, stamping the grass down flat, killing it as they followed a well-worn route. They moved slow and steady, shuffled and lurched forward, their shriveled eyes and empty skull sockets fixed on an unknown point to the south. Wrigley took a pair of field glasses from his belt and gazed northward in the direction of the column's source.

"Shit and piss in a blender," he mumbled.

He passed the glasses to Farmer, who stared through them for several seconds and then handed them to me. I raised them and looked. On and on the dead walked, coming from as far as the eye could see, a distance of maybe a couple miles with every indication that the line reached much further than that, stretching toward a hidden mouth maybe fifty miles, maybe a thousand, to the north. The corpses passed out of sight south of us and showed no signs of fatigue or wear. This forced march of the damned, this measured torrent of rot and putrefaction, this scar upon the quiet earth—the sight of it drove home what Birch had said about the living being like carrion bugs against nature's new order. We were six living men against an irresistible wall of dead flesh, and I didn't need to see the others' faces to know how small each and every one of us felt in its presence.

Some of the slitbacks began to slow down as they passed our position, causing those trailing them to bump together. They danced clumsy circles for a few minutes, tangled up in one another, until one of them fell over and broke the clog. The others stomped along, crushing his twitching body into the soil, but more came and got hung up right there in front of us, distracted, sidetracked from their journey—and it didn't take long to figure out it was us throwing them off. They hadn't seen us but they were starting to sense us.

As silent as we'd come, we retreated up the trail, hoping we hadn't lingered long enough for them to track us. Past the marsh the path rose to a low hill and we dug in there for a couple of hours to make sure the dead weren't following. Nothing came up the trail and when we felt sure nothing would, we hurried back to the pickup, jogging every other mile to reach it before dusk.

The whole ride home Wrigley rambled on, saying nothing, just asking himself all sorts of pointless questions as he tried to put some explanation to what we had seen. The rest of us sifted the murk of our thoughts. No one wanted to voice it but the meaning was clear. Baxton, where the dead had been gathering, stood to the south. This was no random migration, but a pilgrimage with a known destination, and that meant something no one had yet guessed at—that meant the rotting slitbacks, the mindless dead, the stinking, fucking wormfeeders were walking with a purpose.

8.

CREDIT WHERE CREDIT IS DUE, Weichert played the hand dealt him as well as anyone could once my hunting party returned with news of what we'd seen. He kept it quiet until he met with his deputies and then he had them spread word to the others, quietly, so as not to spark a panic, but putting everyone on guard. Next he organized eight armed groups, six men each, to camp three miles outside the complex in the direction of the dead march and stand guard. A rotation of scouts posted deeper in the woods kept watch on the walking corpses, and after a week of waiting for something to happen, when the corpse parade showed no sign of abating, Weichert turned to Birch. There had been an ugly incident, too; it shattered Camp Cady's air of relative freedom and put everyone on a razor's edge, which meant Weichert couldn't afford to wait things out.

Three days after my party turned with its report, a slitback wandered into the parking lot, strolled by the cars, stumbled over the rough ground, and trudged up to the front door of the mansion. No one saw it. Too many men were posted to the west of the compound, leaving parts of the perimeter exposed. A woman, Nancy Morris, exiting the mansion walked head-on into the thing and before she could make a sound, the slitback ripped open her throat, dragged her to the ground, and started gnawing into her stomach.

It fed for awhile, piling up scraps of eviscerated intestines and organ meat, slurping down what it could until three children turned up the walk and disturbed it. They screamed and fled. Smart kids, but too bad they didn't have a decent weapon among them to end things before they really got started. Their commotion attracted the slitback. It went after them, leaving its fresh kill to clamber to her feet a couple minutes later and straggle off toward the infirmary with her guts dangling past her waist and dragging through the dirt.

After losing sight of the children the first corpse wandered the yard until he met Chester Lang making repairs to the old gazebo. The carpenter fought back with a hammer, caved in the slitback's skull, smashed his brain, and then chopped the thing down to manageable bits with a hatchet. Came away with a dozen or so nasty bite wounds and a six-inch gash along his abdomen, but Chester lived.

Across the compound dead Nancy Morris got as far as the open grass outside the women's longhouse, which also housed the infirmary. Della saw it first and while everyone else went scrambling to lock the place tight, she stepped outside with her gun drawn and put two rounds through dead Nancy's head. Took her off her feet long enough for Della to go to work with a scalpel and a hacksaw, concluding poor Ms. Morris' existence as a flesh-eating zombie. Should've ended there, except all the activity over the intrusion meant no one noticed three more slitbacks coming from the east.

Skeletal and rotted, crawling out of the woods like enormous beetles snuffling and clacking for prey, they found their way to the garage where each one killed a man. Of course, those three partly-eaten dead men got up, too, driven by their burning hunger for flesh, and so six slitbacks roved into the heart of Camp Cady, and yeah, we can all call that a big, bad day for Tom Weichert and his rule of law.

Down at the greenhouse, hard at work in the cellar, Birch and I missed all the excitement. I heard all about it later from Della. Took Weichert's men an hour to round up all the dead ones and when the last had been put down and set afire, the body count numbered twenty-three residents, four killed by stray shots fired by Weichert's deputies. A riot almost broke out then and there, but it had been so long since most folks at Camp Cady had seen a slitback that shock won over outrage. That wouldn't last long, though. The happy illusion of life at Cady's had been irreparably shattered.

Not surprising, Della was smarter than I was about it. The night of the attack she decided we ought to leave in another day or two, three at most.

"Camp Cady is no safe haven anymore," she said. "What's the point in hanging around? Besides, Christopher is up to traveling now."

I wrapped my arms around her, reveling in the flush of having just made love and not wanting to talk about such stuff but knowing Della was right.

I said, "Probably a good idea. The dead march isn't that far off. Only a matter of time before the secret about this place gets out among the dead. It's just that Birch has been up to something new, and I'm curious to find out what. He hasn't been this intense about anything since I met him."

"Well, tell him to hurry it up. I've been swiping supplies from the infirmary, putting together a little stockpile," she said. "We'll need some food, too, and our camping gear and stuff, and weapons."

"And the car," I said. "Got to figure a way to load up and sneak out of here without getting shot. Birch said he might be able to help us with that. I'll talk to him tomorrow."

"You think he ought to come with us?"

I shook my head. "Doubt he would. And, anyway, much as I like him, he scares the shit out of me sometimes."

"That woman who died today," said Della. "When I started cutting her up, she sprouted eyes like the slitback that killed Mason. Every time I took one of her limbs off an eye blinked back at me. Felt like having cold beetles crawling under my skin. There was hatred in those eyes. I sliced them apart to stop them from looking at me, but another one popped up for every one I destroyed. The others saw them too. There were eyes in all the slitbacks today. Not everyone here already knew about that. Got folks more frightened than ever."

I told her about Birch's wall and some of his ideas, and she listened, her quiet body warming me, her gentle breath brushing my neck. Her gentle heartbeat thudded against my chest.

"I don't care what they are or what they want, Cornell. I just want to get away from them. Promise me that, all right? That we'll go away from here, away from all this horror, and find our own, safe place? Okay?"

"Promise," I said.

I kissed her and slid my hand along her body to feel her heat, and she welcomed my touch.

That morning I made Della wake up early and after a stop by the infirmary to pick up Christopher, I took her and the boy into the woods to the place where Weichert had dumped all of Cady's taxidermy displays when he'd had the longhouses cleared out for housing. Cady had been a real enthusiast and so the three of us stood amidst animals from six different continents, each one expertly preserved though now soiled and weathered from being left outdoors, torn and punctured from being used for target practice. Among them were two black bears; an array of big cats that included a leopard, a tiger, and some cougars; an alligator and a crocodile; three spider monkeys; a wolverine; a group of raccoons; a wolf, a dingo, and one other that I felt a special attachment to—a jackal.

It looked exactly like the one I pictured in my mind.

With their fur matted down, their paws spattered with mud, and dry leaves clinging to them, the animals looked all the more lifelike. I kept expecting them to move, but they never did. I glanced over my shoulder every so often to peek at the jackal. Could've sworn I felt him looking back, but I ignored it. Della didn't know about the jackal, and I didn't want to tell her. Sharing that kind of secret can change how people think of you, not often for the better.

Besides, we had work to do. Birch had given me a set of long hunting knives. I handed one each to Della and Christopher and showed them how to use it. Science wasn't all Birch and I had been up to down at the greenhouse.

"Birch used to be in the Marines, maybe some kind of Special Forces, too, based on some of the things he's said, but he don't like to talk about it much," I told Della. "He's adapted his military training to fight the dead close up. Got a system of a cutting them so their joints are useless without having to sever their limbs. We learned the hard way a legless body can still drag itself across the ground and bite you. A severed hand or arm can still claw you. Just like with Mason.

"Birch says you sever the spine and that leaves them burdened with their own dead weight. Then you clip the shoulders and hips the right way, and you got a trunk straddled with limbs like a plastic doll whose rubber bands have snapped. Since they're half dried out already, you can slice into them a lot deeper than you'd be able to cut a living person."

I showed them what Birch had taught me: the proper way to hold the knife, how to thrust and slice, where to place the blade, how to keep moving so they couldn't grab you.

"Don't cut too deep. You might get your blade stuck or cut the limb all the way off," I said.

"I'm not that strong," said Della.

"Neither are the dead. A lot of them are rotten inside," I reminded her. "Five blows is a lot, I know, but the slitbacks are slow, so it works if you keep your head."

"What if there are too many of them?" asked Christopher.

"Run," I said. "Nothing else you can do."

"Well, why don't we just shoot the fuckers?"

Della smacked the boy in the back of the head. "What'd I tell you about that mouth of yours?"

"Give me a break," Christopher complained. "We're out here learning how to slice up the walking dead in five easy steps, and you get on my case about swear words?"

"Little fucker's got a point," I said, grinning.

Della scowled at me for a moment, then turned away to hide the smile creeping into her face. "You boys must be closer in age than I thought."

"You know how to use a gun?" I asked Christopher.

"My brother taught me. I'm a good shot."

"All your family could handle one?"

"Could after the dead started walking."

"How many slitbacks were there the last time you saw them all alive?" I asked.

"Cornell!" Della snapped.

"It's all right," I said. "I just need to make a point about thinking a gun in your hands is a magic wand that's going to solve all your problems. They got in close, right? Overran you, and you couldn't get in a good crippling shot, and one bullet, even at point blank range, doesn't do much to hurt them does it? And maybe you ran out of ammo, no time or room to reload, and then all you had was a club, something blunt they could grab, two or three of them latching on to it maybe, and pull it away from you."

The exuberance left Christopher's face, and his stony glare made it clear I'd struck a nerve. His mussed sandy hair twitched in the breeze, and he looked more like a child in that moment than any other time I laid eyes on him. His eyes welled up a bit, but he squelched any tears hoping to escape. Della watched the two of us staring one another down, waiting to see who might break, wondering where to direct her rising anger.

"Guess a knife is a handy thing," Christopher said in a voice just a hair above a whisper.

"Save your life, maybe," I said.

Christopher stepped toward me. "Show me that last move again, okay?"

After that we practiced for a long time, and Della never uttered a word about what I'd said to Christopher. They caught on quick. Our blades flashed through the shadows time and again until they knew the pattern as well as I did. When we were done, I turned and hurled my knife toward the jackal, landing it dead in the side of the thing's neck. A puff of dust spewed out but the jackal didn't come to life, snarling as I saw it in my mind. Its glass eyes bored through me, stale and indifferent as they stared straight ahead into forever as if nothing in the world could ever kill their owner. I'd never seen a real, living jackal, but I couldn't imagine there'd have been any more life in one's eyes than I saw in this one.

9.

WEICHERT KEPT THE lid on for two days before he showed up at the greenhouse, bright and early, stepping through the doorway while Birch and I were spiking our coffee with a touch of Johnnie Walker. The mood at Camp Cady was getting bleak and the sheriff had to act. He waited just inside the door for a minute, watching us through the lattice of morning shadows, and then he glanced once at the wall of body parts, before averting his gaze toward a row of African violets among the few plants Birch had kept. He moved toward us past the long plant tables laden with Birch's equipment, eyeballing the gadgets and experiments in progress.

"Time for a talk, fellows," he said.

Weichert's attitude bore a touch less antipathy and a few degrees less arrogance than usual, undoubtedly due to the humbling security breakdown, maybe even an after-effect of Wrigley reporting how I'd helped the hunting party stay alive. Birch sensed it, too, because he refrained from the usual verbal lashing he saved up special for Weichert. I suppose it's true that troubling times bring folks closer together—at least when their instincts for self-preservation converge.

"All right," Birch said. "Want some coffee?"

He filled another mug from the pot and then tipped the whiskey bottle over its rim, pausing a moment to see if Weichert would turn it down, then letting the honey-colored liquor splash in to mingle with the dark brown.

He handed the mug to the sheriff, and said, "Let's talk downstairs in the lab."

Birch had taken to spending a lot more time in the greenhouse cellar. He hadn't lied about having equipment down there. Half of the machines and gadgets I couldn't name, but Birch worked them like a virtuoso, setting them up, priming them, letting them run, and studying the results. He recorded his data on three laptop computers, and he kept a dozen notebooks scattered around, each one dedicated to a different strain of research. I tried reading them but Birch's tech jargon and calculations only got jumbled up in my head. Lucky I had the man himself to translate.

He'd launched half a dozen new experiments he wouldn't tell me about, and he'd gone back to looking for an organic cause behind the walking dead, something viral or bacteriological, re-treading work he'd done months ago in hopes of spotting an overlooked loophole or some new inspiration. The slitback curse wasn't contagious, though, and their bites spread nothing other than the standard infections connected to dirty wounds, which steered Birch toward the theory of a bacteria that settled into a body at the moment of death, or one already present but only fully activated when its host expired, perhaps even by some other bacteria, one that thrived in decaying human tissue.

Birch was no optimist. He hadn't changed his views about what was really behind the resurrection, but intellectual curiosity drove him. Birch the man might not have needed answers, but Birch the scientist couldn't stop asking questions. Some days that frightened me. Birch made few—if any—mistakes, and despite his beliefs, he tortured himself working every angle he could imagine that might unlock the secret. He was so thorough it got to the point I believed him when he said if there was a reason to be found under a microscope or in a test tube that he would've found it by then. A man like that—one who's exhausted all rational options, who's sweated blood working to prove himself wrong—well, when he tells you there's only one answer to be had, no matter how much you hate the idea of what he's saying, you know odds are he's right.

Take someone like Weichert, though, who won't accept anything that doesn't fit his expectations—his crystal clear, box-framed picture of the world—no matter how bold the evidence, a man who's hell-bent on reconstructing an impossible way of life.

Put the two together and there's nothing to do but sit back and wait for the shouting to die down.

Every day the pressure of maintaining Camp Cady punched at Weichert with pneumatic consistency. He needed solutions from Birch, not more questions, but that's all Birch could offer. He and I had talked all week about what was happening in the far, western meadow, spinning over ideas and theories, broad guesses and wild notions, so when Weichert sat there and demanded hard and fast conclusions, Birch told him the only thing he could.

"I don't have enough information to say anything for sure and you don't like my guesses, so I can't help you much, Tom," he said.

Honest, yeah, but not what Weichert wanted to hear.

Their verbal artillery escalated. Each man jabbed the other's insecurities and fears; neither gave an inch toward compromise. Though they had known each other less than six months, their argument had the character of two old men who've been taking each other to task decade after decade until they don't know any other way to communicate but to fight. They wanted to help each other, sort of, in a strange way. Birch would've given Weichert answers if they were his to give, and Weichert wanted to believe that a man in a lab with clever machines and tremendous knowledge at his disposal could solve any problem.

That's when I stepped in and slammed my coffee mug on the granite countertop, sending a fine crack through the mug's pale ceramic.

"Shut up, both of you," I said. "Just shut the fuck up."

I spoke with tone of voice I'd once relied on to send terrified bank employees and their customers into fits of trembling before I even drew my weapon. Birch and Weichert listened.

"It's real simple," I told them. "Two of you standing here hashing words with each other gets no one anywhere. No agreement is gonna sprout out of this. Hear me? You want to keep some people alive? You want to know what's going on down in Baxton, why the dead are marching south, what it is that's keeping them on their feet? Go to the source. Go to Deadtown. Go and see for yourself."

Fuck me and my big, dumb mouth.

Once the shock wore off Birch and Weichert's expression, I saw in their eyes that they thought I was right, that we had to go, and that they'd already made their decision. From down in the recesses of my mind laughter bubbled up, high-pitched and shrill, only it wasn't laughter really but the cackling of my hated, constant companion, that savvy fucker who knew the day I was fated to die but would never tell me: the jackal I would never be free of until I was free of everything in the world.

That night I tried to convince Della that going to Baxton would be a good opportunity to get the lay of the land between Camp Cady and Lohatchie, that I'd go, come back, and then we'd sneak ourselves away for good. She said nothing for a long time then she told me she wanted to go with me. We both knew Weichert wouldn't allow it and I knew she didn't really want to leave the compound without Christopher, but I loved her for saying it.

Christopher was getting stronger every day, and I was beginning to see the benefit of him coming with us, another set of strong hands, another pair of sharp eyes. Better for Della to stay and get things ready for our departure.

We argued about it until there was nothing left to say, and then we spent the small, black hours of the night cocooned in our room, wrapped tight together, Della holding onto me like she needed to imprint the sensation of my body against hers, like she wanted to trap the heat of my breath, my life in all her senses. We fell asleep entangled, glued together with sweat, but Della woke before the sun rose and slipped away without waking me. She didn't want to say goodbye, and I didn't go looking for her. That way it was just another day like any other. I left the car keys hidden where I knew she would find them, inside a little box she used to keep her odds and ends, and then I went to meet Weichert at the greenhouse.

Once he'd taken up my suggestion, he put together a dozen men, including us, to make the trip. Plan was to take three jeeps down the highway as near to Baxton as was safe then hike across the open wilderness and come at the town from the northeast to avoid the dead line. By the time I finished packing and got to the greenhouse,

Weichert and his group were already milling around, ready to go, and waiting on me and Birch.

"Nice of you to join us," he said.

"Where's Birch?" I asked.

"Downstairs getting some equipment."

Morning spread through the trees, telegraphing the sweltering day ahead of us, but at least there was clear sky in every direction. Weichert's men roamed around, unhappy, jittery, and I didn't hold a case of nerves against them. No one wanted to go on this trip, including me, and it had been my dumb idea.

"What do you think we'll find down there?" I asked Weichert.

"Bunch of stinking, rotting dead people," he said. "Doing what stinking, rotting dead people do."

"Hey, Weichert," I said. "What if there is no *why*? What if it's just one of those things that *is*, you know? No reason, no logic, just nature."

Weichert turned to me with a stony glare. "You've been spending too much time with Birch and his superstitious bullshit. There's got to be a reason. There's a reason for everything. You get lucky and maybe you'll be the one to find it out."

Birch appeared, pulling an oversized backpack across his shoulders as he exited the greenhouse. He paused to straighten it then spat a wad of phlegm into the dirt.

"You need to use the bathroom or you ready to go now, princess?" Weichert asked.

"Why? You want to hold my dick and shake it?" grumbled Birch.

Weichert shook his head, paying no mind to the murmur of laughter that rippled through the men. He turned and stalked up the trail toward the parking lot. The men followed, and Birch and I fell in at the rear. As we left the clearing behind and stepped onto the narrow trail, a distant bird cawed, a lingering, porcelain sound like a lonely dirge crackling under a cathedral ceiling. We planned to be gone three, four days tops, but I wondered if I would ever see Camp Cady or Della again.

10.

BIRCH SHOOK ME AWAKE. I shot upright and reached for my gun, settling down only when I felt his hand pushing back on my chest and saw his haunted face. He sat cross-legged atop his rumpled sleeping bag, his eyes two pale patches in the dimness of the barn.

"Fuck, Birch, you scared the hell out of me," I whispered. "What is it, goddamn it?"

"Keep your voice down," he said.

We'd covered thirty-five miles that day, traveling the road out of Camp Cady and through the town, picking up the highway and then leaving it behind two exits above the one for Deadtown. Birch's pet name for Baxton had stuck with the men. It had been slow going though. The road worsened to the south, blocked by massive jams of forever motionless cars crammed together like racers waiting for a start flag that would never fly. There were accidents, too, moments of kinetic chaos preserved in three-dimensional freeze frames. Corpses occupied some of the wrecks, the remains of folks who gave up or got trapped and died where they sat. Chewed-up arms and half-eaten faces hung out of broken windows, their ruined bodies stuck inside twisted metal, some pinned behind cracked steering columns or under caved in roofs. Our presence stirred them, and they tried to wiggle loose for fresh meat. We gave them wide berth and kept moving.

Where the road was impassable, we drove over the shoulders, and twice we forced a path, eight or nine of us heaving and pushing to clear a car or two off the road while the others kept watch. Traveling the back roads wasn't much better, but it was easier to get around things with open fields, parking lots, and lawns at roadside. We stopped fifteen miles away from Baxton, and there, with the sun bobbing low like a warning buoy, we made camp at an abandoned lumberyard, pulled the trucks into an old warehouse, and hunkered down for the night.

Weichert assigned guards. The rest of us went off to sleep. Dusk was barely behind us but we were exhausted. In the morning we'd be hiking to Deadtown across fields, back roads, and rough ground, following a man named Grant, who said he could find a route to keep us off the main roads.

Birch shifted and his nylon sleeping bag whispered under him. "I got a bad feeling about Baxton."

"Hundred thousand or more slitbacks hanging out there? So do I," I told him. "You woke me up to tell me that?"

Birch slid up against the barn wall and leaned back. "No," he said.

The two of us had crashed in a corner, away from the others. Birch frightened some of them, and none of them much liked us. A few had been openly hostile, blaming me and Birch for getting their sorry asses dragged along on this expedition, but the way I saw it, as long as Birch and I were right there with them to do the dirty work, they could shove their complaints where the sun don't shine. Imagine trying to tell that to a gang of nervous, armed men, and you can imagine why Birch and I kept to ourselves and kept our voices low.

"Remember I told you about my dreams?"

"Yeah."

"Just had one," he said. "Used to hit me once a week, maybe, but I've been having them a lot lately, two or three times a night some nights. Usually wake up screaming and sweating bullets."

"They're just nightmares," I told him.

"I hope you're right. What we're going to find in Baxton, well, I think we're not going to like it. In fact, I got such a black fog over my thoughts right now, I'd bet you half of us here never leave Deadtown alive."

"You saying we should turn back?"

"No," he said. "That's the screwy part. I think we're doing the right thing going there. I'm just sure it's going to get ugly."

"Shit, man, what'd you dream tonight?"

"It's not what I dreamt so much as it is how I felt dreaming it," he explained. "I was standing at the heart of a gray desert like the surface of the moon, thick dust all around me but the air as clear as perfect water. I was gazing up at a night brimming with stars, more than I'd ever seen in my life, and then one-by-one they started winking out, going dark. I thought about how each one might be a sun, and how maybe there were worlds out there freezing over or flash-burning to ash, all life on them dying in an instant as their star exploded or went dead and black. Started wondering how long before our sun burned out. But then all at once they weren't stars anymore, but eyes, infinite in number, all of them looking down from the abyss of space like the eyes on the specimen wall. As each one blinked and disappeared I felt something drawing closer from beyond them, a raw, unfocused energy, a thing vast with potential but lacking purpose. Like the fury of a nuclear bomb when that smoking, glowing dome of destruction just keeps spreading, eating up everything in its path. Behind me, someone laughed, and it echoed through the air. And then I woke up."

"You had that one before?"

"No. Mostly I dream about the dead. They're all around me, going about business as usual as if they hadn't died until they realize I'm alive. Then it's like that scene out of *Invasion of the Body Snatchers*. Remember that? All the pod people start shrieking at the normal folks? Fuck me. I watched too many horror movies growing up. Stuff gets all wound up in your subconscious and comes farting back out when you least expect it."

"Guess so," I said.

Time passed marked only by the abstract sounds of men sleeping and the creaks of tired boards as the warehouse swayed a little in the stiff wind. A howling gust kicked up and sent the trees across the field rustling like rainwater pattering down. Outside the guards passed by, crunching their feet against the earth.

"Had a dream like that myself once," I said. "Everyone in the world was dead except me, and it was like business as usual. Guess is it's going around. Probably a lot of people dreaming that dream. Hard not to, I think."

"You're probably right," Birch said. "But I got a notion that maybe sometimes there's someone on the other end of my dreams, sending them to me, watching me through them—watching us, maybe. I want you to remember what I told you. Okay? Everything I said here tonight and everything we've talked about the past weeks. The others will follow Weichert, even the ones who can think for themselves, because when push comes to shove security, company, and what's safe and expedient will win out over what's hard and best. You're not built that way, so I think you've got a chance at surviving. Weichert's going to get a lot of people killed. I don't know how but I feel it coming. Maybe you can save some folks, maybe not. Might already be too late. Goddamn, stupid, fucking thing to come waltzing down here into the middle of a city full of undead corpses, but the kicker is, you're right. It's the only way to find out what's going on."

"Let's hope we all get back to Camp Cady to put whatever we learn to good use," I said, and it was partly a lie because my top priority when we got back to Camp Cady would be getting Della, Christopher, and myself as far away from there as possible.

"Whatever. Just remember the things I've said. And think about this—when was the last time you got sick? When was the last time you met someone who was sick? Since the dead rose up, you hear about anyone dying from AIDS or cancer or diabetes or pneumonia? I haven't. Just accidents, infections, gunshots, and being killed by the scarecrows."

"Knew a guy in prison had the flu or something. Killed him and he became a slitback," I said.

"Hunh," said Birch. "Exception that proves the rule, I suppose. Or maybe it's tied in with why some of the dead rot and others don't."

"What are you getting at?"

"Tried some new tests last week," said Birch. "Compared living cells with dead ones. Started with my own and moved onto samples from some of the others around the compound. Fed them a story about using live cells to find a cure for the undead."

"But that's not what you were doing."

"I don't know exactly what I hoped to accomplish. It was just something new to investigate," he said. "Bottom line is you do everything you can to keep from getting hurt too bad tomorrow, all right? If I die here, someone has to bear the truth forward. Understand me? Maybe it's a small thing but it's important to me. Someone has to know and live to tell whoever is left alive just how important living is now. You know where all my work is. You can figure out enough of it to make it useful. You're smarter than you think, my friend."

"Birch, man, no matter how smart you think I am, I don't understand a quarter of what you scribble down in your notebooks. I don't know what to tell anyone. So hit me with the plain English, Mr. Wizard, and tell me what the hell you're talking about."

"Time hasn't slowed down for just the cells of the dead, but for the living, too," he said. "Aging, disease, deterioration, all of it has stopped or slowed to a crawl. Not for everyone, maybe, but for most folks. We still heal at a normal rate, which has me puzzled. And we can still die, as we saw the other day. But barring violence, mishap, or suicide, you keep yourself intact, and you just might live forever."

"You're fucking crazy. Anyone ever tell you that?"

"First thing I say to myself every morning. But being crazy doesn't make me wrong."

"And you tell me this shit now?"

"Wanted to make sure you'd be careful tomorrow. Don't do anything stupid. Don't be a hero," he said. "I never told you, but some of the stuff that's come to pass these last few months, that's stuff I dreamt ahead of time. That's why I took my equipment and left my lab when I did. I dreamt how and when the three men who came with me were going to die, and it all happened the way I saw it. I knew I'd be leaving Camp Cady on an expedition like this, and I knew someone like you would be part of it. If I'm right you've got a bigger part to play in what's unfolding here than you expect.

"I got a bad feeling about myself for tomorrow. Something pivotal is coming and I feel terribly connected to it. I think the dead watch us, Cornell. Those eyes of theirs are meant to see something inside us we can't see ourselves, like they're passing judgment on our sins. I've done a lot of bad shit in my life, you know? Ah, fuck it, anyway. I'm just a 'mad scientist.' Go get me a lab coat and a Tor Johnson look-alike, and I'll start practicing my hysterical laughter. Anyway, you play it safe tomorrow, so you can go back and tell them what they need to hear, all of them. You tell them about my dreams."

"Birch, I haven't been inside your head. I haven't dreamt your dreams."

"Yeah, well, I got a feeling you will," he said and then he lowered himself into the shadows and lapsed into slumber. "Get some sleep, now."

"Fuck you, how am I gonna sleep after that?"

Birch didn't answer. A quiet few minutes ticked by and he started snoring. I closed my eyes, but too many thoughts spun through my mind, mostly questions about what Birch had told me. I wondered if the living and the dead were connected in some deeper way than that of predator and prey. I wondered what Della was doing, if she was lying awake in our bed, thinking of me, maybe glancing out the window at the high quarter moon in the misty sky and listening to the murmur of the woods. I tried to summon her face from memory but failed. Birch's words consumed me. I thought about waking him up and making him talk, but he wasn't one to say more than his piece. So I lay awake until morning and ran scenarios through my head, looking for the single perfect backup plan that would guarantee I made it back to Della in one piece and still breathing. But there wasn't one. There weren't many situations I couldn't find a way to control or manipulate to some degree, but this was one of them. I hoped to hell I could roll with whatever punches came down tomorrow.

Hours later the sun rose and probed the cracks in the walls with blades of dusty light. Something strange came on the morning air, a sensation like a heavy fog on my skin, and I thought of the blind energy Birch had described. It made me despondent and angry, made me want to go out and smash something, hurt someone, find all the slitbacks I could and hack away at them until my muscles grew too weak to lift a blade. I wanted it over and done with. I wanted no more to do with it.

I scolded myself for not having sense enough to keep my mouth shut, for bringing this on, but I had to face the fact that a big part of me wanted to be here. All that had happened, all that I'd seen, and everything stretched out ahead of me with Della at my side compelled me forward. It was one thing to run and hide, and hope the dead never caught up or caught us off guard, but sooner or later, the time would come when there'd be nothing to do but make a stand. It's the way life goes, and if I had to meet the coming darkness head on, hold my ground in the face of Birch's holocaust nightmare, I wanted to be prepared.

I walked out into the dampness of the yard to take a leak. If what Birch said about the living was true and we could no longer age and die after a fashion then everything I'd ever done and said in the name of immediacy, every stolen and breathless moment of passion that had ever fueled me seemed now to amount to little more than a hot puddle of piss.

The apricot sky lightened above the horizon.

A cold calm settled over me.

11.

THEY CAME FOR us on the outskirts of town, pouring out of every street and alley, every front porch and storefront, a gushing stream of dead flesh wrapped in a ripe miasma of putrescence that flowed onward like a river. Rot and dry sores blemished their green-black flesh, and their tattered clothes crinkled with matted dirt and crusted bodily fluids. They looked unreal in the daylight, like movie props or animatronic amusement park monsters. Remnants of life clung to them in bits of jewelry and identification badges, in shredded uniforms and the tatters of once-fine suits, in T-shirts emblazoned with rock band logos and bicycle shorts that sagged over wasted flesh. Their faces, though, all bore the same hungry, hollow-eyed, thoughtless death mask. Greedy mouths hung wide on busted jaws. Eager hands grasped with awkward, splintered fingers, gesturing for more, always more, telegraphing their lust for warm flesh.

Weichert shouted.

The men heeled around and ran. Stopped short.

The dead spilled out from the spaces behind us, on all sides of us, clogging the road and drawing into a circle that tightened with every shaky step they took. A billowy cloud crossed the sun throwing down a shadow like the fist of heaven rising to smash us.

We shouted and opened fire, throwing round after round into the crowd of lifeless meat, but still the dead ones shuffled closer. We tightened together, a dozen men standing paralyzed at the center of lonely intersection on the cusp of a town that had once been a place for the living but was now less hospitable than a desert on Mars. Deadtown is what we called Baxton, and everywhere were the empty sockets of ravaged faces, the eternal grins of skulls shorn of flesh, the gelatinous sheen of organs bloated by decomposition. Something I'd said to Birch the first week we met came back to me, and I knew I'd been right—this world was no longer for the living. We were feedstock at best and at worst, intruders, an infection, an invasive species to be consumed and controlled.

The dead must have known we were coming and laid a trap that left us nowhere to run, no way to fight back. We'd been wading through their stink all morning, listening to their mournful chatter, but that was no less than we expected on the approach to Baxton. Now useless gunshots popped around us, but neither Birch nor I drew our weapons. The tired dread in the scientist's eyes told me that his premonition had come true: he'd found what he'd expected here in Deadtown—and perhaps a great deal more.

An explosion ripped the air. An abrupt gust of heat and a bone-jarring concussion knocked me to my knees. Men rushed past me in a furious line, fleeing the street toward the narrow passage that had suddenly opened in the wall of slitbacks.

Someone had thrown a bomb into the mob.

Weichert must have been holding out on us when it came to munitions, and I prayed he had another dozen of whatever the hell he had used.

Birch and I hauled ass with the retreat. Pavement underfoot gave way to grass, grass to dirt and gravel as we rounded the corner of an auto garage and turned toward a high, chain-link fence in the distance. Behind it across an open field stood a towering water tank, its lofty catwalk accessible only by a single staircase winding around one of its support columns.

Slitbacks swept in from all sides, closing ranks like a giant, arthritic hand. Two of our party, Coogan and Daniels, stumbled and screamed; their bodies twisted as gray arms snatched them up, and they rode a tide of clutching, dead fingers, kicking hard and wailing for help, while the rest of us kept running. Stopping—even slowing for half a second—would equal suicide. I glimpsed splashes of red as the dead split open Coogan's and Daniel's skin like orange rind to reveal the juicy bits underneath, and then the men disappeared beneath scrabbling, gray bodies.

Three more men—Janson, Libby, and Tanner—fell along the way, firing blast after meaningless blast into the arms of the fetid meat that embraced them. After seeing how the dead handled Coogan and Daniels, they didn't wait to be picked apart. At the point of absolutely no return, each one turned his weapon on himself and cheated the final horror of being eaten alive. Made no difference to the dead. They divvied up the warm bodies like lazy butchers.

The forward men were scrambling up the fence now, flipping themselves over, and dropping to the clear ground beyond it. Birch and I pumped our legs harder, driven by the cold wave of death tickling our asses. At the fence Weichert shouted, shoved his men up and over, and then waved like a lunatic for me and Birch to pick up the pace. We did. Our fingers wrapped around rough aluminum and our feet left the ground. Chain link rattled and shook. A sudden weight struck below us. I grabbed for my gun before I realized it was Weichert bringing up the rear, and then I climbed faster as he overtook me. Weichert, Birch, and me—we all hit the top rail of the ten-foot fence just as the slitbacks slammed into the mesh and jolted the whole structure. But then were over, tumbling, slamming against hard ground, and rolling, crawling, scraping to get back on our feet. No question the weight of the dead masses would bring the fence down; it was just a matter of whether or not we'd reach the water tank ladder before it did.

Seven of us had survived the gauntlet, and four were already out of sight overhead, climbing higher and higher toward the catwalk. Again Weichert brought up the rear. I felt an unexpected burst of gratitude and admiration for the sheriff. Much of a hardcase as he liked to be, he was no coward bearing his authority like a crutch, but a granite-minded man doing what he believed was necessary. Birch and I mounted the narrow metal risers. Weichert followed. We were twenty feet up when the fence caved and folded like cardboard under the press of the dead. A swarm of black figures rambled over it, building up an enormous pile of flailing corpses as the front-runners toppled in the tangle of aluminum poles, chain link, and cold flesh. Their clumsiness bought us precious seconds, enough for the men up top to find positions and start shooting the first slitbacks to reach the stairs. In their excitement to catch us the ranks surged forward, mashing their fallen into the ground. I pounded the last steps upward, hit the catwalk, turned back, and pulled Weichert up the rest of the way.

All around the base of the tower the slitbacks churned in a festering, unbroken skin of corpse flesh that blanketed the earth. They filled every street and open space, every stretch of ground, stood on every rooftop, every car and truck, and way off in the distance at just about the limit of our sight, more ambled in to feed the crowd. I'd never seen so many living people in one place and of one mind, let alone such hordes of the dead. Estimates of a hundred thousand at Baxton were pitiful. Had to be a half a million. Had to be more.

Round after round snapped through the air as Weichert and the others dropped a shower of lead to cover the stairs. They were good shots and it didn't take much to tip a slitback off balance. They always got up again, yeah, but you could knock them right back down, which meant we'd be safe as long as our ammo held out. At the rate of fire, though, that wouldn't be long. Then the dead would clamber up and force us to fight hand-to-hand, and that's when our lives would be measured in minutes, ultimately seconds.

Birch grabbed my arm and pointed toward the center of Deadtown.

"Look," he said.

A red light shone bright despite the late morning sun. It rose from the distant avenues of town.

"Coming this way," Birch said.

The luminescence shimmered and pulsed as it crept through the low canyons of Deadtown streets, emanating from an unseen source.

"What is it?" I asked. "Fire?"

Birch shrugged and then hailed Weichert to come look. The sheriff's face kind of twitched when he saw the glow, and he swore under his breath.

"You got any more of those grenades or whatever it was you blew up back there?" I asked him.

"One," he said, lifting the edge of his coat to reveal a grenade clipped to his belt. "Scavenged them after that army troop passed us by months back. Wish I had a hundred more. Figure all this one is good for is taking along as many of these scarecrows as I can when I go."

A last volley of shots crackled, and the guns fell silent. I feared the men had run out of ammunition but they hadn't. They were waiting for the next slitback to hit the stairs, but it looked like the corpses had given up. A smashed-up pile of them lay quaking and rolling in the shadow of the tower. None of the others made an approach. They bobbed in the wind like saplings, their heads craned upward in our direction. Everywhere among them I saw eyes in strange places. Eyes peering out from dry blisters and scabby excavations. Eyes staring from the cracks in smashed skulls. Eyes dangling from the stumps of snapped fingers. One slitback missing its lower jaw unfurled a swollen, bloody tongue, and an eye prodded from its tip.

"What the fuck is that shit with the eyes all about? Huh, Birch?" blurted Weichert, staring toward the scientist, but Birch didn't answer.

"Language, Sheriff," I said. "You don't want to wind up in your own swear jar when we get back to Camp Cady, do you?"

Weichert wanted to glare at me, but a grin cracked his façade. He tried to hide his laughter at first, but then he let go, almost doubling over as his gut kicked with big-voiced guffaws. Some of the other men chuckled with him; the rest looked at their leader like he'd lost his mind.

"Hell, that's a good one," Weichert said, when his laughter died down. "Get back to Camp Cady. Heh. Yeah, right. Then I'll open an ice cream shop and retire. Son of bitch, but that tickles my funny bone."

After that the seven of us watched the red light creep onward, filling the town with a sickly pink luminescence as it came. The dead crowds rippled along like confetti making way for the wind. Nearer it came until it reached the main road beneath the tower and emerged from behind a house on the corner. Then we saw him: a gaunt man, clean and perfect, garbed only on a pair of tattered blue jeans and dirty boots, looking like any living man might except for the sanguine glow radiating from his body and the fact that the dead did nothing to interfere with his passing. He crossed the street, the field, ambled over the fallen chain link fence and stood below us, looking up—and all the dead turned with him, mimicking his gaze like army of robots, turning a half a million or more corpse faces toward us, and with them the countless pallid specks of eyes among the rot of the dead arrayed. I thought of the stars from Birch's dream. The Red Man raised a hand and flashed us a smile and a two-fingered peace sign.

He started up the stairs.

With weapons ready we watched the bizarre figure climb, his aura fading as he rose, before it blinked out altogether as he crested the last step onto the catwalk, and faced us. His skin looked pasted over his bones, etched into the spaces between his ribs, glued to muscle and tendon. Two black pits scarred his face—one above his left eye, the other through his right cheek. I looked for the telltale rise and fall of his chest, but no part of him moved. He stood as still as the dead except for filthy wisps of his thin, dark hair twitching in the wind.

"Welcome to Deadtown. Been expecting you," he said.

His voice rattled like a rat scratching inside a metal pipe; it warbled and echoed like his teeth were falling out and rattling around his mouth; it popped and sizzled like frying meat, and escaped him like coffin dust floating from an unearthed grave. Every syllable cut us like razors.

"Don't move," said Weichert.

We tightened around the sheriff and raised our weapons. Birch grabbed my arm tight enough to hurt and spun me toward him. His face had turned pure white, and the breath had left him. He started to speak, but a gun blast drowned out what few sounds he managed.

Guy named Owens had shot the Red Man, and now our visitor was looking down at his chest, fingering the fresh, dry wound to the left of his sternum. The bullet had passed through him as if he were paper. The Red Man grabbed the shooter and seized his gun, tossed the weapon aside, and then, lifting Owens by the waist, raised him up and hurled him over the catwalk railing. Owens screamed as he plummeted into the eager horde waiting to receive him. The sounds of his flesh tearing and his joints snapping mingled with the grumblings of the dead.

"I have business with some of you," said the Red Man. "But I don't mind adding the rest of you to the ranks of my followers. You're all bound there sooner or later. Don't be so stupid as to think shooting will help you. You folks died the moment you came to Deadtown. You died the moment you were born."

"Who are you?" asked Weichert.

The Red Man surveyed the rows of the dead sprawling in all directions, and said, "The Lord of the Dead, I am, yet, only a humble shepherd. Witness ye my sheep."

A vein in Weichert's forehead throbbed, and he ground his teeth together. "What's your name?" he demanded. "Tell me how you can just walk around with the dead like that."

"Easy. I'm one of them," answered the Red Man, and then he pointed at Birch and said, "As for the rest, why don't you ask him?"

Everyone looked at Birch. The scientist's body quaked, and a sheen of perspiration drenched his face. He tightened his hands into fists and pushed ahead of us.

"No," he growled. "No. You're dead, Stradley. I killed you. I fucking killed you years ago before all this shit happened, and there's no way you can be here. No fucking way."

The Red Man shrugged. "Remember what you said before you shot me?"

Birch struggled to dredge the answer from the pits of his memory; his expression told me that the Red Man had sent him hunting through some painful territory.

"I told you that you weren't God and that if you wanted to meet God, here he was in my hand," Birch said.

"And I replied, 'Just because you wish it doesn't make it so,'" the

Red Man added in a voice that creaked like a distant transmission heard over a dying radio. "Then you squeezed the trigger so that I might hear your God speak and feel his awful, burning touch."

The Red Man darted toward the water tank and snatched the hand of one of the men, Napoli, who'd pulled his automatic in hopes of hiding it behind Birch long enough to get off a shot. He forced Napoli's wrist back until the gun barrel pressed against his forehead, then reached in with his other hand and pulled the trigger. The shot sounded like close thunder, and Napoli's brains painted the side of the water tank. Stradley caught the body as it crumpled, lifted it up, and threw it to the hungry dead.

"More food for my followers," he said. "Who will be next to serve?"

No one moved. Birch stared at the shining gore, peppered with bits of bone and hair, dripping down the faded blue façade of the tank.

"You still think you're God," Birch said.

"I came back from the dead, didn't I? Is that not a trait of the divine?" the Red Man said in his guttering, spastic voice, but then he shook his head. "But, oh, no, I *know* I'm not God, and I have you to thank for that, Birch. Truth is, God is dead and gone. He left us a long, long time ago. The living taught me that, taught all of us that, and that's why we've come back—to help you all find the cold light of the universe. See, death is the only God there is, and death is a perfect God because one day all people, no matter how they live their lives, must become his eternal disciples."

12.

GOING BACK A couple of decades, now, Birch told us, there lived a man named Darrel Philip Stradley, a man of small measure by most standards, a failure and an outcast, a man fueled by the pain of his many inadequacies. Except one day Darrel Philip Stradley found his calling, heard it beckoning him from the infinite night while he emptied the trash out back of the mini-mart where he worked. With the souvenirs left by the five-year-old who had thrown up on the magazine rack and the wilted vegetables from the sandwich bar as witnesses, the voice came to him out of the heavens and though he tried to ignore it at first, it refused to leave him be. It told Stradley to do things, to say things, and when he complied he felt good and people listened to him, respected him—some of them, anyway, and who gave a fuck about the rest? So Stradley followed the path yawning before him toward his perfect place in the world and a destiny he could never have imagined.

In time he attracted others to his side, and he shared with them the gift of his vocation, the magnificence of the things the voice out of the void imparted to him. The voice never quieted for long, and Stradley always had much to tell his followers. He went from working a minimum wage job and masturbating in front his television every night to leading a host of devotees; and when his little band numbered more than 200 they got organized and took up together on the outskirts of town. Stradley's acolytes donated their life's savings to the cause; they bought an old farm with a centenarian house and built little shacks scattered over acres of fallow ground.

Away from the world, living in a reality of their own construction, Stradley and his faithful cut an existence out of the land; and in the name of their beliefs, they did things to one another that most folks would call unnatural. Took awhile for the rumors to spread, but soon enough they did: whispers of cannibalism and necrophilia, of people burnt alive in sacrifice, of rows of cages half-buried in the woods where Stradley kept those who offended him, of people tied high up on trees and left there naked for days. Every now and then someone from the farm straggled into the local emergency room with acid burns or low-dose strychnine poisoning or teeth cracked off above the gums. Others came with infections and lacerations and patches of missing skin that wouldn't heal. The police visited the farm every time, but no one talked; there was always a story to explain it all away, always a dozen or more folks ready to back it up. And the cops feared pressing too hard because by then there were nearly 400 living at the farm and they were armed with everything from pitchforks and machetes to shotguns and automatics.

So on it went in the world of Darrel Philip Stradley, a man rejected by society; rejected by a mother who'd beaten him, and a father who'd sold him to his friends sometimes for as a little as a bottle of gin; rejected by siblings who had whipped and tortured him; rejected by women who had mocked his awkwardness and insulted his affections—a man inevitably led by life down a dark path of transgression.

Stradley mortified his flesh. And the faithful followed.

Stradley purged his soul. And the faithful followed.

Stradley fasted for weeks. And the faithful followed.

None of the faithful matched Stradley's fervor, though, and none attained the heights of "transcendence" that Stradley claimed for himself. A long time after he died, the faithful still spoke of his miracles:

how he'd entered a trance and floated himself off the ground, how he'd healed with the touch of his right hand and maimed with his left, how he'd made the sun and the moon stand still in the sky, how he'd once turned the waters of a nearby stream to blood, and how a red aura sometimes embraced him like a full-body halo. No one but the survivors of Stradley's farm believed the stories, of course; for everyone else psychologists explained it with big ideas and handy theories about "group think" and "mass hysteria."

All the while that was happening, though, the outside world pressed in with its suspicions, investigations, and persecutions driven by fear of what might rise from that group of strange and isolated people. Knowing well their fear, Stradley and his faithful saw to it that every man and woman on the farm had a gun to their name and bountiful ammunition. Then Stradley went a step further. With the money he had gleaned from the faithful still wandering in now and again, and numbering hundreds more around the country (including one manic-depressive millionaire aging into dementia), he gathered a small stockpile of death: nerve gas and disease specimens. He meant to use them before the police came around banging on the front door for the last time.

That's when Birch entered the picture. Stradley's black market dealings got him noticed by government intelligence agencies and they acted fast. Another month's delay, maybe just a week's might have permitted a tragedy. Birch was on the scene as a bio-weapons expert, qualified as much by his security clearance and Marine Corps experience as his scientific credentials, when a mixed group of Special Forces and agents from the Federal Bureau of Investigation raided the farm on a cold, clear night. They came out of the dark, moving with precision and determination, working under orders to kill anyone who resisted. It was a secret operation, an illegal use of military troops on native soil, a desperate move to prevent disaster, and any hint of it in the media was squelched hard and heavy until the cover story—a disastrous raid on a violent, right-wing militia plotting revolution—took hold and became accepted fact.

The firefight was heavy, though, with casualties on both sides. Most of the farm complex burned down in the aftermath; the little shacks went up like kindling and spat columns of smoke into the sky. Charged with securing Stradley's stockpile, Birch's group located it in the cellar and Stradley along with it. When Stradley moved to open one of the gas canisters, he and Birch exchanged words and Birch fired.

Three shots: two through Stradley's head, one through his right lung.

13.

FIFTEEN YEARS LATER the wounds still showed on his reanimated corpse. Stradley caressed each one as Birch spun his tale about what should've been the demise of Darrel Philip Stradley, and when Birch finished talking, Stradley looked us each in the eye, paused, and then he laughed.

"Fifteen years," I said, looking at Birch. "He should be rotted away to bones and dust. Only the recently dead can get up and move."

Birch shrugged, as lost as I was.

"You're right," croaked Stradley. "I shouldn't be here by any normal reckoning. Learned some things when I died, though, like where I'd been right and where I'd been wrong during my life. All those things my faithful said I did were true. The world condemned us for how we lived but there was holiness in it, and purity, too, just not the polite kind. We were mad monks living in the wilderness, neglecting the needs of the flesh so that the spirit might thrive. And no one's spirit thrived more than mine. I believed in everything we did. Oh, how I *believed*—more than anyone else there ever could—and I was rewarded for it. My spirit was elevated. I became like a saint, like a bodhisattva, like a holy man with the power of Heaven on Earth, and what I learned of the universe I doled out to my followers."

Stradley gazed down at the bristling plane of the dead gathered to Baxton. The nearest of them still dripped red from the morsels his leader had provided. He smiled, and it was an awful thing to see, skeletal and reptilian, like a crack in the bottom of the earth.

"Holy men don't rot when they die," he said. "Crack a history book if you don't know what I'm talking about. I lay underground in a pauper's grave, still as stone for many years, a lost relic of myself until I felt my body—changed but not really decayed—stirring to rise up and walk again. And, oh, the things I saw while I was dead. The souls all around me, a chaotic multitude like grains of sand swirling and boiling in a dust storm, an endless fabric of raw energy adrift in the void. A billion or more dead crying out for the Word, ready to hear any word telling them what to do.

"And there were others like me there, souls that remembered, souls that understood that the dead had been abandoned. The clamor only grew as people went on dying and more souls poured into the emptiness bringing their anger with them, their rage at what they found waiting on the other side, their hatred for those who survived them. They forgot who they were. They became no more than what they had felt in those first moments of death. There were some voices of love and mercy, sure, but they were few and faint, and easily silenced. And when the needs of the dead hit a fever pitch, I was there to answer. *We* were there to answer, all the saints and the holy men, the magicians and the shamans and the devils, speaking with one voice, and we said, 'Rise.' And the dead listened."

Stradley's feral, hideous voice faded into the wind and then even the wind died and stranded us at the heart of a shattering silence. Birch hung his head like a guilty child. Weichert mumbled a mantra of nonsense words through his gritted teeth. The others stood by him, rigid with fear, faces contorted by confusion, guns clutched tight like talismans.

Stradley said, "Once there existed a God to tend all souls, but He died or went away. Perhaps we killed him with our perversions of his name, or maybe he just abandoned us out of disgust. Who cares? But with only the void to shelter them the dead recognized that there simply was nowhere else for them to turn but back to the flesh that had once served them. But the flesh they found waiting was rotten and suffused with corruption and insufficient to accommodate so many righteous and angry ghosts."

Stradley raised his arms above his head and crimson light streamed out of him. His skin bubbled and twitched, coruscated like it was infested with maddened bugs, and then a hundred or more bloody seams appeared, snapped open with liquid rents that jetted sprays of blood, and revealed eyes covering every part of his body, each one blinking in unison against the warmth and brightness of the sun.

"Many souls dwell in me," Stradley said. "The souls of the dead who demand what was once theirs: living flesh."

He grabbed one of the men by the scalp, tugged him up close, and bit hard into his arm, gnawing, working the joint until the limb popped loose. It was Grant, our guide, and I think he went into shock and never felt any pain because he made no sound even when Stradley threw him to the corpses, keeping behind Grant's arm for himself. Blood dripped over Stradley's body as he sucked on the torn limb. Blood coated his swarm of eyes, bled into them, nourished them.

"So the dead have come back to feed on the living because somehow, somewhere along the line, we killed God?" I said. "That's what you're telling me? Well, what about all you dead sons-of-bitches who lived and died before us. Weren't you the ones who did the killing?"

"Don't believe him," Birch said. "He was insane when he lived, a con man, a megalomaniac. There's more to this, Cornell. I swear it. Trust me. The world isn't finished with the living yet."

Stradley spat a hunk of gristle onto the catwalk. He dipped a finger into the bloody stump of Grant's arm, then reached out like lightning, and traced something on my forehead. His touch lasted only a moment, but it drained all the heat from my body. I shuddered. I wanted to panic, wanted to run. My knees bent, and I nearly fell.

"The dead know no mercy," he said.

He crushed his thumb against Birch's forehead the same way, daubing a little "X" there, and then he shoved by us to get at the others. We could do nothing as he killed them. He ripped out Lee's throat, gutted Ferring, and dropped them dead and hemorrhaging to the catwalk. He moved too fast for Birch or me to act, but when he reached Weichert, the sheriff fought back. He jabbed at Stradley's many eyes with a knife, and they popped and spewed gore, Stradley shrieked. There was no hurt in his voice, though, no anguish or fear, just elation at whatever pain Weichert brought him. He welcomed it, and he let Weichert do his best with the blade.

Remembering the techniques Birch had taught me, I drew my knife out and sliced across the side of Stradley's neck, bringing the cutting edge down exactly right, biting into his spine. Something snapped and Stradley's head lolled forward. He staggered a moment, then punched Weichert in the chest, sending up a little burst of red light as he cracked bones and slammed him backward. He turned and crushed me against the water tank. A crimson haze filled my eyes and the world faded into it for a moment.

Stradley touched his hands to the bloodless wound I'd carved and clutched it tight. It glowed red for a minute and when he lifted his fingers, he was healed, his head once more secured to his body. He looked at me, shrugged.

"You tried," he said.

He hefted Ferring's corpse over the railing and dropped him out of sight. Weichert waved to catch my eye and nodded to me. His face was pale and dripping with sweat. He lifted the flap of his coat, showed me the grenade hidden there.

I got the hint.

When Stradley turned back to him, Weichert—choking and gasping for air—spat blood and saliva in the dead man's face. Stradley's skin drank in the moisture. I scrambled away, my chest barking with every breath, signaling that Stradley had broken one of my ribs; I ignored it, grabbed Birch, and bolted for the far side of the tower.

Too soon the grenade detonated.

The catwalk bucked and the tower shook. I stumbled forward into the air, lost my grip on Birch, and came down rough, smashing my face against coarse metal. Iron scraps darted through the air followed by a jet spray of water that hit my legs and shoved me toward the edge of the catwalk. A flood gushed out of the tank. I grabbed on to the platform, digging my fingers into the sharp grooves of the metal mesh. Water swamped my legs, rushed past, and cascaded down in a heavy waterfall that punched into the dead below.

Something jabbed my arm.

Straining back, I saw Birch hanging over the side of the catwalk, clutching the edge with one hand, digging into my side with the other.

"Remember my dreams," Birch shouted over the roar of the water. "Remember what I told you."

I tried to grab his hand, but his wet fingers slipped loose and the raging froth carried him away. I hollered his name into the falling river. A flash of red sparkled below me, and then I closed my eyes and focused on holding tight. Water flowed for what felt like hours, cold and hammering, pawing at my legs, freezing me, filling my ears with thunder, and drowning out the world. Everything became a roiling, wet spiral. My hands ached and cramped. Pain lanced my wrists. The edges of the metal grooves sliced my fingers. My body teetered on the edge of failure and just when I was sure I could hold on no longer, when I could feel my feet creeping over the catwalk edge and dangling into empty air anxious to take me, the outpouring abated. The pressure diminished. The flow of water slowed and then died down to a feeble stream.

I flopped over on my back and panted.

After awhile I forced myself to sit up and looked at the gaping hole blown in the tank, the darkness inside it. No sign of Weichert. No sign of Stradley. I peered over the catwalk edge and saw the dead below scattered and broken by the floodwaters, wriggling like ants in the rain. An enormous puddle spread outward from the tower, swamping the field, and a steady stream trickled through the air, draining like ice melting off the corner of a snow-capped rooftop.

I was alone.

I screamed, loud and harsh, straining my larynx to its limits, bellowing to the open sky, venting my anger and frustration to a deaf and uncaring audience, until my voice cracked and faltered and died. After that I thought of nothing for a long time.

Metal bit into my back. Soon the dead would come for me. I was drained and hollow, and I could never fight half a dozen slitback, let alone a half a million. I rolled onto my side and watched the faraway trees dance in the blustery afternoon, thinking that the scene made a fitting last sight and wishing I'd been able to keep my promise to Della. My old jackal friend sat by my side but he wasn't laughing any longer, and as strange as it might sound I was grateful for his presence. There was sympathy in his silence, comfort in his restraint. I should've known then that there was no kindness in him, that the dead world and its scavengers were far from done with me, and that the jackal's kept quiet because even he was horrified by my fate. But a dying man grasps at whatever comfort comes by.

I blacked out and fell into nothingness.

When I woke an endless array of stars glittered in the night like ice crystals in a blanket of virgin snow. I stared at them, waiting for them to be snuffed out like in Birch's dreams, and I listened to the moans of the dead below as I shivered in the cold air brushing over my sopping clothes. I lapsed back into unconsciousness.

In the morning, stiff and aching from lying so long on hard metal, shaking from the chill that had seeped into me, I opened my eyes and crept over to the railing. Still no sign of Stradley or Birch or any of the others. The dead remained, though, holding vigil, tormenting me with their idiot placidity. Why hadn't they hadn't come in the night to devour my flesh?

"Enough of this shit," I muttered through chattering teeth. I forced myself onto my feet, lumbered to the stairs, and began the long descent.

14.

THE DEAD WOULDN'T TOUCH ME.

The moment I set foot on the ground I braced for their rush but not one of them moved. I walked right up to them, shouted, cracked one of them in the face with my shotgun, retrieved from the muddy ground.

Nothing.

Gangly, frail like scarecrows, and dappled with black stains of rot, they watched me. Something about Weichert's preferred name for them stuck in my mind then but I couldn't figure out why.

"What the fuck is wrong with you?" I shouted.

A swarm of silent eyes regarded me.

Nearby stood a dead man dressed in a courier's uniform, his face broken and mashed into a featureless muddle. From each of his crusty wounds peered a stark, rheumy eye. I put my shotgun in his face and blew his head to a fine spray of sticky muck that coated the slitbacks behind him.

Nothing.

Where I walked, the dead parted, and their ranks closed in behind me.

Down among them, thousands of them on every side of me, the stench of their decay was almost suffocating, but to my horror I found that I'd gotten just a little bit used to it. I tore off a patch of my shirt and tied it over my mouth and nose to cut back the worst of it. There was nothing I could do about the endless groaning and gurgling.

I crossed the muddy field, passed the auto shop, and headed toward the street where the slitbacks had ambushed us and the road out of town. I passed the little crater Weichert's grenade had left, moved into the shade of the trees, and kept going. As much as I tried not to, I gaped at the death surrounding me in all its strange and savage glory. Bodies ripped open, limbs hanging by a last thread of drying ligament, dead faces mottled purple and gray, eyeless skulls, organs poking out of flesh split open like old leather, scraps of metal and wood broken off and still protruding from rotted meat—and forever, the eyes. Not all of the dead, but too many to count, tracked me with the pearly studs of those abhorrent eyes.

After awhile I stared back.

Trying to ignore them made it worse. Something had shifted in my mind, changed my perceptions—something that rose out of my disgust and frustration and settled into anger. I glared at every one of the eyes I caught as I walked through the mob and flashed them the stare that had earned me the undying enmity of the law and thousands in loose cash from the hands of terrified bankers.

An odd thing happened then: those dead, white eyes began to flinch.

The longer I looked back at them, the more of them that blinked, twitching odd folds of flesh poorly suited to the purpose, and then some of them started to turn away. I gave back at least as good as I got. They dropped their gaze to the ground, looked off to the side, curled up and retreated into dead flesh. I stared down the dead, my stride growing more certain and confident; I thought of what Birch had said about the world not being finished with the living, and I knew he was right. I didn't understand it, didn't see what role other than food we might yet serve, but I suspected that the dead did, and that's why they didn't take me. The Red Man had placed his sign upon my forehead, marking me for some future purpose.

A hundred yards more and the dead were behind me, a hundred thousand, half a million, however many they were, and I was leaving Deadtown. I walked out of their shadow and the road lay open before me, not a corpse in sight, only the empty Earth, the far horizon, and the path home free and clear.

I did not look back. Not once.

I walked until my legs ached and my body screamed for water, and then I forced myself to keep moving, pushing one foot ahead of the other, grinding for every inch of ground I claimed, staggering onward until the dark made it impossible to go any further. With the day's sun just a memory I found a place without windows in the back of a ruined grocery store, and there I landed hard, and I slept.

15.

I WOKE ONCE THAT NIGHT. Three slitbacks stood over me, swaying like drunks, a stench pouring off them. Maggots crawled over their pitted flesh, and flies buzzed in and out of the ragged shreds of their clothing. One of them wore a hunter's cap, the second a police hat, and the third was bald with the top of his skull caved in like a soft-boiled egg. Their multiple sets of misplaced eyes glowed in the dimness. I reached for my gun but by the time I brought it around, they had turned and shuffled away.

I leapt up, slammed the door behind them, and then barricaded it with office furniture. I sat up, expecting them to return or others to come, but nothing stirred in the corridor. After a few hours I dozed back to sleep. Brought me no rest, though.

My mind came alive with dream visions of a sweeping darkness populated by the eyes of the dead, rolling and churning like waves in a stormy ocean. I hunted for safe shelter but found none. A dry, granular rain pelted my skin and peppered me with sooty smears; in the distance a pillar of light lanced far into the night. I ran in its direction, drawn by the rabble of voices rising from it, fighting the slowness of dream-running and hoping to find others. But all the voices were dead voices. When I neared the light, I saw it came from the glow of millions of souls ascending out of an infinite field of graves and pouring into the sable heavens. As each one reached the pinnacle of its flight, it shimmered and snuffed out like a candle flame.

I felt a black line of annihilation crossing the universe, withering all it touched, yawning far and wide, reaching to incomprehensible dimensions, and behind it lurked a wicked, faceless will. I sensed it—malicious, greedy, born of dread and despair, brazen and unstoppable, and hollow with an infinite hunger aching to be filled.

Left me sweating and cold when I woke, and I began to understand what had been behind that perpetually haunted look I'd seen in Birch's eyes. Goddamn dream was as real as anything I'd ever experienced awake, and I felt the presence Birch had described, almost tangible, like it could reach into my head and touch my mind. It made me glad for the daylight, and at dawn I shook it off as best I could, relieved myself in the back corner, and headed out.

I needed to find Della.

Stradley had known we were coming. Maybe he had spies among the living or maybe Birch's dreams really did connect him to something outside himself, something also connected to Stradley. Or maybe he had seen through the eyes of the slitbacks that had invaded Camp Cady. The dead pilgrimage ran not far from there, really, and it didn't take much to get me wondering what had happened back at the compound while we were gone. I worried about Della and Christopher, about what I'd find when I returned.

I moved along the back of the grocery store, checking each cluttered aisle as I passed. There was nothing left but junk and spoiled food. Still, my hunger drove me to search the debris, an effort rewarded with a lonely bag of marshmallows hidden under a pile of dented pots and pans and broken glassware. I tore it open and shoved three into my mouth. Marshmallows never go bad.

Up front past the cash registers where the glass windows had all been smashed in, something crashed.

I shoved the marshmallows into my shirt, hefted my shotgun, and eased out along what had been the produce aisle. I glimpsed a man stumbling through the wreckage of the front entrance. The sun at his back blanketed him with shadow. He didn't move like a slitback, though.

I wrapped my finger around the trigger, and said, "Something I can help you with, champ?"

Startled, the man jerked forward, stumbled, and fell to his knees, spouting a string of unintelligible grunts and waving his hands. He came out of the light, and as my eyes adjusted, his features came into focus. It was Birch, his clothes smeared with blood, his eyes glassy and wild, his forehead tagged with the same sign I bore on mine, and he looked like he'd aged ten years overnight. I marveled that he'd survived falling off the water tower. He gestured toward his open mouth, spitting and snarling a little. A trickle of blood dribbled over his lips, and I saw that his tongue had been ripped out.

"Sonnuvabitch, Birch," I said. "I'm glad to see you alive, but what the fuck happened to you?"

I hooked my arm under his and hefted him back to his feet. We moved outside into the warming morning. It wasn't easy for him, but Birch made it clear that Stradley had mutilated him and that a group of slitbacks had led him here in the night and left him for me to find. No doubt there was a lot more to tell. All the time I'd slept on the water tower and walked out of Deadtown, Birch had been with the Red Man, alone if you didn't count the dead, a man he had killed.

I didn't want to think about it. It was clear Birch was too tired to act it out or scribble it all down, and anyway my first priority was getting back to Della. Moving together Birch and I traced the rest of our path back to the lumberyard where we had camped two nights ago. It was early afternoon when we got there, and we took one of the jeeps and drove back up the highway. Birch nodded off right away, and I sank into loneliness greater than any other I'd ever known. There were more slitbacks along the road now than there had been on our way down, as if with things in Baxton over and done the dead had started spreading out. They roamed the road and combed the wrecked cars for food though there was none to be found. They watched us roll by. Some of them turned and staggered after us, so I hit the gas and let them grow small and vanish in the rearview mirror.

I kept the pedal to the floor, drove with abandon, and the world became a place of streaks and blurs. Ruined cars formed a slalom course along some stretches but I didn't slow down, and no matter how much the jeep jerked and swerved, Birch slept through it. The speedometer needled quivered all the way right and the whine of the engine drilled into my head. I hit a few slitbacks along the way and they went down beneath the wheels or burst in a mess of viscera that spattered the windshield.

I told myself to slow down but I couldn't. No matter how I tried, I couldn't bring myself to ease up on the accelerator. It was like my leg was locked tight, my arms riveted to the steering wheel, my back welded stiff to the seat. Only when I saw the oncoming car across a clear stretch of road was I finally able to break the spell.

The driver of the car must have noticed us about the same time. Our vehicles screeched to a stop, maybe a quarter mile between us, separated by a grassy ditch between the lanes. There were no slitbacks here, but we'd passed half a dozen just a couple hundred yards back, and I wasn't happy to be stopped. Seconds ticked by and no one moved. I tried to see who was in the vehicle, but the sun glancing off its windshield made it impossible. Then I recognized the familiar shape and blue paint of the car. It was Mason's. I prayed that meant what I hoped it did, but just in case it didn't I made sure my gun was loaded before I left the jeep.

A second passed, ten, twenty, and then the driver's side door of the car flew open.

Della leapt out.

She raced toward me. My loneliness evaporated.

Della jumped into my arms and wrapped herself tight around my torso. We clung to each other and kissed and then stood there awhile, holding on, afraid to move apart, savoring one another's touch. We might've stood there forever if Christopher hadn't rose from the passenger side of the car and shouted, "Get a room, losers."

I laughed, and it surprised me. I hadn't thought I still had it in me, but seeing Della alive, Christopher with her, and the old car that had carried us so far went a long way toward raising my spirits.

In Weichert's absence order broke down in Camp Cady. His trusted deputies tried to hold it together, but there was too much fear, too much uncertainty. People started taking weapons and supplies without permission, and Della had acted fast. With Christopher's help she grabbed what she could and packed the car full of food, gear, and guns. Many of the folks at Cady's had benefited from her medical attention, and they were generous toward her. No one tried to take what she gathered, and no one tried to steal Mason's car out from under her.

The same morning I walked into Deadtown with eleven other living men, an army of corpses poured out of the woods and into Camp Cady. The dead line had broken formation in the night. Della couldn't guess how many slitbacks came—there were too many to count and the men who'd been on watch in the woods were among them. They overran the camp, slaughtering the living as they went. Della and Christopher reached the car and bolted. Others tried to follow. Some of them made it. Some of them didn't. Those that did headed for town and went north. Della came south, looking for me.

She said it was like when Mason died. Nothing left to do but run to stay alive.

"Lucky you found me," I said.

Della's eyes glistened, and she said, "I had to try, you know?"

"Yeah, I do."

She licked her thumb and rubbed my forehead with it, scrubbing. "You got some blood on your face."

The remnant of Stradley's touch—painting me with the blood of the dead, smearing me like a rancher marking his brand.

"It won't come off," Della said.

I pushed her wrist away. "Leave it. I'll worry about it later. I've got a lot to tell you."

We woke Birch and helped him over to the car. The jeep would've been a good choice, but with gas as scarce as it was we felt safer opting for mileage. Besides Mason's car had served us well and it was already packed. Christopher and Birch crushed into the back seat with the packages and boxes Della had brought. Della, thinking of all I had told her about Birch's research, had grabbed the scientist's computers and notebooks, whatever fit into two boxes. Birch stared at it all for a long time, then dug out a mostly empty notebook and started scribbling. I slipped behind the wheel with Della riding shotgun and turned the ignition key. The engine growled. I let it idle for a minute, then shut it off and rubbed my eyes.

Della took my hand. "What is it?"

"Where the hell are we going?" I said. "Nothing but the dead in every direction."

"That might be," said Della. "But one way or another we're going home."

Going "home," I thought, as if the word still meant something, but I started the engine again, put the car in drive, and roared off toward the south, planning to speed past the exit for Deadtown without even so much as slowing down. I told Della and Christopher about Birch's theory that the living were sort of immortal now, but they didn't much believe it. I didn't know how much of it I bought myself. The Red Man had made the other side of death sound a whole lot like what we had in life, just maybe a little worse, a little more pointless. Living forever didn't sound too bad, but even if Birch was wrong, I wasn't going to let the dead rotting bastards kill us. Way I saw it, none of us owed the dead so much as a stray tear for their suffering or even a handful of dirt for those wise enough to stay in the ground. We were back on our way to Lohatchie and wouldn't stop moving until we got there. We traveled the cenotaph Earth, roaring past its ragged, angry denizens, and I started wondering if "scarecrows" wasn't a lot closer to the truth than anyone had realized. The dead were ferocious and horrifying, all right, but they were only restless bags of lifeless skin and bones, and if they truly desired living flesh, they couldn't afford to wipe us all out, and maybe that meant that in the war between the living and the dead, we had—despite appearances, you understand—already won. Who could say? But my four-legged friend had abandoned me for the time being; there was no hint of his cackling from the dark places of my mind, and though I knew the jackal came and went as he pleased, I took that as a good sign.

Ode to Brains
by Adam P. Knave

Gnnahhh. Unnghh grannnh, huurrrr, ughn nnnnr. Graanh uhh ghuun nuuuhg grannhhh.

Ghuun grannnh huurrrr. Ughn nuuuuhg, gnnahhh uhhn fuuhg, ghah. Huurrrr ghunn grannnh naahg gnnah uhh.

"Fnuuh," hunng gruunhh. Gnnahhh: fuh hunnguh hurrr uhhnfg. Gruun. Ruuhhhggg, uuhn funaaaa. Aaahhrrgg.

Huunnaag frug gunhf. Uhhn aag ruhhfug, aannuuh. Gnnahhh nuuuhg naahg haanuh funaah.

"Huggfunaaaa," gunnfa hanaaaa, "grraaahhh, uhnng, grrrunnnaa."

Gnnahhh ruhhfuhh fuuhg grannnh funaa. Nuuuhg, ghah, huurrr grunn.

Grannnh fuh huggfunaaaa, aag nuuuhg naahg gnnah. Uhhna grnnah uhhn uhhnfg. Hunng gruunhh naahg.

Bang!

Thud.

ACCoMPLiCES

STEPHEN BLICKENSTAFF (Cover Artist) is an unassuming lad, with a quiet, gentle demeanor and a taste for the truly dimented. Though he best known for the cover of The Cramps' *Bad Music For Bad People* album, his artistic output has, much like the Blob, multiplied exponentially. The merest fraction of his artwork may be viewed at his website, the eponymous www.stephenblickenstaff.com.

JAMES CHAMBERS ("The Dead In Their Masses") "writes stories that are paced fast enough to friction burn a reader's eyeballs," says Horror Reader.com. His tales of horror, fantasy, and science fiction have been published in *Bad-Ass Faeries*, *Crypto-Critters*, *Dark Furies*, *The Dead Walk*, *Hardboiled Cthulhu*, *No Longer Dreams*, *Sick: An Anthology of Illness*, *Weird Trails*, and *Warfear* as well as the magazines *Bare Bone*, *Cthulhu Sex*, and *Allen K's Inhuman*. His short story collection, *The Midnight Hour: Saint Lawn Hill and Other Tales*, was published in 2005. Access his virtual presence at www.jameschambersonline.com.

JOHN L. FRENCH ("Fast Eddie's Big Night Out") is a crime scene investigator for the Baltimore Police Department. He has been writing short fiction for over ten years. His stories have appeared in *Alfred Hitchcock's Mystery Magazine*, *Hardboiled*, *Futures Mystery Anthology Magazine* and many more. His next book, a collection of his Bianca Jones stories, is scheduled to be published by Die Monster Die! Books. John can typically be reached at bpdlab@yahoo.com.

BRUCE GEHWEILER ("Ragged Bones") is an editor, publisher, seminar leader, and consultant, as well as the author of numerous short stories and books. He owns and runs Marietta Publishing, a respected small press publishing company. Locate him within the vast labyrinth of the world wide web at www.mariettapublishing.com.

C.J. HENDERSON ("A Large And Rattling Stick") has been a professional writer for over a quarter of a century. He has produced everything from novels to comic books, including an encyclopedia. His works have been translated into a half dozen foreign langauges, and yet he will still work for food. His work here is but his latest attempt to coax chicken legs out of the public at large. www.cjhenderson.com

D.J. KIRKBRIDE ("Married Alive") was born the mall-infested state of Ohio some 42 years ago, D.J. took to making stuff up at an early age when he realized that reality was boring. After questionable schooling still being paid off and some menial jobs, D.J. took his leave of the Buckeye state, eventually landing in southern California despite his fear of the sun and the physically fit. While writing for various publications and constantly changing his facial hair at every whim, D.J. dreams of one day being paid substantially for both. He is also the founder and senior editor of The Footnote (www.thefootnote.com), where he can be be usually found, hanging out with all the wrong people.

ADAM P. KNAVE ("Ode To Brains," "High Noon Of The Living Dead") is a Writer of Things in NY where he lives with his wife and two cats. He dabbles in interpretive dance, competitive mocking and fibbing in bios. He welcomes hearing from readers via pulse@hellblazer.net and openly admits to having more of his writing up at www.hellblazer.net.

STEVEN A. ROMAN ("Laundry Day") is the writer/creator of the horror graphic novel *Lorelei: Building the Perfect Beast*, as well as the author of the novels *Final Destination: Dead Man's Hand* and *X-Men: The Chaos Engine Trilogy*. His most recent short fiction appeared in the anthologies *Doctor Who: Short Trips: Farewells* and *If I Were an Evil Overlord*. He lives in Queens, NY, where only the trendiest ghouls hang out.

NATE SOUTHARD ("Of Cabbages & Kings") writes comics and prose. Nate Southard lives in Austin, Texas. Nate Southard has a girlfriend. Nate Southard has two dogs and two cats. Okay, they're really his girlfriend's. Nate Southard has worked as a cook, bar back, and pizza maker. He is also the author of two graphic novels showcasing the plucky inhabitants of Millwood in their ongoing struggle with hordes of the living dead, as well as numerous non-zombie short stories. He can be found online line at www.natesouthard.com.

PATRICK THOMAS' ("Zombie And Spice") Dept. of Mystic Affairs stories have appeared in *Hardboiled Cthulhu*, *Crypto-Critters 2*, *Through The Drinking Glass*, *Shadow Of The Wolf*, and *Hard Times At The Harvest Moon*. In addition to his DMA tales, Patrick is the author of over 75 published short stories. He co-edited *Hear Them Roar* with C.J. Henderson, and is co-editing the upcoming *New Blood* vampire anthology. His novellas have appeared in *Go Not Gently* from Padwolf, and *Flesh And Iron* from Two-Backed Books. Patrick also writes the syndicated satirical advise column *Dear Cthulhu*. Visit his website at www.patthomas.com.

LASZLO XALIERI ("2 Dead 2 Walk," "The Spare"), despite the Hungarian-Italian-sounding name, is an unabashed southerner who has lived all but two years of his life in Georgia. That's the one in the U.S.A., not the one in Eastern Europe. In the spirit of worldly brotherhood though he drinks as much *arak* as bourbon. Xalieri is a published novelist, short story writer, poet, essayist, pundit, and is the author of the five-year-running "Tales from the Third Lobe" column at www.TwoHeadedCat.com.

Printed in the United States
87258LV00001B/1-99/A

9 781890 096373